A GENERATION
OF VIPERS

ARROW™

A GENERATION OF VIPERS

Clay Griffith and Susan Griffith

TITAN BOOKS

ARROW: A GENERATION OF VIPERS
Print edition ISBN: 9781783294855
E-book edition ISBN: 9781783295791

Published by Titan Books
A division of Titan Publishing Group Ltd
144 Southwark St, London SE1 0UP

First edition: March 2017
10 9 8 7 6 5 4 3 2

TIBO3917

Visit our website: www.titanbooks.com

A CIP catalogue record for this title is available from the British Library.

Printed and bound in the United States.

ARROW™

A GENERATION OF VIPERS

1

My name is Oliver Queen. I lived a life of privilege before I found myself trapped in a merciless jungle for five years. I learned to survive and returned to the real world. But until I help others survive too, I will remain in that jungle.

The Green Arrow followed the latest-model SUV. It drove under the speed limit and did nothing to draw attention. Despite the blacked-out windows, he knew there were four men inside, and they were heavily armed.

He crunched over the gravel rooftop to the edge and peered down at the dimly lit road below. The SUV paused at an intersection as if debating direction.

"Right," Green Arrow murmured to himself.

The SUV turned right as he predicted. He waited for it to pass by ten stories below before firing a cable arrow to the building across the street. He swung out high over the empty pavement and hit the building on the opposite side with his feet at just the right angle to minimize the impact. Climbing to the roof, he sprinted to the opposite side in time to see the black SUV pull to a stop right below him, as expected.

Most of the buildings on this street were dark. Windows were broken and some boarded up. Streetlights had been restored so the car doors opened and four men emerged into pools of yellow. They wore black fatigues with dark stocking caps. Two of them pulled heavy assault rifles from the backseat. The other two drew pistols from holsters.

Green Arrow mapped his steps. The two Pistols would go inside the building. He would rappel down to the street. Flash-bangs for the two Rifles. Blunt arrows would put them down. By then, the Pistols would turn to the noise. He'd take cover behind the SUV. The Pistols would come out guns blazing—these types liked to come out guns blazing. It should be simple to take them both down as they hit the door. Certainly the unexpected could happen, but he trusted himself to manage the scene and react properly.

The cold autumn wind ruffled Green Arrow's hood. This was reminiscent of the old days when he fought alone.

A shudder of excitement passed through him. He almost smiled with nostalgia, but he didn't do that sort of thing. Those early days had been simple, although they hadn't seemed that way at the time. Before the partners. Before the team. Before the names: the Hood, the Vigilante, the Arrow, and now the Green Arrow. Tonight he had nothing to depend on except himself, and no one to protect except himself.

Alone. The hunter and his prey.

There were no voices in his ear feeding him information. No eyes in the sky tracking his targets. No one in a command center watching his back, protecting his flanks.

This was not his jungle. While he knew his home of Star City like an animal knew its hunting grounds, Central City was still new to him.

When an army of metahumans ran roughshod over Central City last week, the city's protector, the Flash, had been overwhelmed enough to ask Green Arrow to join the fight to bring down the metahumans. But the situation had proven worse than metahuman criminals.

The Flash was losing his powers, and the process was killing Barry Allen, the man behind the mask.

Arrow checked the time.

Barry would be undergoing a "procedure" right now in hope of healing his illness. That was why Green Arrow was patrolling the streets of Central City without support from the team at S.T.A.R. Labs who were helping Barry. Criminals didn't keep convenient schedules.

Far below, the Pistols went to the front of the building. The faint sound of glass breaking tinkled in the air. Green Arrow counted to five to let the Pistols get well inside the shop. He drew a metal rod about six inches long from a loop on his tunic. A touch fired the tip hard into the concrete at his feet. He tugged once to test the anchor, and leapt over the side.

The high-pitched whine of the polymer cable playing out accompanied the sight of windows flashing upward. His boots touched the sidewalk in near silence. Releasing the device, he snatched a high-tech compound bow off his shoulder, pulled an arrow from the quiver on his back, and fired. A white flash shocked the air and a sharp snap traveled through his body. He was prepared for it; the two riflemen were not.

They doubled over, twisting away, stunned. Two blunt-tipped arrows flew at them, impacting chest and upper back with audible thumps. The black-fatigued men crumpled to the asphalt street.

A pistol shot exploded behind him accompanied by glass flying out from the shop windows. Something small buzzed past Green Arrow's head. He dropped as another shot fired and the windshield of the SUV behind him exploded. He rolled toward the street. Heavy bullets gouged chunks of concrete out of the sidewalk. The bottom of the open driver's door passed over him and he sprang to his feet, pressing his back to the SUV. The two gunmen inside the shop were closer to the front than he had anticipated. They carried .50 caliber Desert Eagle semiautomatics.

Typical. These guys hadn't come for a fight, but they'd brought cannons anyway.

Two jagged holes blasted through the driver's door. Green Arrow pulled another shaft and pressed back against the open driver's seat, sheltering behind the wheel. The engine block would give him temporary cover. Half the door ripped away. The men were trashing their own transportation, which was stupid. However, they weren't rushing out like Butch and Sundance, which was smart. They were using cover and their firepower.

The front of the vehicle rocked when several slugs pounded into it. Steam geysered up from the punctured radiator. Green Arrow leaned around the door, brought up the arrow, and let it fly through the empty front window of the store. A heavy *whoomp* preceded a cloud of tear gas billowing up inside the shop.

One man stumbled out into the clear air, trailing spirals of smoke. He coughed and gagged, covering his face with one arm, and fired wildly into the air, unable to control the massive pistol with one hand. Bullets flew in all directions, smashing windows high above, cracking the sidewalk, and punching more holes in the SUV.

Green Arrow drew and shot just as a bullet ripped off another hunk of the door next to him. A jagged piece of steel punched into his Kevlar and bounced to the asphalt. The tranq arrow hit the gunman solid in the thigh to avoid probable body armor on his torso. The weakening man squeezed off another booming round that spun him around and threw him to the ground. He scrubbed at his face, trying to get back to his feet, before stumbling flat against the cement.

The archer continued to study the smoke roiling out of the storefront for signs of the last gunman. No motion visible from inside. The gunfire had ceased. Green Arrow slipped in a crouch around the rear of the SUV. He paused to kick an assault rifle across the street out of the reach of one of the black-suited men who was groaning and fighting to recover.

Green Arrow inched up along the passenger's side of the vehicle; gunfire exploded from the shop again. He dove inside the rear door. Thundering blasts from the pistol ripped through a fender and exploded a front tire. One of the headrests exploded in chunks of foam and the rear window blew out.

The archer pulled an arrow and pressed the bottom of his boot against the running board. Launching himself away from the vehicle, he flew low over the ground, nocking and firing. The shaft burrowed through the smoke and disappeared into the shop. Green Arrow hit, bounced, and rolled.

Booming shots blasted out of the tear gas and whipped past the archer as he came to his feet and scrambled toward the shop. He leapt into the air and somersaulted, feeling something tug at his tunic. Arrow slammed against the wall, recovered his feet, and spun to aim an arrow toward the shop window.

He waited.

In a second, someone was going to die.

2

"Okay, Barry, we're going to activate the magnetic field and see how the plasma reacts."

Barry Allen stood inside a ring of huge equipment, a modest version of the S.T.A.R. Labs particle accelerator that made him the Flash. He wore his red costume, and a circular piece of machinery was clamped to his chest.

Barry was the Flash.

He was the fastest man alive.

Well, that was debatable, because he'd met other speedsters who were faster. However, they were from the future or another Earth, so Barry still made his claim with confidence. That is, until recently.

Several weeks ago, Barry started to experience issues with his speed powers. He began to vibrate at a different frequency from reality, quite literally, sometimes for a few seconds, sometimes longer. The cause of the phenomenon turned out to be an anomalous energy in his body, temporal plasma he had acquired while shutting down a destructive singularity that had opened over Central City months ago.

Being the Flash meant Barry Allen reacted fast. Being Barry Allen meant the Flash was particularly susceptible to the fear of losing those closest to him. Those emotions were killing him. When under stress, neurotransmitter biochemicals coursed through his body, primarily cortisol, as they did to anyone. He was different, however, in that he was the host to an anomalous plasma that was destroying him. The cortisol rush was the very thing that activated the plasma which then used the Flash's speed force for fuel to spread and overtake his body.

Two other people worked keyboards at a nearby workstation. Cisco Ramon, the young engineer who had spoken, in jeans and a t-shirt that proclaimed WILL WORK FOR KARMA. His long black hair was shoved behind his ears. Caitlin Snow, doctor and biochemist, was similarly young but more professional and restrained in appearance. They both tried unsuccessfully to hide hints of concern on their faces.

"So what's the best we can hope for?" Barry asked.

"The best," Cisco answered, "is that the magnetic field will attract the plasma, pull it out of your system, and funnel it out of your body through that inertial channel on your chest. We will capture and contain it in the magnetic mirrors surrounding you."

Caitlin glanced at her bio-readouts. "Barry, your heart rate is rising."

He took deep calming breaths. *Be still. Breathe.* He heard Oliver's instructions in his head.

"Better," she reported.

"Let's see what happens," Barry called out. "Ready when you are."

"This may sting a little." Cisco winced and pressed a key.

Barry screamed.

He imagined every cell in his body rupturing, exploding in a burst of fire. The horrific scraping in his brain eclipsed the sound of his own screeching lungs. The image of Cisco and Caitlin wavered through ripples of air that could have been heat or could have been the severing of reality, the rupture of the dimension.

Barry experienced the numbing terror of a loss of certainty, having transported beyond the agony with no idea where he was. He couldn't feel or understand anything.

"Barry!"

He heard his name from somewhere.

"Oh my God. Barry. Wake up. Barry!"

A cool sensation slid into him, jostling his attention.

Bright light. A dark shape suddenly blocked it. Eyes stared at him. Frightened eyes.

Barry told the shape to move.

"I think he's coming around."

Caitlin appeared out of the darkness. She held a syringe dripping something from the glowing tip of the needle. Cisco's face pushed in next to her.

"Did it work?" Barry mumbled.

"Um... no." Cisco grinned with relief that Barry was talking. "It didn't work *a lot.*"

"Plasma still there?" Barry slurred.

"Still there. All we did was agitate it."

"Yeah, I felt it."

"We'll know more later." Caitlin spread Barry's eyelids and shined a bright light into his eyes. "When we examine the results." Her face looked more pensive than usual.

Barry flexed his fingers and toes. Feeling was returning. He smiled, or thought he did. A slight tilt of his head showed him the familiar med bay of S.T.A.R. Labs.

"How long have I been out?" he asked.

"Not long." Caitlin straightened and checked a saline bag that was nearly empty. "Ten minutes."

Barry raised his arm to see the IV needle taped into his hand. His skin was red and blistered.

"I'm burned."

"Yes," Caitlin said. "Thank God nothing life-threatening. And you do still have a small bit of your healing factor active, so the worst will pass. But it's going to hurt for a while."

"So the magnetic field agitated the plasma." Barry started to sit up but felt Caitlin's hand on his chest. "Maybe if we used more power—"

"No!" Caitlin exclaimed.

"Yeah, that's not happening." Cisco stood back and crossed his arms.

"But we got a reaction," Barry said.

"We did," Cisco replied. "But the plasma seems to have bonded to your speed force. It's using your power. If we zapped it with enough energy to drive it into our electromagnetic channel, you couldn't survive it. So, yes, we could use more energy to remove the plasma, but there wouldn't be a Barry left behind."

"That's not optimal."

"No, it isn't." Caitlin folded her stethoscope. "But we have other options. Felicity is working her angle in Star City for the Markovian technology. And you have the meditative techniques that Oliver is teaching you."

"Right. Be more zen."

Caitlin pulled up his sleeves and pointed to his arms.

"When I was fixing the IV, I saw this. How long have you had it?"

Barry looked at her in confusion until his gaze followed hers. Long black streaks twisted along the length of his arm like veins.

They *were* veins. His veins.

The shock on his face must have been plain.

"I gather they're new then." Caitlin kept her face neutral, as any doctor worth her salt would, so she didn't alarm her patient. He lifted his shirt and saw the telltale dark lines stretching across the skin of his abdomen.

"Crap. It's getting worse. I thought we were slowing it down."

"We are," Caitlin replied. "If we had done nothing, I'm not sure you'd be here talking to us. I'll run more tests on you and we'll see what new information it gives us."

"How much longer do you think I have?"

"That's not a question we're asking," she snapped. Then she settled and said, "Just don't stop what you're doing. Every second you buy me is time we can use to find a cure."

Barry nodded.

"Right." Cisco hefted the magnetic channel. "I'll get this thing working so it doesn't rip your atoms apart."

"Sounds fantastic." Barry sighed and flopped back into his pillow. "I liked it better when I just ran fast and hit guys to solve my problems."

"Good times." Cisco nodded in agreement.

"And we'll have them again," Caitlin assured them both as she strode from the room. "I have no intention of letting this damn plasma take someone else I care about."

"Oh, she's feisty." Cisco winked at Barry. "There's no stopping her once she gets like that. Look out."

Barry's gaze drifted to the blackened veins bulging along his biceps while Cisco checked his cell.

"Uh oh," Cisco muttered.

"What?"

"Nothing." Cisco tried to look innocent. "It's nothing he can't handle."

"He who?" Barry pushed himself up in bed. "*He who?*"

"Oliver." Cisco held up his phone, displaying a red blinking dot on the map of Central City. "Remember that militia group that was talking about robbing the gold exchange? Well, they're robbing the gold exchange. And Green Arrow is in the middle of it."

"Gotta go." Barry swung his feet onto the floor with a grunt of pain.

"You're in no shape to—"

Barry was gone in a flurry of papers blown off tabletops.

A red streak swept across the street and rushed into the shattered shop with a gust of wind.

"Flash! No!" Green Arrow shouted.

His words barely stopped echoing when a red-suited figure appeared on the sidewalk holding up a semiconscious man with one hand. The Flash held the heavy semiautomatic pistol with two fingers.

"This the last guy?" The Flash grinned. "You okay?"

"Get down!" Green Arrow pressed against the wall and turned away.

A blast from inside the shop threw out a shower of glass and wood shrapnel amidst a thick wave of tear gas. Green Arrow turned back coughing to see the sidewalk empty.

The Flash stood farther down the street still holding the gunman, who wore a gas mask. He whistled. "Man,

I hope their insurance will cover that."

Green Arrow heard a noise. He pulled a blunt-tipped arrow and loosed it at a rifleman on the street who sat up cradling his assault rifle. The arrow clipped the man's head and he fell over unconscious.

The Flash zipped back up to Green Arrow with a look of admiration for the knockout shot. Arrow took the .50 caliber pistol from the Flash, ejected the magazine, and cleared the chamber.

"Check him for weapons," Green Arrow said, "and be careful."

Before the sentence was finished, the Flash had his hands full of knives, ammo magazines, and two small revolvers. He nodded his head toward the smoking storefront. "This area was pretty hard hit by Weather Wizard's tornadoes anyway, so a little bomb arrow won't make much difference I guess. So all this for gold?"

"Yes." Green Arrow went to each of the other gunmen, depriving them of their small arsenals. "They had heard rumors that the owner of that coin shop didn't clear out his inventory after the storms."

"Hm. He didn't?" The Flash took long plastic zip ties from Green Arrow and secured all the gunmen's wrists and ankles.

"We'll find out when the tear gas clears. Or the police will." Green Arrow spoke into his comm link. "Cisco? Are you online?"

"Right here," Cisco replied over the comm. "C.C.P.D. is on the way, G.A."

"Don't call me G.A."

"Green Arrow?" The militiaman squinted up through red eyes and struggled against the zip ties. "You're in the wrong place. This isn't fair." He looked over at the Flash. "You gonna let this happen? This is your city, ain't it?"

The Flash pointed down at the man. "You're lucky he got to you first."

"Oh please." The militiaman lay back on the street. "You may be fast, Flash, but you won't kill us. You're a good guy. That guy, though. Everybody says he's nuts. I almost died!"

Police sirens drew closer. Flashing blue lights appeared a mile up the avenue. Green Arrow stepped over to the cable still hanging from the rooftop. He slid the bow over his shoulder and took hold of the rappelling device.

"Flash," he commanded in his altered voice, "stay here and talk to the police. Then meet me back at base."

"Base? Oh, oh yeah. Base." The Flash waved. "You got it."

"We have things to talk about."

The Flash smiled, but suddenly went deadly serious when he saw the stern expression on Arrow's face.

"We do?" The Flash swallowed nervously.

The archer triggered the cable recall and was drawn skyward into the darkness.

3

Green Arrow entered the Cortex at S.T.A.R. Labs. Barry was already back. He sat in civvies, long legs dangling off a table. His Flash costume now covered a mannequin that stood in a lit alcove across the command center. Caitlin and Cisco sat at their workstations and streams of data flashed over the monitors. The Cortex was almost barren in its cleanliness, not too different from the operations space he kept under Palmer Tech back in Star City. The three turned to greet Green Arrow with smiles of congratulations.

The archer stared at the faint black lines on Barry's forearms.

Barry self-consciously rolled down his sleeves.

"So I assume the magnetic channel didn't work," Green Arrow said.

"Not as such," Cisco replied. "But it showed us some interesting possibilities."

"Barry, can I see you?" Green Arrow walked up the ramp into the med bay.

When he heard Barry enter the room behind him, he said without turning, "What were you doing out there?"

"Out there? Talking to Cisco and Caitlin."

"Not now. On the street earlier. Why were you there?"

"Um…" Barry's voice was hesitant, unclear why he was being questioned. "…because you were facing four goons with guns."

"I face four goons with guns every day. That wasn't *your* job, Barry."

"Look, I'm sorry for helping you out. What's the issue, Oliver?"

"The issue is –" Green Arrow spun around and pinned the younger man with his intense gaze, "– you asked me to help you, but I can't do that if you won't listen to me."

"But you were—"

"It doesn't matter what I'm doing. It only matters what you're doing."

"So I should just sit and meditate while you're under fire?"

"Yes. You have one job now. Work on controlling your emotional responses. You practice in the morning with me, and in the evening by yourself. Without fail."

Barry Allen slumped his shoulders. For a second he looked like a kid on the wrong end of a scolding he didn't understand. He struggled with arguing or apologizing because he genuinely didn't know which was appropriate.

"Do it now." Green Arrow refused to reach out or soften. "Go work."

"Look, I can't just stop being the Flash. Isn't that the reason you're here, to keep me running while Caitlin works on a way to fix the anomalous plasma in my body?"

"No. I'm here to train you."

"Right. So I can run."

"No."

"Then what's the purpose?" Barry's hands slapped against his thighs in frustration.

"You're training so you can learn how to train." Green Arrow peered out from inside the hood. "I thought you understood that. This isn't about you being the Flash. It's about survival."

"The goal of all this work I'm doing has to be so I can keep being the Flash. So if I have to stop being the Flash in order to practice, that seems counterproductive."

Green Arrow stood quietly for a moment. He pulled the mask away from his eyes and pushed back the green hood. He was Oliver Queen now and some of the hardness slipped away. He did feel sympathy for Barry because he remembered his own earliest days training. It seemed like a lifetime ago when he first fell under the influence of Yao Fei back on the island of Lian Yu. Oliver had felt as if he was being misled and bullied, but he needed the rigor and strain because otherwise the island would have consumed him.

Unlike Oliver, Barry was no privileged trust-fund kid washed up on a dangerous island. He was the

Flash and had several years of the severity of being a metahuman Super Hero under his belt. His experiences were far outside those of everyday humanity. Barry had endured incredible rigors, both physical and psychological. Still, apparently his mind worked very much the way a normal young adult's would. That had to change, and change soon, or Barry was going to disappear forever under the terrible threat building inside his own body, his own Lian Yu.

"Let's go." Oliver made for the door of the med bay.

"Go where?" Barry followed. "You know, communication is our friend. We talk a lot more in Central City than you guys in Star City."

"Trust me, I know."

Oliver led him past Cisco and Caitlin, who suddenly pretended to be engrossed in their work. The two men left the Cortex and went down to the sub-level. A huge tunnel ran around the perimeter of the circular building. It was once the home of S.T.A.R. Labs' crowning achievement, the particle accelerator. Now it was a tomb-like structure curving infinitely away both ahead and behind. The curved walls of the Pipeline, as they called it, showed new cracks and fissures from a recent battle.

Oliver and Barry walked silently past dangling wires and ruptured pipes. The archer turned into a short hallway that led to a chamber—a cell. The particle accelerator tunnel had been modified into a makeshift prison to hold metahuman criminals too dangerous for traditional incarceration. The Pipeline prison was empty now, but the cells remained. Oliver and Barry entered one of them. It was bland, featureless, and disturbingly sterile.

"Cisco," Oliver said, "do you hear me?"

"Roger that, G.A.," came a voice from above. "I mean… uh…" He trailed off into silence.

"I want you to close and lock the door. Then shut down communication and visual contact. In an hour, you can check on us and—"

"Wait a second," Barry interrupted. "What if something happens?"

"Then it happens," Oliver said.

"I mean like a metahuman attack in the city."

"I know what you mean. Cisco, go ahead."

"Cisco, wait!" Barry called out, and then gave Oliver a reasonable smile. "Okay, I get the point. I'll try harder from now on."

"No, you won't."

Barry grew angry. "You can't lock me up to make me do what you want."

Oliver stared.

"No, really." Barry laughed now. "Oliver, really, you can't."

The archer removed his bow and quiver, and sat on the hard floor. He folded his legs into a lotus position and then raised his eyebrows at Barry as an invitation to join him.

"I promise." Barry held up his hand in the Boy

Scout salute. "Okay? Promise. I'll practice twice a day. No distractions. No rescues or crime fighting. I'll just sit and breathe even if Deathstroke is hitting you with a crowbar." He pointed toward the door. "So let's go."

Oliver didn't budge.

Barry leaned casually against the wall. "Listen, they'll tell you that I can follow through. Hey, Cisco, Caitlin. Tell him. I'll practice like I'm supposed to. Right?"

The door slid shut and locked.

Barry rolled his eyes. "Are you kidding me? Come on, Cisco. This isn't right."

"Shutting down communications," Cisco announced. "See you boys in an hour."

"Don't!" Barry yelled up at the ceiling speaker. "Hey! Cisco. Caitlin. Open up. Hey! Guys?"

Oliver remained in the same position.

Barry huffed in disgust and swayed off the wall. He settled next to Oliver while muttering under his breath, "I could just vibrate through the door if I wanted to."

"No, you can't." Oliver laid one hand atop the other in his lap. "This is the cell where you kept Reverse Flash. Get into position and we'll start with breathing."

"This is so bogus."

Groaning, Barry drew his lanky frame into a lotus position and unconsciously began the specialized breathing regime Oliver had taught him. It wasn't long before the tension left his face and, as his breathing grew deep and regular, he settled into the proper frame of mind.

"Remember, Barry, associate this mindful state with your trigger. The microscope you owned when you were a kid. Remember the calm. The timelessness. No rush. No hurry. Follow your process. Everything ahead of you. Step by step. One foot in front of the other."

Barry settled deeper into a meditative posture.

Oliver followed suit. He began to breathe. Air filled his lungs, held, and released. And again. And again. He was always amazed by how well it worked. Oliver hadn't actively practiced meditation for years until last week when he started instructing Barry. It felt good to return to it.

The world slowed. He felt the texture of the floor beneath him. The pressure of his knees and feet. The impressions of his fingers touching. His mind drew inward.

Oliver still saw Barry across from him, but his thoughts wandered. He let them. There was no value in forcing the mind. Let it guide you; let it teach you.

He smelled wet soil and foliage. The air chilled. The distinct and familiar scent of evergreens washed over him.

Lian Yu.

It meant *purgatory* in Mandarin. Oliver spent the better part of five years on that frigid rock in the North China Sea fighting for his life. In some ways, he realized he had actually lost that fight. When he left Lian Yu, there was little left of the Oliver Queen who had washed up there.

In the early days, when he still believed he could get away from the island with some shred of his previous identity, Oliver recalled Yao Fei sitting cross-legged in front of him in the dripping fir forest. The sun rose in the distance behind Yao Fei, throwing his stern face with its scraggly beard into shadow inside the green hood he always wore.

"You are staring at me," Yao Fei had said quietly on that morning.

"I'm waiting for you to say something," Oliver replied.

"Then I will. Stop looking at me. You don't need to know what I look like. You need to see yourself."

Oliver smirked.

"Is that funny?" Yao Fei had a bit of an edge to his question. He pushed back the green hood, angling his head in a threatening position.

"No, it's just so… zen."

"How would you know?"

Oliver tightened his muscles in the lotus position. He closed his eyes and began to chant softly.

"What's that noise?" Yao Fei asked sharply.

"It's my mantra."

Yao Fei chuckled. Oliver smiled too, feeling like he had finally struck a common chord with the general. Suddenly Yao Fei's hand flashed up with a stick and slapped Oliver hard across the face.

"Ow! What the hell are you doing?"

"Every time I hear you making those ridiculous

sounds, I will hit you. That will be my mantra." The general set the stick on the ground next to his leg. He straightened the tattered remains of the People's Liberation Army uniform he wore. "Now, start again. Breathe. That is all you need to do."

"Sitting in the woods breathing won't get me off this island." Oliver rubbed his sore face and looked around at the deep green forest surrounding them like a cage.

"You have spent your whole life thinking the universe is here to help you, but it does not care whether you live or die. You must learn to survive in that universe now." Yao Fei's hand inched toward the stick. "Breathe."

Oliver's mind wandered off the island and more ghosts slid past. His father's last seconds spent explaining his sins to his son while they bobbed helplessly in a life raft in the North China Sea just before putting a pistol to his own head.

Oliver recoiled at the sound of that gunshot.

"Oliver?" Barry's gaze shifted. "You all right?"

Oliver breathed heavily through his nose. The calm was gone. Worse, he had broken Barry's concentration.

"Yes. Sorry."

"Isn't this supposed to be relaxing? Your face was all twisted like you were in pain."

"How did you do?" Oliver stretched out his legs and twisted to loosen his muscles.

"Pretty good." Barry continued to watch Oliver with concern. He checked his phone. "It's been nearly an hour. That time passed like nothing. I feel a lot better."

"Did you blur today?" Oliver jumped to his feet and reached out to help Barry stand.

"No, not today. It was two days ago." Barry thought. "No, three. I really think this is helping."

"Good. When it happened last, were you running?"

"Yeah."

"Did you see anyone during the blur? Reverse Flash?"

"No, not that time. It was just a blip really. I came back in a few seconds. And today when I ran out to help you with those goons, I didn't blur at all. I think you're helping. Sorry to be so dense about it."

"It's hard." Oliver wondered if Barry really thought the exercises were helping, or if he was just trying to make Oliver feel better. That would be typical of Barry. "Has Caitlin checked your levels today?"

"No, but everything's good."

Oliver raised a doubtful eyebrow.

"Well," Barry added, "the levels were up a little, but so little it was insignificant. The rate of the plasma increase has definitely slowed. We're on the right track. When are we going to Markovia to retrieve what we need from this Wallenstein guy?"

"John's working on it."

"John is?"

"His wife, Lyla, is head of the government agency A.R.G.U.S." Oliver continued stretching. "So John's gathering the latest intel. Don't want to go in blind, not against Wallenstein. Don't worry, it'll come together soon."

"I know. I'm just a little impatient to get back to normal." Barry paused. "I'm not supposed to be impatient, am I?"

"No. There's no reason for impatience as long as you are working. And you are. Step by step. Stay in the moment. And I'm not saying you can't be the Flash while we wait. But control your emotions. Keeping your mind steady will hold down the plasma in your system, and hopefully keep your blurring to a minimum. You have to be able to use your speed and not have it go out of control and feed the plasma. All you can control is yourself."

Barry nodded in agreement.

"Oliver, I want to thank you. We called you originally because we needed help on the streets with Pied Piper and his metahumans. But I should've thought about you for this other issue I'm going through. Nobody has your focus, and even though I don't always act like it, I really appreciate you bringing your expertise to help me."

"It's been an hour," Cisco's voice crackled over the speaker. "Everybody okay?"

"We're good." Oliver retrieved his bow and quiver. "Open up."

As the door slid away, Barry's gaze locked on Oliver's tunic. He took a deep breath and reached over, tugging on the green Kevlar costume.

Oliver looked down to see a hole in the heavy fabric

of his tunic dotted with dried blood. One of those .50 calibers had just nicked his ribs. A fraction of an inch the other way could've been death. Fortunate, but Yao Fei would've reminded him the universe didn't care one way or the other. The archer slung his bow on his shoulder and briefly touched the cloth hood crumpled behind his head. The stale institutional air beneath S.T.A.R. Labs still carried the faint scent of the dangerous Lian Yu forests.

4

Felicity Smoak grabbed her coat and her tablet and headed for the door out of the underground command center for Team Arrow, the lair or, more humorously, the *Arrowcave*. Her attention was so focused she literally bumped into the broad chest of John Diggle.

"Oh, John. I was just going to call you."

"Then where are you going?"

"I was going to call you from outside, where I was going." Felicity noticed the grim face. "But what's wrong? Is something the matter with Lyla or your daughter?"

"No, they're fine," was his gruff response.

"That's the same kind of *fine* Oliver uses when he's hiding the fact that the world is about to end."

John grunted.

"Oh my God, is the world about to end?"

"Not quite so biblical." John let out a pensive breath. "Lyla is worried an incursion into Markovia could compromise A.R.G.U.S. operations. She wants us to stay out. I explained Barry's situation, and she understands, but answers to people high in the government and that puts her in a precarious position. She knows we have to go in, but trust me, it just doesn't make for a very pleasant date night."

Felicity smiled. "Oh. Okay."

"That's it? *Oh. Okay.*" John shook his head.

"I've got something that may save your marriage and help Barry at the same time. You're welcome. That's what I was going to call you about. While I was nosing around looking for more information about the research done in Markovia, I found leads to similar work here in the United States at the same time."

"That's a coincidence."

"Maybe not. The programs may have been related in some fashion I just don't know yet. And even so, parallel research programs on big subjects aren't rare. Like when Hollywood brings out two blockbusters about singing killer whales at the same time."

"Uh huh."

"It's just that Markovia made public announcements about their research, and then it apparently went nowhere, whereas the American research was kept under wraps in case it went nowhere."

"And where did it go?"

"Nowhere." Felicity slipped into her coat as they went up the ramp out of the Arrowcave. "But we're going to see if we can find it. The research was done at Queen Consolidated years ago, before it became

Palmer Tech. I've called up all the old files, including old Queen data tapes they had to dig out of the archives. If we're lucky, we may not need to invade Markovia, and the Diggle house will be its usual love nest."

"Have you told Oliver?"

Felicity scowled. "I don't have to tell Oliver everything. He's busy in Central City getting in touch with Barry's inner Flash. I can do a little groundwork on my own."

"So what we're looking for is here in Star City?" John brightened, holding the door.

"I think there may be information at one of Queen's former office buildings. In the Glades."

John's humor faded. "That's a bad area, Felicity."

"Hence you coming with me." She waited by his car.

Once he was behind the wheel, they headed downtown. Soon they were passing into the impoverished neighborhood called the Glades. It had once been home to factories and businesses, but now was blighted and decayed, not even worth the money to tear it down.

They pulled up in front of a brick building that in its glory days had stood tall and glittering in the sun. Now its windows lay shattered and cracked. The walls dripped rust across the graffiti scrawled over its surface. Weeds had grown from mere stunted sprouts to tall grasses and even a few oak saplings reached up to the first floor.

"You're sure it's in there?" he asked her.

"Yes. Well, no. But this is where the records lead."

"Let's check it out then."

Felicity's shoes crunched on the broken glass scattered about the ground as they approached the main doors. The frames hung empty and they stepped through into the lobby. It was also empty. Anything that wasn't nailed down had long since been hauled away. Felicity expected that to be the case throughout the building. Her stomach knotted.

Her shoe sunk into something soft and wet. Thank goodness she hadn't worn her best heels. John reached out to steady her as they found the stairwell.

"Which floor?"

"Tenth," she told him. "Not too bad, right? It could have been worse. It could have been the eleventh."

John produced a flashlight and shined it ahead of them. The stairwell smelled terrible; devoid of air for years, it was musty and stale. Dirt and debris had piled up on the sides, though the center appeared clear enough.

"Looks better than I thought it would, really," Felicity said.

"People live here."

A look of horror swept over her face. "It's leaking and rusting and it smells of... garbage," she put politely, but that wasn't the only pungent smell.

"It's got a roof. That makes it viable housing." John scanned the dark landings above them. "So what are we looking for?"

"I don't know exactly. The project was intended

to create small, stable wormholes in order to generate plasma energy. The lead scientist was a man named Jackson Straub. He ran the program—from what I can tell, he *was* the program—until he left Queen Consolidated, and the project was mothballed after that."

"Where's this Straub guy now?"

"He's dead. Heart attack, I believe. He died a few years after leaving Queen, but it wasn't suspicious that I could find. He was nearly eighty years old. For most of his years with the company, his office was here."

A barely discernible 10 lingered on the door ahead of them. John signaled for quiet as he turned the knob. It swung open with a rusty squeal that made them both wince.

The hallway had natural light due to the fact that some rooms had no doors and shafts of sunlight dappled the floor. Nature's colors abounded in areas of green as weeds sprouted in the sunshine while moss crept to claim the shadows. More graffiti was scrawled across the walls.

An old man whose tight black curls were now aged white opened the nearest door and leveled a baseball bat at them.

"Get out of here!" he shouted.

"We're just passing through," John assured the man.

"Pass through faster. There's no room for no more here."

"Pretty sure I don't want to stay here," Felicity muttered.

John pulled out what cash he carried in his pocket: a couple of twenties and a fifty, and handed it to the old man. Eyes darted to the cash, probably more than he had seen in a year.

For a moment, Felicity watched pride and desperation fight a small war over his features before the gnarled arthritic hand snatched up the money.

"I ain't got anything to tell you."

Felicity thought it funny he told them that after he took the bills.

"Just for interrupting your day," John told him patiently. "We'll be done here quickly and on our way."

"Don't take nothing. It don't belong to you."

"Well, as a matter of fact, it—"

John grabbed Felicity and tugged her along before she could finish her sentence.

"What room are we looking for?"

Felicity pulled out her tablet and opened a schematic. "Office 1025C. Far left side."

"Let's hope it doesn't have a current occupant."

They squeezed past overturned desks piled in the hallway, along with other fixtures that were barely recognizable. At the end of the corridor they found the office. It looked like it was being used as a storage room or a dumping ground. Another room lay beyond this one with an actual door still on its hinges.

Light fixtures hung by mere wires as the decaying ceiling could no longer support them. Wallpaper rotted like flaking skin. A vine crept in through broken glass and took up the whole bay window; limited light shone in, but it was enough.

"I can't see how anything would still be here," John muttered.

Old computers sat moldering on desks. Felicity rummaged through the drawers. Most of the paperwork was gone, either hauled away when the building was decommissioned or burned for fuel by the residents. She didn't know what she expected to find after all these years.

A sense of sadness fell over Felicity. The ghosts of technology lay everywhere. The detritus left behind waited for nature to take its course; relics of the past long forgotten, abandoned in a desolate landscape.

A tin garbage can stood nearby. Inside were ashes. She blew through the top layer but there was nothing left. But then by her foot she saw some half-burned scraps that had escaped the fire to drift down to the damp floor where the embers were snuffed out.

She flicked the scraps about with a finger. Fragments of spreadsheets, datebook pages, and some office memos. Most were not applicable until her eye caught two words—*plasma shielding*. She plucked it from the litter.

They scrounged for a half hour more, but found nothing else. Just when they were about to move onto the next room, something made John jerk upright and immediately Felicity paused in her work.

"What is it?" she whispered.

He held up a hand for quiet and she fell silent, listening for what he had heard. Painstaking seconds of stillness passed but nothing happened and Felicity's wild heart rate slowed to a more normal pace. Finally, John relaxed and nodded at her. She continued to search through the tumbled desks and toppled filing cabinets.

A soft scrape interrupted her thoughts. Rats, maybe.

John heard it too and he moved to the outer door, motioning her back out of sight. She crouched behind a barricade of desks.

Shadows moved out in the hall. Squatters? Maybe they were just curious. *Please let them be curious*, Felicity prayed. She heard no footsteps at all. That was never a good thing.

A face peered into the door and she shrunk down farther behind her barrier, pulling a Taser from her satchel. The figure wore a heads-up display over his right eye and sported a telltale earwig. That sort of tech ruled out gang members or irate residents.

John quickly grabbed the man and yanked him into the room to sprawl across the floor into the metal desks Felicity hid behind. The towering structure teetered and she pulled back just in time to avoid a falling drawer.

A second commando dressed in black fatigues pointed a 9mm pistol at John. With a swipe of his leg, John kicked the weapon out of his hand. Grabbing the still-outstretched arm, he yanked him into the room but then swung the body to slam against others crowding into the door. John blocked and punched, using all his considerable skills.

The man sprawled on the floor in front of Felicity rose to his feet, furiously drawing a knife. He moved toward John's unprotected back. Felicity lunged at him, pressing the Taser against the man's shoulder. The electricity crackled, arching the man backward. Felicity jumped aside as he flopped onto the floor. She sidestepped him and darted back behind the metal desks as bullets pinged all around her.

"Move to the next room," John commanded.

Felicity crawled over a broken desk and struggled with the door. It moved stiffly, its hinges rusted and warped. But slowly it opened. Behind her she heard John fighting and she turned back, desperate to help.

"Go!" John ground out, ducking under a blow and stiff-arming a man that rushed him.

She shoved the door the rest of the way open with a shoulder and a determined shout. The next room was piled with as much debris. The only other way out was the window. Outside the dirty glass, she saw a rickety, rusted mockery of a fire escape. Half the bolts were gone and it listed off the brick wall. She looked back to the door where John fought to hold ground.

"There's a fire escape," Felicity called, "sort of."

Outnumbered, he gave ground, darting into the room with her. "Get on it!"

"It's not safe!"

"Safer than here!"

Felicity gingerly climbed out onto the unstable fire escape. Flakes drifted down as the entire structure shifted. She clutched onto the rusting rail, feeling the sharp iron filings dig into her palm. She started climbing down when John yelled at her.

"Go up!"

"Up?" she shouted back incredulously, but she started heading for the roof. They were two floors from the top. Her hand slapped the edge of the roof just as John leapt out on the fire escape below her. The added weight caused the structure to pull away. Felicity held on. The iron assembly shuddered again as two commandos jumped onto it after John.

"Jump!" John shouted over the ringing footfalls coming up from below her.

She did. Her waist hit the edge of the retaining wall, pushing her breath out in a rush. Her legs kicked free over empty air. Squirming, she flopped ungracefully over onto the roof. As soon as she had solid footing again, she scrambled to reach back for John.

The fire escape slammed back against the brick wall with a rusty screech of twisting iron. The two commandos wrestled to hold onto John until they realized the structure was falling apart beneath them. It was every man for himself. All three struggled to reach the top.

John leapt for Felicity. She reached out and grabbed for his hand. A gasp of relief escaped her lips that turned to one of alarm as she took John's full weight.

The fire escape wrenched free of the brick and

collapsed, taking the other two men down in a tangled rumble of wreckage.

"I can't hold you," she shouted.

John braced his boots against the wall and pulled himself up onto the edge of the roof. Felicity let out a spent breath and collapsed next to him.

The roof door slammed open and five more goons piled out. The soldiers moved without speaking, operating off hand signals.

"Come on." John climbed to his feet, pulling her up too. "We have to go."

They ran for the far side of the building. Felicity saw the edge of the roof coming up. She shot a look at John sprinting next to her.

"What's the plan?" She dreaded the answer.

"Get you to safety."

"There's too many for you to handle alone." Felicity slowed her pace, but his hand was firm on her arm.

"Don't stop."

She didn't, but then the gap between the buildings yawned wide and she knew she wouldn't clear it. John grasped her belt and heaved her across.

"No, wait!" she shouted.

A red shape flew past her as she tumbled onto the opposite roof.

"Cavalry's here," the new figure quipped. A bowstring twanged as she released her arrow while vaulting in midair. One of the paramilitary men flew back from John.

Speedy.

She wore a red version of Oliver's hooded outfit. Speedy landed and rolled. Three arrows fired in rapid succession. One pinned a commando to the rooftop. The second disarmed a man, while the last slammed a blunt end into a third commando and punched him to the ground.

Speedy leapt among them, drawing a gleaming short sword. The blade struck, but didn't kill. Flat-bladed blows instead of deep cuts. She moved between her enemies like blood in the water, a mere wisp visible before dissipating. Both she and John moved among their targets like a well-oiled machine and the men fell before them.

One last commando aimed his pistol at John. The ex-Ranger rolled forward under the shots. Coming to his feet, he grabbed the wrist and twisted, causing the man's nerveless fingers to open and drop his pistol. Then he stepped up like a boxer and slammed a fist into his unprotected jaw. The man collapsed to the ground.

Felicity cheered John and Speedy from her spot on the far roof. Then she winced from a pain in her hip. She twisted to look, but she didn't see any wounds.

John searched the unconscious men and came away with nothing important. He shook his head at Speedy, and they turned and jumped the gap over to Felicity.

"Are you okay?" he asked.

"I thought I was shot." Felicity smiled. "But I'm not, so yay."

"I could've sworn they caught me too, but I don't see any blood." John flexed his arms and legs to his satisfaction. "So we're done here?"

"Yes. I'd like to leave," Felicity said. "It looks like Straub's project might not be quite as mothballed as I thought. And I think I'll call Oliver now."

5

Barry Allen returned to the cell in the Pipeline once used to restrain Reverse Flash. If he couldn't stop the growth of the plasma in his body, it would eventually cause him to blur out of existence. Barry knew Oliver was right, but no matter how important these exercises were, he still couldn't wrap his mind around the fact that they were more important than being the Flash. If he knew someone needed help, he would help no matter what it cost him. When you ran so fast, it was hard to think about long-term consequences. But this wasn't just about the Flash. The concern on the faces of his family and friends reminded Barry every day that he couldn't be self-sacrificing in this. His life mattered to them.

"Cisco, shut it down."

"Okay," came the reply. "See you in an hour."

The door closed and locked. This was the only way he could keep to the plan, and he wanted to do it. He trusted Oliver Queen. The man had been the Green Arrow for years, and had suffered enormous tragedies but kept working. Barry had only the slightest idea of what had happened on the island where Oliver spent five years. He had seen the terrible scars on Oliver's body. There was no telling what scars the man had on his mind.

Barry sat in the middle of the floor, feeling a little silly folding his legs into the lotus position. Meditation had never been his kind of thing. These tricks—not tricks, Oliver would chide him, *techniques*—had enabled him to shift his focus in moments of stress, slow his mind, calm the fight-or-flight reactions. By slowing the flood of cortisol in his system, the plasma became less aggressive. He had actually stopped several blurring incidents when he felt them coming on by using the mental trigger that Oliver had provided him. Barry smiled thinking of his old childhood microscope. Oliver had asked him for something that Barry associated with serenity. Nothing came close to that old microscope for dredging up warm memories of excitement, comfort, and discovery; days when Barry had everything to look forward to.

He settled into his breathing routine. Predictable. Repeatable. Effective. Like science. His heartbeat slowed. He felt himself sitting in the cell, but the environment didn't matter. He could've been anywhere. And soon he was.

Barry saw himself in his laboratory at the Central

City police headquarters where he worked as a CSI investigator. His lab was crowded with folders and evidence bags of cases waiting to be worked on. The tools of science that would allow him to find answers, to discern knowledge out of chaos, also surrounded him.

The lights were low. He sat at his desk, eye pressed to the lens of a microscope. The familiar steel and plastic smell filled his nose. He adjusted the knob to bring a simple hair into focus. The textures and lines fascinated him. So complex and intricate. A world of sophistication hidden in a haze of simplicity. Those mysterious relationships drew Barry to science the way some were drawn to poetry. Everything had meaning. Everything had value.

"Hello, Mr. Allen. Hard at work?"

Barry spun in his chair to see a man in yellow leaning against the counter.

Reverse Flash. Eobard Thawne.

Or Harrison Wells.

Barry resisted the urge to attack the man in the yellow version of his own Flash costume. Any time he saw that yellow suit, he instantly went into fight mode. The face of Harrison Wells made it worse. Wells was the man young Barry had idolized, and who had then trained him to use and manage his speed. It nearly broke Barry when he realized Wells wasn't trying to make the Flash better, only faster to suit his own purposes.

Barry kept one hand on the microscope, realizing

with dread that he was in a blur. The plasma had seized him. It was happening despite his exercises, despite his calming trigger.

"Nowhere to go, Mr. Allen?" Harrison Wells smiled. "Your little mind trick won't work now. Oliver Queen might be helpful if you need to learn to shoot an arrow into a target of concentric circles, but if you think he can save you, you are mistaken."

Barry lunged at Wells…

…and clutched nothing but a handful of papers. The man in yellow stood next to the window with the skyline of Central City behind him. Barry was now in his red Flash costume.

"We'll beat you," he said. "We've beaten you before."

"No, you haven't. Remember, I'm not Wells or Thawne or Reverse Flash or whatever you think of me as. I'm *you*. I'm a creation of your mind. I am the singularity plasma tearing through you. Soon, you'll lose control of your mind, and then your body. You will blur out forever and vanish from your world." Wells held out his hand, palm up, to reveal a small sphere of energy like a crumpled ball of lightning. "I've got your life in my hands. They can't save you, only you can do that. It's just that simple. But you don't know how."

The Flash streaked at him again, swung a fist that swept through the empty air and obliterated half the glass in the window. A heavy wind sprang up inside the room and poured out of the broken glass as if in a pressurized airplane cabin. Loose objects went airborne. Books and papers slapped against him and flew through the hole in the glass. Barry tried to grab them, but they moved too fast.

Through the broken panes, Barry saw a swirling black mass outside like the singularity that had churned over Central City. The wormhole that infected him with plasma. However, when he looked through the glass that remained in the window, it appeared to be a beautiful summer day. Green leaves. Blue sky.

The detritus of Barry's science, of his reason, roared past him into the void. Harrison Wells stood by the desk with a yellow finger pressed down on the microscope, anchoring it against the gale. Papers and files flew. Posters and charts ripped from the walls and slipped out the window. The evidence board he had used to trace his mother's murder case ripped apart. Wallpaper tore free. No, it wasn't wallpaper. It was the paint itself. In fact, all the color bled from surfaces and swirled in the air. The actual shapes of normal objects were pulled from the moorings of their reality and thrown into the tumult. The very concept of Barry's laboratory spun before his eyes and funneled out into the churning anomaly.

Harrison Wells smiled, looking at his index finger still pressed down on the microscope.

"It's getting heavy," he said.

The Flash stared into Wells's eyes, silently pleading for him not to let go. But the man in yellow lifted his finger and the microscope shot for the window.

"Run, Barry."

The Flash flew after it. His hand bumped the lens tube, fingers scrabbling awkwardly as it hung for a second. The microscope elongated in the air and turned into a black spiral in the emptiness. Barry tried to catch it but it was like gathering the wispy seeds of a dandelion floating free. The microscope disappeared through the hole in the glass.

The Flash spun on Wells. His red and the other man's yellow were the only colors left against the black mass. He gathered his muscles to run, thinking only of pummeling Reverse Flash to a pulp. The figure in yellow transformed into a line of color vanishing into the distance. The Flash gave chase.

Barry slammed into the door and crumpled to the floor of the cell. On instinct, he leapt to his feet, ready to fight.

He was alone inside the small chamber in the Pipeline. He was dressed in jeans and a plaid shirt. His hand came away wet and red from his mouth. Black veins pulsed under the skin. He staggered back against the wall, catching his breath, slowing his heart rate.

He dug his phone from his pocket and clicked to check the time. It had only been twenty minutes since lockdown. He was trapped until Cisco opened the door. Barry slid down the wall and wrapped his arms around his knees.

* * *

When Barry shuffled into the Cortex, Caitlin looked up from the computer, expectant, intent on asking how his meditation session went. The look on Barry's face must've told her everything she needed to know.

"What happened? Did you blur?"

"Yeah." Barry sank into a chair. "While I was meditating. I couldn't stop it."

"Let me take some blood." Caitlin tapped him on the arm.

"Don't you have enough blood by now? What more can it tell you?"

"I won't know until it tells me. Now come on."

Barry really didn't want to go through any more testing, but he followed her into the med lab and dutifully hopped on the table. Caitlin went through the routine with practiced speed. Within a few minutes she had three vials of blood and went to a microscope to prepare a slide. Barry stared at the instrument as she put the slide under the light and pressed her eye to the lens.

"How's it look?" Barry asked after a minute. When she didn't straighten immediately, he turned to the dark monitor on the wall. "Put it on the screen."

Caitlin hesitated, but her finger touched a toggle on the microscope and the display flickered onto the monitor. Red blood cells were easy to see. Unfortunately so was the colorless plasma from the singularity.

"Did you treat that sample with cortisol?" Barry asked.

"No. The plasma is now visible without the catalyst."

"That's not good." He breathed out in suppressed concern. "It's really growing, isn't it?" Barry pretended to study the screen with detached objectivity.

"I won't have numbers until I analyze these samples."

"We don't really need numbers to know." Barry offered Caitlin a smile. "I'm not sure these exercises are really helping anymore."

"What's with the 'tude?" Cisco leaned in the door. "Everything we're doing is helping. And once we get that Markovian tech, it's game over for the plasma. Felicity said that tech was designed to generate temporal anomalies. We only need a wormhole to create a reservoir for the plasma inside you. We can exploit the plasma's diffusion matrix and channel it out using our magnetic field inducer. So between Felicity and Caitlin and—hello—me, we can make that puppy siphon the plasma out of you like a singularity Hoover."

"*If* we can secure the tech that is currently housed in the mountain castle of the terrorist Count Wallenstein in Markovia. *If* we can make it work. And *if* it actually does what Felicity thinks it does."

"Dude, that sounds like a first semester problem where I went to engineering school. Or the plot of a really cool comic book."

Barry smiled briefly. "I just keep wondering that if someone had come up with a wormhole generator, don't you think we'd know about it? Yet this thing went into mothballs."

"Nah. Successful projects disappear every day. The everlasting light bulb. Cold fusion. Calorie-free ice cream."

Barry laughed and shook his head.

"What happened here?" Caitlin stepped up to Barry, peering closely at his face. "Where'd you get that bump?"

Barry touched a painful knot on his forehead. "Oh. That must've been when I ran into the cell door chasing Reverse Flash. During the blur."

"*Thawne* Reverse Flash or *Wells* Reverse Flash?" Cisco asked.

"Wells Reverse Flash. He always looks like Wells in the blurs."

"What did Reverse Flash do this time?" Caitlin asked while she retrieved a bottle from a drawer.

"He… um…" Barry shoved his hands in his pockets. "He let my microscope fly out the window."

"Wow!" Cisco whistled in amazement. "Sounds like there's quite a party going on in your head."

Barry bristled. "That microscope meant a lot to me."

"I totally understand." Caitlin daubed ointment on the bump on Barry's forehead. "When I was eight, I got my first Zeiss Axioskop. What did you have?"

"I don't remember the brand name." Barry looked a little embarrassed. "It came from Sears. It wasn't a Zeiss, I can tell you that. Aren't those things thousands of dollars?"

"I don't know. I didn't pay for it. I loved that scope!" She stood quietly with a smile of bliss on her lips. "One summer I tried to sequence my gerbil's genome. I couldn't finish it, but it was a wonderful summer." She collected herself self-consciously and picked up a vial of Barry's blood. "The gerbil was fine."

"I will never understand you biology types." Cisco rolled his eyes. "Weirdos."

A shadowy figure appeared behind Cisco. It towered over him, staring down. The engineer jumped with a shout of alarm.

Oliver Queen stood behind him in the door.

"Holy cow, man!" Cisco put his hand over his heart. "Make a noise or something before you roll up on a guy."

"I just heard from Felicity." Oliver looked past Cisco to Barry. Everyone tensed with anticipation. "There's trouble. I'm going back."

"Okay. I figured something like that." Barry caught his breath, feeling his stomach turn. "Let us know something when you can."

"You're coming with me."

"What? I have a job. I can't just—"

"Find a way. Take a vacation. Detective West will cover for you. We might need the Flash."

"Oliver, I've lost some of my speed." Barry ran his hand over his hair, head down. "And I can blur out at any time now."

"We're running out of time." Oliver turned and walked away. "Pack a bag. We're going to Star City."

6

The big windows in the apartment meant the sun came roaring in as it crested the neighboring skyscrapers. Oliver Queen turned his face away from the light with a groan, stretching out his arms above his head. His eyes opened gradually to squint at the woman lying against him. Felicity Smoak smiled. She was always smiling. How was anyone that happy this early in the morning?

Her fingers trailed across his skin and her smile faltered for just a moment. She didn't say anything but he knew what was going through her mind. So many scars crisscrossed over his flesh. Knives. Guns. Acid. Whips. Arrows. Shark bite even.

She leaned over and kissed the newest one, still aching but healing. Her lips barely touched it but his muscles reacted even so. He drew in a sharp breath, though it was hardly from pain.

"I'm sorry," she told him quietly.

He lifted her chin. "Don't be."

"It looks painful."

"I've had worse." He shifted closer to her, groaning slightly as some of his other aches and bruises made their presence felt.

"I know." Her gaze trailed to the multitude of other scars. "So many," she whispered. "You're going to be a stove-up old man at age sixty."

"I doubt I'll get to sixty," he remarked simply.

Felicity's smile fell and immediately he regretted his answer. Watching the light fade fully from her round face made him ache inside.

"Don't," she told him looking him square in the eyes. "You don't get to joke about that."

"You're right." He brushed a lock of blond hair from her face. "I'll live long past sixty and you'll get to push me around in a wheelchair."

"I push you around now." Her mouth quirked.

"Yes, you do." He gathered her into his arms. "And you're adorable when you do."

Felicity curled up against his warm skin, hiding her face against his chest to keep the day at bay a bit longer. An old wound puckered under Felicity's fingers as they rested across his ribs.

"I'm just glad you're home."

"Me too." Oliver's arm draped over her shoulders. "So tell me about this Jackson Straub you mentioned on the phone."

"So much for romance." Felicity shifted, looking up at him. "The big news is I think Straub may have

actually designed a working wormhole generator."
As she turned her head, her hair brushed against his
bare skin. "Do you remember anything about Queen
Consolidated testing this technology here in Star City?"

"No. But something that potentially dangerous
wouldn't have been done in town. Regulations and
city zoning orders wouldn't have permitted it."

"I'm not sure Queen Consolidated was overly
concerned with regulation." Felicity raised a cynical
eyebrow. "But in this case I think you're right. If the
company wanted to conduct very dangerous tests,
where would they have done it?"

"Queen Consolidated owned a lot of property."

Felicity reached to the side of the bed and retrieved
her tablet. She started typing, or more precisely
hacking. He regretted starting the conversation.

New rule: No work in the bedroom.

"Let's see." Felicity had already called up the defunct
records of his family's old company, subsumed now
into Palmer Technologies. "Real estate, gas companies,
an old shopping mall. A farm." She looked at him
curiously. "Really? A farm?" She shook her head. "I
don't want to know." She turned back to her screen.
"Oh, wait, a mine. A coal mine!"

"We owned a coal mine? Why?"

"It doesn't say. But a mine, depending on how deep
it was, would be a great spot to test something like a
plasma-generating device. It would suppress electrical
conductivity and plasma is ionized—"

"I'll take your word for it."

She kissed him. "Thank you."

"So even if this device was tested in this coal mine, you don't think it's still there, do you?"

"It's probably not." She looked back at her tablet. "But every lead takes us closer. The lack of records on the servers means we have to search for information the old-fashioned way."

"Tell me more about this scientist, Jackson Straub. Who was he?" Rising from the bed, Oliver slipped into a pair of pajama bottoms, dropped to the floor and began vigorous push-ups.

"He came to work for your father about twenty-five years ago. A top researcher. Very highly paid for a long time. Until he quit."

"Why did he quit?"

"He retired, technically. He was getting up in age. Straub wrote a final report that I've read where he explained how the device simply never operated. He believed the fundamental concepts were unsound. The project was shelved by the company because they'd already sunk a ton of money into it and gotten nothing out of it. And Straub retired."

"A failed device isn't very useful to us. Or do you think there is more to it?"

"I'm not sure. Straub didn't leave behind a lot of personal papers. His personnel record is pretty cut-and-dried, standard paperwork but nothing else. The only real glimpse of his personality is the memo I found in his old office that mentions a request for shielding. It had a tone that makes me think he was fighting for it with higher-ups."

"Do you think this device is dangerous?"

"That's a high probability since it is designed for ripping a hole in space-time."

"Strange that it's left such a shallow footprint." Oliver positioned his left fist against the small of his back and continued doing push-ups with one arm.

"Um… yeah, I guess." Felicity was silent for a minute.

Oliver paused in his workout, glancing toward her. Her eyes were locked on his splayed form.

"Wow, you look good in blue. Brings out your eyes." She jumped as though she shook herself and coughed. "I mean, I've dug through all the files. Not much there. So they must have been wiped from the servers or were never on there to begin with."

"Is that normal?" Oliver switched arms and continued to drive himself up and down, barely breathing hard. He relished the burn in his back and shoulders.

"Scientists can be a paranoid lot, particularly if there was some squabble between Straub and Queen Consolidated. I once knew a guy who kept all his schematics in his head. Sort of like Mozart. Did you know he wrote all his symphonies in his head before he put them down on paper?"

Oliver held himself up on one straightened arm and glanced at Felicity. He shook his head with a smile. He loved her like this. Felicity's mind moved at a dizzying pace, full of odd facts and interesting tidbits. He adored watching it race about him. He didn't understand half of what she said, but it didn't matter.

"If he was like Mozart," she continued, "he may not have put anything on the servers."

"That's not going to help us."

"Just because he didn't put it on company servers doesn't mean he didn't put it somewhere."

"I guess that means we're going to explore a mine today."

"Yes!" Felicity threw back the covers and leapt to her feet. She opened her closet. "I wonder what you wear to a mine. I need some flats definitely."

"You're not going." Oliver bounded to his feet, shaking out his arms.

"What? Of course I am."

"Not after what happened in the Glades."

"You need me."

Felicity stood in front of Oliver, trying to look imposing with her pert little nose and tousled hair. It almost brought a smile to his lips but only because her determined expression released a bit of the tension inside him. The fact she was wearing pink elephant pajamas didn't help.

"Yes, I do," Oliver said. "I need you watching over us, not in the field."

"But I'm your technical advisor. I have an idea what we're looking for."

"We'll have Barry with us. He's a scientist, and he has superspeed in case a gunfight breaks out."

"Oh. Barry's here?"

"Yes. He's downstairs on the sofa. I brought him to continue his training."

"How's that going?"

"I don't know." Oliver gazed off into space.

"Why not? Aren't you the one doing the training?"

"Yes." He lowered his voice. "I don't know what I'm doing. I'm trying to come off as some sort of zen master, but I'm not. I got some training back on Lian Yu, and I've read a bit since I've come back, but I haven't practiced meditation regularly for years. Now I stand around lecturing him about practice, practice, practice."

"You believe what you're saying to him, don't you?" Felicity gave him her even stare. "The point is you have a presence of mind that few men can match. Barry knows that and he's smart enough to tap into it. You get that, right?"

"Sure."

"Then what's the problem?"

"I feel like a phony. Like any second I'm going to ask him to snatch a pebble from my hand."

"It's okay to have doubts," Felicity sighed, "but don't let Barry know that you have them because he believes in you. I do too. Just do what you can for his mind and his spirit, while we work on the technology."

Oliver rested heavily on a table, still not accepting. The

muscles of his arms and shoulders bulged with tension.

"So do you think it's wise to take him out to the mine? What happens if those mercenaries show up again?"

"I'm only going to use his big brain. Not his speed. Not if I can help it."

"Fine. Let's call everyone in."

Oliver took her arms and brought her closer to him. "Thank you."

"Sometimes I really hate staying behind." Felicity raised her face to his. "I feel isolated and in some sort of gilded cage."

"It's not a cage. It's a watchtower. Without you overseeing what we do, we'd be working blind." He put a finger under her chin. "Don't ever think you're not with us. You're always with us."

Oliver leaned in to kiss her, but Felicity pulled back. He furrowed his brows at her. She grinned beatifically and lifted her hand. A paperclip rested in the center of her palm.

"Snatch the pebble from my hand," she intoned. "Maybe then you will be worthy, my son."

"I can never be worthy of you," Oliver whispered, staring down at her.

"Oh my God," Felicity sighed, moon-eyed. "Fine, just take my pebble."

7

A dark opening yawned before the small group in the van. They were all dressed in working gear. John exited on the driver's side in black leather and his Spartan helmet. He checked his weapons as Speedy and the Flash hopped out of the back, together in red. Speedy's feet sank into the mud.

"Well," she muttered, "this is totally out of my element."

Green Arrow walked toward the gaping entrance to the mine, scanning the ground. They appeared to be the first people to walk here in years.

"Let's go. Keep your eyes open."

They passed through the entrance and into darkness. Green Arrow reached for his flashlight but, as if on cue, a row of faint lights flickered to life along the ceiling of the tunnel. Water dripped from the walls, still weeping even after all this time. Piles of debris blown in over the years lined the tunnel. Decrepit timbers and rusted iron beams looked incapable of holding back the wind, much less the full weight of the mountain above them.

The team squelched through the wet ground for thirty yards before the tunnel split. One passageway continued on into the dimness, long abandoned and treacherous. The other tunnel only stretched a few yards more and came to a dead end of rock and timber.

"Overwatch, which way?" Green Arrow asked.

"The branch on the left is the original mine," Felicity's voice crackled in their ears, "but the right has notes on construction from the last few decades. And you're welcome for the lights, by the way. It's the best I can do. Most of the systems are shut down."

"The tunnel on the right is collapsed." John laid a hand on a large cross beam that barred their path.

"From the map I'm looking at," Felicity said, "that rock fall is covering the elevator to take you down."

They got to work.

An hour later, when enough of the wreckage had been moved, Oliver stepped over the final beam to examine the wall beyond. His hand brushed the left side and found a small square seam. A panel. He pried it open to find a single button. He pressed it. Within a minute, a signal dinged and doors slid open on a modern elevator coated in dirt.

Green Arrow stepped in and tested the weight. It held with a slight shudder. Barry and John entered next, and the elevator groaned and shimmied.

"It's not going to hold all of us," Speedy said.

"It will." Green Arrow motioned her in and she regarded him dubiously.

"What do you weigh, Speedy? Twenty pounds soaking wet?" Spartan suggested. "I think we'll be all right."

She gingerly stepped inside and closed her eyes in silent prayer, her body tense. The doors closed and Green Arrow hit the down button. The elevator groaned and something clanged loudly before it started to descend. Speedy exhaled. They sank in silence.

The Flash looked up. "I'm waiting for 'The Girl from Ipanema' to start playing."

Green Arrow almost smiled until the elevator jolted violently. They grabbed for the sides before being tossed to the floor when the elevator slammed to a halt. John went to the door and jammed his fingers into the seam. Green Arrow joined him. Together they pried the doors apart to find a wall. However, there was a two-foot open gap at the bottom, the top of the open door they should have been in front of.

Green Arrow slipped through the space and landed on uneven ground. The elevator had come to a sudden rest atop a pile of debris in the bottom of the shaft.

In the pale light provided by a few bulbs scattered around the vast space, the walls gleamed laboratory-white even though rust or mud dripped from cracks, stirring the illusion that the walls were bleeding. He heard the others climb out of the elevator behind him.

"Well, it could be worse," John remarked.

"No jinxing, please," Speedy warned.

"Overwatch, do you read?" Green Arrow fiddled with his comm.

"Yes." Static filled his ears, but then Felicity's voice crackled. "Any sign of the object?"

"It would help if we knew what it looked like, but I don't see anything yet."

The area was cavernous, industrial in appearance. Numerous doors lined the walls, and above them, a walkway encircled the expansive chamber complete with glass observation rooms.

"Where do we start?" Speedy swept her gaze over the place.

"One door at a time," Oliver told her.

"I don't know about you guys –" she stepped up to the nearest door, "– but I want to see what Dad was hiding down here."

"He wasn't hiding anything," Oliver replied quickly. "Merely conducting tests. Better out here than in the city." Even he didn't think he sounded convincing.

The room had been stripped bare to the walls. The next room showed more of the same. Occasionally a table or chair sat abandoned, but that was all. Not even scraps of paper littered the floor.

"They cleaned up behind themselves." The Flash looked around the cavern. "I could zip around and—"

"We'll do it the old-fashioned way," Green Arrow said. "May take longer, but at least it won't cause you to blur."

The Flash looked mildly irritated, but waved at Green Arrow and headed across the cavern at a slow walk. Well, slow for the Flash. John followed after him, searching rooms to the Flash's left.

Green Arrow and Speedy went high, scouring the catwalk and observation booths. Upstairs turned out to be as clean as down below. To Oliver's annoyance, thirty minutes of searching turned up nothing.

"Overwatch, I think this is a wild goose chase." Green Arrow closed the door to yet another empty room. "Back to the drawing board."

"It might not be obvious." Felicity's voice sounded faint and scattered. "Particularly if they hid it."

"So we're looking for a safe of some sort or a hidden storage locker?" Green Arrow asked.

"Or a brick wall instead of a metal wall. Anything out of the ordinary."

"Wait," said the Flash. "She's right. There was a wall that looked different." He jogged quickly across the chamber and stopped before a section of wall that was just a bit off color. "Look."

"It's certainly not the same material." Oliver bent closer and then used an arrow from his quiver to wrench back some of the plaster. A large sheet cracked off to reveal a solid steel door.

"Jackpot!" the Flash exclaimed.

"First we have to open the thing, and I'd rather not risk explosives." Oliver looked around the laboratory. Even though it seemed secure enough, they had no idea of the condition of the supports that held the surrounding rock at bay.

"I can shatter the bolts." The Flash held up his hand in expectation of Oliver's protest.

Green Arrow's lips held a hard line, but he nodded. Barry's expression went from mild surprise to a broad smile. Stepping up to the heavy door, he touched the thick bottom hinge. His arm began to vibrate until his hand was barely visible. Oliver watched in amazement as the Flash pushed his fingers inside the metal like a knife into butter.

The massive door popped from its hinges. Everyone stepped out of the way. The steel slab shifted and fell to the floor with a massive clang. Air hissed out.

Green Arrow's bow lifted as Spartan shined his flashlight inside. Swirling trails of dust filled the beam that played around a small dark room. The only thing inside was an odd contraption sitting atop a table, glinting in the light that brushed across its metal facets.

It was about the size of an office desk, and appeared solid at first glance, a dense chunk of steel. But on closer inspection, it was actually a system of conduits and tubes and pipes of various sizes and shapes. They twisted into each other to create the illusion of solidity.

Peering deeper into the construct, the metals were different colors and there also appeared to be spheres of glass suspended inside.

"Is that it?" Speedy looked over John's shoulder. "It's not very big."

Green Arrow stepped into the room.

"Wait!" the Flash called out. "What about booby traps?"

"This isn't *Raiders of the Lost Ark,*" Spartan cracked.

"What do you think?" Arrow motioned the Flash forward, letting the scientific expert take over.

Barry bent over the device, peering close to examine the cobwebbed mechanics.

"Well, will that little thing open up a wormhole or not?" Speedy asked.

"It is definitely something unusual." The Flash straightened with a grin of excitement. "It's not a weird space heater or anything. Parts of it do resemble some of the temporal tech we've rigged at S.T.A.R. Labs. I think."

"We need to get it back home." Green Arrow looked at the others.

"C'mon, Flash, I think we can carry it together."

Spartan lifted one end of the device with a straining grunt as Barry grabbed the other. Together they managed to heft it off the table. With shuffling steps under the weight, they lugged it out of the vault into the main chamber.

Green Arrow caught shadows moving across the ceiling. His bow lifted and an arrow flew. One of the shadows plummeted to the floor. Ropes suddenly dropped and dark shapes slid down.

"Overwatch, we have hostiles."

"I didn't see them up top." Felicity's reply crackled

with interference. "And I can't read anything where you are. You're too far down."

"Incoming," Spartan shouted as a group of commandos rushed toward them. He and Flash set down the machine and Spartan pulled his pistols. Three men fell under his barrage. "Those look like the same guys who jumped us in the Glades."

The rest of the commandos charged. They carried guns but didn't fire.

The Flash stretched his arms out, spinning them in tight circles. Twin cones of forced air struck the attackers and sent them flying backward.

Green Arrow and Speedy moved forward on the flanks, the strings of their bows humming as they fired bolt after bolt into more attackers descending from the ventilator shafts in the ceiling. The commandos dropped, unleashing a popping hail of bullets from machine pistols at Green Arrow and Speedy. A red streak zipped in front of the archers and the shells fells harmless to the floor. However, the red streak paused mid-stride.

Barry was going into a blur.

"Flash!" Green Arrow shouted, hoping to jar the speedster out of it. Abruptly the Flash moved again at normal speed. A sheen of sweat and a touch of fear graced his features. "You and Spartan get the generator! We'll handle the gunmen."

Green Arrow and Speedy rotated their position. They moved laterally, giving cover to the Flash and

Spartan, who started off again for the elevator lugging the generator.

The commandos wheeled with them. Suitably armed with TEC-9 semi-automatics, and well trained. They wore black assault gear with single lens heads-up displays and no covering on their faces.

Among the anonymous commandos, a face suddenly stood out. The image kicked Oliver in the gut and his bow lowered.

"The generator is mine!" the man shouted. "Let it go."

"Like hell," Spartan snapped back.

The man's gaze didn't waver from Green Arrow.

"It should have all been mine years ago," he sneered. "Isn't that right, *Oliver*?"

Everyone turned to Green Arrow in surprise. This strange man knew his secret identity.

8

"Did he just say your name?" Felicity gasped.

"Is that who I think it is?" Speedy gaped in shock. "Is that Ghasi?"

"Keep Spartan and the Flash covered. Don't get cut off from the elevator." Oliver kept his eyes locked on the man. It was Ghasi. Older and worn, dark eyes more vicious, but Ghasi without a doubt.

"Don't do it!" Speedy shouted but it was too late.

Green Arrow rushed at the man. His bow lashed out, but didn't find the target. Ghasi appeared behind Arrow in a flicker of light, his arm slashing with knives that extended from steel bracers and sparked with electricity. Oliver managed to bring his bow up just in time.

"Don't stand in my way, Oliver," Ghasi snarled at the archer.

"Stop giving me a reason." Green Arrow kicked the man in the chest, sending him staggering backward. He followed with an immediate shot, but Ghasi flickered like dozens of tiny mirrors catching the light, and vanished. The shaft spun through to hit one of Ghasi's men.

Green Arrow backpedaled toward the elevator. Bolt after bolt in quick succession left his bow, each one taking down a target. Speedy joined him, striking commandos on their right. As they drew close to the generator, the commandos lowered their guns; they were clearly afraid of hitting the device.

A blow struck Oliver from behind and sent him flying. His shoulder went numb. He flipped up to his feet and spun around for his attacker, raising his bow despite the sharp needles pricking his skin.

Across the chamber, commandos broke toward the elevator where the Flash and Spartan struggled to manhandle the heavy generator through the narrow opening.

Arrow and Speedy moved as one, back to back, covering ground. They pulled arrows and fired without thinking. Instinctive. Their bowstrings sang as they released bolt after bolt, driving the enemy back again. Wherever the archers' gazes centered, targets fell.

The Flash climbed up inside the elevator and dragged the end of the generator after him while Spartan shoved from behind.

"It looks like a Kurosawa film out there," the Flash muttered to Spartan before waving the rest in. "Let's go!"

Arrow nodded at his sister so she spun and ducked into the elevator. Four commandos rushed from the dark, firing machine pistols. Oliver fired a flash arrow. The room illuminated in a bright glare, staggering the attackers.

"Hit the button!" Green Arrow shouted.

"You're not inside yet!" the Flash called back.

Spartan punched the button. The elevator started rising.

Arrow leapt feet first through the narrowing gap into the elevator, clearing the door just as hard steel slid down over the opening. He was in.

"Please tell me *everyone* made it," Felicity said.

"He's with us," Speedy informed her.

Oliver heard Felicity's sigh of relief.

"Going up, next floor ladies' lingerie, sundries," she told them.

Green Arrow's attention focused on the sound of the elevator as it rumbled upward. Something wasn't right. A hard *thunk* hit the undercarriage.

"There's trouble!" Felicity cursed and then the car rocked to a halt. "They stopped the car!"

"Get it moving," Arrow said with extraordinary calm.

"Trying!"

They heard the sound of Felicity's fingers typing furiously as she hijacked the controls to the elevator.

The elevator rumbled upward suddenly with a ragged jolt. Speedy collapsed back against the wall in relief.

"That was close!"

"There will be more waiting up top for us," Spartan reminded them.

"It won't matter." Green Arrow drew out three arrows to keep in his hand.

"You have a plan?" the Flash asked.

Speedy smiled. "He always has a plan."

The car jerked abruptly again.

"Crap, I hate elevators," murmured Speedy, grabbing onto a rail as the vehicle shuddered to a halt. "Now what?"

"We're going down," Spartan observed.

"Overwatch!" Oliver called.

"I've got you!"

The elevator rocked once more to a halt.

"Damn. These guys are good. They're trying to override the controls, locking me out."

At their feet, a narrow serrated blade sliced through the floor and began to cut out the center of the elevator.

Oliver drew a cable out of a grappling arrow and weaved it through the open sections of the generator. He then attached the cable to a climbing spike from one of the loops of his tunic. After jamming the spike into the elevator wall, he repeated the procedure. Just as he slammed the second spike into the elevator, a section of floor dropped. The generator lurched and sagged a few inches. The cables suspended it securely from the elevator car.

For now.

Everyone pressed against the walls. Through the jagged hole in the floor, faces peered up. A gas arrow made them pull back. The Flash spun his arms to make sure that the gas didn't float back up.

"Overwatch," Oliver called out, "can you get the elevator moving again?"

"Working on it. The electronics aren't in the best of shape."

Heavy boots pounded the roof of the car and it bounced abruptly.

"What now?" Speedy moaned.

Another saw blade began cutting over their heads.

"They are really determined to get this thing." The Flash looked at Arrow. "Who are these guys?"

"We'll worry about that after we get out." Green Arrow readied his bow and then glanced at the Flash. "When they make the final cut, blow that section of ceiling back at them."

"You got it!" the Flash turned his attention upward, ducking his head as sparks rained down. The blade reached its end mark and the metal slab slipped toward them. The Flash thrust up his arms and spun them. The wind blast drove the steel upward. A startled shout indicated it had collided with someone.

Oliver fired a flash arrow right behind it that exploded with a blinding snap.

Speedy jumped up through the hole. With practiced ease, she laid out two blinded troopers.

"All clear."

"Overwatch, you got control yet?"

"Barely. The best I can do is keep the elevator where it is. But I'm picking up chatter from the intercom system. More men climbing up the shaft toward you."

"We need to get out of this death trap," Speedy said.

"Can't leave the generator behind." The Flash laid a claiming hand on the device. "We went through too much to get it."

Oliver fired an arrow up. It hit the top of the shaft, trailing a polymer line.

"Speedy, fire another line up." As she did, he lashed his cable to the generator. "Overwatch, on my mark, release control so the elevator drops."

"All right." Felicity didn't counter his instructions so she must have realized he had a plan.

"Everyone climb onto the roof," Arrow commanded.

Spartan pulled himself up through the hole and then reached down to hoist Barry up. Arrow heard men below clanking nearer using magnetic grips. He climbed onto the crowded roof of the elevator.

"Grab hold of the lines!" When his team all clutched one of the cables dangling from the top of the shaft, Green Arrow looked at his sister. "Cut the generator free from the elevator."

Speedy drew her short sword and flipped upside down into the car. With two clean strokes, she severed the cables that had attached the generator to the walls of the elevator. Now the device only hung from the line stretching to the top of the shaft.

Arrow glanced down to see the shapes of commandos closing in on the open floor of the car.

"Everyone hang on," he said, and then shouted to

Felicity through the comm, "Now!"

Elevator couplers unhooked with a clank and the car hung for a split second before plunging in a shower of sparks. A few screams sounded over the metallic squeal. It crashed far below with a cacophony of twisted steel.

The four heroes and the generator dangled on the two cables. Spartan and Speedy immediately started climbing.

The Flash struggled. "Um, a little help here. I didn't know we were having gym class today."

"Brace your feet against the wall and push back," Green Arrow instructed, demonstrating the maneuver.

Grunting, the Flash tried.

"It would be easier if I just ran up the wall. Or went up on a cushion of air. I can do that."

"You've used your speed enough. Just climb like a normal person."

"A normal *ninja* person, maybe." The Flash looked down to the dark bottom of the shaft. Smoke and dust rose around them. "Seriously, I'm not going to be able to pull myself up. I'm super fast, but upper body strength is not my forte."

"Wait here. Hold onto the guide rail." When the Flash started to protest, Arrow added, "Guard the generator until we can pull it up."

The Flash nodded and swung himself to the side of the shaft and clutched the nearest metal rail.

Green Arrow hauled himself up, hand over hand, to where Spartan and Speedy hung next to a pair of closed elevator shaft doors.

"Get ready." He jammed the tip of his bow into the seam of the door. They all knew what likely lay beyond: more people wanting to kill them. Bracing themselves against the side of the shafts, John and Thea aimed their weapons.

Green Arrow hauled back on the bow and slowly pried the doors apart. As soon as the opening was wide, Speedy fired. The stun arrow burst in the mine tunnel. Oliver wrenched the doors wide. Spartan opened fire, sending anyone still standing out there to the ground or ducking for cover.

Green Arrow flipped around the edge of the door, his bow snapping up, seeking a target. Four men in combat fatigues lay moaning on the ground. Four more men farther back ran forward. Two arrows flew toward them. The first one burst into a net that tangled two of the men. The second arrow hit the shoulder of a man and spun him violently around to collide with his partner. They both went down hard on the stones. Speedy vaulted forward and delivered two savage knockout blows.

"Speedy, help the Flash." Arrow grabbed the line holding the suspended generator. He and Spartan labored to haul up their prize as carefully as they could to keep it from bashing against the sides of the elevator shaft. The Flash helped to steady it as he ascended along with it. When they both reached the top, they were pulled out of the shaft.

Speedy wiped her perspiring face. "Good thing you're almost as thin as I am."

"Funny," grumbled the Flash.

"Let's go!" Green Arrow led the way out of the mine. The Flash and Spartan hefted the generator again. The way out was clear.

They squinted in the bright light of day. Green Arrow saw no hostiles. However, there were plenty of places to hide.

"Speedy, with me. We'll get the van." They raced for the vehicle while Spartan and the Flash defended the generator.

Arrow and Speedy reached the van, but a hail of bullets exploded from the surrounding hills. Before the Flash could race out to help, Spartan grabbed his arm.

"Stay here. They got this."

"They *got* this?"

John bobbed his chin again. Speedy was already behind the wheel and stomped her foot on the gas pedal. The van roared straight for the entrance of the mine. Oliver hung out the window, his legs jammed somewhere inside to keep him steady. Arrows flew from his bow.

Barry reared back because the van wasn't slowing. Speedy spun the vehicle into a mud-spewing 180. The rear double doors appeared a few feet from calm John and wide-eyed Flash at the mine entrance. Spartan yanked open the doors, and they shoved the Straub device inside.

"Go!" Spartan shouted.

Speedy floored it. The vehicle spun out in the mud

just as a group of commandos rushed from cover. Speedy shifted and the wheels found some traction. Amidst smoke, mud, and bullets, they roared away with their prize.

"Holy cow!" the Flash laughed with adrenalin. "That maneuver was completely unsafe!"

Speedy laughed. "It took me three times to pass my driver's test, if you can believe it."

"Heads up!" Green Arrow called out.

Ahead of the van, a single figure stood in the center of the rutted dirt road. He ran straight for them.

Ghasi.

"Ollie?" Speedy let off the gas a little.

"Keep going!" He drew and fired a string of arrows. "Don't swerve off the road. Don't get bogged down!"

Ghasi deflected each arrow that zipped at him using the steel bracers on his wrists. As the arrows bounced away, he sprinted headlong at the van.

Speedy cringed and pushed back in the seat, but kept the wheel steady, bearing down on him.

Ghasi leapt into the air. A foot hit the grill and another touched the windshield. He climbed onto the roof, leaning toward the passenger's side.

Green Arrow saw the crackling trail from Ghasi's charged knife just in time to duck. The smell of ozone filled the air. A crackle of electricity slid just over his head.

Arrow swept his bow across the top of the van, catching Ghasi's ankle. He twisted and sent the man toppling. Ghasi fell to one knee on the roof. With a grunt, he lost balance and tumbled past Oliver, stabbing at him again as he fell from the speeding vehicle onto the rocks. Arrow felt a slight tug at his shoulder and a snap from the electricity as the tip of the dagger touched him.

"Ollie!" Speedy shouted even as she swerved and she wrestled the wheel to keep control. The vehicle bumped onto dry asphalt and picked up speed.

Green Arrow slid inside the van as calmly as if he had just stepped onto a city bus. He glanced in the side mirror, looking for pursuit. The road behind was clear.

"Good job," he said to Speedy.

The Flash turned from the back window of the van where he and Spartan watched for incoming. He shook his head, watching Green Arrow settle into his seat without another word.

"So, Oliver." John pulled his helmet off and kept a steadying hand pressed onto the shaking generator. "Who was that guy?"

Oliver continued to stare straight ahead at the road. His fingers clutched his bow.

"A ghost."

9

BEFORE THE JUNGLE

The Maserati flew down the street. Oliver could feel the car thrum deep in his thighs and shoulders as he shifted gears and sped around other drivers who were unwilling to commit to a 100-mph lifestyle.

When the Maserati swerved through two other cars, missing them by inches, a deep laugh came from the passenger's seat along with a cloud of cigarette smoke. Oliver's friend, Ghasi Lazarov, watched traffic slide past.

Ghasi was Oliver's age, early twenties, with a handsome Mediterranean appearance. He was from Croatia, but seemed more Neapolitan and exuded a studied charm. His sleek expensive Italian suit completed the look. Oliver sometimes envied Ghasi's impeccable style along with his olive skin and dark wavy hair. The man was a walking magazine cover, and he made even handsome bad boy Oliver Queen look like he should be relegated to a safe moms' magazine next to the recipes. Even more reason to step his game up.

Ghasi blew a cloud of smoke toward the low roof.

"This is a bad part of town?"

"Yes. The Glades. Bad for living, but great for parties. Tommy Merlyn throws the best parties in town."

Abandoned buildings. Shuttered warehouses. Businesses and shops long left empty. The Maserati roared past all of them, shiny and new, spitting rainwater from its tires.

"I have family too," Oliver said. "So what's up?"

"It's my father." Ghasi pressed against the headrest with a sigh. "He wants to go home."

"Back to Croatia?"

"Yes." Ghasi blinked as if in thought. "Croatia. I've tried to convince him it's a mistake, but he won't listen. There are family troubles there he doesn't need to be involved in. And he is ill. Too ill to travel now. I tell him to stay here where the medical care is better. If he goes home, he will die. I know it."

Ghasi slid down the window and tossed his cigarette into the wet air.

"I didn't know your dad was sick," Oliver said. "I'm sorry. Is there anything we can do? I mean, he works for my father's company."

"No." Ghasi turned back quickly. "He is a stubborn man. Old world, you know. He has never been comfortable here in America." He smiled. "Don't say anything to your father."

"No, no. I won't. But if you need any help, anything, you just have to ask. You know that, right?"

"Of course, Oliver. I would expect nothing less of you."

"You can have anything but this car." Oliver spun the wheel and the Maserati bounced through the open gate of a high chain-link fence. A very large man in a suit stood at the gate but didn't flinch at the car's arrival.

Oliver sped past a row of empty delivery gates. Music and light spilled out into the night. Squealing to a stop, Oliver got out and left the car for the valet. He and Ghasi headed for a door marked by a weathered old sign saying Freight Office. A deep thumping sound vibrated in Oliver's chest and when he opened the door the music exploded into the night. Light strobed. The beat slammed through them.

Now Oliver was in his element. All the way across the jammed floor: smiles, waves, handshakes, hugs, kisses. Ghasi followed with far less cred than Oliver. Anyone who recognized him knew him only as Oliver's good-looking friend whom they had met or seen at parties before.

At the bar, Oliver ordered a double Scotch neat and a bourbon for Ghasi. The Croatian had become enamored of American liquors, as he had of most American things that were popular or expensive or hard to acquire. Ghasi bobbed his head to the innocuous throbbing dance beat. Oliver turned back to the mob and saw a familiar face cutting through the neon flashes.

Tommy Merlyn. Smiling. Boy-next-door looks. Son of tycoon Malcolm Merlyn and richer than Oliver could think about being. A decent guy with good intentions but little initiative to exert them.

"Ollie!" Tommy shouted in Oliver's ear to make himself heard. "Good to see you, Ghasi. Nice suit."

"Thank you." The two shook hands and Ghasi beamed. "I have to spend twice as much to look half as good as Oliver."

Oliver leaned in. "His father obviously does important research for Queen Consolidated to afford it."

"My father will pay him twice that," Tommy shouted with a grin. "My father will always pay more to win."

"That's none of my business." Ghasi laughed. "My father seems content at Queen. Are we still on for tennis tomorrow?"

"Yeah." Tommy nodded. "Come over whenever. Ollie, are you playing?"

"I don't know," Oliver yelled back. "I'm not in shape for tennis."

"Sure." Tommy shook his head with suspicion. "You're just setting us up. I know you."

Oliver's smile went flat and his eyes turned cold as he stared out over the dance floor. Among the roiling mob, Oliver saw a familiar figure. A young girl bounced to the music with a sheen of perspiration on her face and a wild expression of abandon. Her long hair flew around her tossing head.

"That's Thea!" Oliver turned angrily to Tommy. "She's underage."

Tommy studied the crowd and finally saw the girl too. "Oh, Oliver, I didn't let her in. Sorry, man. I'll get her."

"No." Oliver set down the Scotch untouched and pushed into the flashing, deafening chaos. "I'll do it."

When he drew closer, he could tell she was dancing with a man, or around one. Oliver recognized him, had seen the man at parties and clubs, but didn't know his name. Oliver pushed through the last barrier of sweaty dancers and caught Thea's eye. She stopped dancing with a mildly intoxicated guilty grin.

"Ollie!" she slurred.

"Speedy." Oliver burned a hard glare into her date.

The man tried to maintain a sense of machismo, more annoyed at the interruption than frightened of the angry young man in front of him. "Hey, dude. We're trying to dance here."

"Hey, *dude*," Oliver said menacingly, "she is underage."

"Who are you, her dad?"

Oliver stood deathly still. "I'm her brother."

Thea shoved Oliver playfully. "Come on, Ollie. Don't be a party pooper."

"You're leaving, Speedy. Now."

"No, I'm not. Are you going to carry me out?"

"Yes."

"Hey, man." Thea's date put a hand on Oliver's arm. "Lighten up. We're just dancing."

"You need to back up." Oliver swatted the hand away. "You could go to jail for being with her. But you don't have to worry about that because I would kill you first." Oliver took Thea by the wrist and started to pull her off the dance floor.

"Oh my God, Oliver! You are not doing this!" Thea resisted. "We're just dancing. He's a nice guy."

"Is he? What's his name?"

"Um. Steve. Noah?" Thea broke into giggles.

"You're drunk."

"Are you mad that I beat you to it for once?" Thea pulled her arm away, but continued to follow Oliver, back straight, ignoring the amused crowd around them.

Back at the bar, Thea greeted Tommy with an exaggerated wave and a manic grin. She barely deigned to notice Ghasi: an obvious slight. She slumped against the rail, raising a finger to the bartender, "Vodka rocks, please."

Oliver glowered at her. "Speedy, for God's sake, just stop it." He looked up. "Ghasi, I have to take Thea home. I'm sure Tommy will give you a ride."

Tommy nodded agreement so Ghasi said, "Sure, Oliver. You take the little bird home."

"I'll little bird you," Thea growled and pushed toward Ghasi.

Oliver stepped between them with an annoyed sigh. He took Thea by the shoulders and turned her around.

"Let's go. I'll call you guys tomorrow." He started toward the door with his sister.

It was slow going through the throng of drinkers and watchers. They hadn't made it to the door when the sound of shouting came from behind. Beyond the first layer of dancers, bodies collided violently. Oliver went to propel Thea toward the door when something struck him hard on the back of his shoulders. Thea shouted in alarm as Oliver staggered to his knees.

"I'll teach you to screw with my date, you rich punk!"

The words were cut off and suddenly everyone was screaming. Thea tugged at Oliver's arm, trying to get him back on his feet.

Shaking his head, Oliver managed to stand. He saw Ghasi struggling with another man.

Ghasi had his arm locked around the throat of Thea's former date. Arms flailed. The man tried to shake Ghasi free. The cruel glare on Ghasi's bloody face gave Oliver a shock. It was the face of a man who was able and willing to badly injure someone. Oliver kept an eye out for anyone else ready to join in, but no one was here to fight. They all looked at the two grapplers with disgust and annoyance.

Oliver was certainly no fighter, but he grabbed the man's jacket. "Okay. I've got him. Let him go."

Ghasi grunted with renewed effort, forearm bulging in the expensive fabric of his suit. Thea's dance partner's eyes rolled up into his head.

"Ghasi!" Oliver shouted. "Let him go!"

Ghasi's eyes flicked to Oliver with sudden recognition. He loosened his chokehold. Oliver pulled the gasping man away, but he shook free and squared off. A quick fist caught Oliver on the jaw, staggering him.

Another figure darted in. Tommy slammed into the guy and knocked him onto the floor. Ghasi moved to attack again.

"Hold it!" Tommy put a shoulder out to block Ghasi. "He's had enough. It's over."

The guy on the floor looked up in embarrassed anger. "Three on one, huh? That's how you rich guys do it."

"You jumped me." Oliver worked his jaw back and forth as the guy pointed at Ghasi.

"He tried to kill me."

Ghasi stared at the man, silent and cold. The blood running down his face made the picture all the more chilling.

"Let's go." Oliver took Ghasi by the arm. "The party's over."

They started back toward the door where Thea waited with mouth open wide in amazement. They went outside. The cold wet air reinvigorated them. The dimming vibrations from the music were a relief.

"He ruined my suit." Ghasi inspected his wrinkled jacket that had spots of blood on it.

"Hey, thanks for the help back there." Oliver put a friendly hand on Ghasi's shoulder. "But be careful. You can't choke guys out just because they take a swing at me."

"Yeah," Thea murmured. "You'd be choking guys all night."

1 □

The newly acquired wormhole generator rested in the center of a raised platform in the Arrowcave. Oliver, John, and Thea stood staring while Felicity and Barry prowled around the machine and fiddled with controls.

"Should you be doing that?" John asked. "Doesn't it create wormholes?"

"*Supposedly* creates wormholes." Felicity scowled at the buttons. "There's no proof it ever worked."

"I can call Cisco," Barry said hesitantly. "No disrespect to your abilities, but there aren't many people with more experience in temporal or dimensional tech."

Felicity flipped a switch and waited. Nothing happened. She snatched up her tablet and connected it to the Straub device with a cable. No one spoke as she swiped and touched.

Oliver stood with arms crossed. Although he watched the proceedings, his mind was far away, thinking of the face of the man in the mine.

"So, Oliver," John said, "you going to tell us who your friend was back there?"

Thea took a deep breath. "Was it really who I thought it was?"

"Yes," Oliver replied.

"You both know him?" John asked.

Felicity and Barry turned to look at Oliver.

"His name is Ghasi Lazarov," Oliver said. "He was a friend of the family."

"He was *your* friend," Thea added. "I was the only one who kept telling people he was crazy."

Oliver gave his sister a smile. "His father worked for Queen Consolidated. This was years ago, before the island."

"Is his father still around?" John asked.

"He's in prison."

"Prison?" Barry exclaimed. "What did he do?"

"He was convicted of spying for Markovia."

"Markovia?" John grew more sullen. "So you think his kid is still working for Markovia now? Some sort of Markovian metahuman strike force? The guy had some unnatural abilities."

"I don't know if he's metahuman," Barry said. "I bet he's equipped with high tech."

"I don't know what happened to him after he left Star City." Oliver made eye contact with everyone in the room. "But clearly he isn't a normal man. And he knows my identity. No one goes anywhere alone. We don't have a good sense of his abilities or his resources, or his purpose."

"We know his purpose," John corrected. "He wants that generator. First the Glades. Then the mine." He shook his head in frustration. "How did he know to be at the mine? Felicity didn't see those guys come in, so they must've been there waiting. Like he wanted us to find that generator so he could just take it away from us."

"Ghasi knows too much about what we're doing," Oliver agreed, "and we have to find out how."

"I'm not worried about bugs in the Arrowcave here." Felicity continued to prowl around the generator. "I have unbeatable security running at all times. But I'll have checks run throughout Palmer for bugs or cameras or any sort of eavesdropping devices. And I'll do a full scan of the company computer systems for evilware."

"Also, check all your employees for any connection to Markovia, as well as suspicious activity or unexplained changes to bank accounts. The Markovians may have left moles inside the company even after we caught Ghasi's father." Oliver turned to Felicity. "Do what you can to keep the lair safe from him. Or at least give us a heads-up if he shows."

"I've got a few tricks. He might vanish from sight, but as far as we know, he's still there physically. He still moves through space even if we can't see him. I can set up scanners to detect air current movements or micro vibrations where there shouldn't be any."

"I can help you rig that up," Barry said.

"Thank you." Felicity gave the speedster a quick smile, but her attention was still devoted to the generator. She scowled at the tablet in her hand. "Even if this Ghasi guy sneaks in here to snatch this machine, it won't do him any good because it's just an empty shell."

"Meaning what?" Oliver joined her to look at the display on the tablet even though he had no idea what it meant.

Barry glanced at the screen too and nodded with understanding. "Ah, there's no operating system."

"Right." Felicity huffed with annoyance.

"So no software?" Oliver asked.

"Sort of, yeah." Felicity tapped the tablet against the generator. "I have no idea exactly how this machine is supposed to actually work."

"We've opened wormholes at S.T.A.R. Labs," Barry said. "I'm sure we can get it going."

"Didn't you use your speed as a power source?" Felicity asked.

"Sure. We can do that here."

"You said you don't have that kind of speed now."

"Oh yeah." Barry slumped in disappointment.

"Plus," Felicity added, "it's not just about opening a wormhole; it's about opening a *stable* wormhole. So call Cisco."

John leaned against the railing around the platform. He rubbed his face in thought. "So does the spy case

Ghasi's father was involved in have any connection to this wormhole machine?"

"I don't know," Oliver said, "but if Felicity could check—"

She was already at her keyboard. The monitors soon flashed with news clippings and scanned corporate and court documents. Oliver recognized a lot of the material. He got a jolt when he saw old news footage of his mother and father, as well as a press conference led by the formidable Walter Steele, his father's right hand and later the second husband of his mother. He felt Thea standing close to him and he put a comforting hand on hers.

"According to the press accounts and court documents," Felicity said, "the technology that was transferred to Markovia was related to agricultural sciences. Nothing earth-shattering." When an image of younger Oliver appeared in the background of a shot outside Queen Consolidated, she pointed and grinned. "Aw, young playboy Oliver Queen is so hunky!"

Oliver ignored this. "Remember, a lot of it was sanitized and buried at the time." He watched the frozen images of his mother and father holding hands as they left the courthouse. "My father wanted to keep proprietary corporate data from coming out in court documents. I gave depositions for the case and even I don't know all the details. So what we're seeing here may not be an accurate depiction of the material actually lost to Markovia."

"It is hard to know what's real when the Queen family is involved." Felicity nodded, her smile faltering.

"Sometimes." Oliver stroked her hair. His phone buzzed. He pulled it out and looked at the screen with an interested grunt.

Felicity pressed against his hand on the back of her head, eyes slipping up to his face. "Who is it?"

"It's Ghasi."

1 1

BEFORE THE JUNGLE

Oliver Queen and Tommy Merlyn stood on the torch-lit plaza outside the Museum of Science and Technology. People in formal wear streamed from cars across the square. A small figure strayed from the crowd and approached the two men. A teenaged Thea looked very adult in a flowing evening gown, clutching a small jeweled purse. Tommy kissed her on the cheek. Oliver gave her a brotherly sarcastic smile.

"Going stag, Speedy?"

"Oddly enough, yes." She iced him with a glare. "It's hard to find a date when your last one ended up in a chokehold."

"Your last date was a predator."

"So it's acceptable for Ghasi to nearly kill him?"

Oliver almost said *yes*, but instead offered, "He started it."

"He shoved you. You think that deserved the beating he got? Ghasi is going to kill someone."

"Oh come on."

"Seriously, Ollie. Ghasi is dangerous. You better say something to him."

"Why would I say anything?" Oliver gave her a smug smile. "I'm not his father."

"He follows you around like a puppy." Thea shook her head in dismay. "God knows why. But if you don't do something about him, he's going to get you into a problem that Mom and Dad can't just buy off."

"You don't even know him."

"I know enough. He's a phony."

"A phony?" Oliver looked at Tommy for support, but his friend merely watched. "I don't know how you can say that. Ghasi and I are practically the same guy."

"Oh, Oliver, it bothers me to hear you say that. I'm going in." Thea started away, but turned back with a smile. "Thanks for covering for me with Mom and Dad."

"No problem." Oliver gave her a reassuring nod.

"You know," Tommy said after Thea had gone, "I was talking to Detective Lance and he said Ghasi has been in a number of fights. Serious stuff. He's hurt a couple guys."

"He's new to America."

Tommy laughed. "Oliver, we're not talking about some scrappy immigrant boy trying to get by on the streets with his fists and his wits. He is the son of a physicist who works for a Fortune 500 corporation."

"I know." Oliver took a deep breath. "But he really is a good guy. You like him, right?"

"Oh sure. He seems okay."

"Oliver!" Malcolm Merlyn appeared from the passing crowd. Tall, handsome, and vigorous. Malcolm was a matinee idol and tycoon rolled into one. Plus beneath the charming sophisticate was the alluring mystery of a man emotionally damaged by the murder of his wife, Tommy's mother, so he had the air of suppressed tragedy in him as well. Malcolm Merlyn dominated any room. He looked like he was born in his tuxedo and black overcoat with flowing white scarf. He spared a perfunctory smile for his son before embracing Oliver.

"I heard what happened to that man who threatened your sister. Good work."

"He wasn't threatening her. He was just too old."

"Still, he deserved it." Malcolm glanced at his son. "You could learn a few things from Oliver." He patted Oliver's back and strode toward the museum.

Tommy stood blank-faced and stoic, trying to hide the embarrassment. "Well, that was pleasant."

"Come on, let's go in." Oliver put an arm around Tommy's shoulder. "Maybe *you* can get drunk and strangle someone tonight."

"My father would be so proud."

They both laughed and joined the flow into the glowing museum. Inside the spacious glass-walled atrium, a string quartet played Mozart while waiters carried trays of champagne and hors d'oeuvres.

A sign on the wall advertised: MUSEUM OF SCIENCE

AND TECHNOLOGY. FUNDED BY A GRANT FROM QUEEN CONSOLIDATED, APPLIED SCIENCES DIVISION. The usual civic suspects wandered the premises, gathering in clutches to chat, laugh, and plot. The cream of the city's elite out for yet another fundraiser, reaching for the checkbooks because they knew they would be asking the same crowd for contributions to their own hobbyhorse later.

Across the lobby, Moira Queen stood with the museum director and the mayor. She looked resplendent in a violet gown that perfectly set off her hair. Totally in her element, attentive and gracious. She nodded a distant greeting to Oliver, waving him over. He went to her side and kissed her cheerfully.

"You may want to find your friend," she whispered.

"You mean Ghasi?" He kept a smile plastered on his face. "What's wrong?"

"He and his father are here, but they seem to be quarreling. I think Ghasi has been drinking, no surprise." Oliver set his half-finished champagne on a passing tray and his mother continued, "I expect you won't ruin this event with some petty altercation."

He stood back with a charming laugh as if they'd been discussing flowers and went to find Ghasi. He found Tommy first and asked him to help search. Tommy nodded and started off.

Mr. Lazarov stood in a corner alone, pretending to look at a display of old electrical equipment that looked to Oliver like it came from a Frankenstein movie. He was short and round with graying hair. His face, though, showed clear evidence of being related to Ghasi; he was a softer version of that rugged visage. When Oliver approached, the man seemed grateful.

"Ah, Oliver," Mr. Lazarov said in his broad accent. "Good to see you. You look so handsome in your tuxedo, but to some that comes so naturally."

"Thank you, sir."

"Not at all." Dark eyes stared off into the crowd, searching for someone.

"Is Ghasi around?" Oliver asked.

"Somewhere, I suppose. We had words. We often have words now." Mr. Lazarov glanced quickly at Oliver with quiet sadness. "Could you go and find him before he hurts someone? He will listen to you. You may be the only one he listens to."

"Yes sir, I will."

"You're a good boy, Oliver."

I'm tired of being a good boy, Oliver thought as he continued his search through the museum. He saw Tommy, but that only resulted in a fruitless shrug from his friend. At one point, he heard two guests holding empty champagne flutes remark about the lack of servers. Oliver looked around and noticed he could only see a few of the once ubiquitous men and women in black suits carrying trays.

He wandered off the main floor to a backroom marked CATERING. Pushing the door open, he saw bottles and cases of champagne, stacks of coolers for storing hors d'oeuvres, and a long row of steam trays. Large oval platters sat unattended. The back door stood open and strange noises filtered in.

Outside in a service alley, people in black suits crowded around a disturbance where feet scuffled, arms flew, and bodies surged in and out of a fight. Ghasi stood in the center, bloody, his tuxedo torn, kicking and punching. Four men struggled to grapple him.

"Break it up!" Oliver shouted.

Some of the bystanders turned around and saw him with shock. They scrambled back to the kitchen. Others ignored him. Oliver shoved through the observers.

He spun one of the grapplers and threw a punch that clipped his jaw. Oliver took a shot to the eye that staggered him. Hands clutched his shoulders. A knee drove up into his stomach and he doubled over, unable to breathe.

Oliver dragged himself up on the brick wall, gasping for air. A fist appeared and he managed to dodge before kicking out and connecting with the man's leg. The guy screamed and clutched his knee.

Oliver felt an exciting surge of confidence until he found himself shoved against the wall. His head jerked sideways from a blow. A hammer shot against his neck drove him to his knees.

"Stay down, pretty boy!" came the warning.

It sounded like good advice, but Oliver climbed back to his feet. Ghasi flew past him, bounced off some trashcans and sprawled to the pavement. When Oliver went to help him, a punch cracked him in the face. He backpedaled and dropped again.

Despite the pain and the taste of blood, Oliver pressed his hands against the dirty ground. Ghasi lay sprawled down-and-out so Oliver had to keep the others from ganging up on him and doing real damage. Staggering to his feet, he tried to focus and raised his fists, waiting for someone else to hit him.

Nothing happened.

Through bleary eyes, he saw Malcolm Merlyn twisting a man's wrist, forcing the guy to his knees. He turned the arm easily and the man went down in a groaning heap.

Oliver looked around wildly for the fight. It appeared to be over. Four or five men either lay unconscious or crying in pain. The crowd retreated, some staring in wonder at Malcolm.

"Oliver, are you okay?" Malcolm stepped over two men and took Oliver's face between his hands. "Can you hear me?"

Oliver breathed heavily, but he nodded, slowly lowering his fists. "What did you do?"

"That?" Malcolm glanced at the prostrate men and shrugged. "Just a little… tai chi I picked up while traveling. Comes in handy."

"What is going on out here?" came the scandalized voice of Moira Queen from the kitchen door. Thea peered out from behind her, staring directly at Oliver with a grin on her face. Moira saw her son amidst the carnage. "Oliver! What in God's name is happening? I sent you to stop trouble, not join in!"

Oliver raised his hands to explain and found his tuxedo jacket hung in tatters from his arms.

"You broke my leg," moaned one of the men on the ground.

"Quiet!" Malcolm jabbed a finger at him. "You'll never cater in this town again." He then said to Oliver, "Take care of your friend. I'll take care of your mother." He hopped over a writhing server and herded people back into the kitchen. "Moira! This has been the most memorable gala in years. Congratulations."

Ghasi had managed to shove himself up on trembling arms. Oliver secured him around the waist and dragged him to his feet. Ghasi teetered and fell back against the wall. His face was red and swollen.

Several men on the ground started to stir so Oliver looped Ghasi's arm over his shoulder and they limped out of the alley. They staggered along the side of the museum and skirted the torch-lit plaza. The faint strains of Mozart filled the air.

A couple blocks from the museum where the city turned seedy was a backstreet bar called the Glossy Starling that Oliver and his friends enjoyed on late nights for post-club slumming. Two bloodied men fumbling through the front door wasn't a completely unique experience there. Still, Oliver and Ghasi received nervous glances as they made their way to the men's room where Ghasi washed the blood off his face. Finally, after drenching his upper body in water, he flattened his wet hair against his head and stared into the mirror. Oliver handed him a bundle of paper towels.

"I knew I could count on you." Ghasi braced himself stiff-armed on the sink, dripping red into the basin. "How about a drink?"

"As long as it's coffee."

Oliver led the way to a back booth where they collapsed.

When a waitress brought coffee, she eyed the two bruised young men in the remnants of formal wear. "Must've been a helluva of wedding, boys."

Oliver laughed with an amiable arch of his eyebrow, then watched Ghasi pour sugar into his coffee.

"So what were you fighting about?"

"Nothing." Ghasi gave a cavalier shrug.

"You were getting stomped by five guys. It must've been something."

"I overheard them talking about your family. They said very unkind things."

"That's it? Of course they said unkind things. They probably hate us because we have money and they're breaking their necks working as waiters. If I was a waiter, I'd do the same thing."

"They should know their place. Back home we wouldn't allow such a thing."

Oliver exhaled in exasperation. He looked at the window where his bruised face gazed back. He smirked at the image of himself as a brawler. He touched a painful spot on his head and winced.

"You might want to call your father," Oliver said. "He was worried about you."

"I'll see him soon enough. Did he pull that befuddled old Euro bit with you? Don't believe him. He's a cunning devil." Ghasi's voice slurred and he covered his eyes with one hand as if he had a headache from the neon sign outside.

"I like him."

Ghasi tasted the coffee and shoved the cup aside with a grimace. "The only thing Americans can't do is coffee. Everything else—liquor, music, movies, cars, women, guns, money—you do better than anyone. Not coffee."

"So they have good coffee in Croatia?"

"How would I know?" Ghasi dropped his head to the table. "I'm not from Croatia."

"You're not?"

"No. I'm from Markovia."

"Markovia?" Oliver sat back and watched Ghasi moan and cover his head with both hands.

"Yes. We just decided to be from Croatia because they won't let Markovians into the United States. This was where my father needed to come… for his work."

"Does my father know that?"

"No." Ghasi looked up suddenly, red eyes narrowing in pain. "You can't tell anyone, okay, Oliver? It's a secret. Our secret, okay?"

Oliver shrugged nonchalantly and started to

speak, but Ghasi grabbed his arm.

"No, listen to me, I'm serious. I shouldn't have told you, but I did. Markovia and the United States aren't friendly. We had to leave our home, you understand, *had* to leave. We can't go back. But if your government finds out we are Markovian, we'll be deported. And we'd be killed the second we stepped off the plane in Markovburg."

"You're drunk." Oliver pursed his lips in disbelief.

"No!" Ghasi surged across the table, scattering silverware in a noisy clatter. Everyone in the bar turned to look. Ghasi's dark eyes held the coldness Oliver had seen at Tommy's party as he choked out Thea's date. It was either threat or fear, he wasn't sure which. Ghasi lowered his voice. "I'm telling you, if we go back, we're dead. You can't tell anyone. Not even Tommy or Thea. Promise me, Oliver. Promise me!"

"Okay, relax. Why would I tell anyone? Croatia. Markovia. What's the difference?"

"Thank you." Ghasi sank back into the plastic upholstery. "It's good to have at least one person in the world you can trust, you know?" He exhaled, shaking his hands as if to work out tension. "Well, I'm stone sober now after that. I need a drink. I'm having a drink. What do you want? Scotch?"

Ghasi started to slide out of the booth, but Oliver grabbed his arm.

"Wait, wait." Oliver reached inside his ragged tuxedo jacket and pulled out a small silver flask. He twisted off the top and poured a small shot into Ghasi's coffee. "Just finish the coffee first."

Ghasi sipped from the cup. He grinned.

"That is better. Thank you. That flask is beautiful."

"Here." Oliver capped the flask and handed it to Ghasi. "Take it."

"Oh no." Ghasi's eyes stared at the bright silver. "I couldn't."

"Sure you can. It's just a little thanks for having my back at Tommy's party, and protecting my family's good name, although both counts were a little extreme."

Ghasi reached out and took the flask. He turned it in the neon light, staring at the reflections.

"But listen," Oliver said, "you need to remember that you can't keep fighting like that."

"I know. I'll wait for you next time." Ghasi cupped his hand around the back of Oliver's head, pressing their foreheads together. Oliver could smell the dried blood staining his friend's white shirt.

"I'm serious, Ghasi."

"Okay, okay. I'm sorry. I'll do better. Soon I'll be as American and as smooth as you."

"You're not going to survive long enough to become an American. Really. I'm not going to cover for you forever."

"I know you, Oliver," Ghasi said. "You don't give up on your friends."

Oliver watched his friend hefting the silver flask in his hand, smiling again and charming, and covered in blood.

1 2

The Glossy Starling hadn't improved since Oliver had gone there with Ghasi years ago after the disastrous museum gala. Oliver swore the bartender and waitress were not only the same people, but wore the same clothes they had that night. He scanned the crowd, noting each person and their location. A few guys at the bar and a scattering sitting at tables and booths. These men were not dive-bar patrons. Their muscles bulged under their shirts, and their posture showed natural physicality that couldn't be disguised. He didn't see Ghasi yet, but obviously his old friend had come prepared.

Oliver went to the same booth in the dark corner and sat so he could see the door. He ordered a Scotch. One of the people at the bar was a slender figure hunched over his beer and phone. It was Barry. Ghasi and his people might have recognized John, but hopefully they wouldn't know Barry. Spartan and Speedy were nearby on a rooftop.

"There's some muscle in the bar," Oliver muttered while leaning on his hand.

"We've got nothing," Spartan reported via comm link.

"Oliver?" Ghasi stood beside the table. "I'm not interrupting anything, am I?"

Oliver suppressed a startled jerk. He smiled casually and extended his hand to the seat across from him. Barry stared over at them, but Oliver gave him a quick glance that sent him back around to his phone.

"Okay, he's definitely weird," Felicity said in Oliver's ear. "He wasn't on thermal, then there was a flash, and he was there."

Ghasi slid in. He wore an Italian suit, as opposed to Oliver, who was in jeans and a heavy cotton shirt. He ordered a bourbon from the waitress as she passed and the two men shook hands. Ghasi seemed to hold Oliver's hand a little long, apparently genuinely pleased to see his old friend again. He sat back, content and relaxed. When his drink came, he lifted the glass.

"Cheers, Oliver." Glasses clinked. "It's good to be back. And here, in our old spot. My God, look at your arms. You must work out twenty-four hours a day."

"I hit the gym when I can." A strange comfort tried to seep into Oliver like a warm shade of the past. It felt alien and unwelcome, but he couldn't stop it. Emotional muscle memory. He worked to stay conscious of it so he didn't slip into the habits of trust that he had long since abandoned.

Ghasi sipped his drink and grimaced.

"What's wrong?" Oliver asked. "You always said America had the best whiskey."

"It's been a few years since I've had it. And this place was never exactly the best example." He drank again. His face softened to a version of the old Ghasi. "I was very sorry to hear about your parents, and Tommy as well. I enjoyed the time I spent in your home. I miss it."

"Thank you. I miss it too." Oliver leaned forward. "So what brings you back to Star City?"

"I'm glad this bar is still here." Ghasi acted like he hadn't heard the question. He signaled to the waitress for coffee, which surprised Oliver. "So many things change. You Americans, so focused on change. So desperate to believe in miraculous transformations— weakling to strongman, scoundrel to hero. But the fact is things never change. People never change."

"Is that true?" Oliver eyed the half-empty bourbon. "I remember you liked to drink and fight, but I don't remember you turning invisible before."

Ghasi shimmered before vanishing. Then he was back.

"Yep," Felicity said, "he went white-hot for a second, then he disappeared totally. Now he's normal again. No one seems to have noticed, though."

Oliver caught a whiff of electrical ozone.

"Some trick, eh?" Ghasi chuckled. "I've got others. I don't know if I can tell you about them. I remember you don't keep secrets well."

"What Oliver Queen is he talking about?" Felicity muttered.

The waitress brought two cups of coffee. Ghasi thanked her and reached into his coat pocket to produce the silver flask Oliver had given him. He poured liquor into his coffee and offered it to Oliver, who held up a hand in refusal.

"We were ignorant young men in our day, Oliver." Ghasi took a long swig of coffee before regarding the flask fondly, and putting it away. "We had no idea what the world was like beyond our little circle of parties. But I found out. When I left America and returned to Markovia, I suffered." He stared into Oliver's eyes. "Suffered, Oliver, in ways you can't imagine."

"I'm sorry."

"Are you? That's nice. They took me and cut me open. They put things inside me. I don't understand it all. They knew how to use a man's own body to fuel amazing things." He held up his hand. "I have miles of biomechanical threads inside me."

"Did you go back to Markovia on your own? You told me they'd kill you if you went back."

"Oh that was a bit of an exaggeration." Ghasi shrugged. "Just to gain your sympathy. I knew they wouldn't be happy, but my father had gotten most of the intelligence they sent him for. He just got caught. Sloppy. I went back because it's my home."

"But they tortured you?"

"They said if I served them, endured the procedures,

I would become rich and powerful. So I said yes."

"So they didn't force you? You agreed to let them do it to you?"

"Of course. We're not all born special, Oliver." Ghasi sipped coffee and jerked his head over his shoulder. "That boy at the bar. He's yours, yes?"

Oliver nodded. There was no point in lying.

"I thought so." Ghasi waved his arm around. "Most of the others in here are mine. But there are innocents too. A little insurance so you don't try anything."

Ghasi thought he had taken control of the ground by positioning his people early this evening, but Oliver had broken into the bar last night after receiving Ghasi's call and hidden a cache of throwing darts and a fighting baton. He had taped them under the table where he sat.

Oliver mapped out a series of moves that would disable Ghasi, and take down three of his men, letting Barry finish the last few after moving the bartender and waitress to safety. But it was still too uncertain, too many innocent people in harm's way.

"I can help you," Oliver said. "You know who I am. You know I have contacts. Stay here. We can do whatever needs to be done to make you well again."

"I am well." Ghasi half stood, turning around and holding up his cup impatiently for another coffee. "I like what I've become. Don't you enjoy your mask and hood? It's fun, isn't it? Running around at night? Killing people?"

When Ghasi had the fresh cup, he spiked it and took a straight drink from the flask too. He stared hard at Oliver.

"I want the Straub device. The wormhole generator."

"You can't have it."

Ghasi twisted his head in confusion as if he didn't fully understand Oliver's simple reply.

"So," Oliver said calmly, "do you want to meet for drinks in another ten years or so?"

Ghasi slammed his fist on the table. "If you give me one more oh-so-clever answer, I will start killing people."

"Stop it, Ghasi," Oliver commanded. "You're not fooling anyone with that Hollywood tough-guy talk. It won't get you what you want."

Ghasi reared back for a moment. Oliver's sudden authoritative tone had snapped the man back to the past, when it was Oliver who made the calls. With a sudden cold sneer, Ghasi wiped his face. His eyes were growing bleary and red. The alcohol was taking a toll. It should make Ghasi sloppy and less effective, but it could also set him off. He had always been a hair-trigger drunk.

"I'm smart, Oliver." Ghasi set his drink aside. "I'm smarter than you. If you check under the table, you will find that I have removed the weapons you hid here." He grinned as Oliver felt under the table to find his darts and baton gone.

"Let's decide this like civilized men," Ghasi said. "My father was sent here years ago to steal the technology, but you sent him to prison before he could finish his work. I'm going about it in a more direct fashion than he did. Bring the generator to me and I won't kill anyone. Simple."

"It doesn't work."

"Nothing personal, Oliver, but you're hardly a mechanical genius. My people can make it work."

"No. You don't understand. There's no operating system. It's just a piece of metal."

"You're lying." Ghasi tensed, but then sat back. "Bring it to me and stop delaying."

"Why do you want it?"

"To make money. A *lot* of money. Oliver Queen-type money."

"Oliver Queen money isn't quite as big as it used to be."

"Your family's company was destroyed by your father's greed."

"I'm trying to make up for that." Oliver could barely keep Ghasi's eyes locked in, but he forced himself. He tamped down the anger and turned it into a quiet smile. "Who's your buyer? Count Wallenstein?"

"Ah. Good call, Ollie." Ghasi nodded his head in admiration. "Yes, Count Wallenstein has run this operation from the days when my father was here spying on your father's company." The liquor had certainly wrecked his poker face. He instantly knew he didn't have a shred of cover, but seemed unperturbed by it. "You're not just an athletic dilettante with a Robin Hood fetish, are you?"

Felicity snorted in Oliver's ear.

Ghasi stared at his coffee, realized there was little more damage he could do to his composure, and downed it. "Twenty-four hours. Call me and I will pick up the device, and this whole thing can be over."

"Or I could end you here."

"My team has crosshairs on your people outside." Ghasi licked his lips and narrowed his gaze. "Little Speedy and the big man my men followed to the Glades the other day. If I say the wrong thing, if I make a suspicious noise, your two eyes in the sky get splattered by armor-piercing rounds. Body armor won't help them, unless they're wearing a Chieftain tank." He raised an eyebrow and pointed at Oliver. "I never thought you would give up your free time to get into this line of work." He laughed. "And I must say, I certainly never expected Speedy to join you. Actually I thought she would be divorced twice and a miserable drug addict by now."

"Shut up." Oliver clenched his fists and started to rise.

"Easy, Oliver!" Thea called over the comm. "Don't blow it. He's just yanking your chain."

"How does that jerk know our operation so well?" Felicity's tone was both worried and angry.

"If you can take him, do it," John said. "I don't see anyone with eyes on us. I think he's bluffing."

Ghasi tilted his head. "Oh, I'm sorry. I forgot how protective you are over your little sister. I apologize."

He smiled as if all the unpleasantness was past. "I'm going out now. It's been a pleasure seeing you again, without a hood and mask. Truly. Wait ten minutes before you and your friend there..." He waved at Barry, who glanced side to side in confusion before waving back. "...leave. The big man and Speedy should stay put too."

Ghasi stood up, leaning down. Oliver tensed as his old friend moved closer. Ghasi put his hand around the back of Oliver's head and touched foreheads like the old days.

"Please don't test me, Oliver," he whispered. "You have no idea what I've become. They made me into something no one has ever seen before. You don't have enough arrows to stop me." He straightened. "You'll pay the tab, yes? I don't have Oliver Queen money yet." He laughed loudly and went out.

Barry watched Ghasi leave, and then turned to Oliver, who waved him over. Barry crossed the bar with many eyes following him. He slid into the booth.

"So," Barry asked, "was that good or bad? I can't tell with this spy stuff sometimes."

"Could've been better, could've been worse."

"Oh. Okay." Barry rolled his eyes and shoved the empty coffee cup aside. The smell of bourbon filled the booth. "Your buddy sure can drink."

"Yes. When I knew him before, that was his only super power."

"Are we going to fight these guys?" Barry glanced

over his shoulder at the icy stares coming from the men around the bar.

"No." Oliver sat back and checked his phone. "We're going to sit here for ten minutes, then leave."

"I assume we're not giving him the wormhole generator, are we?" Barry whispered.

"No."

"You have something else in mind?"

"Always." Oliver crossed his arms, content to wait.

1 3

BEFORE THE JUNGLE

The elevator opened on chaos.

Raised voices. People running. Phones ringing. The executive level of Queen Consolidated was usually a quiet haven of mood music and purposeful but measured activity. However, this resembled the fall of Saigon.

"What's happening?" Oliver glanced at his sister, who stood beside him with the same shocked expression.

"Oliver? Thea?" Walter Steele waded through the chaos toward them. He carried two cell phones and had several folders pressed under his arm. Walter was a top executive at Queen Consolidated, master troubleshooter and Robert Queen's right hand. This was the closest Oliver had ever seen Walter to being upset. "What are you doing here?"

"We—" Oliver pressed against the wall to avoid being run over by a man in a very expensive suit racing down the hall. "We were told to come down for a photo shoot. For the annual report."

Walter grimaced. "I should have called you and told you to stay home. That was my fault, I'm sorry. Go home, please. And stay in the house until you hear differently."

Instead, Oliver followed Walter into the gauntlet, offering his hand to Thea for support.

"What's happening?" Oliver asked. "Is it the stock market?"

"No." Walter put a hand on Oliver's chest as they stopped outside a door labeled PRIVATE. He took a deep breath. "Your father is going to be arrested today on charges of espionage."

"Arrested!" Oliver wasn't sure he'd heard properly. "Espionage?"

Thea laughed. "Dad? A spy?"

"Spy for whom?" Oliver asked. "That's crazy."

The door opened. Robert Queen stood there. He was a tall man, white-haired, handsome, competent, authoritative. He started to speak to Walter, then noticed his children.

Robert Queen looked annoyed at the interruption at first, but then softened and reached out to them.

"You two come in here."

Their father pulled them into his inner sanctum. Walter followed. He put an arm around Oliver's shoulder, which surprised the young man, and kissed Thea on the cheek. Moira Queen stood by the windows overlooking the skyline. She smiled, exhausted, and took Thea's anxious hands.

"Dad, what is going on?" Oliver asked.

"We got a call this morning from a friend inside the Department of Justice to alert me that the FBI has been conducting an investigation. Into me."

"But espionage?"

"I know." Robert laughed and raised his eyebrows. "I was surprised too, believe me. But our friend told us that they had evidence—"

"*Credible* evidence was how he put it," Moira added.

"Yes, credible evidence that I had sold technology to a foreign power on the State Department restricted list."

Oliver noticed personal documents on his father's desk including a passport. Robert followed his son's gaze and with embarrassment began to fit the documents into his coat pockets.

"I'm leaving the country, Oliver. Just until we can get this straightened out."

"But you didn't do anything."

"No, but if I'm arrested, it could threaten enormous amounts of proprietary information. It could cripple Queen Consolidated. This whole thing is a malicious attack on this company."

"Then stay and fight. We'll all fight."

"Oliver," Moira said, "sometimes the best way to fight is to maneuver. We need time and I won't see your father arrested like a common thief."

Oliver stalked across the room. The image of his father slinking away bothered him, even made him worried there was something he wasn't saying.

"What technology were you supposed to have sold?"

"It's best you not know too much about it for your own protection," Robert said. "We do know that the end user was in Markovia."

Oliver spun around with enough force that everyone stared at him.

"What is it, Oliver?" Moira asked.

He didn't want to say anything. Thea's frightened face decided for him.

"You don't know this," he said, "but Ghasi and his father are Markovian."

Moira and Robert exchanged alarmed glances.

"No, Oliver," Walter Steele replied calmly. "They're from Croatia. I vetted Mr. Lazarov personally."

"No, they're not. Ghasi told me they had to escape from Markovia and arranged for Croatian documents so they could come here to the United States."

Robert came toward Oliver. The flinty look in his eyes was unlike any Oliver had seen before.

"Are you sure?"

"Yes, sir. Ghasi was drunk when he told me, and later he asked me not to tell anyone. He was afraid he and his dad would be deported." Oliver looked at Walter. "But that doesn't mean there's any connection to this. His father is a physicist. He was just looking to continue his research."

Robert stayed quiet for a moment before pointing at Walter. "Get our security people to take another look at Lazarov. And call our friend at DOJ and give him this information. Let the FBI know about Lazarov too."

"Dad, I don't think—"

"That's all right, son." Robert clapped his hand on Oliver's shoulder. The man's face was no longer burdened by fear and anger; it was full of cold purpose. This was the Robert Queen Oliver knew so well, and he felt a sense of relief and pride that he had helped restore him. "Nothing will happen to anyone if they're innocent." He smiled at Oliver as he removed the passport from his pocket and slid it back into the desk drawer.

14

Felicity sat in her office high inside Palmer Technologies. She never felt at home here, maybe because her path to this office had been so random. She had been satisfied as an IT manager at Queen Consolidated until the darkly handsome Oliver Queen asked her to do some off-the-record snooping in the company computers. It turned out darkly handsome Oliver was really the mysterious vigilante, the Hood, so she joined his war on corruption. She took a side trip to a relationship with Ray Palmer, genius entrepreneur who scooped up Queen Consolidated. It was Ray who anointed Felicity as CEO of his company. She knew she was capable of the task, but never felt completely deserving.

Felicity double-checked the data on her screen. In fact, it was the second time she had double-checked it. The intercom buzzed.

"Ms. Smoak, Beth Copeland from Archives and Records is here."

"Send her in." Felicity's hands started to sweat.

The door opened and a woman crept in, worried but composed. She saw Felicity and smiled perfunctorily. Gray-haired, mid-50s, thin. She stood silently.

"Hi, Beth. Sit down."

The woman perched on the edge of a chair in front of the desk with her hands clasped in her lap. She still didn't speak.

Felicity sat up straight. "Beth, I want to talk to you about the Jackson Straub files."

"I believe I brought you everything we have from the QC archives, but I can do another search."

"No." Felicity cleared her throat. "Um. Is there anything you'd like to tell me about that?"

"No." Beth looked down.

"Are you sure?" Felicity stared hard at her, imagining she was coming off as an ogre of a boss, which was her intent.

"No."

"Beth, when I requested Jackson Straub's records a few days ago, did you alert someone?"

"What do you mean? I followed the usual retrieval protocols."

"See, I don't think you did. I think you called someone to tell them I was interested in Jackson Straub. Did you?"

"I… don't understand." Beth shifted in the chair.

"I know what happened because you used a company cell phone to make the call. The number you called was local, but it leapfrogged to an exchange in Markovia."

"Markovia?" The woman shook her head in disbelief. "I never called Markovia."

"And the day after you made that call, fifty thousand dollars appeared in your bank account."

"I hit the lottery," the woman replied in a panic.

"No you didn't." Felicity rolled her eyes. "Just tell me. I've got all the proof right here." She spun the laptop.

Beth peered at the screen, studying the data. "How can you have that? It's illegal for you to have my private information. I should report you."

"Report me?" Felicity laughed, but turned the computer away from Beth. "I'm going to report *you*. You're a spy."

"A spy?" Beth's mouth went wide. "I'm not a spy. I've worked here for thirty-two years. And I didn't sleep with the owner to get *my* job!"

"Well, that's just mean." Felicity sat back. "And to think, I wasn't going to send you to prison."

"Prison!" Beth slammed her hand on the desk. "I'll call my guy in the FBI and he'll have you arrested for hacking into my accounts. Markovia! Shows what you know. That phone number is FBI headquarters in Washington. I'm going to sue you."

"Beth, that number connected to Markovia. Did your guy tell you he was with the FBI? Did it ever occur to you that the FBI doesn't make cash payments for tips?"

"Sure they do. They always offer rewards. They gave me twelve thousand back when they contacted me years ago, after the spy trial. After that guy went to prison for spying."

"For Markovia."

Beth pursed her lips in thought. "Oh yeah, that was Markovia too, wasn't it?"

"So someone approached you a decade ago and gave you money, and offered you more money to call a number if anyone in the company ever started looking into Jackson Straub's research. Right?"

"Yes." Beth sat back, staring off into space. "The FBI."

"It wasn't the FBI, Beth. It was an agent of Markovia."

"But he said he was FBI. You can't do that if you're not one." She raised her eyes to Felicity in desperation. "He didn't have an accent." Beth put her hands to her cheeks. "Oh my God. Am I a spy?"

"Technically yes."

"But my father is a veteran." The woman covered her face. "This won't affect his pension, will it?"

"I doubt it. We're not looking to prosecute you."

"Oh thank God!" Beth gave a shuddering exhale. "I really thought he was from the FBI. Honest. I'll give you the number, Ms. Smoak."

"I already have the number, thank you." Felicity poured a cup of water and hurried around the desk to hand it to Beth. "I do think it would be best if you took retirement."

"You're firing me? Just for this?"

"You're not being fired. I'm recommending that you retire. With full pension."

"This is the only job I've ever had." Beth started to cry.

"Besides spying you mean? Sorry. Just a little joke to lighten the moment."

Beth gave Felicity a sour look. "I'm not sure I can live on my pension. I'm glad I have that fifty thousand."

"Oh." Felicity held up a finger. "Yeah, you should probably divest yourself of that."

"What?"

"You can't really give it back to Markovia, but you should donate it to charity. Anonymously."

"Really? I was going to put a down payment on a beach condo."

"We have to insist you donate it."

"Who's *we*?"

Felicity took an unwilling breath and nodded toward the drapes. A gloved hand pulled the curtains back and Green Arrow stepped out. Beth went rigid in the chair with a yelp of surprise.

"Ms. Smoak is offering you a bargain." Green Arrow's voice rumbled. "Take it."

Beth continued to stare, dumbfounded.

"We believe your story." Arrow's eyes glowed from inside the shadow of the hood. "For now. But if you do anything to cast doubt on what you've said today, I will see to it that you pay for your crimes."

"I-I didn't commit any crimes," Beth stammered.

"Then prove it. Do as we ask."

"Okay," came her meek reply.

Felicity took the empty cup. "All right, Beth. You

can go. You should prepare and file your retirement papers tomorrow. And obviously don't tell anyone about this. Do you understand? Anyone."

"Yes, ma'am." Beth continued to stare at Green Arrow without moving.

"Okay then, Beth." Felicity smiled and took her by the arm, prompting her to stand. "Off you go."

"Yes, ma'am." Beth stumbled over the edge of the chair, recovered and continued backing toward the door. She bumped into it, felt wildly for the doorknob, grabbed it and pulled the door into herself. She swallowed hard and slipped out.

Felicity closed the door and leaned against it. "I didn't really want to do the Green Arrow guilt trip on her."

"Do you believe her?"

"Yes."

"Do you think she's somehow been leading Ghasi to us?"

"I don't see how." Felicity returned to her desk. "First of all, she wouldn't know anything to tell him. Even if she could've known to send him to the old office in the Glades, she couldn't have had any idea about the mine. I have swept this office building and our lair and our equipment several times, and I would bet my... my... something really important that there are no bugs here. I don't know how Ghasi has anticipated our moves."

Green Arrow's phone buzzed. "Barry just texted that Cisco is in town. He's going to vibe the generator."

Felicity sat with eyebrows knit. "He's going to *what* the generator?"

Cisco Ramon slumped in a chair and clutched a large coffee. Barry sat with him near the brightly lit mannequins where the Arrow team costumes rested when not in use. Footsteps alerted Barry to the arrival of Green Arrow and Felicity.

"We are so glad you're here." She hugged the listless Cisco. "Where's Caitlin?"

"She stayed behind in Central City to keep working on the plasma issues."

"Ah, okay." Felicity rubbed her hands together. "We'll get the wormhole generator working now. What did you think of it?"

"I haven't shown it to him yet," Barry said. "I thought he should be properly caffeinated first. The red-eye from Central City is a killer."

"I'm ready." Cisco took a slug of coffee. "Let's get going."

"Over here." Oliver shoved back his hood and pulled off his mask. He moved past Cisco toward the main bank of computer consoles.

"Am I just going to look at it on screen?" Cisco sat up. "I've got to go where the generator is so I can get up close and personal."

"It's right here." Oliver pointed to the device that sat on the floor in center of the raised platform.

"That cannot be a wormhole generator." Cisco came forward slowly, shaking his head with a smug grin. "A wormhole generator needs a big power source. Like designed by Jack Kirby. Like bigger than the Arrowcave. Like S.T.A.R. Labs big."

"No, that's it." Barry came up behind him. "We think."

"Well, you've got to be wrong." Cisco stepped onto the platform, setting his coffee on the console. He stared down at the device. "This thing here couldn't possibly generate enough power. Maybe this is a scale model that your guy Straub built. You know, like a little model of a steamboat or a rocket ship, just to get a sense of proportion."

Felicity moved next to Oliver. "We really think that is the whole thing."

"I got doubts." Cisco paced around it. "So tell me more about Jackson Straub. Is he really smart, because I'd never heard of him before I read those few papers he wrote that Barry sent me."

"Seems to be," Barry answered. "His early research was pretty tough stuff. Once he joined Queen Consolidated, he stopped publishing."

"Well, it's pretty cool-looking, I'll give him that." Cisco knelt and peered into the metallic facets of the device. "Hm. That's interesting."

"There's no operating system." Barry joined Cisco next to the generator. "We're looking for it now, but we're hoping you might be able to do a little, you know." He held out his hands and wiggled his fingers like a magician casting a spell. "Just in case you see the world being sucked into a black hole. That would give us a heads-up that the thing is really dangerous."

"Any chance you can see where Straub hid the code for the operating system?" Oliver asked.

"I'm not a Magic Eight Ball." Cisco rubbed his hands together. "Okay, here we go." He held his hands out over the device, took a breath, and then grabbed hold. He squeezed his eyes shut. After a few seconds, he released.

"What?" Barry asked. "What'd you see?"

"Results cloudy. Ask again later." Cisco clutched the generator again and concentrated. Thirty seconds passed. He let go. "Nope. I got nothing."

"No vision at all?" Barry helped him stand on exhausted legs.

"Nada. Sorry." He glanced down at the generator. "Maybe this thing is just a boring hunk of metal with no life."

Oliver let out a long breath.

"Felicity, why don't you and Cisco do what you can to analyze this generator, pick up what function you can from the structure. Barry, you get with John and Thea to scout out sites where Ghasi's forces might be holed up."

"And you?" Felicity asked.

"I'm going to prison."

"Oliver Queen to see Dmitrij Lazarov."

The uniformed prison guard consulted a clipboard with a nod. He eyed the famous playboy and checked the clipboard again. He studied the ID card created for Oliver at the gatehouse.

"Okay, Mr. Queen, empty your pockets." As he talked, the guard went to a caged-in window and grabbed a heavy Ziploc bag. "All items such as your wallet, phone, watch, pens, and pencils must be left here before you proceed."

Oliver emptied his pockets and dropped everything into the bag. A squealing metal detector wand slipped over Oliver. The guard pressed a code into a pad on the wall and pulled open a heavy door.

A long wall, the upper half plexiglass, was divided into semi-private stations with chairs and old-fashioned telephone receivers.

"Take a seat at the first chair, Mr. Queen. I will have

Lazarov brought in. When he arrives, you will have fifteen minutes. Do you understand?"

"Yes. Thank you." Oliver settled into a cheap metal chair and waited. It took ten minutes before a door on the other side of the plexiglass wall clanked open and Lazarov came into view. The man looked much older than Oliver remembered. He was stooped, his hair thinner and completely white. Once he had been round and soft, but now his frame was lanky and his face angular and hard. The man resembled his son much more now.

Lazarov nodded thanks to the guard on his side and shuffled forward, squinting at Oliver. Sitting slowly in his chair, he picked up the receiver. The old voice crackled through the phone, familiar but strange.

"Oliver?"

"Hello, Mr. Lazarov. Thank you for seeing me."

"Certainly. I am a little surprised. I don't get many visitors. Even the FBI agents stopped coming after a while."

Oliver had gone through Lyla and her A.R.G.U.S. contacts to clear this meeting. The feds weren't usually keen on convicted spies having unofficial visitors.

"How have you been? You look good."

"Please, Oliver. I look old. Prison, even medium security, is not conducive to an easy life. Still, it could've been worse. At least I'm here rather than Iron Heights. Did your father have something to do with that?"

"I believe he did."

Lazarov tightened his lips. "Robert Queen was a good man, at heart. I'm sorry he died, but I was very glad to hear about your return from the boating accident. I always appreciated your friendship with Ghasi. Moving to America was difficult for him."

"He seemed to take it well enough."

"In some ways." Lazarov chuckled. "Once he met you. He admired you so much, Oliver. He wanted to be you. He dressed and acted like an American playboy, no offense. But he grew so angry. Angry at me, at everything."

Oliver glanced at the wall clock. "Mr. Lazarov, I only have a few minutes with you. Could I ask you something about your time at Queen Consolidated?"

"Of course, Oliver." Lazarov watched him kindly.

"Do you remember a man named Jackson Straub?"

"Yes." It was hard to tell if a slight smile crept over the old man's lips. His eyes flicked downward and he appeared to be thinking. "Why do you ask?"

"Do you know what his field of expertise was?"

"He was in applied sciences, as I recall." Lazarov bit his lower lip in contemplation. "A physicist. Cambridge man. Very smart."

"What did he work on at Queen?"

"Why are you asking about Jackson Straub? More important, why are you asking *me*?"

"Ghasi is back in Star City," Oliver said without pause.

"What?" Lazarov jumped in surprise. He pressed

forward. "He's here? Have you seen him?"

"Yes."

"How is he?"

"He seemed fit enough."

"How could he be in the United States?" Lazarov whispered.

"He's not here legally, Mr. Lazarov. He's working for Count Wallenstein."

"Oh no no no." Lazarov seemed to melt in pain. His eyes welled and his grip tightened on the phone. He pressed a hand against his face, shaking his head.

"Mr. Lazarov, Ghasi is here looking for the results of Jackson Straub's research. He's looking for the wormhole generator."

"No." Lazarov shook his head firmly. "You are lying now. You know that Markovia already has that research. That's why I am here. I stole the designs for Straub's wormhole generator and sent them to Wallenstein, who was the head of Markovia's Secret Research Services."

"And you tried to frame my father."

"Please forgive me, but once Wallenstein had Straub's plans he wanted Queen Consolidated to be ruined so their research into the same technology would cease and only he would have the wormhole generator." Lazarov laughed sadly. "It was a mistake because the frame attempt led them to me. It turned out not to matter. The generator didn't work. Neither Markovia nor America profited. And I went to prison. All for nothing."

"Was Ghasi part of it?"

"No. He was not an operative."

"He is now. Apparently Wallenstein sent him to retrieve our own Straub device. The count must believe the American generator could work."

"Do you know where it is?"

"Yes, but your son and Wallenstein don't realize it won't do them any good. There's no operating system and we have none of Straub's notes to recreate it."

"Ah. I see. Well, I only stole the schematics for the device itself. Jackson kept the operations inside his brilliant head. And he is dead now, God rest his soul." Lazarov looked through the glass with that same strange smile. "Oliver, I want to see my son."

"That's not possible."

"You must make it possible. I will answer all your questions about Jackson Straub and his work. I know a great deal because I became Jackson's friend. Of course, I did so because I wanted to steal from him."

"I can't arrange it. You are a federal prisoner and Ghasi is in hiding."

"Fine. Then don't." Lazarov shrugged with a smug grin. "I have kept my secrets for years. I'm happy to continue keeping them. There are things I never told Count Wallenstein and his lackeys in Markovia. Things you need to understand. You have my terms. Let me see my son and I will tell you what I know."

"Why should I trust you?" Oliver said into the phone.

"What choice do you have?" the tinny voice came back.

"Oliver," John said, "you do realize that the man is a spy. He lied to your father, lied to Jackson Straub, who he claimed was a friend, he lied to this country, and you said he even lied to his bosses in Markovia. He lies for a living. He's in prison because he's a liar."

Oliver remained quiet.

"So if Jackson Straub did keep the operating system in his head," Felicity asked, "which I totally called by the way, and Lazarov admitted he never possessed it to send to Wallenstein, what could he even tell us?"

Oliver remained quiet.

"We can figure out this device." Barry's voice sounded fatigued. His eyes were ringed with dark shadows. "We just need a little more time."

He stood at a white board filled with scrawled formulae, holding a marker with more jammed into his back pocket. He frantically wiped out several strings of equations with his sleeve and began to write again with amazing speed. When he stopped to ponder, the faint black veins were visible on the back of his hand. He took a deep dismayed breath and wiped half a board clear again.

"We don't need to deal with a spy. Right, Cisco?"

"This can't be the whole device!" Cisco threw up his hands. "Something is missing. I have no idea what this part is even supposed to do. This is either the worst design ever or the greatest. I can't tell if these are hypermetals or what. Is he generating his own magnetic field with… that thing there? And where's the containment?" He tugged anxiously on his long hair. "How are we supposed to make an operating system for it if we don't even know how the designer wanted it to work? If only I could vibe an operator's manual."

Oliver remained quiet.

"Even if we did agree to Lazarov's terms," John continued, "the man is in federal custody for espionage. You can't check him out like a library book. No way will the feds let him stroll. And Ghasi isn't going to walk into the friendly confines of a federal correctional facility to see his dad. It's a non-starter."

"Oliver," Thea added from her spot sitting on a tabletop near the generator, "this can't be about any guilt you might have over Ghasi and his father. You didn't turn Mr. Lazarov into a spy and you didn't send Ghasi to Count Wallenstein. Don't make this about wanting to see a happy family reunion and thinking something good and Christmassy will come out of the meeting between them."

"Not to mention how he's been spying on *us*," Felicity said. "Although I don't know how."

"John." Oliver finally spoke and all eyes turned toward him. "Call Lyla and have her secure a temporary release for Mr. Lazarov on A.R.G.U.S. authority. I'll call Ghasi and arrange a time to meet."

John gave a grim look at the floor before pushing off the rail.

"Barry," Oliver said quietly, "it's time for your exercises."

Barry nodded and capped the marker without question. He stood back, studying the formulae with a critical eye and pointed at one of the lines of calculations. He shook his head and as he started away, he stumbled.

"Whoa!" Cisco jumped up and grabbed him by the arm. "You okay, man?"

"Yeah, yeah." Barry grinned and waved off Cisco with a friendly pat on the arm. "Just tripped. My shoe's untied."

"No, it's not," Cisco replied.

"Oh." Barry looked down at his feet. "Well, I thought it was."

He chuckled and left. Cisco watched him go before returning slowly to the Straub device.

"Oliver, are you sure about this?" Felicity said nervously, searching his face for some clue what he was thinking. "You're asking a lot of Lyla."

"We need information." Oliver held his phone in his hand. He looked at her, and then started to dial. "Barry doesn't have time to wait."

1 6

BEFORE THE JUNGLE

"He's been calling me for the last week." Tommy Merlyn showed Oliver his phone with a list of missed calls and messages from Ghasi. "He's starting to call from other numbers so I won't know it's him."

"Have you answered?" Oliver slumped in a chair in the library of the Queen estate.

"A couple of times by mistake. He wants to know where you are and why you won't return his calls. I said I hadn't heard from you, that I thought you were in Europe. How long is this going to go on, Oliver? Why don't you just talk to him?"

"I shouldn't. The FBI said not to. And my father said not to. And Walter said not to."

Tommy's phone rang and he glanced at it. He held it up again. "C'mon, Oliver. You can't treat him like this. You need to say something."

"What can I tell him?" Oliver sprang to his feet and paced the expensive Persian rug. "If I give anything away, I could get my father in trouble with the feds."

"I just can't believe Ghasi's dad is a spy." Tommy shook his head. "He seems so harmless."

"I know, but they've found evidence against him. And there's proof that he planted evidence against my father to cover his activity." Oliver grew silent, trying to quiet the anger at the thought of someone attacking his father and the family. "The feds are just waiting to build a stronger case before they move against him."

"Do you think Ghasi knows?"

"No," Oliver replied quickly. "I don't know half the stuff *my* father does. Neither do you."

"Less than half," Tommy muttered.

"I feel terrible for Ghasi. He's going to be in a tough spot."

"You think he'll be deported back to Markovia?"

"Not if I can help it." Oliver clenched his fists. "We have a lot of influence and I'm going to use it."

The door opened and a private security guard stepped in. Dark suit with a bulge at the armpit and coiled earpiece. Face like a slab of iron. "Mr. Queen, we have an incident outside. Ghasi Lazarov is at the front door demanding to see you. Shall we get rid of him?"

Oliver exchanged an alarmed look with Tommy.

"What should I do?"

"You just said you can't talk to him."

"Yeah, but if I don't," Oliver said, "he'll just keep coming around or bothering you. Or he might do something stupid. Dangerous stupid."

Tommy shook his head. "If the FBI said don't, I wouldn't."

Oliver considered the range of possibilities. Ghasi was unpredictable at the best of times. This situation could spill over onto others, and that wasn't right. This was Oliver's mess.

"I'll see him." He nodded sharply and went for the door.

"Are you sure that's wise, Mr. Queen?" the security guard asked. "The man is emotionally distraught. He could be a threat to himself or others."

"I'll see him." Oliver took a deep breath and steadied his nerves. He didn't want to face Ghasi, who was anxious at the best of times. Tommy followed, which gave him some comfort. As he headed toward the front door, he saw it was open and Ghasi stood on the portico outside beyond the broad backs of two plainclothes security men. Ghasi's first reaction on seeing Oliver was relief, but it quickly changed to resentment.

He stepped back when Oliver pushed out between the guards. "Well hello, Oliver. How was Europe?"

"Hi, Ghasi. Sorry about all this."

"All what?" Ghasi laughed harshly. "Lying to me or not answering my calls or something else? Hello, Tommy. Nice to see you… here."

Oliver studied Ghasi, who wore tight jeans with sneakers and a t-shirt, but his heavy denim jacket could've hidden a pistol.

Ghasi glared angrily toward the security men.

"Oliver, could we step away from them for a second? Somewhere private?"

"We can't let you out of our sight, Mr. Queen," one security guard said.

"We'll just be out on the lawn." Oliver held up a cautioning finger to the man. "We'll stay in full view."

He and Ghasi started off the portico. Tommy stayed where he was until Ghasi said, "Come on, Tommy. You're welcome to join us. I have no secrets. Apparently."

The three men gathered on the grass fringe in the shadows of the gothic Queen mansion. Ghasi lowered his head to hide his mouth from the security guard. "Oliver, what the hell is happening?"

"I've been busy. Sorry."

"Not with you." Dark eyes flashed up. "My father was placed on administrative leave and he's been locked out of his lab. There are people watching us, following us. Government agents have come to our home and questioned us. They know we are from Markovia. How did they find this information?"

"The government suspects your father is a spy."

"And why do they suspect that?"

"Look, Ghasi, if he's innocent, there's nothing to worry about."

"What the hell are you talking about? We're Markovian and everyone knows now. His career is ruined no matter what. We'll be sent home and probably murdered."

"We won't let that happen."

"Oh, you won't?" Ghasi snapped. "You are our champions now? First you ruin us, then you pick us up. How American of you. Should we show gratitude?"

"Someone tried to frame my father." Oliver breathed out slowly. "Documents were planted in company servers implicating him as a spy for Markovia."

Ghasi's anger melted away. He suddenly became a kid far from home in danger of losing his new place of safety. His eyes grew frightened.

"Oliver, please," he nearly whimpered. "I can't tell you what happened but I know my father is innocent. We can't go back to Markovia or we will die. I must beg a favor from you."

"I want to help you." Oliver's tone softened. He felt miserable for his friend. Maybe Ghasi truly believed his father was innocent. "I'll do anything I can for you."

"Thank you, my friend. We need twelve hours."

"What do you mean?" Oliver blinked in confusion. "Twelve hours for what?"

"To get away. We do have some resources, but we need you to help distract the FBI." Ghasi smiled in a sly, friendly manner. Old chums on a caper. "You are so good at lying, Oliver. Twelve hours. We can be gone by then."

Oliver glanced at Tommy, who looked very suspicious. "Ghasi, I can't lie to the FBI."

"Why not? You lie to everyone. You are an expert. You will do this for a friend, yes?"

"No."

"Six hours then? Please, Oliver. You must do this for me."

He knows, Oliver thought in stunned surprise. *Ghasi knows his father is a spy, a Markovian agent, a provocateur who tried to misdirect law enforcement onto my father. Ghasi knows and he's down to his last option to escape the consequences, preying on friendship.*

It hurt more than it should have.

"So it's all true?" Oliver shook his head, mouth gaping open, stunned. "You knew about it? You would've sat back and watched my father go to prison? After all we've done for you?" He grabbed Ghasi's collar and punched him as hard as he could. Ghasi stumbled to the grass, staring up in surprise.

"You are sentencing us to death then?" Ghasi gathered his anger and screamed, "You are murdering us!"

The security men launched themselves from the portico, but Oliver held up a hand to halt them. They still walked forward slowly with hands inside their jackets.

"Get out of here!" Oliver shouted. "Get off my property!"

"You pretend to be a man." Ghasi climbed to his feet. "But that is all you do. *Pretend*. When I need you, you are nothing." He pushed a finger into Oliver's chest. "Whatever happens now is on you."

Ghasi walked toward his car. Oliver watched him slip behind the wheel and screech off. The car sped out of sight and the roar of the engine vanished into the background. Oliver's heart pounded wildly in his chest. He took a deep breath and reached for his phone, exchanging a glance with Tommy. He hit a single button and waited for the familiar voice.

"Dad," he said. "You need to call the FBI. Mr. Lazarov is going to run for it." Oliver hung up and dropped his head. His voice was monotone and lifeless. "Tommy, I need you to distract the rent-a-cops."

"What are you going to do, Ollie?"

"I don't know yet, but I need your help to do it."

Tommy sighed, wide-eyed. "Okay. I'm your man."

Oliver dropped into a crouch as if distraught. He almost conjured tears but that seemed a bit much. He heard Tommy's footsteps moving away. His friend's hushed voice asked the three security men to give Oliver some privacy. *Step inside. Let him have a moment.* More footsteps shuffled to the door and Oliver heard it click shut.

He leapt to his feet and ran. A motorcycle sat next to his Maserati in the wide circular drive. Digging the keys from his pocket, he straddled the bike and kicked it up. The sound of a door.

"Mr. Queen!"

The security chief's shout was lost in the rumble of the motorcycle. He fishtailed across the lawn and turf rained over the pursuing man. Oliver wrangled the motorcycle out onto the street and sped off toward Ghasi's home.

He weaved through traffic, unsure why he was doing this. Not even sure what he was going to do. If things looked desperate, Ghasi might do something stupid, very stupid. Oliver couldn't bear that being on him. He hunched over the handlebars and twisted the throttle. When he turned onto the street where Ghasi lived with his father, he saw one car in the driveway, but it wasn't Ghasi's.

There was a van parked at the curb, a dark nondescript van like the FBI would use. When he skidded to a halt in front of the house, Oliver saw the front door was open. Figures moved inside. He dismounted and started for the door. A tall man in a black suit stepped out to block him with curt professionalism.

"Mr. Queen, is there some reason you're here?"

Oliver stopped, trying to see beyond the agent into the house. Someone appeared in the doorway. It was Mr. Lazarov and he looked at Oliver with terrified, pleading eyes, much like his son had.

"Who are you?" Oliver asked, but he knew already.

"Federal Bureau of Investigation, sir." The man held up an ID.

"Oliver!" Mr. Lazarov cried out. "This is not right. Tell your father I have not done what these men say. Please, Oliver."

"Mr. Queen, you'll need to leave," the FBI agent said quietly.

Two dark sedans screeched up to the curb. More federal agents poured out, wearing windbreakers labeled *FBI*.

"Doesn't he get a lawyer?" Oliver drew closer to the agent at the door.

"Remove yourself from the property now or *you'll* need a lawyer."

"Just because he's not American doesn't mean—"

A heavy hand clamped on Oliver's shoulder and he found himself staggering across the lawn. In a second he was at his motorcycle. The agent released him.

"Mr. Queen, do you know the current location of Ghasi Lazarov?"

"No!" Oliver jerked his shoulder back for effect.

Beyond the stern FBI agent, Oliver saw Ghasi's car turn the corner down the street and brake hard. He could see Ghasi through the windshield. Their eyes locked. He tried to stay calm, but when the agent noticed his attention and started to turn, Oliver blurted out, "He might be at a bar named the Glossy Starling. He always goes there."

"The Glossy Starling?" The agent turned back to Oliver.

"Yeah. It was like his second home." Oliver stared at Ghasi. He could sense uncertainty and anger. He silently urged Ghasi to back up, get out of sight and get away. But Ghasi's unpredictability might include ramming the FBI van. Oliver waited.

The car jerked and reversed out of sight.

Oliver let out a breath, causing the agent to peer suspiciously at Oliver. "If you have any contact with Ghasi Lazarov, you will alert the Bureau."

Oliver nodded and straddled his motorcycle. He sat slumped, waiting for his hands to stop trembling as the FBI agents all entered the house. He saw the scared face of Ghasi's father as the door was shut.

Oliver started the bike and wheeled it around. Speeding down the street, he expected to see Ghasi's car idling around the corner. He didn't.

Oliver never saw his friend again.

1 7

Oliver sat in the back of a nondescript panel truck, dressed in civvies. Mr. Lazarov sat next to him in an old brown suit with a white shirt and a tie ten years out of fashion. Lyla and two A.R.G.U.S. agents, a man and a woman in casual clothes, sat on the low bench across from them. The truck had rumbled to three locations so far, called in by Ghasi, only to have him cancel. Each call had come from a different phone so Felicity hadn't been able to trace them.

"Do you think he will really talk to me?" Lazarov bobbed his knees up and down, tapping his feet against the truck floor.

"Yes."

"But he's changed the location three times already."

"Just tradecraft. He's smart and he doesn't fully trust A.R.G.U.S."

Lyla gave Oliver a sidelong glance. She stayed quiet, but he knew she had pulled a lot of strings to make this happen. He didn't know the extent to which she'd lied to her superiors, and didn't need to. John had said that once she understood this was important to Barry's future, there were no questions.

"Or you, Oliver," Lazarov said. "I suspect he's worried you could turn him over to the authorities."

"I won't."

Lazarov patted Oliver on the knee in a grandfatherly way. "You're a good boy."

Lyla worked to suppress a smile.

Oliver sat back against the rattling side of the truck. John and Thea were following at a distance in the van, but Ghasi had probably seen them already. Barry was in reserve and could get to any eventual meeting spot in seconds, if needed, so they always had that bullet in their gun.

Oliver's phone rang.

"Yes?"

"Aparo Square," said Ghasi's recycled voice. The call ended.

Oliver repeated it to Lyla and she buzzed the driver. Aparo Square was a trendy urban park downtown. While it was a chilly November night, there would still be a crowd in the area. The neighborhood surrounding the square was a popular site for bars and restaurants. It gave Ghasi two things he wanted—cover in case he needed to disappear and innocents in case he needed to threaten. If this was indeed the meeting spot, he would have men pre-positioned to do mayhem if necessary.

The two A.R.G.U.S. agents did final checks on multiple 9mm pistols and hid them under coats and inside boots. Lyla said, "Mr. Lazarov, you understand the rules of this agreement, sir. You cannot touch your son. You must maintain at least six feet of distance. You cannot accept anything from Ghasi, and you cannot give anything to him. You must be in clear sight at all times. There will be guns trained on you."

"I-I don't want trouble, ma'am," he stammered. "I only want to see my son."

Lyla nodded. "Overwatch, any telltales on Aparo Square?"

Oliver felt odd letting Lyla handle the contact with Felicity, but he was just Oliver Queen now and he had to assume Mr. Lazarov didn't know his other identity. He could hear Felicity's response. "I read a lot of heat signatures. Large crowd out tonight. But I can't separate out the evil Markovian commandos, if that's what you're asking."

"That's what I'm asking," Lyla said. "Thank you, Overwatch, and stand by."

Oliver checked his phone, noting a blip on the map that was the truck and another that was the van with John and Thea. Their van had rushed ahead and was stationary a few blocks from the square. A red dot appeared on the map and then reappeared halfway across the cityscape. The Flash. He moved far too fast for the phone's processor to track.

The truck stopped. A panel slid open from the front

to report they were a block from the square. Oliver held his phone, expecting another call from Ghasi to brush off the meeting.

Lyla and Lazarov both stared at him. Nothing.

"Okay," Lyla said, "we're getting out. Mr. Queen, with me and Mr. Lazarov." She turned to her two agents. "No action unless I order it." They nodded.

Lazarov let out a breath and rubbed his hands together. He smiled nervously at Oliver. The agents swung open the back door and stepped out. Cold air rushed in. Oliver and Ghasi's father followed with Lyla behind them.

The truck had pulled into a space reserved for city service vehicles and promptly displayed the proper sticker on a rotating section of its bumper. Passers-by glanced curiously at the people piling out of the back of the truck, but since those people acted like it was nothing, it must be nothing. Oliver and Lyla blended into the evening crowds with Lazarov beside them. The agents drifted into obscurity nearby.

Aparo Square was a triangular plaza set between multiple crossroads. A few people sat at concrete tables playing chess. Couples strolled leisurely, while groups of homeless gathered along a low brick wall, smoking and staring into the distance. A small band of street musicians drummed in the center of the square.

Lazarov gasped and pointed. Ghasi stood with several men in military fatigues, but not mercenaries. These were rumpled bearded men in old greens and desert tans. When Ghasi spotted his father, he straightened off the wall, handed one of the men a pack of cigarettes, and came forward alone. Oliver could see Mr. Lazarov trembling.

Ghasi waited next to the drummers. A collection of five men and women boomed out rhythm on kettle drums, bongos, and steel drums. Lazarov took small steps as if hesitant to reach his son. When he finally got within a few feet, he raised his hands but quickly lowered them, remembering Lyla's warning about touching. Ghasi watched his father with a blank face. Lazarov wiped his eyes.

"Overwatch, Ghasi is stationary twenty-five feet to my southwest. Five feet south of Mr. Lazarov. There is a group of five just ten feet to his north. Can you mark him?"

"Got him."

Lazarov was speaking to his son, but Oliver could hear nothing but thunderous drumming via the earpiece connected to the wire the old man wore. Lyla put her finger to her ear and cursed. Ghasi was smart, but so were they. The drums faded into the background and Lazarov's voice became clearer. Unfortunately he was speaking Markovian.

"Translator," Oliver said unnecessarily because the line already crackled. A computer-generated voice kicked in with its measured pace. Given the dry mechanical voice, Oliver could only get a sense of emotion from watching the body language of the two men and listening to the tone of the Markovian still audible underneath the English. The translation came across a few seconds after the original so it was disconcerting to follow.

"How are you?" Lazarov was saying. "You look thin."

Ghasi shook with a huff of disdain. "What have you told them?"

"Who?" Lazarov drew closer, motioning for his son to be cautious.

"Oliver. And the government. They've asked you about Jackson Straub and his research. What have you told them?"

"Nothing. Are you living in Markovia now? Are you married? Tell me about your life.

Ghasi sneered. "Tell me about Straub and his work."

"Son, I'm not here to pass intelligence. That's in the past. I have nothing to say. Can't we talk about you, please?"

"You would betray Markovia?"

Lazarov squared his shoulders and tilted his head. "I heard you are serving Count Wallenstein. You count him as a patriot, do you?"

"What has Oliver promised you? Money? Freedom?"

"He promised me nothing except the opportunity to see you."

"In return for your knowledge about Straub?"

"Well yes, that is true, but I'm not going to tell him anything. Just as I won't tell Count Wallenstein anything. I am no longer a spy. I am only a prisoner. And a father."

"And a failure at all of them."

The next few seconds passed in surreal disjointed speed. Oliver listened to the last few seconds of Ghasi's translation as Ghasi was already moving. A glint of steel shone. Lazarov grunted in surprise. His son disappeared.

Oliver jolted into action. "Ghasi stabbed his father! Overwatch, have you got him?"

"He's gone!" Felicity reported. "He just disappeared from my screen."

Oliver ran to Lazarov, who staggered. The attack had been so fast, the surrounding crowd didn't notice. It was only Oliver shouting and running that attracted attention. He caught Lazarov and lowered his weight to the ground. A spreading red stain colored the man's white shirt. He clutched his stomach and looked puzzled.

Lyla was at their side summoning her team in the truck with a med kit. Oliver pulled off his jacket and bundled it up, pressing it onto the wound and holding it. The drumming group stopped and peered at them in confusion. Oliver searched around, looking for anything out of the ordinary. He saw nothing. A growing sense of unease filled passers-by who realized an accident had occurred, asking what happened. Heart attack? Did the old man trip and fall?

"Spartan, Speedy, anything?"

"No sign of hostile activity," Spartan replied. "No movement. Nothing."

Lazarov muttered nonsense until Oliver heard the translation in his ear again.

"Why?" he mumbled in Markovian. "What did I do?"

"He's not the man you knew," Oliver answered in English. "Hold on. You'll be fine. We have a medic coming." He caught a glimpse of a red streak moving through the street and along the sides of buildings. "Flash, anything?"

"No," the Flash answered. "I don't see his goons anywhere."

"Okay, come down here." Oliver hesitated. He didn't want to stress Barry's limits, but there were no options. "We need a medical evac fast."

Lazarov held his hand up in front of his eyes, staring at the blood on it. He looked at Oliver. "Jackson Straub's generator worked. He told me that it worked."

Oliver continued to press the coat against the wound. "He reported that it didn't."

"He had doubts."

"About what?"

"Your father. The government. Himself." Lazarov coughed. "He kept the code, the operating instructions, separate. Installing and uninstalling when needed. He didn't want anyone else to be able to use it."

"You never sent the code to Markovia?"

"No. I was only able to steal the plans for the device. And then I went to prison."

"Then how do you know it worked?"

"He told me. He used to come and talk to me. When we worked for your father, we often took our lunches together. He always wanted to go to the museum and look at the Tesla display. I didn't mind. It made him happy. He loved Tesla. He said Tesla was the only person he would've trusted with his research. That Tesla saw things no one else did."

"Mr. Lazarov, do you know where Straub kept the code?"

"No."

One of Lyla's men arrived with a medical kit, but she held him back. Oliver felt his hand sinking into the dark, sodden jacket on the old man's stomach. There was nothing a field dressing could do for this wound. He watched the face grow pale. "If you did know where the code was, would you tell me?"

"Yes," Lazarov groaned, struggling to breathe. "I wish I could help you, Oliver. You're a good son."

Oliver looked up to see the Flash at his side. "He needs emergency surgery if he's going to survive. Star Memorial Hospital is ten miles south on Alexander." The hero in red lifted the gasping old man. There wasn't a hint of reservation in Barry's eyes. When Oliver took his hand off the wet jacket, the Flash vanished in a streak of crimson. "Felicity, call the hospital and alert them."

"Already done."

Oliver scanned the plaza, wondering if Ghasi was

watching, perhaps merely a few feet away, smiling. His hand clenched. He looked down and realized his hand was red and dripping with the father's blood.

18

The Star City Museum of Science and Technology bustled with excited shouts from school kids and the stern commands of teachers. However, the late afternoon hour meant that the herds of field trips strolling across the museum's vast halls would soon ebb.

"Ah, young minds being broadened," Cisco murmured, casting his arms wide. "It does my heart good to witness it."

Barry watched a young kid of about twelve fascinated with a solar thermophotovoltaic device.

"I remember coming here on a school field trip. I'd always heard about this museum. It was the highlight of the year."

"Me too." Cisco nodded impishly. "I tried to hide out overnight. They had a figure of Albert Einstein and I thought he might come to life so I could talk to him."

"That doesn't sound like the mind of a genius at work."

"I was eight." Cisco pouted.

"Excuses, excuses."

Barry scanned the crowd, but didn't see the one person he wanted. Oliver was here somewhere. For such a noticeable and famous man, he could slip into obscurity in the blink of an eye. Instead of meditation, Barry wouldn't mind learning that particular ninja skill. Though as a speedster he supposed that really wasn't necessary.

They walked to the Inventors Wing where both remembered a Tesla exhibit residing, including numerous original devices and objects owned by Tesla himself. When they entered the wing, it held only a display on the history of computers.

"Hey, what gives?" Cisco looked around in confusion. "Don't tell me they got rid of it!"

"Let's hope not." Barry spotted a school kid playing with an interactive display. "Hello there. You wouldn't happen to know where the Nikola Tesla exhibit went, would you?"

"Who?" The kid regarded them with a frown.

"The horror!" Cisco grabbed at his heart and staggered back.

Barry smiled, withholding his own pained expression.

"He was one of the most incredible scientists of the twentieth century! He was responsible for figuring out the alternating current electrical system we have today. Not to mention the rotating magnetic field we all use in half our electrical products."

"I thought that was Steve Jobs." The kid gave him a blank look.

Cisco gasped again in horror.

"Regardless," Barry said to his friend before looking back to the boy, who stared at Cisco with alarm. "Do you know what happened to the exhibit? It's supposed to be right here."

"Oh that old junk? It's up front, isn't it? Didn't you guys come in the front door?"

"No, we didn't. Thank you." He turned to Cisco. "That's a relief, eh?"

"Old junk?" Cisco grunted. "Probably hidden behind a light-bulb exhibit."

They joined the flood of overstimulated third-graders to the main atrium. They passed under the painted-over remnants of a sign still partially visible: MUSEUM OF SCIENCE AND TECHNOLOGY. FUNDED BY A GRANT FROM QUEEN CONSOLIDATED, APPLIED SCIENCES DIVISION.

The late-afternoon sun shot through the glass walls and cast orange highlights on a display labeled FANTASTIC VICTORIANS. Standing behind an H.G. Wells time machine and an elaborate brass ray gun stood the lifelike figures of Nikola Tesla and Thomas Edison surrounded by incredible and whimsical Gilded Age technologies.

"Steampunk!" Cisco whooped with excitement. "Yes! Now all is forgiven. Makes me want to break out my Professor Sebastian Hornswoggle cosplay."

Barry's eyes widened in delight. "Are you kidding? I was Lord Phineas Fogbottom for Halloween in high school."

They high-fived.

"You two are reading about an eighty-five on the geek meter," Felicity interceded over their earpieces.

"Oh please." Barry flashed Cisco a grin. "We know you have one too."

"Come on, admit it," Cisco urged.

There was a pause before Felicity said, "Miss Eliza Babbage."

"I knew it!" Cisco laughed. "The three of us next Central City Comic Con. It will be a blast."

"Focus, people," came a stern voice.

Cisco spun around to see Oliver Queen gazing down at the engineer, his face expressionless and strict.

Gulping, Cisco muttered, "You should blend some of this steampunk with your costume. It would be kicking."

Oliver merely continued to stare.

"Focusing." Barry grabbed Cisco's arm and pulled him toward the exhibit, searching for something that might trigger an idea as to where to look for anything Jackson Straub could've hidden there.

"This operating system could literally be written or installed on anything even back when Straub designed it," Cisco said. "It could be as small as a microdot or as big as my head. So it's time to bring in the big guns." He pulled out a small handheld device with a rectangular digital readout. "Thank you, Felicity, for the sweet Palmer technology. This baby should detect any high-tech circuitry."

"Bottom line," Felicity cut in, "there's a good chance thousands of lines of code were packed away on a computer chip of some sort. And if so, that scanner *will* find it."

They started a methodical search of the exhibit, but kept it slow and hidden to keep from drawing the attention of the guard who was staring out the windows daydreaming about the end of his shift.

It could be anywhere. Anything. They could ignore much of the added steampunk material since most of that was new or cobbled together from other exhibits in the museum. That left only a few key pieces of original Tesla equipment. They held the device as close as they could to each object.

And nothing.

Cisco sighed. "If it's here, we're not going to find it this way. Maybe Straub used some old tech just to throw folks off the track. Maybe he wrote it on paper." He made a face. "We'll need to start tearing through these exhibits to look inside for the code."

"That will go over well with the guards," Felicity said.

"Oliver," Barry asked, "what was it that Mr. Lazarov said about Straub and Tesla?"

Oliver drew closer. "Something along the lines of Tesla *saw things no one else could see.*"

Barry stood in front of the cased, wax Tesla, breaking the figure's line of sight. Then he turned to look where Tesla's attention lay. It was staring almost accusatorily at Thomas Edison.

Cisco saw what Barry was up to. He went to Edison and ran the scanner over him, but nothing lit the readout.

Barry turned back to Tesla. "No one else could see," he murmured. He couldn't stop looking at Tesla's face. Especially his eyes.

"Cisco, hand me the scanner, will you?"

Cisco tossed Barry the device. "You see something?"

"Maybe. Does his left eye look a bit different than the other?"

"It's a dummy. I kind of expect it to look a bit wonky."

Barry watched the guard strolling across the atrium. The autumn sun created garish streamers of light that might block Barry from sight if the guard did turn back. He leaned over the rail and waved the scanner at Tesla inside his Faraday cage. The scanner went off with a sharp ping.

"Whoa. That's it!" He glanced at the readout. "It's showing high conductivity. There's a microprocessor in that eye or on it. A contact lens?"

Cisco checked the still-disinterested guard and climbed over the rail. He slipped closer to the mannequin.

"The code is in Tesla's eye!" he whispered in amazement.

Felicity's voice came dark and sinister. "Bring me the head of Nikola Tesla."

"Dun dun duuuuun!" Cisco intoned ominously. He reached out and touched the case.

The guard turned at the echoing notes, but Oliver had positioned himself exactly between the man and Cisco.

The longhaired engineer went suddenly rigid.

Barry grabbed Cisco before he hit the floor, steadying his reeling friend. They both bumped the exhibit case and something metal fell hard to the floor with a clatter.

"You all right?" Barry asked anxiously. "What happened? Did you vibe on Tesla?"

Behind him, Oliver intercepted the approaching guard.

"He's fine. He's got a condition. We're sorry. We can pay for damages."

"What? No." The security guard came forward to check on Cisco, who held his head in his hands. "What are you guys doing?"

"Urgh, I'm dizzy." Cisco sagged heavily against Barry.

"Maybe you need to head home, son, and leave the exhibits alone," the guard suggested.

Another security guard turned the corner to observe the commotion.

"A good idea." Oliver signaled Barry and Cisco to extract themselves from the exhibit. "Let's go."

They made it outside the museum before Barry could wait no longer.

"What did you see?"

Cisco's face was pale as he fidgeted on his feet.

Whatever it was, Barry thought, it was bad.

"I saw a wormhole generator, pretty much the same as the one you guys have." Cisco drew in a deep breath. "At first there were a lot of people standing around it. Lights flashing. Then everybody starts shaking hands with this one guy. And it's clear that he's won the generator or bought it or something."

"Who was it?"

"It was that guy you know." Cisco looked directly at Oliver.

"You'll have to narrow it down," Oliver replied.

"The guy with the bow and arrows. You know, the handsome guy. Kinda smarmy. With the dark hood."

"Malcolm Merlyn?"

"Yeah, that's the guy. He got the generator. That's bad, right?"

"It wouldn't be good."

"But Malcolm Merlyn isn't even involved." Barry regarded Oliver. "Is he?"

The archer's mouth twisted in distaste at the name. Malcolm Merlyn had been a friend of Oliver's father and led the sinister effort to destroy the Glades, primarily out of vengeance because Malcolm's wife was murdered there. Malcolm had trained in martial arts and maneuvered himself into the leadership of the ancient and nearly mythical League of Assassins, from which he had eventually been expelled. Now he was a free agent of chaos in the world, one of the most unpredictable and dangerous men alive.

"Not that we know of," Oliver said.

"There's more." Cisco's voice lowered to a near whisper. His eyes didn't waver from Oliver.

"Great." Barry's gut knotted.

Oliver merely stared back at Cisco. His head tilted almost curiously, not at all unnerved. "Do you want me to guess?"

Cisco hesitated but then said quietly, "I saw you die."

Back at the Arrowcave, everyone was talking at once. Oliver let them talk. He had stopped them from discussing it over the open comm and out in the streets for fear of being overheard.

Felicity's face held only dread as he stood across the console from her. She almost glared at Cisco.

"What do you mean Oliver is going to die?"

"Well, it's what I vibed." Cisco shrugged apologetically.

"What does that even mean?" John asked. "You're like a psychic?"

"More like a fortune teller, but both are cool, I guess." He sighed. "Vibing is more like seeing possibilities."

"So it's not *fact*." Thea had her arms crossed and she stood beside her brother.

"Well, sort of. I don't really know for sure. Somewhere it's going to happen."

"What?" Felicity was trying to grasp what exactly

he was saying. She looked up in alarm at Oliver. "What does that mean?"

Barry stepped in. "It's like he's seeing glimpses of a possible future from one of the many Earths in the multiverse."

"Possible future," John clarified. "So in *one* of these multi-worlds, Oliver is going to die. But there are thousands of them?"

"More than thousands," Barry said. "We think."

"How do we know it's not *our* world? Can we stop it?" Felicity's questions came at a frantic pace.

Cisco shrugged again, wishing there was some way to make this news easier. "We really don't know. Just be ready, I guess."

"How will I die?" Oliver spoke for the first time.

Everyone turned to look at him. Cisco squirmed but then answered.

"You looked beaten to a pulp. There was flaming wreckage everywhere. You were slumped over the generator."

"How do you know I was dead?"

"Your arm was ripped off. And you had an arrow sticking out of you."

"But how do you know I was dead?" he asked again.

"Your arm being ripped off isn't enough proof?" Cisco asked incredulously.

The blood in Felicity's face drained. She swung her chair to face Oliver.

"What do we do?"

Oliver remained a mask of calm. "We go back to the museum and get the code."

"No, about the vibe!"

"There's nothing to do about that. We've already taken every precaution we can for all of us to come through this. To do anything more would be jumping at shadows and a waste of energy. We proceed as planned."

"That's it? Preventing your death isn't a waste of energy. Who else uses arrows? Oh crap. Malcolm. We need to find him."

"Right now, Malcolm isn't even in this scenario," Oliver said. "Let's not worry about something that might have no bearing for us."

Felicity remained upset, but all he could do was go over and lift her chin to look at him.

"It'll be fine," he said. "It's only a museum heist."

Her lips pursed in her telltale pensive pout.

He kissed them and then nodded to the others.

"Suit up."

Green Arrow and the Flash paused in the darkness outside the back entrance of the museum. A small mechanism magnetically clamped to the door whirred softly.

"Just another second," Felicity muttered in their ears. The lock clicked open. "And there!"

The two men slipped inside and pulled the door shut behind them. A few lights high on the wall lit the interior. There was no sign of guards.

"Anything outside?" Green Arrow whispered.

"Speedy and I are in position on the roof," Spartan answered. "All clear so far."

"Stay sharp," Green Arrow replied.

The Flash looked at the archer. "I could just run in and be out before—"

Green Arrow held up his hand. "No need to risk a blur for something this simple. If I can't acquire an item from a public museum, I should give up the business. This way is effective, just a bit more leisurely."

"A bit?"

"Humor the slow people."

"I always do."

Felicity broke in. "I've got the security system. The corridor looks clear to the atrium. I've modified the camera feeds into a continuous loop, so you should be good."

Green Arrow slipped around the corner and jogged down the hall.

The Flash followed after. "You keep watch while I snatch Tesla's head."

"And that's a sentence that can't come up too often." Cisco's voice came through the comm.

"Probably not." The Flash hurried to catch up to Green Arrow, who was already disappearing into the main wing of the museum.

"Cut the unnecessary chatter," the archer told them. "Keep your eyes and ears open."

"I've disabled the alarm on Tesla's case so it should be easy enough to vibrate through and get the lens," Cisco announced. "Or are we cutting through it with a diamond-tipped arrow?" He sounded excited by that prospect. "Man, this is just like a spy movie."

"Do you have a diamond-tipped arrow?" the Flash suddenly asked.

Green Arrow regarded him with a furrowed brow and then nodded, pulling a graceful green shaft from his quiver. The Flash grinned and took it.

They paused outside the entrance to the main atrium decorated in the Victorian style with grand banners. Everything seemed quiet inside. Both Tesla and Edison remained in their corners. The electricity was shut off. The exhibit was dead.

Oliver moved inside. He waved Barry toward Tesla and began a slow circuit of the room.

The Flash turned his focus to the case. It was a full body enclosure. He didn't want to destroy the display. Vibrating in would be precarious because there was too much risk of damaging the object.

He lifted the arrow with a smile. His hand vibrated and the arrowhead blurred. Using the diamond-crusted tip, he sliced the glass in a perfect circle.

Cisco nearly squealed in his ear. "Oh my God, you're doing it, aren't you? Using the arrow to cut a hole?"

"Yes."

In seconds it was cut and he caught the disk of glass as it toppled out. Studying Tesla's eye closely, the Flash saw the round lens sitting atop the wax eyeball. He removed a glove and stretched his hand through the hole toward the mannequin's motionless face. It felt like a game of Operation.

He used a fingernail to delicately catch the edge of the lens and pop it from its perch on the eye. The flexible disk floated away from his fingers out into the air. He shifted with sudden speed and snatched the lens before it fell to the ground or drifted somewhere out of sight. He drew his arm slowly back through the hole and held up the lens with two fingers.

"Well?" Felicity blurted out.

"Hang on. I think we got it." The Flash pulled out a small device from his belt. It unfolded into a pair of eyeglasses with very thick rims. He opened a small compartment between the two eyepieces and slipped the small contact lens inside. Snapping it shut, he put the glasses on and pressed a small stud on the side. The glasses hummed.

Through the viewer, he saw symbols projected in front of him. Hundreds of thousands of lines of code scrolled through the air.

Barry let out a low whistle.

"This is it all right. We can crea—"

1 9

Green Arrow realized the Flash had stopped speaking in the middle of a word. He turned to see the Flash with Ghasi standing next to him.

Ghasi held a syringe. It was jammed into the base of Barry's skull and the Flash stood frozen, mouth open. Ghasi pulled the viewer from the Flash's face. He smiled at Oliver.

"Ghasi's there!" Felicity shouted.

Green Arrow launched himself just as Ghasi shimmered and faded from sight. He grabbed an arm, now invisible, and struck out where the other man's chest should be. A blow slammed against Arrow's jaw, but he held tight.

Green Arrow's hand struck again and his feet stepped instinctively, knees up to block. With quick lightning blows, he mapped out his invisible opponent's position. Feeling the moves and twists, predicting where counterblows would fall.

Spartan's strained words came over the comm. "Trying to get to you, but we've got hostiles approaching."

The Flash shuddered and his eyes blinked, coming awake. He yanked the syringe from his neck.

A figure coalesced in front of Arrow and a fist crushed into his chest. Oliver crumpled backward onto the floor. He slammed through one of Tesla's generators. Pain radiated around his ribcage.

Ghasi reached for his belt and tossed a capsule at the Flash, who was distracted by Arrow's violent tumble. Something black oozed around the speedster. Soft folds of foam slipped up over Flash's legs and torso, trapping one of his arms too. The Flash toppled to the floor. Ghasi kicked him and the dark cocoon slid across the floor as if on a cushion of air.

Ghasi grinned. "Frictionless foam stolen from Kord Industries."

Green Arrow extracted himself from the wreckage and threw a sedative dart at Ghasi, who deflected it with a metal bracer.

"Stay down, Oliver. I don't really want to hurt you, but I'm not averse to it either."

Arrow drew and extended his bow with a snap of his arm. He pulled an arrow and let fly. Ghasi blocked it too, almost bored with the exercise by now, but a second arrow following close caught the viewer in his hand and carried it away. The arrow shattered the glass case around the mannequin of Edison and plunged square in its heart. The viewer still dangled from the shaft.

Ghasi cursed and ran for Edison.

Green Arrow looked down at the Flash, who held onto the footing of H.G. Wells's time machine.

"Get the lens!" the Flash yelled. "I'm okay."

Ghasi stretched for the lens dangling precariously against Edison's chest when an arrow punctured his hand and pinned it to the mannequin. He screamed.

"Don't move!" Green Arrow called. "Or I will drop you!"

"Be careful," Felicity said into their ears. "He is white hot."

With a grunt, Ghasi pulled his hand free with the arrow still protruding. The viewer shook free and fell to the floor. He spun and deflected a shot singing straight for him. He grabbed a cast-iron and mahogany work table, easily weighing five hundred pounds, and flung it across the room.

Oliver dove aside. The table roared over his head to smash glass and crack wood, tearing a swathe through Tesla's display and punching a crater in the wall.

Green Arrow rolled to his feet, arrow ready. Ghasi knelt amid the shattered glass and tangled gearworks that tumbled off the table he upended, searching for the viewer. An arrow fired, but again Ghasi ducked and let it slip past, missing only by inches. He came up with the viewer in his grasp.

Oliver snapped off several smoke arrows. They popped into the floor near Ghasi just as he sparked and vanished. Smoke billowed to fill the room, swirling noticeably where the invisible form pushed through it.

Ghasi rushed into the face of a barrage of arrows. Some burrowed harmlessly through the smoke, but others ricocheted out. Ghasi appeared in front of Green Arrow, stretching out his hand with the arrowhead still protruding from his palm.

Oliver felt his own arrow slice through his hood and into his neck.

Ghasi tightened his grip on Oliver's throat, driving the razor deeper. "It's over now."

"No," he rasped.

"If I wanted to kill you, you'd be dead. Although if I move a fraction of an inch, you *will* bleed to death."

"Like you did to your father?"

"Yes. He's alive because if I left him alive I knew he would babble everything and I could follow you. It's over. I win."

A red streak appeared. Oliver felt a painful tug at his neck as Ghasi flew to one side. The Flash stood there, his scarlet suit smoking. He was unsteady on his feet, but his ferocious gaze pinned Ghasi.

"*Low* friction maybe," the Flash said. "Not frictionless."

The Flash streaked at Ghasi in an instant and swung at the kneeling man. Barry's fist stopped dead against Ghasi's chin like he had punched a building. The Flash cried out in pain and his arm dropped numb to his side. Even so, he grabbed for the viewer with the other hand, but Ghasi vanished in front of their eyes.

"No!" the Flash shouted, desperately sweeping the air around him with his good arm. He sped through the room, a crimson line crisscrossing. Then he zipped through the rest of the museum.

"Spartan, Speedy, what's your situation?" Arrow said.

"Hostiles are retreating," Spartan answered. "We're coming to you."

Felicity asked, "What about the operating system?"

"Ghasi took it," Green Arrow replied.

"What now?" John asked.

Oliver tried to focus his eyes to keep the room from spinning. His fingers and toes were cold.

"I think I have a problem."

"Yeah," Spartan responded, "I hear sirens approaching."

"Not my point." Oliver fought to keep the shadows from closing over his vision.

The Flash returned to stop in front of Oliver. He shrugged with dismay. "Gone. Couldn't find him." Then his expression turned to alarm. "Oliver? Crap, he's bleeding badly."

"Oh my God!" Felicity cried.

"Almost there!" Speedy shouted.

The Flash knelt to pick up Oliver and froze; his body quivered translucent. Oliver could actually hear a faint sound like a bee's wings.

The Flash jerked back into reality. "I just blurred, didn't I?"

"Yes."

"Sorry. I lost concentration. I'm fine now. I can get you to a hospital."

"No. Can't risk it."

Spartan and Speedy sprinted into the room. Both of them covered the angles with their weapons as they ran for Arrow. Spartan bent down and gently lifted the edge of the green hood away from the tunic collar. Arrow felt blood sluice hot down his shoulder.

The Flash stepped back to give Spartan room to work.

"Oh man," Spartan muttered, "that's close to your carotid. Can you breathe?"

"Yes."

"Good. Dizzy?"

"Yes." Oliver's heart pounded laboriously as it struggled to keep what little blood he had moving.

"Blood pressure dropping, but I got you." John pulled off his helmet, which Speedy took. He slid a small metal case from a pocket in his fatigues. "I'll do a quick field dressing to stabilize. Felicity, prep some whole blood and saline."

"Is he okay?" Felicity's voice quavered.

John hastily folded gauze into a thick pad and handed a roll of white tape to Speedy to pull strips. "He's bleeding like a pig, but not dying. Don't worry. He'll be fine."

Arrow appreciated the easy confidence John showed despite the fact that he had lost a large amount of blood already. The big man's sure movements calmed him. His breath grew steadier. The world was starting to black out when he saw John look up with bloody hands.

"Okay, Flash, he's yours now."

Oliver felt himself lifted from the floor. Barry's cowled face looked down at him. Before he could say anything, the world was a blur.

20

IN THE JUNGLE

Oliver crouched motionless in the mud. He had been there so long he barely felt the cold and wet on his knees. Ferns tickled his face. His breath sounded like thunder in his ears. He wiggled his toes to bring them back to life, barely feeling the rough wood of a bow in one hand and the arrow and bowstring between the fingers of the other.

Footsteps and the rustling of branches reached him. He couldn't pinpoint the location. It could be ahead of him or to the rear. Keeping his head straight, he let only his eyes slide back and forth. He couldn't see anyone.

Yao Fei had told him not to move. *Stay down and stay still. Do not engage any targets.*

The men patrolling the island were heavily armed mercenaries with high-powered weapons. Oliver was a wet, hungry, miserable trust-fund baby with a homemade bow and arrow.

Two low voices now accompanied the footfalls. That was comforting; if the soldiers knew Oliver was around, they would've been silent. Or they would've killed him already.

Oliver thought about breaking and running. Now was the time; if he waited, there was more of a chance he'd be caught.

Something moved beyond the layers of dark green in the forest. Oliver's heartbeat jumped.

Two men coming his way. He started to rise up so he could see beyond the thick ferns, but he stopped.

Yao Fei said stay still.

Surely he didn't mean that Oliver shouldn't protect himself. He couldn't sit here while those soldiers blindly stumbled over him.

Breathe, Oliver reminded himself, hearing Yao Fei's voice in his head. *Stay calm. Stay still. Stay silent. Let the moment happen. Be ready.*

Low cedar limbs swayed as two camo-clad soldiers strode into a clearing only twenty-five feet away. They stopped to get their bearings. Calm and assured, assault rifles cradled in the crooks of their arms.

Oliver struggled to be still. He expected arrows to fly into the two men. Where were the arrows? Why didn't Yao Fei kill them? The soldiers would see Oliver in a second. A few ferns weren't sufficient cover.

He should run. Maybe Yao Fei was waiting for him to distract the soldiers. He would bolt, the soldiers would turn in surprise, and arrows would drop them. Is that what Yao Fei wanted?

One of the soldiers laughed softly and rattled his

gun. Oliver tensed his legs, ready to go. He stared at the soldier's face. If the man looked this way, their eyes would meet, and Oliver would go then.

The man turned his head directly to Oliver. Somehow he didn't react and Oliver managed to stay still, although inaction was far more difficult than action at that moment. The soldier continued his leisurely study of the forest before tapping his companion. They started in a slow stroll directly at Oliver. He remained still despite an electric charge that wanted him to run for it. The fern that brushed their legs slapped back into his face. Their footsteps moved past him. Oliver fought not to turn and look for them. Soon the sound of rattling ammo belts and the soft whisper of voices faded into the distance.

Oliver almost moved in relief but stayed still instead. He breathed slowly in and out, watching the forest, listening for any change around him.

"You lived," came a voice close to his ear.

Oliver still did not move. There was no reason. If it was Yao Fei, all was well. If it was not, he was already dead.

A familiar laugh snorted. "You may move, if you can."

Oliver slowly turned his head on a wrenching neck. Yao Fei settled back into the thick ferns with a smile. Oliver unfolded his arms to sharp pains. After a few seconds, he braced himself in the mud and leaned over, stretching out his aching legs. He set the bow aside, working his fingers.

"I thought they had me." Oliver massaged his thighs, suppressing a hiss of pain. "Where were you?"

"I was watching."

"Where? I didn't see you."

"I was there, even so." Yao Fei pushed back his green hood and smiled.

"How about I get one of those hoods so I can hide too," Oliver snapped angrily.

The general laughed.

"I don't understand you, Yao Fei. You had those guys out in the open and you didn't do anything."

"I can have them in the open anytime. I have seen these two patrol this sector many times. I was not testing them. I was testing *you*."

"Don't you want to kill them?" Oliver scowled in confusion.

"If I had, they would not return to their base to say this sector is clear. If I had, we would soon be overrun by their colleagues looking for me."

"But what if they had found me?"

"They wouldn't find you if you did what I told you. They always take this exact path because it is the easiest, and they know it in their minds."

"What if I had moved? What if I panicked?"

Yao Fei replied with dead calm, "I would have killed you before you gave yourself away to them. I would still be safe."

"What the hell is that supposed to teach me?"

"To do as I say."

Oliver looked into the cold face. The man wasn't being glib or cute. He was serious. In the simple expressionless answer, Oliver recognized a plain truth. He had no control over his world; perhaps he never had.

Yao Fei popped to his feet and offered Oliver a hand up. "When you live in a jungle, you do not fight the jungle. You survive it. Sometimes it means killing. Sometimes it means not being killed." He tossed Oliver the makeshift bow.

Oliver pointlessly straightened his filthy, sodden clothes. "I'm not going to die here. I'll survive. I'll beat the jungle." He hung the bow across his back, growing weary of the philosophical doubletalk. "I'm getting off this island one day."

"You may leave the island, but you will never leave the jungle."

Yao Fei drew up his green hood and slipped into the forest without a sound.

Oliver stared at the ceiling.

Needs dusting up there.

At the sound of a ping, he glanced at the readout. Temp normal. Blood pressure a little low but stable over the last twenty-four hours. He sat up and pulled the clip off his finger. He twisted his head, testing his stiff neck.

"What are you doing?" Felicity scolded from her computer across the Arrowcave. "Stop turning your head all around. John said to keep the wound stable for a few days. You want to gush blood all over the place?"

Oliver hopped off the table and steadied himself. Dizzy.

"Are you dizzy?" Felicity shot up in her chair.

"No."

"Oh, you liar. You were almost killed three days ago. Just like Cisco said! Just be still!"

Her expression wasn't her usual one of wistfulness. Instead it held loss and fear.

The island had taught him that life was fleeting, and to worry about it being snatched away from you was time wasted. But she didn't.

She couldn't. Only life mattered to her and how to preserve it. She was much like Barry in that regard.

"This had nothing to do with the vibe. I survived. And if it did, then the danger is passed."

"We don't know that."

"No, we don't."

"That doesn't make it any easier." She leaned against him, her head on his shoulder.

"No. It doesn't. It shouldn't. But fretting about it isn't going to change anything."

She pulled her tablet toward her. "I've looked for Malcolm, but there's no trace of him. But I'll find him."

"I'm more worried about Barry than Malcolm. I've already wasted three days. I need to get out there and find Ghasi."

Oliver turned toward the mannequin dressed in his green costume.

"Oh no you don't!" Felicity shouted. "You need to rest. John and Thea and Barry are out there finding Ghasi."

"Well, we didn't find Ghasi." The Flash strode down the ramp into the cave followed by Spartan and Speedy.

John pulled off his helmet. "Lyla says A.R.G.U.S. has no leads either. Ghasi's people are in the wind."

"He played me like an amateur." Oliver shook his head angrily. "How did he know where we were? He said he *followed* us."

Thea replaced her bow and arrows in the wall locker. "He's been a step ahead of us the whole time."

Oliver's mouth was a grim slit. "We led him right to it. If he had been standing in the same room with us, he couldn't have read us better."

"Well, he does turn invisible." Barry raised an eyebrow. "So maybe…"

Everyone paused and looked around the chamber. A shuffling sound came from the entrance. All heads turned. Cisco walked in studying a tablet. He looked up and froze in mid-step.

"What?" he asked meekly. "What'd I do now?"

"Nothing." Barry smiled in relief. "We thought you might be somebody."

"Okay, well, that's insulting but whatever." Cisco waved the tablet. "This code is amazing. Even this small sample is sophisticated beyond belief."

Barry shook his head. "I wish I could've remembered more of it to show you, but I didn't get much of a chance to study it. Even with my super-fast comprehension, it was outside my comfort zone."

"I don't doubt it." Cisco handed the tablet to Felicity. "It's outside mine."

"Robert Queen was good at finding talent and keeping it to himself." Felicity looked up quickly at Oliver. "Nothing personal."

"He didn't build Queen Consolidated by accident," Oliver replied. "And he hired you, didn't he?"

"Very true." Felicity raised a finger. "Your father was the only one who believed in Jackson Straub's crazy ideas—wormholes, practical plasma generation—years before Harrison Wells opened S.T.A.R. Labs. Well, fake Harrison Wells. Reverse Harrison Wells." Felicity squinted in annoyance. "I don't know how you guys keep all your multi-versions straight."

Barry offered her a supportive smile. "After a while you just stop trying or you'd spend every day with a headache."

"I already have one." She suddenly asked, "Does that mean there's an evil version of me?"

Cisco leaned on the console. "Maybe you *are* the evil version of you."

Felicity froze in amazement. Cisco mimed blowing his mind, complete with fingers waving away from his head.

Oliver felt the tightness in his chest ease. If there was one thing this group knew, it was how to relieve tension.

"If we have this part of the code," Felicity mused, "could we extrapolate the rest?"

"Like they did with frog DNA to fill in dinosaur DNA in *Jurassic Park*!" Thea exclaimed.

"And that worked out really well." Cisco looked thoughtful as he pointed at some aspect of the code on the tablet screen and Felicity hummed in agreement. "The answer is *maybe*… if we had Harrison Wells, which we don't. This Straub guy's approach to wormhole generation is way different than ours because he didn't have the World's Fastest Man as a battery. Without more of Straub's code, I just don't know what he's doing here. Or here. Or here. Or anywhere. It's like being given a page from the third Harry Potter book and trying to summarize the whole series. It would take us months or years, if we're lucky."

"You have got to be freaking kidding me!" Felicity shouted.

Everyone turned to see her staring at her computer, standing, her face a mask of rage.

"What's wrong?" Oliver ran to her.

"Look!" She pointed at the screen. "Look!"

Oliver fought with his blurred vision. He saw what appeared to be an email with a strange, old-fashioned letterhead.

Count Von Wallenstein.

"What the hell is that?" he asked.

"It's an invitation!" Felicity was still shouting. "An invitation!"

The rest of the team gathered around her, looking at the document too.

"Calm down," Oliver said softly. He rubbed his eyes. "An invitation to what?"

"The count is holding an auction. He's inviting special guests to bid on an item of special value."

"What sort of item?" John asked. Then he opened his mouth in realization. "I got a bad feeling I already know."

Felicity clenched her fists and tightened her mouth, fighting her anger.

"It's a generator! A *wormhole* generator."

"How did he get one so fast?" Thea looked incredulous.

"More than likely he built one back when Ghasi's father stole the plans. But obviously it never worked. Now that he has the operating system, he has a complete unit." Felicity gave an exaggerated sarcastic smile. "He's selling my technology—well, Straub's technology, Palmer's technology— and is inviting me to bid on it!"

"That is cold." Thea glanced at Oliver. "What do we do about it?"

Oliver straightened with a comforting hand on the seething Felicity. He took a deep breath and exchanged a glance with John.

"We're going to Markovia," he said. "Wheels up in twenty-four hours."

Beyond the main terminal at Star City airport were the hangars of the private jet services. Palmer Technologies maintained a Bombardier Global for corporate travel. It sat on the tarmac in the bright November sun with fuel hoses trailing out of it. Maintenance crews consulted checklists.

The Palmer Tech van pulled to a stop at the corner of the hangar. A man in a pilot's uniform noted Felicity in the passenger's seat and left his companions to approach. He gave her a polite touch of his cap brim.

"We're on schedule, Ms. Smoak. You're free to board when you wish. We need to finish fueling and make a few last-minute checks, and we're good to go. Mr. Queen. Mr. Diggle. Good to see you both." He nodded at Thea, Barry, and Cisco before walking away.

"Here we go." Felicity climbed out of the van.

While Oliver and John hefted duffel bags on their shoulders from the rear of the vehicle, Cisco asked,

"Is this trip dangerous? I mean, we're allowed to go to Markovia, right?"

"Sort of," John said. "The visas we have are very limited. America and Markovia are not friendly at the moment."

"If something goes really wrong, you'll want to get to the American consulate in Markovburg." Oliver checked a green hardshell case full of arrows.

"State Department closed that last month," John corrected.

"Then your only hope is the border," Oliver said. "How fast can you run?"

"I'm good." Barry gathered several bags.

"Wait." Cisco stood amidst the luggage chaos. "So if something goes wrong, they'll arrest us?"

"No." Oliver handed Cisco a suitcase.

"They'll probably just kill us." Thea passed by carrying her red case and smiled at Cisco.

"Do I get a cover story?" Cisco clutched a bag. "Like I'm a harmless engineer who's come to study the Markovian highway system?"

"Relax." Barry put an arm around his shoulder. "They're just messing with you. You know, Team Arrow humor is dry."

"Hilarious," Cisco muttered.

"It'll all work out," Barry said. "We've been through worse."

"Have we? At least we've always been in Central City. If there were problems, I knew where to get a hamburger. And I spoke the language."

Barry laughed, and the crates and duffels made their way onto the plane. All the gear was stored in the rear of the main cabin rather than in the cargo hold. Fuel hoses uncoupled and the tanker pulled away. Jet engines began to whine.

Everyone settled into seats. Intelligence reports on Markovia came out for study. Bio-facts on Count Wallenstein. Historical data on Wallenstein's castle. And of course headphones and tablets, the usual accouterments of a long plane trip.

"Oh crap," Cisco mumbled from his chair. "This thing is busted."

He fumbled with the conductivity sensor. The device was pinging.

"What's wrong with it?" Barry asked from across the aisle.

"I don't know. Look." Cisco pointed it at Barry and it hummed. Then he aimed it toward Felicity and it pinged.

"It's not supposed to do that." He stood up and pointed at Oliver: hum. "See? It has to be recalibrated to—"

Ping.

The device was directed at John. Cisco frowned. Aimed at Thea: hum. Back at John: ping. Oliver: hum. Barry: hum. Felicity: ping. He adjusted a dial. "Are you two wearing any weird tech?"

"No." Felicity looked at John, and he shook his head.

Cisco held the scanner close to Felicity and it hummed.

"Oh," she said. "You fixed it."

"Don't move." Cisco started at her head and moved the scanner down her neck and shoulders, along both arms, and then across her back and toward her waist.

Ping.

Felicity's eyes went wide. He finished scanning her with no new pings before turning to John, who raised his arms to his side. Working his way around the seats, Cisco played the scanner along John with a hum until it reached his right calf.

Ping.

Cisco studied the readouts on the scanner. "I think we found Ghasi's bug. There's definitely tech under your skin."

Felicity exclaimed, "He bugged John and me? How is that possible? Why just us?"

John sat in one of the plush leather seats and drew up his pant leg. He pressed his fingers into his calf. "In the Glades. They tagged us. Remember we both thought we'd been shot." He stopped and squeezed harder. "Yeah. I feel it. Maybe half an inch in." He looked at Oliver. "I'm getting it out."

"We're not set up for surgery," Oliver said. "Let's go back to the cave."

John scoffed. "Just numb it with a local and cut it out. It's nothing."

Felicity put her hand on her side. "But..."

Oliver lifted Felicity's blouse and pressed deep into the flesh over her right hip. After a moment of probing, he felt something small and hard. It wasn't muscle. "You're right. It's in there." He looked up at her. "We do need to take them out. They might be moving deeper. It's shallow right now. A quick incision and it's gone."

She made a disturbed squeak while John pulled out a med kit. He checked a small bottle of Novocain and prepared two syringes. After a pause, he jammed one needle in his calf and injected it. He pulled out a small scalpel.

Oliver reached for the knife. "I'll do it."

"Why?" John tapped his calf, testing the numbness.

Cisco winced. "He's going to operate on himself?"

Barry tried to look tough through a grimace. "Looks like it."

John pressed the scalpel into his skin and made an incision three inches long with impressive assuredness. He spread the cut with his fingers and peered inside. Then he cut deeper. "Hand me those tweezers, will you?" Oliver slapped the instrument into his hand. John inserted the tip into the incision and began to explore. He hissed. "Probably should've waited for the Novocain to work better." With his face set in effort, he pressed into the wound. After a few grunts, he withdrew the tweezers.

In the bloody tip, something wriggled. About the size of a small maggot. Barry opened an empty glass sample jar and held it for John to drop the thing inside. It clinked against the glass. Barry screwed the lid on. Everyone crowded around to stare at the little object.

"I've got one of those inside me?" Felicity groaned.

Cisco took the jar. "That is so cool." Then it stopped moving. He shook the jar and it rattled like a tiny ball bearing.

Felicity pulled up her blouse. "Let's get the Novocain in me and that thing out. And someone tell the pilot to stay on the ground until we're finished cutting on me."

Ten minutes later, Oliver applied a small bandage to her hip and they had two objects in the jar. The one from Felicity also went lifeless a few seconds after Oliver removed it. Cisco scanned them and they gave only the slightest spike with a faint ping.

"Could they be powered by the host body?" Barry wondered. "That's how Ghasi explained his powers. Some sort of parasite-tech."

"Maybe." Cisco shook his head. "Awesome."

John said, "But they could still be bugs. And Ghasi could still be tracking or eavesdropping on us. We should destroy them."

"Oh, but they're so beautiful," Cisco argued.

"You can examine the pieces, but we can't take the risk." Oliver took the jar and tossed it to Barry. "Smash them."

Barry gave Cisco an apologetic shrug and vibrated his hand into a blur for thirty seconds. When he stopped, the jar was filled with tiny shavings. The bugs were shattered.

Cisco then used the scanner to check all the equipment and luggage in case additional bugs found their way inside. No sign.

Felicity continued to stare at the tiny wreckage in the vial. Her expression grew harder. Her voice quavered with emotion.

"So Ghasi could listen in to everything we said?"

"Probably." Cisco handed her the jar.

"*Everything*?" she repeated and looked at Oliver. "He listened in to all our conversations. Not just our tactics. But all our most private moments."

"It's okay now." Oliver put his arm around her shoulder. He shared the anger she felt, but he kept his tone steady. There was no sense in launching into a furious spiral.

"I'll kill him." Her face reddened as she squeezed the vial in her hand.

"Not if I get there first," John added. "He listened in on me and Lyla too. And my daughter. He's got no right to have anything to do with my daughter!"

"Listen!" Oliver announced. "We have other issues to worry about. I understand your feelings, but there is more to this mission. Keep your eyes on the prize."

Felicity and John breathed heavily and both nodded. They muttered agreement.

"Thank you." Oliver gripped her hand. "Would you please inform the pilot we're ready to go now?"

Felicity sat gingerly in a seat and pressed the intercom. "Captain, thank you for your patience. You can take off when ready."

"We've got a hold from the tower, Ms. Smoak."

"Bad weather?" Felicity glanced out the small window. "It looks clear."

"No, ma'am. I'm not sure why. They said to stand by."

Across the tarmac, several black sedans sped toward them. All eyes went to the windows as the cars braked around the jet. Doors flew open and dark-suited figures emerged.

"Oh no," John moaned.

Barry craned to see past him. "Are we under attack?"

Lyla stepped from the rear of one of the cars. She wore a crisp black suit, all business. She pulled off her sunglasses and signaled toward the cockpit for the pilot to shut it down.

"What the hell?" John squared his shoulders. "She cleared this trip."

Thea patted him on the back. "Nice knowing you."

The co-pilot helped open the door and lower the steps. John went down ahead of Oliver, who lingered behind at the bottom while John strode across the tarmac toward his wife.

"John," Lyla said before he could speak. "I'm sorry, but you're grounded."

"What? Why?"

"I got an angry call from the Director of National Intelligence this morning when he found out someone was going to Markovia besides me. He rescinded your visas."

"But you're still going?"

"Yes. I'm the director of A.R.G.U.S. Wallenstein invited me."

"He invited us too! Well, he invited Felicity, but we're her team."

"I'm sorry, Johnny. This is from very high up."

John moved closer to his wife. His expression was pained. He took her hands.

"This can't happen. We have to go. You know why."

"Because of Barry. I know, John, we've talked about this. But I can only do so much. I already put my credibility on the line to get Lazarov out of prison, and that almost blew up on me."

"I get that, Lyla. But this is so much more important."

"It's always important."

"Not like this," he said softly. "This isn't about national security or politics. This is about the security of the world. You know me, I used to think the Flash was the craziest thing I ever saw. I'm still not used to seeing what that kid can do, and I've seen it close up. But you and I know the world has never seen anything like him. He can run up the side of a building. He can walk on water, for God's sake. He can run so fast he can go back in time. He's the most powerful being on the planet."

Lyla remained silent.

"But it's more than that," John said. "He's got a good heart to go with it. That's what makes all the difference. The world *needs* him, and in return he needs our help." John glanced back quickly at the jet where the faces of

Barry and the others stared out of the windows. Oliver waited patiently at the base of the steps. "Lyla, that kid is going to die if we don't help him."

"I love you for your conviction." She squeezed his hand. "I only wish…"

"He's going to die," John breathed.

They stared at each other for a long minute.

"Let me ask you something," Lyla said. "If I say no and I take off for Markovia, you guys will still go. Right?"

"Right."

"So you're saying I need to arrest you all to keep you out of Markovia?"

"Right."

Lyla nodded and slid her sunglasses back on.

"Sara is with A.R.G.U.S. handlers, so I'm not worried about her. But I swear to God, Johnny, if our daughter's first words are *safe house*, I'm going to blame you." Lyla checked the time on her phone and then looked over the top of her glasses with a coy smile.

"I've got an A.R.G.U.S. C-130 Air Command ready to bolt, so I'll see you all in Markovia." She kissed John on the cheek. "Maybe I'll let you pick me up in the bar." Without another word, she spun and started for her car.

"That's my wife." John turned back to the jet with a grin.

2 2

Oliver watched the ground drop dizzily from under the cable car. The gondola swayed as mountains rose white-capped and craggy. Dark dagger-like stones passed by the wide windows. Harsh winter wind howled in a steady roar that drowned out the music playing through the speakers.

"There's the castle." Barry pointed ahead.

A sprawling structure perched on top of a peak like an eagle crouching, spreading its vast wings over a valley filled with prey.

"Castle Wallenstein." Cisco studied an old Markovian guidebook. "Well, that's not very ominous-sounding. They could have named it something so much better, like Mount Doom or Despair Peak."

The gondola swayed hard and Thea slumped against the seats, refusing to look out over the dizzying drop.

"Oh man, my stomach is flip-flopping all over the place. I should've just stayed in town. How much longer?"

"Almost there," Felicity assured her.

The top of the mountain was a plateau several miles in diameter and covered by a densely packed medieval village. A wall ran along the edge of the plateau with a single gate at a narrow winding path that ran haphazardly down the mountain. The picturesque village sloped up toward another bastion protecting a grand spired keep. That citadel was brightly lit with spotlights, casting thick shadows over its gothic facets.

The gondola jerked as it passed over a cable guide tower. It dropped slightly, coming in straight now.

"I don't like going in naked." John rubbed his head as he studied the figures now visible on the walls. "We don't know what's waiting for us up there."

"They would just take any gear from us the minute we walked in." Oliver came to stand beside his friend. "As soon as we're inside, the Flash will bring it in."

"He can bring all of it up the side of a sheer mountain?"

Barry stepped in between them. "Are you questioning my speed or are you afraid I'll blur?"

"Both." John leveled a stare at Barry.

"It's as easy to run up a mountain as an office building. Momentum's the thing."

"Office buildings aren't coated in snow and ice."

"Cleats." Cisco held his head. "Modified his shoes with cleats. He'll have lots of traction."

John let out an exasperated sigh. "What happens if you do blur?"

"Hopefully Oliver's sessions will give me an edge there." Barry shrugged. "If not, it's a long way down."

"That doesn't make me feel any better."

"Me neither," Barry confessed.

Soon the gondola slid over the thick town wall. It clanked the last few yards into an overhang and bumped to a stop. A second cable car scraped out of the hangar and headed down to the small town of Fürchtenstadt at the base of the mountain.

Men in dark-brown uniforms stepped up to the outside of the gondola.

"I feel like we're in a World War Two movie," Barry murmured as the door slid open.

"Hello," Felicity announced as they disembarked. "I'm Felicity Smoak of Palmer Technologies, Star City, USA. I believe I'm expected."

A burly, square-faced man scanned his tablet. Several seconds passed as he scrolled. His eyes lifted to take in the group. "*You* are expected, Ms. Smoak."

"They're my plus five." Felicity lifted her chin with as much determination as she could muster.

"We have a car waiting to take you to the castle." The man guided them up narrow steps to the blustery street where a black van waited. Everyone looked at Oliver, who nodded and climbed in. He scanned the interior. It was a normal hospitality vehicle with no barrier to separate the driver from the passengers and no discernible traps.

The door shut loudly, making Felicity jump. And Cisco. Oliver placed his hand on her knee. Cisco looked at him pleadingly for a second, but at Oliver's scowl he turned to a more sympathetic Barry.

The van started off, rumbling through the narrow cobblestone lanes barely wide enough for the vehicle to pass through. The dark gray stone walls gave a sense of a medieval prison, but one that held no inmates. No windows glowed warm in the cold evening. Only an ominous foreboding greeted them. The van rolled ever upward, sliding occasionally on the ice.

As they neared the castle, Wallenstein's security force grew thick on the ground, identifiable by their dark woolen coats, furred hats, and machine pistols.

Ahead loomed the bulk of the main castle. It was a grand gothic structure, heavily extended and expanded in later centuries to give it an ominous fairy-tale presence. High towers hosted guards with heavy machine guns. More men with Uzis patrolled the grounds inside the wall.

"I agree with John." Thea watched the guards through the van window. "I'm feeling entirely too naked."

Felicity pulled out her tablet. "There are over twenty-five buyers on the guest list already. This includes Pyotr Alistratov, the former KGB gangster from Russia. General Pyeng from China. Tom Kolingba, the Congolese coltan warlord. And someone named Simon Fowler."

"British arms dealer with known links to global terrorism," John growled. "Those are bad guys. All of them."

The door opened for them and they exited the van.

Men in dark uniforms waited. They climbed wide stone steps to a portico. Another man waited with a tablet, looking incongruous before the granite doorway with deep carvings of knights in battle.

The entry hall was cavernous and lavish. Every wall, every corner, every surface was covered with objects of beauty: huge portraits, original tapestries, furniture of exquisite workmanship, fixtures and vessels of gold and silver and porcelain, laden with jewels. John let out a grunt to show even he was impressed.

"Felicity Smoak?"

Five burly men in black suits surrounded them. "Would you come with us, please?"

Felicity's eyes widened and she turned to Oliver wondering what she should do. Calmly he turned on the famous Queen charm.

"Is there a problem?" he asked.

"Please come with us. All of you."

Oliver's gaze swept the room. Numerous men in dark suits watched them, guns tucked under their coats. His team was unarmed. The caper couldn't end here.

He nodded at Felicity.

She looked at the security officer. "Of course." Immediately she exuded the calm and authority she portrayed when acting as head of Palmer Technologies. The men led them to a door that opened into a large room. More obvious wealth filled the chamber along with a man sitting at a huge gilt desk. Oliver recognized him.

Count Wallenstein.

Oliver exchanged a glance with Barry. The speedster tensed, waiting on his signal.

Wallenstein gained his feet slowly. He was a distinguished, elderly man. His white beard was trimmed into a goatee and his head was nearly shaved. He wore a uniform of green and gold with acres of ribbon and fringe that would look more at home on a major general in a Gilbert and Sullivan operetta than any historical figure. To Wallenstein's credit, he had stopped short of a monocle and riding crop. Still, he had the confident air of a man who had the upper hand in all things.

"Ms. Smoak, a pleasure to meet you."

"Thank you." Felicity's eyes widened, but she forced a smile as easily as Oliver had a moment ago. "Count Wallenstein, I believe."

The man bowed and moved around the desk toward them. "I'm pleased you took me up on the invitation. I feared you would refuse."

"Why wouldn't I want to come to see what happens to *my* technology?"

Wallenstein laughed.

"You have some gall to invite me after you stole Jackson Straub's operating system," she snapped. "Not to mention the technical specs you stole a decade ago." Felicity waved her hand around the room. "How much of this stuff did you steal?"

Thea gave a low groan. "Maybe it's not a good idea to accuse our host right now."

Barry glared at Wallenstein. "I think it's good to know where we stand here."

"Indeed!" their host proclaimed, grinning broadly, showing abnormally white teeth. "We are all comrades here. I would not have sent for you if I didn't want you here. Though I am surprised you took me up on my offer. I expected a ground assault was more your style."

"Hence the guards every two feet," Oliver said.

"I'm not naïve," Wallenstein replied. "When you get in the shadows, Mr. Queen, bad things happen."

Oliver took an odd pride in those words. Obviously Count Wallenstein knew their identities, but likely didn't care. Wallenstein knew a lot of secrets and only revealed them if it profited him. They were currency.

"We're not looking for a fight. We're here to bid on the generator."

That brought another bellow of laughter from the count. "Isn't that delightfully ironic? I'm sure Ms. Smoak does command impressive funds, but not even you can compete with the capital of your competitors."

"We emptied all our piggy banks," Cisco muttered.

"I don't really trust any of you." Wallenstein's lean frame sank again behind his desk. "However, if I send you away you will just try to steal it, wasting my precious time and resources, because I've taken precautions to make its theft impossible. I want nothing to interrupt the festivities. I worked too hard and too long for this event."

"So you intend to kill us?" John's jaw set like stone.

"I could." Wallenstein's voice turned cold as the ice coating the streets outside. "I'd prefer to be civilized about it. We Wallensteins have always valued culture and grace."

"So we're prisoners?" Oliver asked.

"Not at all. I will give Ms. Smoak the same opportunity as all the other guests." He extended something the size of a credit card to Felicity.

"How generous." She took the card. It had her name and a barcode. In the center was a dark square that looked like a biometric thumbprint pad.

"No one else gets a card?" Oliver asked.

"No. Just Ms. Smoak. She is your official bidder." Wallenstein twisted a bulky gold and emerald ring around his long finger. "I've arranged a large suite for you all. One of the best in the castle. I'm sure you won't all mind staying there. Think of it as a vacation, all expenses paid. Eat and drink as much as you like. I already had your luggage sent up."

"After you've searched it," Barry snapped.

"And surprisingly found nothing of interest. It's hard to believe you came all this way without your toys."

"Maybe we don't need them," Oliver remarked.

"It's hard to be the Green Arrow without a green arrow."

"I wasn't always the Green Arrow." His gaze never veered from the man at the desk. "Once I was an assassin."

"And I wasn't always just a businessman." Wallenstein narrowed his eyes, but his smile returned and he touched something on the desk, causing the door to open. "See that they are settled, Bernhardt."

A big guard nodded and gestured. "This way."

They were escorted to a magnificent section of the castle. The northern wing had a sweeping view of the many levels of castle rooftops as well as the walled town surrounding them. Their luxurious accommodation consisted of five rooms with private baths off a lavish sitting room.

"Wow," breathed Cisco. "I'm afraid to touch anything."

"You'll have to." John tossed his coat onto a large Ming vase. "We need to sweep the place."

While others searched the room, Felicity pulled out a heavy military-grade laptop and set up the scanning apps to detect listening devices. Then she checked the card Wallenstein had given her for trackers. It seemed clean.

Oliver went to the window where he began to map out the town in his mind. Eyeing the rooftops and towers, he sought access points and hiding spots. He judged distances and angles. If this castle and town became a battleground, Oliver wanted to know the winding layout as well as he knew the concrete and glass of Star City.

Before him lay a new jungle.

I have to learn to hunt it.

23

A gust of wind and snow blasted through the open window. Barry appeared in the middle of the room holding a large hardshell case. He wore all white and he was out of breath.

"Take a break, Barry." Oliver took the green case from him and set it on an eighteenth-century sideboard. He unsnapped the latches. The case was full of arrows, shiny and green.

"There's only one more." Barry pulled the white balaclava off his head and huffed for air. "It's really snowing out there now."

The main door clicked and everyone turned. Cisco and Thea entered. Oliver pointed to the corner where a similar case rested, but this one was red. Thea smiled and wrestled it to the floor.

"Ah, I feel better now!" She pulled her bow from the case and snapped it into full length with a jerk of her arm. "So how do we hide our weapons from

Wallenstein now that we've got them?"

"He's not spying on us." Felicity sat at a baroque table in the corner under a sparkling chandelier. She tapped busily on her laptop. "Maybe he won't do room searches either because that would be gauche for a sophisticated host."

"Cisco and I didn't see a ton of security around the castle," Thea said. "A few cameras and the guys with guns, but no sign of super high-tech stuff. Maybe this guy is an old-school gentleman's agreement type."

"No." Oliver closed his green case. "He's just selective about what he protects."

"True." Felicity nodded vigorously. "There's some of his network that looks like he borrowed the protection from a 1990s AOL firewall. But there's a core that's a black hole. I can't get near it. Yet."

"You think he doesn't care if his guests have guns and arrows?" Barry asked. "Or do you think we're the only team with weapons?"

"I assume some or all of the other guests are smart enough to get guns inside too," Oliver answered. "Wallenstein's primary concern is that none of his guests shoot *him*. He doesn't care if we kill each other."

"You can tell from just looking around this place," Thea added, "this whole thing is theater to him. He obviously appreciates drama. I mean, who lives in an old castle on top of a mountain these days unless it scratches some itch."

"All right, time to go." Barry went back to the

window, his breath misting. "I'm going to run back down the cables and pick up the last of our luggage."

"Don't slip," Cisco warned.

"Thanks. And please leave the window open." He tugged on the balaclava and paused to take a deep breath. In a white flash, he was gone.

"Whoa!" Cisco leaned out the window. The wind tossed his long hair. "That is cool."

"What?" Thea joined him. "Where is he?"

Cisco pointed. They could see the long cables reaching into the snowy darkness.

"I don't see anything," she said.

"He's gone now." Cisco drew back inside. "It was just a little ghosty shape moving along the cables. You might not have been able to see him anyway. I've got an eye for it after all this time."

There was a knock at the door.

Oliver activated the magnetic lock on his case, as Thea did on hers. While they carried the cases into one of the bedrooms, Felicity clicked out of the castle's private computer network and into a live kitten web feed.

"Who is it?" she called out cheerfully.

Another knock answered.

Oliver and Thea came out, closing the doors to the bedrooms. He made sure everyone was in position, and went to the main door. He opened it.

"Hello, Oliver." Malcolm Merlyn smiled. "I'm just down the hall. Isn't that convenient?"

Oliver didn't react. The tension in the room behind him crashed against his back. Felicity gave an audible gasp, which delighted Malcolm. He stood in his black tunic and trousers, similar to the garb of a ninja.

His name hadn't been on the guest list, but Malcolm likely was one of the John Does because Malcolm Merlyn was a man who didn't officially exist.

"I come bearing gifts." He held up a bottle of champagne. "May I come in?"

"No," was Felicity's quick response.

"Come now, Ms. Smoak. That's no way to greet someone who holds the key to your future. The way you act, you'd think I was here to do you all in."

Thea moved quickly to Felicity in the hope of stopping her from doing something rash.

"Might as well let him," Thea said. "He'll just come walking out of the bathroom at some point anyway."

Oliver stepped aside and Malcolm strolled into the room while throwing his head back in amusement.

"Ah, I had hoped you'd be here," Malcolm said when he saw Thea. His eyes lit up with a genuine shine. "It's always good to see my daughter. Your wit travels well."

Thea merely crossed her arms and glowered.

"What do you want, Malcolm?" Oliver shut the door.

"Nothing. Just a social call. We're all here in Markovia on a business conference. Let's have dinner one night."

"Let's not," Felicity muttered.

Malcolm managed a theatrical pout at her. He exhaled, surprised that his breath misted. Then he saw the open window.

"Hm. You like it brisk, don't you? Where's Mr. Diggle? Oh, he must be with his wife. How domestic." He eyed Cisco. "I know you, don't I?"

"Maybe," Cisco replied hesitantly, peering at Oliver for guidance. "I shouldn't say because you're a bad guy."

"Hardly." Malcolm frowned. "Just a… guy."

The wind gusted and Barry stood in the middle of the room holding a duffel bag. He saw Malcolm and his eyes widened, dropping the bag.

"It's the Flash!" Malcolm extended his arms in delight. "I assume you are, although you're not wearing red. My goodness, Oliver, you've brought the Fastest Man Alive with you and you're using him as a bellhop. Well, Flash, I can tell you that if you're interested in an organization where your talents will be appreciated, we should talk later."

"Is this a fight?" Barry raised his fists expectantly. "Are crazed ninjas pouring out of the closet any second?"

"No," said Oliver, although Cisco looked toward the closet. "Malcolm, if you have anything useful to say, do it and get out."

"How typically impolite of you, Oliver." Malcolm shook his head in criticism. "You were always a little disingenuous; it was your great failing as a young man. I do have something useful to say." He held up the champagne. "You might want to break out the crystal because I am proposing an alliance." He scanned the room. No one reacted to his announcement. "In any case, I propose we combine our resources to outbid the competition for Count Wallenstein's device. It will be difficult for either of us to match the secret services of certain world powers or the cash reserves of major criminal gangs. However, *together* our chances are improved. What do you say?"

Oliver opened the door and stood next to it.

"Don't be too hasty." Malcolm lowered the bottle. "It's our duty to keep that device out of the wrong hands."

"Your hands *are* the wrong hands. Get out."

Malcolm sauntered to the door where he set the champagne on a small table before stepping out into the hall. "As strange as it seems, Oliver, I'm the only one you can trust here. We're in the same boat, you and I."

Oliver slammed the door. When he turned back into the room, the faces of the team were pale and somber. Felicity's hand gripped the table as if that alone was what was keeping her upright.

"Oh God," she whispered. "Does this mean the vibe is coming true?" She sought out Cisco.

"Um… not necessarily."

"But this is bad, right?"

"Well, it isn't good," he admitted.

"It doesn't mean anything." Oliver came toward them. "The odds that he would be here were high. This sale of the Straub device will bring every rat out from every hole."

"Is Malcolm right?" Thea checked the bottle and gave an expression of approval. "Do we have more in common with him than with anyone else here?"

"No," Oliver replied simply. There was nothing more he could say. He couldn't be more emphatic than that. He would never have anything in common with Malcolm Merlyn, the man who had seduced Oliver's father into ruin, the man who had tried to destroy half of their city, the man who had killed his own son. He would not be the one to end the Green Arrow.

"Yeah, we don't need him." Thea stalked the room with the icy nervousness she always showed when she encountered her father. "No matter how much money he stole from his old company or the League of Assassins, he can't compete with the people here. He needs us. But we have our own ally here. Lyla and A.R.G.U.S., right?"

Oliver nodded thoughtfully. "Probably."

"Probably?" Felicity jerked in surprise. "Isn't Lyla on our side?"

"*She* is," Oliver said. "But we can't trust her superiors. She can be overruled. Securing the generator ourselves, free and clear, is the cleanest solution. So we need to find out where Wallenstein is keeping it."

"I can help you there." Barry reached for the ski mask and pulled it off his face. Trickles of dried blood caked his skin under his nostrils.

"Barry!" Cisco exclaimed.

"What?" Barry looked around and checked out his

chest and arms. "What's wrong?"

Oliver stepped closer. "You're bleeding. From your nose."

"Oh." Barry wiped his hand across his face and looked at the flaking red on his white gloves. "I can explain that. When I was coming back with the last piece of luggage, I thought I'd take a quick run around the castle to see if I could locate the generator."

"And?" Felicity asked.

"And I did." Barry grinned and then looked embarrassed. "It has an energy field around it."

"Like a force field!" Cisco exclaimed. "Force fields are always cool. What kind was it?"

"The invisible kind." Barry wiggled his nose delicately between two fingers.

"You couldn't vibrate through it?" Cisco asked.

"No. I'm not as fast as I used to be. And there were guards around, so I couldn't exactly come out of the speed force to experiment."

Felicity returned to the table and opened her laptop. She tapped for a few minutes. "I do see a huge diversion of power to a single purpose."

"Can you shut it down?" Oliver asked.

She typed a few more moments.

"No. Net yet anyway. The grid controls are inside that black hole I mentioned and the pathways keep changing. Maybe if I can get some feelers into his main servers, I can... nope." Felicity balled her fists in frustration. "He's got some good people on this. We'll see *how* good. Don't worry, I'll get it eventually."

Oliver picked up the bottle. His first instinct was to throw it out the window. He wanted nothing to do with Malcolm Merlyn, not even something as minor as a gift of champagne. Malcolm never acted without an agenda, no matter how small, how incremental.

He looked at the faces around him. Everyone's expression was preoccupied and brooding. Felicity's was approaching tortured.

The team needed a moment. Despite the urgency, they weren't going to make a move tonight. It was best if they could spend a few hours together as friends rather than as a squad of soldiers.

Oliver retrieved crystal flutes from the sideboard and then peeled the foil from the neck of the bottle.

Everyone's attention stayed on Oliver with varying looks of stunned surprise. Barry returned in normal clothes in time to hear the pop and his hand zipped out to catch the flying cork. Oliver filled a glass with the sparkling wine and handed it to Felicity with a nod.

She looked hurt that he would give her the first glass of assassin champagne. Then with a small exclamation she went to one of her bags and pulled out a small zippered case. She removed a tiny bottle. Unscrewing the eyedropper top, she carefully squeezed several drops of liquid into the champagne. Felicity held the glass up to the light and watched the bubbles rise.

"Looks good," she said.

"Hold up," Cisco said. "You guys travel with poison-testing equipment?"

"Detection for a full battery of poisons and toxins." Felicity zipped the case shut. "When you're going to eat a lot of meals in a castle full of killers, yes, it's good to pack some."

Oliver proceeded to pour champagne in all the crystal glasses, handing one to each of his team.

The door swung open and John appeared. His face was stern.

"Oliver, we got big trouble. Malcolm Merlyn is here."

"Don't remind me," Felicity murmured.

"We know." Oliver handed John a glass. "How's Lyla?"

"What the hell is going on in here?" The big man stared at the champagne and then at everyone in confusion.

"Mission prep." Thea raised her glass.

"Euro style." Cisco offered a hesitant grin.

"We just spoke to Malcolm," Oliver said to John. "In fact, he gave us the champagne."

"What!" John held the glass away from his face. Felicity gave him a thumbs-up sign and he relaxed.

"Also Barry located the generator," Oliver continued, "but it's too tightly secured to go after it. Felicity is working to compromise the network. Once that's done, we'll make our move." He raised his glass. "But not tonight. To success here and beyond." He nodded toward Barry.

Barry raised his glass to Oliver. "In every possible universe."

The glasses clinked and they all drank. John looked around with accepting amusement. Felicity clutched her glass but her anxious attention was on Oliver.

"Malcolm does have good taste in champagne," Thea conceded with a satisfied sigh.

"I could run to town for cheese," Barry said.

The other side of the bed was empty.

A faint line of light showed under the bedroom door. Oliver could hear the sound of tapping from outside.

He threw back the heavy down comforter and slid out into the frigid air. No matter how much Wallenstein modernized the rooms, it was still a castle in wintertime. And it was cold.

He cracked the door open. Across the sitting room, Felicity crouched over the glow of her computer. On the screen, multiple windows flashed off and on as she swept through data at an incredible speed.

The fireplace glowed a dim orange and untended logs snapped their last soft forlorn sparks into the chimney. The champagne bottle sat on a low table near the sofa with empty glasses around it.

A single crystal flute full of champagne rested next to Felicity. It was untouched from the time she took only the barest sip after Oliver's earlier toast.

He padded across the floor, reaching her shoulder. She didn't notice, continuing to type and scan, murmuring softly to herself as she did.

"Felicity."

"Oh God!" She spun around in alarm. "Why are you sneaking around?"

"Shh." Oliver smiled gently. "You'll wake everyone else." He knelt next to her. "I'm not sneaking. You just didn't hear me."

"Po-tay-to. Po-tah-to."

"Still trying to get into the network?"

"Among other things."

Now that he was facing her, it was clear that Felicity was angry. Not at him, but at her task. It wasn't just her usual hacker frustration at an unsolved puzzle or indignation that someone thought they might be smarter than she was. She was furious to the point of tears or outright hitting something.

"Don't stress like this." Oliver took her hand. "Come to bed and we'll attack it in the morning. You'll get it."

She shook her head silently, biting her lip.

"Are you all right?" Oliver asked.

Felicity stared at him. She nodded.

"You shouldn't stay up all night," he said.

"You stay up all night all the time. Why can't I?" She squeezed his hand. "You go out and fight. You protect people. Why can't I fight? Why can't I protect the people I love?"

"Okay." Oliver was surprised by her sudden passion. He kept his voice calm. "I'm sorry. You're right." He kissed her hand. "Do you want to talk about anything?"

"No," she whispered in a strained voice. "I just

want to work right now. I just have to work."

He stood up and reached for the champagne glass to clear it out of her way.

"No," Felicity said quickly. "Don't take that."

"I'm sure it's flat by now."

"I'm not drinking it." Felicity touched the stem of the glass. Her eyes were hard. "I'm just looking at it."

She went back to the keyboard. Efficient and machinelike. Her focus locked on the data again as if she had pulled up a hood of her own.

He crossed the room and set a log on the fire. He prodded it with the iron poker. Sparks flew and the wood flamed bright. Oliver returned to the dark bedroom. He closed the door, leaving Felicity to her work. The crackling of the log blended with the clicking of her keyboard.

2 4

Barry walked with Felicity and Cisco along the narrow lanes of Castle Wallenstein. The town outside the citadel was quiet and nearly empty, like a museum display. A light snow had begun to fall again through the winter sky. The dusting made the gray stone buildings look Christmassy. Snow-capped gargoyles watched them cross a courtyard where a fountain stood frozen. Atop the fountain, a weathered knight held up the head of a dragon.

"It's nice to get out for a few minutes," Cisco said. "Spent all morning down in that dungeon where you saw the generator being set up for the demonstration today."

"Did you see it?" Felicity asked.

"No. It was covered. All the engineer types from every group were down there setting up their testing equipment. Wallenstein's people said he is offering complete transparency. That's why he let us bring our own monitors."

"Did you get a better idea of when he is going to do

the demonstration?" Felicity asked.

"Nope." Cisco scraped together a snowball and hurled it at the stone knight, missing by several feet. "I get the sense he does stuff when he feels like it."

Barry sat on the edge of the wall around the fountain, breathing with effort. He was surprised by how quickly the fatigue hit him. The air seemed thin, as if it couldn't fill up his lungs.

"Are you all right?" Felicity asked.

"Sure. Just the altitude." He knew it wasn't the altitude. They knew it too. "So do you *really* think that little generator can open a wormhole?"

Felicity paused, waiting for Cisco to answer. Then they both stumbled over each other to express their unending confidence in the generator and their ability to make it work.

"Okay, okay." Barry grinned at their enthusiasm. "I get it. Don't worry. I trust you guys. I know we'll get it to work."

"Yeah. That's what we meant." Cisco blew into his cold hands. "Don't worry about it. Just enjoy your European vacation because, you know, this place is pretty cool."

"I know." Barry gazed up at the gothic spires. "It's like Disneyland but with secret agents and killers."

"Open a few B&Bs and a gift shop, and Count Wallenstein could make a fortune." Cisco shoved his hands deeper in his coat pockets.

"He does okay stealing and selling advanced

technology and weapons." Felicity stared up at the knight, whose ferocious face was blackened with age. "A coffee shop would be nice though."

Church bells rang across the town.

"This is it!" Barry jumped to his feet with a start. "Time to see the generator in action. Come on."

Barry, Cisco, and Felicity rushed back to the citadel and fell in with the flow that swarmed the entry hall. People streamed downstairs and passed through a thick carved lintel down a curving passageway. Torches flickered in wall sconces. As they descended, the air grew damp. The walls were drizzled with moisture. The floors had been altered with rubber strips to give traction on the slick stones.

Finally, the crowd funneled through an open doorway. There were two men on either side of the door, each wearing medieval livery with the Wallenstein crest of a decapitated dragon's head dripping blood. They didn't appear to be armed.

The room beyond was the size of a grand theater, but low and deceptively oppressive. Maybe it had once been an armory or a stable for storing livestock and food during sieges. It was plain but lit by modern fixtures. On the far side, a curtain obscured the spot where Barry had seen the generator last night. Five heavily armed soldiers in black fatigues stood in front of the drape. Their faces were covered by balaclavas and dark sunglasses. Barry wondered if they were the same men they had fought in Star City. They cradled FAL assault rifles and machine pistols hung on their hips.

Barry saw Oliver through the crowd and they went over to him. Felicity bumped into General Pyeng. The general glared at her in alarm and two of his men crowded between him and Felicity.

"Sorry!" She backed away. "No harm, no foul."

"Terribly sorry." General Pyeng nodded to her. "I am a bit on edge because there was an attempt on my life yesterday."

"Really? By whom?"

"I have no idea. That's the problem." The general watched Oliver with suspicion. "It could have been anyone here. And I'm not the only one who has been targeted."

"There are a lot of untrustworthy people here." Felicity looked at the crowd surging around them. When she glanced back General Pyeng was glaring at her. "I don't mean you."

The general gave her a curt bob of his head and moved away flanked by his bodyguards.

"I think I insulted General Pyeng," Felicity said to Oliver.

"He's been insulted worse. He killed thousands to suppress rebellions in Xinjiang. He'll get over this."

"Oh. Then I don't feel so bad." Felicity watched the general slip through the crowd. "Where are John and Thea?"

"They're looking around the castle." Oliver stood silently for a moment. "Testing security in a low-key way."

Barry couldn't keep his attention off the curtain. His heart raced and his palms sweated at the thought of the device hidden there holding the key to helping him, ridding him of the blurs and the recurring nightmares of Reverse Flash ruling his mind. He could finally trust himself again, trust his powers again. He let out a nervous breath and Oliver turned to him.

"Easy, Barry." Oliver's voice was quiet and solid. "Be still. Breathe."

"I'm still. I'm breathing." Barry shook out his hands to fight the nerves. "I just want to run up and grab the thing and run out of here."

"Don't worry," Oliver said. "We are not leaving without it. You have my word."

"Exciting, isn't it?" Malcolm appeared behind Oliver with a polite grin. "This device is the future. And the only one thing more important than knowing the future is owning it. My offer still stands. Don't be stupid like you usually are."

As Malcolm vanished into the crowd, Cisco muttered, "He really is kind of a big jerk, isn't he?"

The lights dimmed. A spotlight illuminated the center of the drapery. A shadowy figure moved behind the line of soldiers to make a dramatic appearance in the circle of light.

Cisco put a cupped hand over his mouth and leaned close to Barry. "Starting at forward for your Chicago Bulls, at six-seven from the University of North Carolina, Count Wallensteeeeeein."

Barry laughed, grateful for the joke to ease the pressure. They earned stern silent rebukes from General Pyeng and an iron-faced Russian officer. He shushed his friend.

Count Wallenstein waited silently, commanding the room's attention. He wore a uniform typical of the late nineteenth century: a stiff gray tunic about mid-thigh length with a high collar; red-striped blue trousers tucked into black boots that shone to a reflective gloss; and a half-cape fastened with gold brocade.

"Ladies and gentlemen," the count began, "behind me is a device that will alter our world in a way comparable to petroleum, to steam, to fire itself." He waited for an amused rumble to slip through the crowd. "Yes, it's true. This device will shake the foundations of the world economy as we have known it for centuries. In five years, nothing will be the same. Empires will fall. Fortunes will be lost and gained. A new era of humanity will begin.

"Man has long dreamed of limitless energy. Energy to apply to all aspects of human endeavor. Energy that will allow us finally to build without restriction, to travel without limitation, to develop without concern. Clean, inexhaustible, and free." Wallenstein smiled. "But you know that nothing is free, not even the key to the gates of Heaven."

Cisco whispered, "Finally, the sales pitch."

Wallenstein signaled to his man Bernhardt and the drapes were swept aside. Cisco and Felicity pressed forward with much of the crowd. The machine behind the curtain looked virtually identical to the Straub device they had found in the coal mine outside Star City. Wallenstein set his hand on top of it like a proud father.

Sitting next to the generator was another machine slightly larger than the generator itself. Two technicians came out on stage and began to work on that machine, tapping instructions into a control pad. Lying on the floor between the two machines was a circular mesh with numerous small devices connected to it via an array of cables and wires.

Barry whispered to Cisco, "Are those the testing equipment Wallenstein let you install?"

"Yeah. Everybody had their own gauges and meters to attach to that mesh. We'll see."

Wallenstein waited for a nod from one of his techs. "Proceed." The tech hit a switch and a blinding red beam shot down from the ceiling into the center of the mesh. In a second it flashed off, leaving Barry's eyes flaring in the darkness.

"That," Wallenstein said, "was a petawatt laser. If you will come forward and consult the meters you installed this morning, you will be able to set a baseline for the demonstration to come."

Oliver nodded to Cisco, who nearly leapt with excitement. He worked his way down to the stage with about two dozen men and women to prowl around the mesh. They knelt to inspect the small gauges and meters on the floor. Some of them consulted with their neighbors and made adjustments to their devices.

"Looks legit so far," Cisco said when he returned.

"Now, ladies and gentlemen, it is time." Wallenstein held up his hands like a circus ringmaster. "Prepare to witness the birth of the future."

He motioned his technicians off stage. His soldiers approached the crowd where they set up a cordon to keep them at a distance. He took a pair of heavily insulated gloves from the top of the generator and pulled them on with a flourish. Wallenstein put a finger to a simple toggle switch.

"I give you the power of the universe." The switch clicked down. A loud snap came from inside the generator. The lights in the room went off. From deep inside the complex mechanical scaffolding of the generator, a faint red light shined. It seemed to flicker, then vanished.

In the air above the mesh mat, a small pinprick of light appeared. It was about four feet off the floor. It grew brighter and revealed a disturbance in the air. The disturbance moved in a spiral, surrounding the light. The glow brightened to reveal a small but growing vertical hurricane whirling in the air.

A wormhole.

Barry felt a tightness in his chest. The air was thin and hard. He looked at Cisco, who studied a meter in his hand. Some people in the crowd backed away, disoriented by the change in the atmosphere. The wormhole expanded. Barry made ready to run for the generator if the whorl continued to grow.

The plasma settled into a vigorous six-feet-diameter disk and spun in front of the crowd. Barry waited. The whirlpool didn't cause chaos; it didn't suck objects into the air. The feeling of that giant singularity churning over Central City came back to him. The destruction it caused. The death. The mourning. His breathing remained steady despite the memories.

Suddenly all the meters and gauges on the floor shattered in a shower of sparks. Some in the crowd reacted with alarmed shouts or screams. Some broke for the doors.

Barry didn't move in because the wormhole hadn't changed appearance. It wasn't growing out of control. It wasn't causing damage. He'd give Wallenstein a little more time before he took action.

Wallenstein raised his hand holding a device like a remote control. The generator snapped again and the wormhole wobbled, losing its shape like a bent bicycle tire. It grew hollow and empty from the center out until finally the accretion disk wisped away to nothing. Wallenstein waited a few seconds before reaching out to flip the toggle switch up. His two techs rushed to the generator. After a minute of testing, with the nervous crowd watching, they gave him an okay signal. The count turned to the group.

"What you have just witnessed was a stable wormhole. Unimaginable energy drawn from another dimension in time and space. Your monitors were in no way capable of measuring the output of the wormhole, but in those few seconds of existence, you saw nearly two zettajoules of energy. That is equal to the current potential reserves of petroleum and natural gas left on planet Earth. All created by this little device before you."

"That is magnificent, Count Wallenstein," Alistratov called out, "but how do we harness that energy? What use is it to us?"

All heads went from that man to Wallenstein. The count regarded him calmly. "We will provide options for that purpose, Gospodin Alistratov. You will be given specifications that will allow you to build the device. Given that I have invented the water, surely your people at the Federal Security Service can manage the hose to run it through. Shall I come to Russia and string your power wires?"

Most of the crowd laughed, dismissive of Alistratov's question now. Colonel Kolingba called, "May we come forward to see the device now?"

Wallenstein glanced at his technician and nodded. "By all means. Please be careful. It may still be warm."

Felicity and Cisco nearly ran to the stage to investigate the generator, and the meters that Cisco had left attached to the mesh.

Barry started up too but Oliver caught his arm.

"Was that real or just a parlor trick?" Oliver asked.

"It was real. I've been near a wormhole, and that's what it felt like. Smaller, but the same thing. No doubt."

One of Wallenstein's liveried servants appeared

carrying a stack of folders with the family crest and handed them out. Barry opened his to reveal sheets of complex data readouts. He recognized some of it as energy measurement statistics. They were impressive. He noticed several other sheets that appeared to offer information on the materials integrity of the generator itself. Those numbers didn't look as impressive, if he was reading them right. He'd have to check with Cisco to be sure.

Cisco and Felicity returned, and before Cisco could speak, Oliver said, "If you two are done here, let's go back to the room."

Oliver led the way to their suite, silencing Cisco and Felicity every time they started to talk about the test. Once inside, Felicity turned on her laptop and activated the noise-cancelling signal that should disarm any bugs.

"Okay," Oliver said, "so what's the story?"

"That device is the real deal," Cisco said. "That Straub dude was a bona fide smart guy. Still not sure exactly how that thing works, but I'm getting there. The generator opened a real wormhole and then shut it down on command, just like Wallenstein promised. And it's pretty believable it had the potential energy level that he said."

Barry showed him the stats of generator integrity, pointing at the section he had questioned. Cisco perused them.

"Oh. Hmm." Cisco ran his finger along the data,

double-checking it. "Yeah, that's not good."

"Why do you think he'd let that info out?" Barry asked the engineer. "Did his people just miss it?"

Oliver looked at the paper with a scowl. "What does it say exactly?"

"The generator isn't safe." Barry pointed at a column of numbers, as if that would make it clearer to Oliver.

"How so?" Oliver asked.

Cisco drew another meter from his coat pocket that he had hidden during the demonstration. He called up data on its screen.

"Oh man," he said. "It looks like that wormhole was *not* stable. Energy signatures were all over the map. As it is, it can't be used safely in industrial-scale energy production. Plus, according to these figures, eventually the generator would've shaken itself apart and the wormhole would've collapsed."

"Isn't that just a materials problem?" Oliver asked. "Make a stronger generator."

"Engineers hate people like you." Cisco smiled. "But even if we could, it won't matter because the matrix trigger that the wormhole is founded on isn't powerful enough." He pulled yet another small gauge out of another pocket. "It's just what I thought. It's a power source issue. He doesn't have the Flash to start it up, so that wormhole just won't stay open. It's like when you try to start your lawnmower with a bad air-gas mixture. It coughs for a few seconds and then cuts off."

"Or a Maserati," Felicity said to Oliver. "I know the

Queens didn't start a lot of lawnmowers."

Oliver smiled at her.

"In some ways," Cisco continued, "the shortcomings are good because at least it won't become a planet-destroying singularity like the one we had in Central City."

"So this device isn't what we need for Barry after all?" Oliver crossed his arms.

Barry sighed.

"Not so fast." Cisco continued flipping through the data readouts. "I didn't say that. I think it is, with some modifications. It really does open a wormhole with a plasma signature similar to what we've found in Barry. The problem is, however, that the wormhole isn't self-sustaining and it's possible the generator could fail prematurely. That means a catastrophic collapse."

"Catastrophic?" Oliver repeated.

Cisco made an explosion noise and outlined a rising mushroom cloud with his hands.

"Yeah." Barry tossed down his folder. "Wallenstein isn't really selling limitless energy. His device is a crappy generator, but it's a really, really good bomb. He knows it and this data is his way of making sure everyone here knows it. Someone here is going home with a doomsday weapon."

"Oh, I hope it's me." Felicity clapped her hands sarcastically.

2 5

Barry picked lint from his black trousers. Leather shoes reflected the lamplight. He would've been more comfortable in sneakers, but Oliver had been clear: black tie in Markovia meant dress shoes. This wasn't casual-Friday America. Turning around with his arms out, he displayed his formal dress sense.

"This is ridiculous!" Cisco glared into the mirror. He yanked his bowtie loose for the tenth time. "What kind of stupid culture judges a man by the strip of cloth around his neck?"

Barry spun Cisco around to face him. The wrinkled black cloth vanished in a blur of fingers and a perfect bowtie appeared at Cisco's throat.

"Whoa." Cisco inspected it with admiration.

"You are the man." Barry put his arm around Cisco's shoulder and crowded both of their tuxedoed forms into the mirror.

"No. You are the man. You look like James freaking Bond in that tux."

"S.T.A.R. Labs representing. Let's go show this castle what real men are supposed to look like."

They strutted from their room to find Oliver leaning beside the window. Perfectly tailored. Exquisitely coiffed and shaven. Eyes like a very well-dressed bird of prey. Sophisticated but smoldering.

"I'm pretty sure *that's* what real men are supposed to look like." Cisco slumped.

A door opened and Felicity appeared in a long black gown, bare shoulders and arms covered by a diaphanous wrap. Her blonde hair was up with only a single stylish lock falling loose along her cheek. She froze in her tracks to stare at Barry and Cisco.

"Oh my God! You two look fantastic!" she exclaimed. "Those tuxedos are perfect."

"We thought so too until—" Cisco jerked his chin toward Oliver, who looked appropriately confused by the compliment.

Thea slid from her room, draped in red silk, dangling stiletto shoes from her fingers. "Is there going to be dancing tonight? Because I should've brought better shoes if there's going to be dancing."

"This isn't a rave." Oliver smiled. "It's a party for international power brokers."

"Good." Thea put a hand on Cisco to balance as she slipped on her shoes. "If they seat me next to Malcolm, will you switch with me?"

"Uh… yeah sure." Cisco nodded.

There was a quick knock at the door and John leaned in.

"Are we ready, people?" He looked around the room approvingly as he stepped in, perfectly stylish in a modified tuxedo with a traditional necktie. Lyla appeared behind him. Her glamorous gown was white with emerald highlights.

"Why is Team Arrow so much prettier than Team Flash?" Cisco exclaimed.

"Nah, you boys are pretty enough." John regarded Cisco with a grin. "You tie that tie?"

"I did." Barry looked closely at Cisco's tie. "Did I do it wrong?"

"No. It's good."

"Joe taught me. He told me every man should at least be able to tie a tie, change a tire, and make an omelet."

"Roger that." John nodded approvingly.

"Let's go before all the crab puffs are gone." Felicity looped her arm through Oliver's.

They started down together. Other guests were streaming to the main floor and into the gigantic grand ballroom. Iron chandeliers hung in a row down the center of the hall glowing with candles. Torches guttered in sconces between heraldic tapestries. A stone balcony ran along one wall about fifteen feet off the floor accessible via spiral staircases. Medieval guards stood along the balcony in steel bonnets carrying crossbows. The large stained-glass windows had been altered into stained-glass French windows. At the far end of the vast chamber, a small orchestra gathered at the base of a wide staircase leading up into shadowy darkness.

"Holy moley," Cisco breathed at the spectacle. "It's like prom night for King Arthur."

They made their way into the ballroom, spotting others with whom they had made vague acquaintance over the time they'd been at the castle. Eyes followed them as they passed, all locked on either Felicity or Lyla.

One man, Simon Fowler, nodded toward them and Barry heard him stage whisper to his companion, "That's her. I know she's the one who tried to assassinate me earlier. A.R.G.U.S. has wanted me dead for years."

"Oh please, Simon." Lyla turned and looked directly at the British mercenary with a sweet smile. "You're still here, aren't you? It wasn't me." She started off, then turned back. "*This* time."

She slid her arm through John's and walked away in an exaggerated sashay.

They found a table with their nameplates and sat.

"This place seems dangerous." Cisco started to drink from an exquisite crystal goblet, but then stopped and sniffed the water. "Is everybody trying to kill everybody else?"

"Officially, no." Oliver glanced casually at the tables around them. "Unofficially, yes."

Barry whispered to Lyla, "Everybody in the room is staring at you and Felicity. I mean even before you basically threatened to kill the big mean guy with the scar."

"Lyla and Felicity are the big threats at the auction." John patted his wife's hand. "Lyla is carrying the president's credit card and Felicity runs Palmer Tech. We are literal nobodies compared to them."

"Glad to hear it." Cisco lifted the tablecloth and peered under the table.

"My credit card isn't what I'd hoped." Lyla sipped water. "My predecessor at A.R.G.U.S. made a lot of enemies in Washington, and they're taking it out on me." She shifted the antique silverware. "Even when I sent them a message that the generator is a potential weapon, they claimed it was a fraud. They're willing to back me only to a certain point to cover their own butts, but then they say they refuse to be suckered by Wallenstein."

"So you've only got so much money to spend?" Barry kept his voice calm even though nerves tingled along his limbs.

"Yes," Lyla replied.

A streak of yellow slipped through the room.

Barry jumped. No one else reacted. No one in the crowded room had seen the yellow blur or felt the wind. Of course they hadn't. It was all in his head. When Barry looked back, all eyes at the table were on him.

"Barry," Oliver said, "what just happened?"

He realized he was gripping the edge of the table so hard his knuckles had turned white. Shoving himself to his feet, Barry murmured, "Excuse me. I need a second."

"I'll go with." Cisco started to stand.

"No. It's the crowd or the heat." Barry patted his friend's shoulder. "I'll be back."

Barry slipped between tables. Very few people bothered to stare at him, probably assuming he was just a technician brought by the Americans to perform testing. Cutting across the center of the ballroom, he climbed an iron circular staircase to the long stone gallery. One of the liveried servants with a crossbow watched him as he went to a pair of French windows and pushed them open. The frigid air slapped him.

His phone buzzed and Barry hung his head. It was time to meditate.

Again. Always.

He rested on his elbows on the thick railing of the half-moon-shaped balcony and looked down the side of the mountain into the valley. Faint yellow lights twinkled in the darkness below. The wind roared around the castle, rippling his tuxedo. He turned around and leaned back against the balustrade, staring up the castle wall to the gargoyle protectors on the edge of the roof. Stars raked the sky in the cloudless night.

The phone buzzed again.

How much time did he have left? How long before Reverse Flash swept in, demanding Barry come with him with a power he couldn't refuse? Barry wouldn't be able to fight his way back to the real world. The plasma would eat him alive. He stared at his hands. Even in the dim light he could see the spidery threads across them. They seemed darker than before.

Would he just be dead or would he be trapped in some strange, surreal world where he was alone with Reverse Flash? What would happen if even the man in yellow stopped coming?

When his phone buzzed a third time, Barry yanked it from his pocket to silence it. On the screen he saw a name:

Joe.

Barry's throat tightened at the sight of the simple name flashing on his phone.

The phone beeped and he saw the words *Missed Call*.

Barry hit the button. "Joe! Are you there?"

"Barry?" The familiar voice of his adoptive father crackled. "Is that you?"

"Yeah, hey, it's me. I almost missed you. What's up? Is something wrong?"

"No, Barry, everything's fine. Sorry to call so late. I don't even know what time it is in Markovia. Did I wake you up? Am I interrupting something?"

"No." Barry's eyes burned listening to Joe's voice. He just wanted to hear the man talk. It made everything seem normal. "No problem. I'm just at a party."

"A party?" There was a pause. "I didn't think you guys would be doing much partying over there."

"Yeah, me either." Barry laughed. "It's a pretty

swanky castle though. I'm wearing your tuxedo."

"Oh good. I'm glad that old thing is seeing a little more action. Well, I don't want to keep you then—"

"No!" Barry clutched the phone closer. "Don't hang up. I'm good. I can talk. I'm standing outside. I'm not even at the party right now. How are you doing?"

"I'm good, Bar. Everything is fine here."

"For real? Any problems? Because I could get back."

"Listen, don't worry about anything. I just—" There was a pause and the rustle of the phone changing hands. "I just wanted to hear your voice. You know, check on you. I haven't talked to you in a week or so, and that's a long time. How are you?"

"I'm fine."

"For real?" Joe echoed Barry's phrase. "Because I could get *there* too."

"No." Barry smiled. "I'm good. I'm… I'm good."

"Getting worse?"

"A little, yeah. I've seen—" Barry caught himself. It was best not to go into any details on an unsecured phone. "I mean, it's okay. About the same. The auction is pretty soon and then we'll be home. So how's Iris?"

"She's good," Joe replied, clearly unhappy about changing the subject but understanding. "She's working. She's pretty much been working since you left for Star City."

"Don't let her do that."

"*Let* her?" Joe chuckled. "Who are you talking about? You think I got any power over her?"

"Right, right. Listen, tell her I'll call her if I get a chance. But we'll probably be home before I do. It's really pretty over here. It's been snowing. It would be a nice spot for a vacation."

"If not for the despotic warlord crime boss running the place, you mean?"

"Uh, Joe, this is an open phone line."

"Oh yeah. Sorry... about that despotic warlord crack, whoever is listening. How's the food?"

"Food is great. Not as good as yours though."

"Attaboy." A deep breath. "You'd tell me if there was a problem, wouldn't you?"

"We got this over here, Joe. I'm going to be fine."

"I know. Man, I called to reassure *you*." Joe's voice had a familiar catch in it that Barry recognized. "Oliver taking care of you?"

"Yeah, since you're not here, someone has to."

There was silence.

"Oliver and his guys have been amazing," Barry continued. "It's embarrassing how much they're doing for me."

"I knew he would. So you think the auction will go your way, right?" The question was almost desperate for reassurance.

"I think so."

Another silence.

"I mean, yeah," Barry said. "Can't really talk about it on the phone, but yeah, don't worry."

"I'm not worried."

"Me either."

He heard Joe take a halting breath.

"So," Barry filled the silence, "you want anything special from the Castle Wallenstein gift shop?"

Joe laughed a little too loudly before his voice grew soft.

"Just bring home Barry Allen. That's all I need."

"Okay."

"Well, you get back to your party," Joe said quickly. "I just wanted to call and talk to you for a second."

"Thanks, I needed it. Be home soon, Joe."

"Love you, son."

"Love you too."

Call Ended.

2 6

"Oh, I'm sorry. I didn't know someone was here."

Barry opened his eyes. A woman stood at the French windows. She smiled, regarding Barry with warm brown eyes and a curious thoughtfulness mixed with blatant appraisal.

"Aren't you cold?" she purred, her voice soft. She closed the stained-glass door behind her with a soft click.

"Me? *You* must be freezing." Barry stared at her as he put away his phone. She was tall with long black hair. He noted the strength of her bare shoulders and arms, and the roundness of her hips accentuated by her gown. He started to remove his jacket. "You should go back inside."

"No, please." She joined him at the railing, placing a hand on his chest to prevent him from taking off his coat to give to her. When he relaxed, she didn't move away and, in fact, pressed against him as she gazed out over the snow-covered valley. "It's a beautiful night, don't you think so?"

"Mm-hm." Barry felt the warmth from her body. Her perfume slipped around him.

"I have a confession," she said. "This meeting isn't entirely an accident. I saw you this morning. I'm not following you," she added quickly. "I just wanted to speak with you."

"Why?" Barry's voice cracked a little more than he wished.

"You seem different." She lowered her head with a sly smile. "So many pass through here and they're all the same. Everyone thinks they are powerful and irresistible, but they are cold and soulless. I can tell you are another type of man. A good man." She paused for a moment to watch the distant blur of the cable car approaching through the night. "I am surprised to see you here with these people."

Barry let her continue nestling beside him. Obviously she was very cold, but didn't want to complain. She probably came out to escape one of those soulless types. If she needed a place of refuge, he was happy to grant that to her as best he could. It was the decent thing to do.

"So are you here for the auction?" he said casually.

Her dark eyes flicked up at him with a hint of disbelief. Barry kicked himself internally—that wasn't very international sophisticate of him. Of course she was here for the auction. *Way to be a corn-fed schoolboy from Central City.* She was probably imagining him grinning with a long stalk of hay in his teeth.

"Let's not talk about that." She pressed harder against him. "Tell me about your home. I imagine it is very clean and warm."

"Um." Barry shifted uncomfortably, but still didn't move away. "Are you sure you don't want to go inside?"

"No. That is the last place I want to be." Her hand brushed his. Her voice softened into a plaintive hush. "Would you like to take the lift down to Fürchtenstadt? There is a small restaurant there with a marvelous wine cellar. Do you like wine?"

"Yes. Sure. I mean, I don't think I can go tonight… right now, I mean. My… uh… friends would wonder."

"My friend would wonder too." She smiled. "I would like for him to wonder. To wonder for the rest of his life."

"Are you in trouble?" Barry glanced back at the door. "Do you need help? Do you want to defect or something? Do people still do that? My friends can help you."

She brought one hand up and draped it lightly on her bare shoulder. Her red nail polish showed dark against her flesh. She paused as if she was fighting an emotion.

"It's too dangerous. Not here. We should take the cable car down."

Barry placed a hand over hers.

"Barry."

Oliver stood at the French windows with a suspicious look. He stared hard at the woman. She stroked Barry's cheek with her long fingers and gave him an expression of amusement. Without a word, she started for the door, offering Oliver a quick glance as she passed.

"Wait," Barry called out.

Oliver closed the door and leaned against it. He grinned. "What was that all about?"

"That woman needs help. She was going to tell me, but you scared her. I should find her."

"I wouldn't." Oliver held up his hand.

"No, really. She came out looking for my help."

"Did she ask you to go somewhere private? Did she seem vulnerable? Was she attracted to you?"

"Well, yeah." Barry raised modest eyebrows. "That's not outside the realm of possibility. We may not all be Mr. GQ of Star City, but I have a boyish appeal that gets a little mileage."

"Yes, you do." Oliver couldn't stop his annoying smile. "She was a spy, Barry. She wanted information from you. She read you as a guy who wants to help others, so that's the route she went. She was good."

"But she…" Barry thought back over the encounter. His exasperation with Oliver turned to embarrassment. "So all the leaning and breathing and invitation to wine… oh man. Wait. Was she going to try to kill me?"

"No, you're not important enough. She was playing you for information."

"I just thought I was doing great with her."

"Sorry."

"Sorry?" Barry's pensive face split with a grin and

a loud laugh burst out. "Oh man! That's fantastic! Me! Barry Allen getting smooched up by a femme fatale!"

"That's a good thing?" Oliver regarded him with a confused squint.

"Good? It's great. That is a Moose and Squirrel moment!"

"If you say so."

"I wish Joe and Iris could see this." Barry arched back against the balustrade and stared up. Bright white clouds rolled in front of the serene stars. "They'd get a kick out of it. I think Iris would really like this castle." He saw Oliver giving him an odd stare. "What?"

"Nothing." Oliver crossed his arms and leaned on the corner of the wall. "You. You're so… I don't know. You get excited because a spy tries to get information from you." He laughed. "It's unexpected, given your circumstances."

"Ah, yeah. My circumstances." Barry shrugged. "I guess every so often I suddenly just look at myself and realize *this is not the life I expected*. Not long ago I was a forensic scientist. I mean that was pretty exciting, but nothing like this. The Flash. Castles. Wormhole generators. Hot spies." He pointed at Oliver. "Hanging out with Oliver *freaking* Queen."

Oliver looked down.

"I mean," Barry continued, "doesn't that hit you every so often? I know your life before was pretty awesome too, but doesn't it just wash over you sometimes, no matter what the *circumstances* are, just how crazy cool life is?"

Oliver stared at Barry, pondering. He shook his head slowly.

"It's hard," he murmured, "for me to see life through those old eyes."

"Is it?"

"Yes. I remember that old Oliver Queen, but he's gone. For the best."

"You think?" Barry heard the weight in Oliver's tone. He lifted himself on the railing and sat, feet dangling, back to the abyss. Thick white snowflakes tumbled down around them.

"Yes. He didn't survive the jungle. He wasn't a soldier." Oliver opened his black tuxedo jacket to reveal the stark white shirt. "This is a different man you're looking at."

"Oh yeah?" Barry nodded. "I think maybe that old Oliver Queen is still in there. I mean, I didn't know him, but I see a guy sometimes who seems a little different. I see him a lot when you're with Felicity."

Oliver stood silently.

Barry hopped down onto the balcony. "I like soldier Oliver with the hood and the bow, I owe that guy a lot, but I'd like to hang with the other Oliver too. If you ever decide to come out of the jungle." He nodded toward the door. "You going in?"

"I'm staying here for a while."

Barry put a comforting hand on Oliver's arm as he passed. He tilted his head toward Oliver.

"Man," Barry said, "she smelled really good too."

"They always do," Oliver replied.

Barry laughed and went inside.

Oliver watched the frozen lifeless mountains for several minutes. Spotlights from the towers passed over him several times, reminding him of a prison. His breath hung in the snowy air. So cold. So barren.

He thought about Cisco's vision of him lying dead over the generator amidst a rain of burning wreckage.

Oliver had little fear of prophecy. He had seen such things before, and he had found the future could be changed. He didn't need the ability to run through time to know that.

He recalled Barry's face when he had realized the women had been a spy. The amazed grin. The bubbling laughter. The pure engagement in the moment.

Amused, Oliver brushed the snow from his hair and sleeves. He buttoned his jacket and went back inside where it was bright and warm. He walked along the gallery above the grand ballroom. Small groups on the floor below conferred, broke apart, and came together with new members, probably to talk about the previous group. The jockeying for position was feverish. Alliances were being made and unmade with each minute.

Oliver smiled to see John and Lyla dancing near the orchestra. So casual. They could've been in their living room with only their infant daughter watching instead of waltzing before a crowd of assassins and agents.

Oliver stood at the rail. On the ballroom floor beneath him, Felicity and Cisco sat at the table writing furiously on a napkin and debating. Still working on the problem; always working on the problem.

He didn't see Barry at the table, or anywhere in the ballroom. Maybe he had returned to the room to meditate. Oliver couldn't tell if any of his half-baked zen had found its target. If Yao Fei were alive and heard the ridiculous mess he was teaching Barry, his old mentor would never stop hitting Oliver with a stick.

A waiter poured wine for Felicity. The man was serving from the wrong side. Oliver straightened and peered down.

The waiter had something in his hand nestled under the linen cloth he used to catch spills.

Oliver turned and snatched a crossbow from the surprised guard. The bolt was already in place so he pulled it back until the mechanism clicked. When the guard tried to interfere, Oliver kicked him aside. Placing the butt to his shoulder, he raised the weapon, made a rough sighting, and fired. When the heavy bolt flew, Oliver was already in motion.

He ran along the gallery to its end and vaulted onto the rail. The crossbow bolt slammed into the center of Felicity's table, rattling dishes, shattering glasses. She jumped in alarm, but immediately turned to shove Cisco down out of danger. The waiter jerked in surprise too. The cloth on his arm dropped to reveal a metal syringe in his hand.

Oliver soared through the air over the ballroom. Heraldic banners billowed out in his wake. Catching the edge of an iron chandelier, he swung out over the floor. He released, somersaulted, and smashed feet first into the waiter. They slammed into a neighboring table, sending it clattering.

Oliver pinned the man's arm, twisting the syringe loose. A knife flashed. Oliver drew back, tumbling off the waiter and scrambling to his feet. Grabbing a chair, he caught the knife arm in the rungs and twisted. The blade flew away. He spun it back the other way quickly and heard a bone break.

The waiter screamed and then screamed louder when a heavy knee crashed onto his broken arm, pressing it to the floor. John pushed a pistol against the man's head. Lyla stomped his wrist on the other side, aiming her gun down at him.

"Make a move," John snapped. "It'll be your last."

The waiter wisely froze, despite the tears of pain.

"Felicity, you okay?" Lyla called out with her gun still trained. "Oliver?"

"I'm good." Felicity leapt to her feet to check on Oliver. He shifted her away from the whimpering waiter and made sure she was uninjured.

"Um... guys." Cisco peered up over the edge of the table. He waved his fingers around to indicate they should look.

The ballroom around them was a frozen tableau.

Everyone was on their feet, chairs clattered to the floor, pistols extended at their nearest neighbors. Killer eyes narrowed. Fingers twitched dangerously close to triggers.

"Everybody relax!" Oliver called out. "It's over! Lyla, lower your weapon."

She shot him a doubtful glare, but then conceded, slipping her small pistol back into her thigh holster.

"Clear." She held up empty hands.

John eased off the waiter's arm and snatched him by the jacket, tossing him over onto his stomach.

"Anybody claim this bum?" he called out. "Cause we're about to have a problem."

"John," Oliver said, "easy."

"Ladies and gentlemen," came the booming voice of Count Wallenstein from the marble staircase at the far end of the ballroom. "This is a party. Please put away your weapons." His uniform was red and white now. He took two steps down. "Now, please, or you will be disqualified from bidding."

Heads turned seeking tacit agreement to the truce. Finally, Kolingba slid his pistol downward and signaled for his team to follow suit. The Englishman, Simon Fowler, did likewise with his band of mercenaries, followed by Alistratov's Russian contingent and then all the weapons lowered and returned to holsters, pockets, or purses.

Wallenstein snapped his fingers for the orchestra to launch into some soothing Brahms. Nodding his approval, he circulated the ballroom floor, touching arms and thanking everyone for their cooperation and civility. He finally converged with several of his brown-uniformed soldiers, who appeared as if from nowhere on the moaning waiter who still had the uncomfortable pressure of John's knee in the small of his back.

"I apologize for this unfortunate disruption, Ms. Smoak." Wallenstein bowed to her. "I can assure you this man is not one of my staff." Then he turned to Oliver with a knowing smile. "Most swashbuckling, Mr. Queen. Mr. Diggle, if you would stand aside, my men will take him."

"We'd like to talk to him." John glared. "He threatened one of us."

"This is not the United States. You have no authority—not that you have any there either. He will be dealt with."

John stood his ground until Oliver said, "Come on. It's over."

John cursed and dug his knee hard into the waiter's back as he stood up, eliciting a scream. He scowled at the soldiers who lifted the wounded man and dragged him away.

"Please continue to enjoy yourselves," Wallenstein announced. And to Felicity, "Again, my humble apologies."

"Spot me fifty million at the auction and it's forgotten," Felicity said.

Wallenstein laughed and walked away.

The entire room stared at Oliver's group over the

incongruent strains of Brahms. Cisco struggled to pull the crossbow bolt out of the table.

"Well, ain't no party like a Markovian party."

Barry appeared around the servants who carried off a smashed table and swept up broken glass.

"What happened?" He looked confused. "I just walked out for a minute. Did I miss something?"

"Yes!" Cisco exclaimed. "Oliver just Errol Flynned some guy who tried to kill Felicity! Followed by the sound of every gun in Markovia cocking."

"Tried to kill Felicity?" Barry turned in astonishment to her.

"I'm good." She sank into a chair and downed half a glass of water. "If I had a nickel for every nut who tried to kill me, I could live in a castle." Her hands were shaking.

"Everything is fine." Oliver pulled a chair next to Felicity and massaged her neck.

"I'm sorry, guys." Barry scrubbed at his hair. "I should've been here. I was down looking at the generator again."

"There's nothing you could've done," Oliver said. "Felicity is safe. That's what matters. If they try again, we'll stop them again."

"Try again?" Felicity exclaimed.

"They won't." Oliver squeezed her hand and shared a smile with her. He turned to Barry, "You weren't out looking for… you know who?"

"Who?" Barry squinted in confusion, then his mouth opened. "No. No."

"Who?" Cisco asked.

"Oh man, Cisco, you won't believe it." Barry lit up again. His fatigue seemed to vanish as he put his hands on his head with excitement. "Out on the balcony earlier. This woman, totally a spy babe—Oliver said so—she was coming onto me for information."

"No way." Cisco gasped. "Wait, do you have any information?"

"No, but that's not the point. Don't ruin it."

John and Lyla laughed.

"Did that really happen?" Felicity looked at Oliver.

"Yes." He put his arm around the back of her chair. "She was all over Barry. If I hadn't shown up, there's no telling what might've happened."

"Absolutely," Barry said. "She was smoking hot and if Oliver hadn't stopped me, I might've defected to Markovia by now."

Cisco pouted. "Why aren't spy babes coming onto me? I actually *have* information." As he shook his head in dismay, he caught the eye of a woman at another table who was looking at him, and he smiled. "Hey, how's it going?"

She turned back to her companions.

"That's not nice." Cisco held up his wine glass to signal for a waiter to come by the table. "She's probably a mobster anyway."

2 7

Outside the grand ballroom, Oliver and John passed many small gatherings all pressed furtively into alcoves, whispering, consulting phones or tablets. Heads popped up following Oliver and John as they passed before returning to their conclaves with more questions.

At the end of a long stone corridor, Oliver led the way into a dark room. It was a library with a high vaulted ceiling and towering walls full of large volumes. The smell of dust, papers, and leather permeated the air. Their echoing footsteps flushed several people from a stone bench near a window. The startled conspirators evaluated Oliver and John before scurrying into the shadows elsewhere. John watched them go.

"I feel like everybody in this castle is having an affair with everyone else, and trying not to get caught," he muttered. "Ah, here we go."

Just inside the arched entrance to the library was a bar. It was a tasteful installation of wood and dark leather. It was only long enough for five chairs, but the lit shelves behind it were crowded with bottles of excellent liquor.

The bar had been set up in front of an original stained-glass window. Obscure saints suffered martyrdom in many horrible ways. Their stiff medieval postures demonstrated a lack of concern over worldly pain and suffering.

"That's just a little weird," John said. "But I gotta say, if there had been a bar in the library when I was in college, I might've studied more."

Oliver smiled and leaned on the bar, scanning the bottles. The bartender stood attentively nearby. Oliver pointed.

"Tennessee whiskey, please. The bottle with two glasses."

When the bottle came, Oliver took it and poured for both of them. He handed John a glass and they toasted silently. Then drank. Oliver poured another shot for each.

"Good call, man." John took his glass and walked toward another stained-glass window where two overstuffed chairs sat.

Oliver carried the bottle and perched on the seat under the window. John settled into an armchair and put his feet up on the stone wall. He picked up a book off a nearby table to find a thick volume of vellum pages scribed in Latin with curious illuminations.

Oliver stretched out his legs. "So what did you want to talk about?"

"Yeah, don't worry, I won't keep you away from Felicity for long."

"That's okay. Lyla and Barry and Thea are with her. She's safe."

"So Lyla and I have been talking about a couple things. What happens if we can't buy the generator?"

"We steal it," Oliver replied.

"That's pretty much what we figured." John set the heavy book aside. "But there's a whole other issue we need to worry about."

"Such as?"

"You know Wallenstein has the schematics of the hardware." John shifted forward in the chair. "Surely he's made copies of the operating system. We can't leave that sort of technology here in Markovia for him to distribute, or use himself."

"The tech is already in the wild. There's nothing we can do to put it back in the bottle."

"Come on, Oliver. Felicity can come up with a way to hunt it down and wipe it out."

Oliver sat silently for a moment before shaking his head. "I don't think we have time."

"You best make time. You know Barry would agree. If he thought some terror group might get a super weapon because of him, he'd never stop going after it."

"That's why he doesn't get to choose. For better or worse, we've got to watch out for Barry."

"Maybe you just want to get out of here before you have to kill your friend Ghasi."

"Why would I have to kill him?" Oliver jerked around to stare at John, who leveled an equally baleful look.

"Because eventually it's going to be him or you. One, he's not letting you walk out of here with his boss's stuff. And two, more importantly, he blames you for everything bad that ever happened to him."

"This was a lot easier when I was a lone vigilante." Oliver rubbed his neck.

"Yeah, it was a lot easier for *everyone* when you were a lone vigilante." John held out his glass for another shot of whiskey. "But none of us are alone anymore. We all have obligations to others."

Oliver watched the eager eyes of his friend.

"Don't get me wrong," John said. "Nobody wants to help Barry more than I do. And I am in this to the end, believe me. But there's more to do here."

"I agree with you." Oliver let out a long breath.

John didn't say anything more. He nodded and drank.

"I'd like to hear your take on Barry's situation," Oliver said as he shifted in the stone window frame.

"I hate to say it, Oliver, but he's slipping. Physically and mentally. That kid has always had that enthusiasm, a natural confidence. Plus, he's a scientist so he's used to figuring things out. Not sure he's seeing a solution this time. There's a look deep in his eyes I've never seen before. I've seen him worry about which way to jump, but now he's worried he might not have anywhere to land no matter where he jumps."

"I agree with you." Oliver exhaled and shook his head. "Barry has always been consumed with keeping his people and his city safe. That's kept him from worrying about himself, but now he seems to have left that decision to me."

"You are the *senior Super Hero* on site. And he respects you. Barry has father issues. Look at the way he latches onto father figures. His own dad. Joe. That Harrison Wells guy who did such a number on him. The Reverse Flash one, not the other one from the other dimension… or somewhere. Anyway, Wells is really in Barry's head. And now you too."

"So you think he's falling into the same relationship he had with Wells, but with me?"

"Doesn't matter if he is or not. You don't have any choice right now. If that Jedi zen stuff you're doing has any hope of working, you've got to stay the boss. It's like having a top sergeant you trust under fire. That means everything, and you mean everything for Barry right now."

"Not sure that's a good thing," he said, dropping his gaze back to John.

"You can hold him together. You've done it for all of us many times."

Oliver nodded his unconvinced thanks.

Slow footsteps approached. John's hand went to his pistol.

A figure appeared between the bookcases and marched toward the window where Oliver and John sat. When the man moved into the light, Oliver leapt to his feet.

It was Ghasi.

"Oliver, it's good to see you again." Ghasi extended his hand to shake.

Oliver instead put his hand on John's arm to prevent him pulling his weapon. Ghasi nodded with acceptance and put his hands in his pockets. He was dressed in a tuxedo like all the men that night. It was odd to see Ghasi here in his homeland, comfortable and placid. Oliver still associated him with Star City, trying to be American, whether via parties or fistfights. This reminded Oliver that they were on another man's turf.

"I'm not here to fight," Ghasi said. "This is a night for a party. In fact, I wouldn't mind joining you in a drink. May I?"

Neither Oliver nor John moved or said anything.

"Ah. I see how it is." Ghasi looked hurt and excluded. "Oliver, I was the one who suggested to Count Wallenstein that Ms. Smoak be invited." He leaned against a bookcase and crossed his feet at the ankles. "And I'm very glad you could make it. Sorry I haven't made time to speak to you until now. Mr. Diggle, good to see you as well without your helmet."

John rose from the chair and put his back against the stone wall with his hand hovering at his waistband. Ghasi ignored the threatening action, turning purposefully to Oliver.

"I want you to know," he said, "that the man who

attempted to assault Ms. Smoak has been dealt with."

"Figures," John muttered before snapping, "Did you ask him anything before you *dealt* with him?"

"I took care of him myself." Ghasi's attention never wavered from Oliver. "I know Ms. Smoak is important to you."

The attempt at a rapport chilled Oliver. There was still some vestige of the old Ghasi there. The smile was close, the voice similar. The expectation of approval clear. But it was as if an old friend was now a dangerous predator.

"Is that why you came here?" Oliver asked. "To tell me you murdered someone so I could thank you?"

"Well, you've become very judgmental and ungrateful." Ghasi twisted his head uncomfortably. "I had hoped we might still have some bond, particularly since we're both in the same business."

"We are not in the same business." Oliver's reply was cold. "Not even close."

"If you say so." Ghasi smiled with a sense of superiority. "We won't be much longer anyway. Once I receive my cut of the sale, I'm going to retire. Italy. Tahiti, perhaps. So by all means encourage your friends to bid high."

"Is this all about money for you?"

"What else is there?" Ghasi had yet to move, still resting casually against the bookcase. "Patriotism? I hope someone blows Markovia off the map one day. Family? I stabbed my own father because he failed me." He cackled and glared viciously at Oliver. "Friendship?"

"Ghasi, listen to me, I can get you money if that's what you want. You don't have to stay here. You don't have to be under Wallenstein's thumb. Come back to America with me. I told you back in Star City, I know people who can help you."

"*Now* you want to help me? Now!" Ghasi's knuckles clenched so hard the crack was audible. "It's too late for that, Oliver. You can do nothing for me. Once this auction occurs, I will become richer than you ever dreamed." He sneered with mock politeness. "For old time's sake, I will give you a piece of advice, Ollie. Don't try to take the generator. You won't survive."

"You know that device isn't really an energy generator. It's a bomb. And potentially a big one."

"I don't care."

"You want some of these people your boss invited here to have a weapon like that?"

"I don't care," he repeated, enunciating the words clearly.

John snorted derisively and said, "Guys like you never have trouble sleeping at night, do you?"

Ghasi breathed out heavily, his eyes flashing anger before recovering smug indifference.

"Do you toss and turn over all those poor Afghans you killed, Mr. Diggle?"

"Yes. Every damn night." John shifted against the wall. "But that was war."

"Everything is war." Ghasi grinned like a skull. "Only you Americans try to draw pleasant boundaries around it. The Wallensteins understand how war and life are intertwined. They are a proud family with a long history of facilitating conflict. They shipped weapons to the Christians in the Holy Land. During the siege of Constantinople, they supplied the Turks. They financed the conquistadors in the New World. They gave money to Napoleon. They assisted in building the Nazi war machine. Then they supported the Red Army that tore down the Reich. Finally, they helped the capitalists put an end to the communist empire. The Wallensteins have destroyed many empires and now it's your turn. Unless, of course, you can buy the generator. You may buy a few more years of supremacy."

"Thanks for the history lesson," John growled.

"That sounds pretty political for a mercenary." Oliver eyed his old friend.

"Just because I don't care doesn't mean I don't know. You always thought I was an idiot, but I am much smarter than you. I understand the power of this device. Count Wallenstein has been after it for years. That's why he sent me and my father to America all those years ago."

Ghasi sighed. "I loved those times in America with you and Tommy. My father would've gone home and I could've stayed. Happily ever after." He stared at Oliver with eyes clouded by anger. "Except for you. You made me into this."

Ghasi reached inside his jacket. Oliver bounded

up and grabbed his wrist. Ghasi's other hand flashed up. Oliver blocked. Counterstrike. Another parry. Step inside. Knee lock. Elbow strike. Duck. Swing. Block. Chest pressed against chest. Hands gripping the other's arms.

In the space of five seconds, the two men struck, parried, and counterattacked ten times. John barely had time to surge forward with his pistol pointed at Ghasi's head.

Ghasi froze and offered Oliver a mocking smile. He raised an eyebrow and inclined his head toward his arm that was still inside his tuxedo jacket. Oliver released the pressure and Ghasi slowly drew his hand out.

He held a silver flask.

Oliver recognized it as the same one he'd given Ghasi the night of the museum gala years ago. He unlocked himself and stepped back.

Ghasi thumbed the stopper off the flask and offered it.

"Since I am not invited to drink with you and Mr. Diggle, I have brought my own. But I will share with you."

"No thanks." Oliver's eyes flicked quickly to John, who lowered his pistol but stayed ready.

"You gave me up." Ghasi swirled the flask, watching the light flicker off the silver. "You're going through all this to help this Barry Allen. But when I asked you for help, you spit on me. You sent them to arrest my father. I barely got away. No thanks to you, Oliver."

He drank again and exhaled. His voice was cold like a tomb. "You were supposed to be my friend!"

Oliver stayed quiet. He watched Ghasi, preparing for a possible attack.

"Nothing matters now." Ghasi shook his head with his eyes closed. He snapped the lid on the flask. "Play the game, Oliver. Follow the rules and everything will be fine. If you ruin this for me, I'll put an end to everything you love." He slid the flask in his jacket and turned away.

When Ghasi stalked up the aisle and vanished, Oliver let out a breath and leaned against the wall next to John. Footsteps faded into the distance, lost in the sounds of voices and music. Oliver had seen many lost causes turn to victories, but this one seemed like a waste.

"Oliver, that guy is not your project," John said. "You know that, right? You have no stake in his life. We have too much riding on this and he's in our way."

"I know."

"If we have to take him down…"

"We will."

28

Barry roamed the lanes of the village without noticing the architecture or others who walked near him. The sun shone in patches. Ice and snow crunched underfoot. His mind wandered to the man in yellow again. A clammy sense of dread filled him.

He stopped to gather himself. His skin tingled. The dark veins covered his arms, legs, chest, and neck. Like an unstoppable rash, it was spreading through his cells, waiting for the speed force so it could feast again.

A hot flush washed over Barry and his knees weakened. It was similar to what he had felt at the banquet last night. He knew the exercises weren't working as well. The meditation was failing. Nothing helped.

The plasma was winning.

Barry wondered if they should just go home before he disappeared. He didn't want to fade away here in the middle of another country. He didn't want Joe and Iris to open the door and see Oliver standing on the porch with an expression that instantly told them Barry was gone. That wasn't fair to them.

"Are you sick?" came a voice.

Barry straightened, fighting dizziness.

A figure strolled toward him. Casual. Unhurried. Thick corduroy pants, a heavy sweater, and ski boots. He could've been heading for the slopes, if there were any. The figure came on slowly and paused in a shaft of sunlight.

Ghasi.

Barry tensed, but tried to keep his breathing calm. The effort must've been obvious because Ghasi regarded him. His expression was a mask of concern, which seemed legitimate.

Drops of sweat rolled down Barry's face. He braced himself against the wall.

"I'm fine." His claim sounded weak even to him. "It's the… cold."

"Ah." Ghasi didn't believe him. "Sit down for a moment. Catch your breath." He indicated a stone bench a few doors away. "Relax. I'm not a danger to you."

Barry actually believed him. He cautiously stepped toward the bench and lowered himself with a harsh breath.

"I would like to speak with you anyway, if you don't mind," Ghasi said.

"I don't think we have anything to say to each other." The sun streamed down between the slate roofs and Barry raised his face to the heat.

"You are Barry Allen, the head of S.T.A.R. Labs."

He sat back in surprise. He was rarely, if ever, described that way. Technically he was the head of S.T.A.R. Labs. Harrison Wells, or Eobard Thawne, had left it to him when he *died* the day of the singularity. That version of Thawne, the one who had pretended to be Wells, had dissipated into the time stream, gone everywhere except for the constant terrible memories festering in Barry's mind.

"I suppose so. I really don't have much to do with the business side."

"Mr. Allen, I can help you." Ghasi sat on the bench and crossed his legs.

"Can you? By stabbing me like you did Oliver? Or like you did your father?" Barry stopped talking.

"I know you have a… condition that is dangerous to you," Ghasi said, "and your health is deteriorating. That's why you want the wormhole generator."

"How did—" Barry shuffled angrily. Ghasi shouldn't have this information; it was no concern of his.

"Remember, I had bugs planted in two of Oliver's people for days. I could overhear conversations. I know everything about you."

"Then you know I could beat you senseless before I even finish this sentence."

"But that's not your style." Ghasi smirked. "The Flash would hardly pummel an innocent man."

"You're hardly innocent."

"True. I can't pretend to understand exactly what

your situation is because you're a—what do they call you—metahuman. It's some type of plasma energy infection. It sounds terrible. But I can offer you help."

"I've got all the help I need."

"Have you? That's not what I'm hearing. Count Wallenstein has the device you need and he has some of the world's leading experts in biochemical energies. My remarkable abilities, which you've seen, are created by exploiting the power generated by my own body. I'm implanted with multiple offensive technologies driven by my biochemistry. I am my own fuel. Your situation seems to be something of the opposite. You are fueling your own end. You may have intelligent allies, Mr. Allen, but the count's people are specialists in exactly what you need."

"So you think I'm going to turn on my friends for some vague offer like that?"

"No, of course not. I just want you to be aware of your options. It's your life. Your condition is not improving. And I can assure you that if you're depending on Oliver Queen for salvation, you're lost."

"Well, you're not exactly his biggest fan, so I'll take that with a grain of salt."

"You don't know Oliver."

"I think I do."

"Exactly. You *think* you do. Everyone thinks they do. You may know the Green Arrow, but you don't know Oliver Queen."

"He's the same guy."

"No. Not even close. The Green Arrow is nothing but a mask. Oliver Queen is a pathological liar who will tell anyone anything to get his way. He cares for no one but himself. Look at him. Look at all the people he has lost, yet Oliver goes on, untouched. He has dragged people into his fantasy world and made them believe it's some crusade other than furthering his bizarre daydreams. And he has lied to you."

"Is that right?" Barry sneered. "I'm going to head back now. Thanks for the chat."

"Oliver admitted to Ms. Smoak that he has no idea what he's doing for you," Ghasi continued. "I heard him say it. He's a fake. Trying to save you with paperback zen. Of course he's not so concerned that he would tell you the truth because then he might lose another worshipper, the only thing Oliver truly loves."

"You really think I'm going to believe you?"

"No. More's the pity. We could save you here, Mr. Allen. Truly, we have the technology and the knowledge. However, you're determined to be yet another name on a tombstone for Oliver to mourn over while his toadies beg him not to blame himself. 'Poor, poor Oliver,' they'll all say. 'Don't be sad that you couldn't save Barry Allen. It isn't your fault. It's never your fault.'"

"Man, you really hate him, don't you?" Barry gave his best dismissive guffaw. "Maybe you should look in a mirror before you give life advice."

He turned his back and walked away. Barry listened

for Ghasi to move, to strike out at him. No sound came from behind him except a sad sigh.

The sun had slipped below the roofs. The slush had hardened into ice again.

Felicity worked furiously at her keyboard. Code whooshed past her eyes. Just symbols to most people. To her, the stream represented the secrets of Castle Wallenstein. She was walking a maze, taking turns on instinct and being rewarded by moving closer to the center. The next turn was based on inference rather than instinct, earned from her growing understanding of how the count's security system worked. Another turn and another tantalizing cascade of data showed she was still on the right track.

Then a dead end. A giant shrub where an open path should be.

"Oh you are freaking kidding me!" Felicity threw up her hands.

Oliver and Thea stood at the window studying the castle and town. They exchanged knowing glances at Felicity's latest outburst.

"Maybe you just don't have the power in a laptop," Oliver said over his shoulder.

"That's got nothing to do with it." Felicity scowled. "I could hack Citibank with a smartphone. Wallenstein must have a team of guys chained to the server changing code at random intervals. Little castle gnomes typing away, getting in my way. There's no trace of the plans for the generator anywhere on the system. Which means that black box I keep running up against must be his super-secure server. The only thing I know about it is that it's here in the castle. Somewhere."

"So if we find his server," Oliver said as he walked to the table where she sat, "we could destroy every existing copy of the generator plans?"

"I can't say that for sure, but we are dealing with a man who lives in a castle high on a mountain. We've seen how he protects the generator but leaves the rest of the castle open. He's got a sanctum sanctorum mindset. Put all your eggs in a basket and then put tanks around your basket. It's a workable security model unless someone manages to put their hands on the server. Then they have your nest egg."

"Can you make something that will copy the plans off his server and then wipe it?"

"Of course. But I can't push code through his security. We will literally have to find the server and plug the code into it."

"We can do that." Oliver looked at Thea. "We'll find the server."

"And you'll have to get back out alive," Felicity added.

Oliver paused. "That too."

Thea sat on the edge of the window ledge. "There are two hundred and sixty-four rooms in Castle Wallenstein according to Cisco's guidebook. When

John and I snooped around, we discovered there's also an extensive sublevel."

"Dungeons!" Felicity exclaimed and pointed at the floor. "If I was a crazy medieval techno-baron, I would put my gold in the dungeon. That's probably where the server is located. Easier to control access. More shielding from EMP. Discourages all but the most determined archers." She smiled at Oliver.

The door opened and Barry came in. He instantly stared at Oliver, and then offered a strange uncomfortable grin.

"Oh hey."

"Everything all right?" Oliver cocked his head curiously.

"Yeah, sure. Was taking a walk and I ran into your admirer. I had a chat with Ghasi."

Oliver grew very still. His jaw tightened.

"Nothing happened," Barry said. "He mainly talked about you, Oliver."

"I'm sure. What'd he say?"

Barry hesitated, suddenly uncomfortable. "He said you don't really know what you're doing, in terms of helping me. And that you know you don't, so you're lying to me."

Felicity clenched her hands under the edge of the table. She looked at Oliver, pretty sure she was managing to keep her face calm.

"He's lying." Oliver didn't bat an eye.

"Oh yeah, I know. He's just trying to throw a wrench

into our group." Barry nodded with relief.

Felicity knew that Oliver had said exactly what Ghasi told Barry, but that didn't make it true. Oliver was helping Barry; it was clear. Once again the fact that Ghasi had overheard all her conversations with Oliver via the bio-bugs sent a hot stake through her.

Felicity tried to ignore the rage, or at least channel it. Oliver's comforting hand pressed into her shoulder. He could tell what terrible thoughts were burning at her. Felicity dove back into the castle's system to dismantle Wallenstein's security. If they wanted to play with her secrets, she could find their secrets and use them like a knife to gut them.

2 9

Green Arrow absorbed the night. His mind shifted gratefully into the mode of a hunter, hidden inside Yao Fei's hood, glad to leave Oliver Queen behind.

Below him John and Lyla walked through the shadows. They held hands, shoulders pressed together, whispering, listening.

Amazing.

A spymaster and an ex-army ranger. This was a romantic getaway for them. Somehow they managed to steal back a few quiet moments of their normal lives in the midst of this.

John could balance a marriage, a child, and his work. Oliver could barely manage the latter. The times he tried to do more ended disastrously.

Keep your mind on your task, Oliver.

Rumors circulated around the castle like the cold air, and the rumors tonight said that some groups might try to strike early to take out members of the competition. Green Arrow was taking no chances. He and Speedy had taken to the rooftops.

He swept his gaze across the castle precinct as he clutched the wings of a gargoyle squatting next to him. Back in Star City, he knew what was natural and what was out of place, what was a threat. Oliver hated to be unprepared. The disconnection in Central City had been bad enough. Here, it was worse. He could hear Barry's question already. *If everything could be a threat, then how do you discern what is and what isn't?*

Assume everything in the jungle can kill you until proven otherwise.

A small figure slid down the slate roof and crouched next to him. Speedy gave him an *all-clear* grin.

Green Arrow nodded without speaking.

Speedy settled into scanning the rise and fall of the castle complex around them. He welcomed the silence, but it wasn't to last.

"John told me you ran into Ghasi last night," Speedy said. "Everything okay?"

"Yes."

"Don't let that guy rattle you."

"I'm not rattled."

"I think he's in your head, Ollie." She held up her hand. "Don't argue with me. You know it. Just admit it and get past it. For all our sakes."

Green Arrow scowled, furious at himself all over again.

"I just keep thinking that if I had seen the problem

back when I had the chance and fixed it, none of this would've happened."

"Stop it!" Speedy slapped her hand against the roof. "There was nothing you could've done for him."

"You don't know that."

"I *do* know." She stared her brother straight in the masked eye. "I told you once he was a phony. But he's much worse than that. You can see that now."

"That's now." He looked away, breathing mist into the sky. "It was different then."

"No, it wasn't," she continued quickly. "Ghasi is hollow. He always wanted to be Oliver Queen, but not the real Oliver. Only the superficial stuff. Celebrity. Women. Money. Action. There was nothing else to him. I can look in his eyes and see the emptiness. You feel sorry for him because you think he's some lost soul. But he's not. He is where he wants to be. He blames you. He blames his father. He blames everyone but himself for what's become of him."

Speedy furrowed her brow, trying to make Oliver grasp her argument. "Ghasi doesn't understand his demons because he doesn't think he has any. You faced yours on the island. Then you helped me face mine when you came home."

"What demons?" Arrow scoffed. "You were a kid and you acted like a kid. Now you're an adult, and you act like an adult."

"I was an addict, Ollie. And I know another addict when I see one. Ghasi is one."

"And I didn't help him." He lifted his bow. The nocked arrow gleamed in the pale starlight. "Why do I think I can help Barry now?"

Speedy offered a calm smile. "Do you remember you told me once how you felt when you first washed up on that island? Dad had died. You were alone and hungry and scared. Lost and hopeless. Well, do you remember when you went from being helpless to being able to fight back? When you finally had something to take that powerless kid and turn him into something else?"

A smile slid over his lips as he remembered the sound of the first arrow that hit a bullseye under Yao Fei's baleful watch. He remembered the first rabbit he dropped on the run so he could eat. So he could survive.

"Yeah, you do." She grinned with sympathy. Her hand tightened on the bow. "When I was young, I spent a lot of years being powerless. Men. Drugs. Booze. I lived my life following any and all of them." She touched the red mask she wore. "This changed me. This gives me power over my own life. Ollie, I put on a mask to control my demons. But Ghasi puts one on to enrage his. That's the difference between him and us. And that's the gift you gave me. Just like you're doing for Barry now."

"She's right," came Felicity's voice in his ear. "And by the way, everything is clear on the satellite feed."

"You're supposed to be sleeping," Green Arrow said softly.

"I am. I mean, I'm resting. This is relaxing to me." He was about to reply when Felicity admitted, "I couldn't sleep. I'm worried. He's getting weaker. And he's so tired all the time."

"I know. How are you doing with the security?"

"They change their codes every ten seconds. There's not enough time to monitor and implement anything before it resets." Then she launched into various theories on crashing through their systems.

Green Arrow couldn't offer any expertise on the matter so he just listened, letting her work through the problem on her own. She recited a five-minute breakdown of the issues. He understood barely a third of it. And that was being generous.

"Are they that good?" Speedy inquired.

"Yes… and no. I mean, two can play at that game. I've already modified our voice feeds at a five-second cycle. That's the delay you're hearing. Even if they crack my code for five seconds, they'll only get a word or two of ours." She paused. "I think I see something out there. Behind Spartan."

Green Arrow's attention dropped again to the courtyard. John and Lyla were almost out of sight. Behind them something moved. He tensed and his bow lifted.

"Spartan, on your five. I've got them in my sights."

Speedy angled away along the eaves, looking down her own arrow, seeking a better vantage.

"Bogies on the roof!" Felicity shouted.

A chunk of a steeple blew off next to Speedy's head.

The gunshot echoed over the mountains. She spun and dropped to one knee, drawing a bead on where she had seen a muzzle flash. She let the bolt go.

Hers was the second arrow that slammed into the shooter. He fell backward with an arrow in each shoulder. More shots fired. The howling wind whipped the sound away. The two archers ducked behind cover. Figures rushed over the rooftops toward their position, dressed in jet-black fatigues with no insignias.

Green Arrow rose over the top of the stone gargoyle, his bow snapping up; three blunt arrows lodged between his fingers, the first one nocked. The bowstring quivered against the bracer on his forearm as they were released, one after the other. Across the roof, three targets flew off their feet, slamming hard to the slates.

Speedy ducked under a hail of bullets and rolled to her feet on the opposite side of the steeple. She launched arrows and dropped two more.

"To your left," warned Felicity.

Another group ran toward the fray. They were decked out in gray camouflage. Assault rifles lifted to spray the area, blasting away the gargoyle Arrow crouched behind. Stone shards bit his exposed skin.

One of the men in black also went down under the newcomers' barrage. His comrades turned and started firing at the gray team. Everyone lunged for cover. Those caught out in the open fell quickly in the melee.

Speedy crouched behind her jagged steeple. "Okay, who isn't up here on this roof with us?"

Green Arrow glanced into the courtyard. John and Lyla were pinned down behind a massive granite fountain. If the enemy could outflank them, they'd be dead.

"I'm waking the Flash!" Felicity announced.

Green Arrow almost stopped her, but Barry might be able to end this firefight within seconds.

"Do it," he told her.

Gray commandos leapt up and rushed forward. An arrow struck the roof ahead of them with a flash and sharp crack. The concussion sent them reeling. The whisper of black arrows filled the night and dropped commandos from both teams. A dark hooded figure crouched atop a row of chimneys, bow at the ready.

Malcolm Merlyn.

Speedy closed on the stunned grays. She seized the first staggering man and swept his legs out from under him. The impact with the hard slate roof knocked him senseless. A second trooper attempted to grab her, but she yanked his arm, snapping it so the rifle clattered to the ground from nerveless fingers.

Green Arrow dropped two others surrounding Speedy.

Malcolm leapt into the air, pin-cushioning one of the black-suited mercs who scrambled to withdraw. The dark archer touched the roof, rolled, came up next to Speedy.

"Are you all right?" He kicked one of the groaning grays in the chin.

She growled and kept her attention outward where

figures still moved in the shadows.

A red blur crisscrossed the rooftop like a sudden flicker of lightning.

Green Arrow didn't wait to see the Flash work. Despite his trepidation about Malcolm, he felt secure with the dark archer at Speedy's side. No matter how twisted Malcolm could be, he would do anything to protect his daughter.

"I'm going to back up John and Lyla." Green Arrow pulled the grapple rod from his belt and fired the anchor into the stump of the gargoyle. He rolled over the edge of the roof, holding tight as the line whined out. He ran down the side of the castle, but before he reached the courtyard another figure appeared beside him, leaping over his line with sword in hand. The blade arced toward his cable.

Green Arrow flipped backward, jerking his line to the side, and the sword missed by inches. The swordsman was suspended from his own cable. He pushed off and swung out wide, arcing over Arrow to land on his opposite side. The attacker ran back at him along the stone wall. Green Arrow would never make it to the ground before his line could be cut.

He flipped upside down, drawing his hips closer to his recurve bow. He snapped the grappling rod into his belt so he had his hands free to defend himself.

He somersaulted backward, loosing an arrow at the swordsman's cable. The arrowhead just grazed it before the line was jerked out of the way. The swordsman turned to retaliate, running again at the Arrow, his blade striking out this time at the archer. The raised bow deflected three swipes.

The moment Green Arrow tried to move his arm, a burning ache lanced down to his wrist. He'd been hit so clean and fast, he hadn't noticed. He barely dodged another blow as the swordsman crossed their lines again, landing behind him.

Arrow maneuvered to gain distance but their lines were tangled. Gravity swung him back toward his opponent, but the swordsman ran at him, pushing off the wall, flying high over him in a graceful arc.

Green Arrow leapt up as well. The two men met in the air above the courtyard in a clash of steel and flesh. The bow blocked the sword. Locked together, they slammed down against the stone wall. Pain erupted as Green Arrow landed on his injured arm. Twisting, he jammed his elbow into the man's ribs, lifting his bow to block a downward slash of the man's blade. Arrow's boot connected with the man's chest and he kicked off. As he spun away on the end of his line, he loosed a volley at the swordsman and then a final arrow at the man's suspension line.

The cable severed and the swordsman plummeted to the stones far below.

John and Lyla were pinned down behind the grandiose fountain in the corner of the courtyard. A spray of stone erupted as bullets struck the fountain.

John aimed over the low wall and opened fire. Lyla snapped off multiple shots with her 9mm. Men fell into the snow with a spread of red. She ejected the magazine from her pistol.

"Johnny, I'm out."

"Already?" He continued firing with one hand and fished a spare magazine out of his coat pocket, tossing it to her. "How about some fire control."

"I don't carry a lot of ammo in an evening gown." She slammed the magazine home.

Incoming fire cut into stone and created small eruptions in the ice of the fountain. When John's pistol clicked empty, Lyla took out several more of the attacks before she ran out of ammo. The militiamen charged, firing. John and Lyla hunkered below the fountain wall, waiting for their assailants to get close. They came surging over and around the fountain. John drove his shoulder into the first man, who fell back, losing his footing on the snow. He spun around and jabbed his fist into another man's unprotected jaw.

Lyla kicked at a fence surrounding the fountain. Yanking a rail free, she swung her club and connected a solid hit. A man went down. John shoved another man's head into the stone, stunning him. Lyla took out the last commando with a hard crack across the knees.

The husband and wife stood panting for breath, surrounded by bodies. They exchanged a glance and laughed.

Another wave came at them from across the courtyard.

An arrow stabbed the ground in front of the attackers. The thunderous flash-bang startled and stopped them. More arrows sliced through the air, biting shoulders and legs. The stunned militiamen fired wildly in the air, dragging themselves out of harm's way back across the courtyard.

Green Arrow dropped lightly to the ground beside John and Lyla, watching the last of the men stagger away into a small alley. Then came the sound of more chaotic gunfire. Three men carrying machine pistols appeared at the entrance to the lane.

The bow came up, loaded to fire.

"Wait!" Lyla held up her arm. "Those are my guys. They're A.R.G.U.S."

"Typical A.R.G.U.S." John shook his head. "Right on time for the mop-up."

Green Arrow tilted his head in unspoken agreement before saying into his comm, "We're secure down here. What's the situation up top?"

The Flash dropped the load of automatic weapons over the edge of the roof and watched them clatter down the mountainside with a sense of satisfaction. He raced back to Speedy in case the unarmed commandos decided to rush her.

He needn't have worried. Speedy was smashing

the face of one of the men with her bow. The commando joined the other three unconscious men on the ground.

Malcolm dropped another trooper and watched him slide down the slope of the roof toward the abyss. A red streak roared past and snatched up the tumbling figure, depositing him out of Malcolm's reach.

The Flash brushed his hands and grinned at Speedy. "Those were the stupid ones, I gather."

"I look like an easy target," she said.

"Their mistake."

Speedy cast a scowl back at Malcolm as Oliver's voice came over the comm.

"We're secure down here. What's the situation up top?"

"We're good," she replied. "The Flash took care of—"

An object rolled out from under a semi-conscious man at her feet.

"Grenade!"

The Flash went into motion. The grenade was in his hand as he roared off the roof and down the exterior of the castle. In milliseconds, the rough stone of the mountain was under his feet.

A streak of yellow bottomed out his stomach. A flash of panic shifted swiftly over him.

He struggled to find his center but he couldn't stop the force that swept over his body. He was familiar with the feeling now. He could sense the blur happening. He was running down the cliff toward the distant rocky bottom when the world vanished.

In his hand was a grenade seconds from detonation.

3 0

When the red streak of lightning vanished off the side of the castle, Green Arrow waited for the explosion, but there was nothing. And no sign of the Flash either.

Green Arrow raced up the wall of the castle to the roof as fast as the line would retract. "What happened?"

"He blurred!" Speedy bent over the edge looking down into the vastness of the mountain cliffs.

Malcolm crouched at the eaves. His gaze went to Speedy and Green Arrow. It looked as if even the dark archer had never seen anything quite like this.

"Where is he?" Felicity shouted in everyone's ear.

"Not in a good spot." Green Arrow put a small scope to his eye, following Speedy's direction. A small dot of red was visible halfway down the cliffs. It clung to the craggy stones like a burr.

"Did the grenade go off?" Felicity asked, barely holding in her panic.

"No." Green Arrow flipped over the side.

"Wait!" Speedy shouted.

The rappelling line shivered as the archer descended at a mad pace along the castle wall and then the side of the mountain itself. Perhaps fifty yards down the craggy rock face, Flash stood. Facing down, frozen in midstride. He was translucent, suspended in the air four hundred feet from the ground. Green Arrow saw a small metallic object shimmering in Barry's hand.

"He's still holding the grenade. It's in the speed force with him. It's blurred too."

"When he comes out," John's voice crackled, "it'll blow up. Probably in a split second."

"I know." Green Arrow dangled precariously beside the Flash.

"What are you going to do?" John called down.

"I'll stay here," was Oliver's quick response.

"But you have no idea how long it will be!" Felicity argued.

"A couple of hours in this weather," John added, "and you'll be a popsicle."

"I'll make it." It was well below freezing and the icy wind pounded him. He positioned himself as close to the hazy figure as he could, eyes locked on the grenade, prepared to act the moment it became solid. "You and Speedy stay up there and keep my line secure."

"I can help with that," he heard Malcolm through Speedy's comm. "My people will keep the roof clear."

"What people?" Speedy snapped.

"I have people," Malcolm replied. "When you have

money, you can always have people. And they are at your service at the moment."

The assassin seemed to be waiting for a *thank you* from Speedy or anyone on Team Arrow. He didn't get one.

"Maybe it won't be a major blur," Felicity said nervously.

Five hours later, the Flash still hadn't come out of it. Green Arrow hung by a thin cable over the precipice. His Kevlar and leather armor had frosted. The cold seeped into every bone he had ever broken, which was many. He flexed muscle by muscle because his body threatened to shut down.

The moment Barry came out of the blur, Green Arrow would have to remove the grenade from his hand before it detonated. And there was no telling when the moment would happen; it would come with no warning.

He heard something above him, but didn't dare look away from his target. He trusted his people to keep the area clear. A rope toppled down the opposite side of the frozen figure of the Flash. Spartan slid into view wrapped in a hooded parka and thick gloves. He had a pack on his back.

"Any change?"

Green Arrow grunted.

"I have coffee and a warm blanket," John said.

"No time." The archer shook his head. "If he comes

out of the blur and I'm not ready, we're dead. Including you now."

"Let me take over for a while. Get warm. Rest."

"You won't be able to throw the grenade far enough away before it detonates."

"And *you* can?"

"That's not what I meant."

"I can help," Speedy called over the comm. "Let me come down."

"No." Green Arrow didn't want his sister to take the risk either. He didn't want anyone to take it but himself. "I need you up top to keep the bad guys away."

"That's just an excuse," Speedy argued. "Malcolm's hired killers are all over the place up here. He's got our back."

"You suddenly trust Malcolm? I'm hanging by a thread and it's a mile down. It's not just an excuse."

Spartan started to drive anchors into the ice.

"What do you think you're doing?" Arrow snapped.

"Putting up a sling. Keeping you awake. Annoying you. Take your pick." He raised his chin a bit defiantly. "Be your backup when necessary, and don't tell me you don't need it. 'Cause that's crap. I'm not budging. Even if you manage to catch Barry and get rid of the grenade in one fell swoop, you're going to need help getting him back up." Spartan stared at him. "You're always so damn stubborn. Just accept the help. We're all in this together."

Green Arrow nodded though his attention remained

focused on the Flash, never flinching. The night was far from over.

The hazy figure of the Flash shifted and the faint hum coming off him slowed.

"Now!" Oliver shouted.

Spartan jerked into motion, stiffly reaching for Barry but he mistimed. The Flash was still partially blurred and his hand passed right through. He cursed. Then the Flash grew solid and started to drop away from him. A green-gloved hand snatched the grenade from the air. Green Arrow threw it as hard as he could.

The explosion slammed a concussive wave into Green Arrow and Spartan, knocking the two against the cliff face. Searing heat washed over them and shrapnel ripped through the air. The grappling lines twanged and vibrated, but held fast.

Their desperate hands grabbed at the freefalling Flash. Fingers scraped red, but lost grip.

The Flash's limp body tumbled down. Green Arrow flipped in his rigging. His eyes sparkled with bright spots. His bow arm stretched out and he pulled an arrow from his quiver. He fired. The arrowhead struck Barry and a tangle of lines snapped open, the cables enfolding his waist. Arrow braced himself, wrapping his arm around the bow, and locking it with the other.

The cable jerked taut, arresting the speedster's fall, and dragging Green Arrow downward. The line sang as Oliver took the strain of the Flash's full weight. He cried out against the pain. Frozen muscles stretched to their aching limit.

Blood dripped into the open air from a gash on his face. The line began to slip. Oliver's bracing arm slowly pried open. He couldn't hold.

Barry was going to fall!

Spartan swung over beside him, his hand grabbing the bow. Blood coated his arm. His hand slipped. With a curse, he reached over with his other hand. Together, they hauled back on the bow.

Teeth gritted, Spartan ground out, "Now what?"

"I'll hold him while you climb up top and help Speedy pull him up."

"We'll bring you both up."

"Barry first." Green Arrow spit blood. "John, the quicker you do it, the quicker it's done."

Exhausting minutes later, Oliver dragged his frozen limbs onto the castle wall. Barry's dead weight slumped against him. Oliver braced him. Barry moaned and his eyes opened, blinking.

"I've got you," Green Arrow said. "It's over."

3 1

Oliver sat in front of the fireplace in their room, barely feeling the radiating heat. The cold had latched itself onto every bone and muscle. Fingers clutched a hot cup of tea, but they still felt thick and stiff. His other hand pressed the thick layer of bandages on the side of his head. When he lifted his arm, it burned from the sword cut which had taken stitches to close. He and John both had taken shrapnel from the grenade, but thankfully none of it was serious.

"How's Barry?" he asked Felicity as she wrapped another blanket around his shoulders.

"Recovering... slowly. Like you."

"That's bad."

"Yeah. Another blur like that and we could lose him. He's running on sheer fumes. He can't heal himself. His speed force isn't replenishing."

"The auction is tomorrow night." Oliver put his cup down and stared at the fire, his jaw muscles tightening. "We're almost done here."

"I hope so."

He shifted stiffly and stood, feeling like an old man suddenly. He embraced Felicity and pulled her tight against his chest. He relished the feeling of her head nestling into his shoulder.

"See?" he whispered. "Still got two arms."

Felicity didn't respond except to hug him tighter.

Oliver grunted from pain and she released him with morose acceptance. Right now all he wanted to do was crawl off to bed and sleep for a month. But like the rest of his team he still had a lot of work yet to do.

"Our limited supplies are running down fast," he said.

"There are enough armed men around here that finding some extra ammunition might not be too difficult," Thea offered from one of the windows. "I bet I could snag some. Arrows will be hard to come by. We might want to think about using weapons invented after the Middle Ages." She cast Oliver a lopsided smirk.

"We'll have to make every shot count." Oliver got to his feet wearily.

"Always do." Thea studied him the same way their mother did when he used to come in late after a night of bingeing. A mixture of exasperation and worry. "Why don't you get some sleep, Ollie? You look like hell."

"I will." He didn't say anything more but just went in to sit with Barry. The man lying in the bed looked like a kid with blankets pulled up to his chin to keep him warm. Sometimes Oliver forgot just how young the speedster was. Or maybe it was just because he felt so old right now. Oliver sat heavily into the nearest chair, one set back against the wall.

What was he doing? Playing at mentor, playing with Barry's life. A few years on an island listening to a half-mad sensei didn't give him the skill set to deal with this. He was trained as a warrior... a killer. He was reaching in the dark.

He drew in a deep breath.

It didn't matter what name he took: The Hood. The Vigilante. The Arrow. The Green Arrow. That part of Oliver Queen, the man he was before Lian Yu, before he boarded the boat with his father, that carefree kid with a wide-open future, was no more. He hadn't been that young Oliver Queen for a long time, not since he had inherited Yao Fei's green hood. All that was left was a driven man, the soldier who kept his city and his people safe no matter the cost.

The one that would never find peace.

Felicity quietly entered the room. Oliver slouched like a deposed king in a high-backed mahogany armchair across from Barry's bed. Both men were asleep. Lifting a blanket from the dresser, she gently covered Oliver.

He mumbled something in his exhaustion, but he didn't wake.

His face looked so relaxed when he slept, like

the weight of the world had finally slipped from his shoulders. But the bandages on his face and arms said otherwise. New scars to add to his collection.

He looked so vulnerable.

Felicity's stomach gathered in knots. She had tried to tell herself that this vibe business was no different than all the other times Oliver stepped out into the violence of the streets, but it still didn't ease the anxiety crushing against her. It seemed like the odds were finally stacking against them.

Her arms folded tight against her aching chest. She turned to slip out of the room when she saw Barry watching her.

"Sorry." She came over to stand next to the bed. "Didn't mean to wake you. How do you feel? Do you need anything?"

Barry shook his head slowly. "Too tired to even know if I do."

"I'm surprised you aren't starving. I had some sandwiches sent up through room service. I think they're prime rib. You want any?" She nodded at a gold tray set on top of an eighteenth-century sideboard.

"Nah."

"Now I'm really worried. You never say no to food." Felicity settled on the edge of the mattress.

Barry smiled at her, shifting under the covers. He winced.

"Are you sure I didn't hit the ground when I fell?"

"Positive. But you were in the blur for a long time."

Barry worked his way into a sitting position. Felicity jumped up and piled pillows behind him. He sat back against the headboard and took in his surroundings. He noticed Oliver's slumped form in the chair.

"Damn," Barry whispered. "He looks worse than I do. Is he going to be okay?"

"He always bounces back," she assured him. Or maybe she was just assuring herself. "He wasn't going to let you fall."

"I know."

"Barry, no matter what Ghasi said, you can always count on Oliver." Felicity fidgeted uncomfortably. "You know that, right?"

His hand slipped over hers. Even in the dim light, she could see the dark veins bulging under the pale skin. Yet there remained a strength in his grip.

"Sure. I didn't believe anything that psycho said."

"The thing is…" Felicity couldn't help biting her lip. "…Oliver didn't really mean… I mean about not knowing what he's—"

"That doesn't matter," Barry interrupted. "We all have times when we wonder if we're doing the right thing. Me more than most. If he didn't, I'd think he wasn't human." His eyebrow lifted playfully. "He is human, right?"

Felicity laughed. "He may not act like it sometimes, but he really is. And he does know what he's doing. He's just worried, that's all."

"Don't think I don't notice everything he's done for

me. I know he'll always have my back."

"No matter the cost," Felicity whispered as if it was some sort of mantra of her own. But then she glanced at Barry. She hoped she looked relieved, but she could feel the burn in her eyes, the tension in her face, the locked half-smile that she struggled to maintain.

"Hey." He shook her hand on the bedspread. "He's going to be okay. I've got his back too. I promise you that."

"I can't lose him, Barry." Her voice was barely audible. "I know that Cisco's powers are real. I'm scared."

"Listen, Cisco's vibes aren't gospel. The multiverse is infinite and really confusing and lots of weird stuff happens. But if there's one thing I've learned, it's that the future is never set. *Never*. Time is fluid and fate is slippery. People like me and Oliver—and you—*make* the future. And our future has a Green Arrow in it."

Felicity nodded, not trusting her voice. She kissed Barry on the cheek.

"Hey now, careful. I don't want him to wake up and see that. He'd throw me right back off the mountain." Barry grinned at her. "How about those sandwiches? Suddenly I'm hungry."

3 2

IN THE JUNGLE

Oliver trailed Yao Fei through the wet underbrush on Lian Yu. His feet hurt, which took his mind off his aching lungs. Breath misted wet and felt like fire. He had followed the general for what seemed like hours. Surely they had crossed every foot of the island twice already, but without landmarks like neon signs, Oliver wouldn't have known. He started up a muddy hill, feet slipping, hands tearing at rough stems for support. Oliver focused on his mud-caked shoes. One unsteady step after another.

He ran into Yao Fei's back. The general stood still at the crest of the hill and shot a harsh look over his shoulder.

"Be quiet."

"I didn't say anything," Oliver argued.

"Be quiet!" Yao Fei growled again. "Get down."

Yao Fei knelt and Oliver did too, dropping to his knees in exhaustion. The general made his way forward, crouched and silent. Oliver crawled on all fours, staring at the ground, pushing through dripping ferns. A hand grabbed his arm just before he toppled over a cliff. Another hand clamped over his mouth.

Yao Fei jerked his chin below them. At the bottom of the thirty-foot ravine were three soldiers. Two stood and one knelt. Rifle barrels pressed against the bowed head of the kneeling man. The standing soldiers spoke, but they couldn't be understood.

Oliver began to pull the homemade bow from his back. Yao Fei held out a rigid hand, signaling him to be still. The general glanced behind them and crawled away from the edge. Oliver watched, wondering what the man's plan was. Yao Fei kept moving away while the soldiers pushed their prisoner to the dirt, kicking him and cursing.

Oliver scrambled after the general, catching him by the shirt.

"What are you doing?" Oliver whispered. "They're going to kill that man."

"Yes." Yao Fei shook loose, rose, and moved off faster.

Oliver swiped at him, missed, and chased after him. He grabbed the general and spun him around. Oliver didn't see what hit him. His head jerked aside and his knees collapsed. He crumpled into the mud. Yao Fei looked down.

"Do you have something to say?"

"Aren't you going to help him?" Oliver pushed himself out of the muck.

"No."

"But why? You helped *me*."

"You deserved help. I think."

Oliver raised filthy fists. "Who are you to decide that?"

"I am the one doing the helping."

"Then I will." Oliver dragged himself to his feet. His breath came out in angry gusts. "I may die—"

"May?"

"Then I'll die doing the right thing. Isn't that the point?"

"Spoken like a man who has never risked death on his own."

"Shut up. You can hide inside that hood if you want to, but I won't." Oliver thrashed back through the foliage, half expecting Yao Fei to stop him.

He didn't.

Oliver reached the edge of the ravine and knelt. He undraped the bow from his back and pulled one of his few precious handmade arrows. From one knee, he nocked and drew, trying to remember Yao Fei's lessons. Take a breath? Release your breath? Take aim? Feel the target?

The target was a man. A human being. Not a broad tree trunk. Not even a rabbit or a gull for food. A man.

Fingers trembled on the taut string. The tip of the arrow wavered in his sightline.

What if he missed? What if he hit? How fast could he draw another arrow? Could he shoot again before the other soldier opened fire?

A rifle shot cracked and the prone man on the ground shuddered. Another shot jerked him again. The prisoner lay still. The other soldiers laughed.

Oliver's arrow flew, zeroing in on one of soldiers, weaving toward its target. And then slipped harmlessly past him. The arrow plunked into the dirt ten yards beyond the target. The two soldiers saw it and one yelled in alarm, "Yao Fei!"

Rifles popped. The air around Oliver filled with wasp sounds and pieces of foliage. Something tugged at his sleeve as he dived behind a thick tree.

Oliver pulled another arrow as splinters flew. He took a deep breath. Then a strange patch of green to his right caught his eye.

Yao Fei fired down into the ravine, and dropped away.

Oliver spun from behind the tree. One soldier had an arrow in his shoulder and was backing away, dragging his rifle with one arm. The other had shifted his aim toward the spot where Yao Fei had appeared. Oliver loosed his arrow. It flew as if in slow motion, burrowing through the air, flying true and straight until it slammed into the soldier's stomach. The man screamed.

Oliver stared in amazement and then cheered. The first soldier raised his rifle with one arm. Something bowled into Oliver and slammed him to the ground. Bullets hummed overhead. Yao Fei rolled off Oliver and sprinted along the ridgeline, shooting arrow after arrow. The gunfire stopped and the general paused, bow drawn.

"Are you injured?" he called to Oliver.

"No!" Oliver shouted back before he saw a patch of blood on his sleeve. "Oh. Maybe."

He pulled himself up on the tree trunk. In the ravine below the executed prisoner lay in the mud. Oliver's one arrow stuck out of the ground. Nothing else.

"They got away?" he asked with surprise.

Yao Fei stared at Oliver as he returned to the tree. Then he calmly turned his head to regard the lonely arrow below. "What did you learn from this?"

"If you want me to say *don't stick my neck out*, I won't. I'd do it again."

"I hope you'd do it better." The general sat on the edge of the ravine. "Now go retrieve that arrow you shot and missed."

Oliver shook his head and began the painful climb down the slope to retrieve the single valuable arrow.

3 3

Oliver checked the time. He turned to the group in the suite—John, Thea, Barry, and Cisco. Felicity was already down at the auction with Lyla, and the other team leaders.

"Everyone ready?"

John slipped on his helmet while Thea fixed her mask. Barry tugged his cowl over his head. Cisco looked at all the costumed heroes, and dramatically tightened his belt.

Oliver raised his hood. He turned off the lights in the room and went to the window. Checked the time again. A bright spotlight passed outside.

"Let's go," Green Arrow said.

"Uh," Cisco interrupted, "I'm not really built for jumping out of windows and stuff."

"Hang onto Speedy." Green Arrow held up a cautioning finger and waited until another spotlight swept past. "Flash, you hang onto Spartan."

"I can run," the Flash started to argue.

Green Arrow threw back the drapes and pushed open the window. Leaning out into the cold, he scanned the area with a night scope. It was clear.

He fired a line up to the top of the keep. Without a word, he vanished upward. Speedy appeared shortly after with Cisco clutching her back, his eyes closed. Spartan soon rose up behind them. The Flash clung to his back and hopped down with an embarrassed roll of his eyes.

Arrow tried to ignore how pale the Flash looked. Barry's eyes showed fatigue, but he was still determined. They would need his speed, but Oliver wished he didn't have to ask for it.

The four heroes crept low over the rooftop. Green Arrow raised a fist, and they halted. A bow lifted toward a distant figure in the chamber at the top of a tower. The man moved without purpose—he hadn't seen them. After a moment, he disappeared back into the darkness of the tower. Green Arrow motioned his team forward.

Three sets of feet moved soundlessly over the tiles. The red-booted Flash crunched after them. When Cisco tried to tiptoe, he made even more noise.

Green Arrow slipped down to the eaves above the main quadrangle. Below him, he saw a set of steps going down to a door. With a click, the door opened and a technician came out. He closed the door behind him and pressed his hand against the wall. A light glowed from under the man's palm. He walked away whistling cold mist into the air.

Green Arrow reached back and took Cisco by the waist. A drop-line whirred. They touched down in the courtyard with Cisco clenching his mouth shut. Arrow put a finger to his lips and moved Cisco into the shadows of the overhanging roof. The rest of the team slid down to join them.

Still breathing heavily, Cisco studied the biometric pad that looked out of place on the stone wall next to the door. He made adjustments to the tablet and held it up to the palm-reading screen.

"Cross your fingers." Cisco tapped the tablet and it glowed. The biometric reader reflected the light to reveal a faint outline of the technician's handprint on the pad. A scanning light rolled along the door pad.

"And capture!" Cisco then waved the newly scanned handprint against the biometric pad and the lock clicked open. He stepped back with a flourish. Green Arrow kicked open the door, aimed inside, and then motioned the Flash and Cisco in.

Arrow stepped out from under the roof overhang and gestured up at Spartan. *Stay in place. Fifteen minutes.* Speedy had her eyes cast out over the courtyard. Spartan signaled *OK*.

Green Arrow leapt down the steps, moved inside, and closed the door behind him.

They were crowded into a small room of old stone where Cisco labored over the tablet. He mumbled to himself as he swiped and tapped. Then he clenched a victorious fist.

"Oh yeah. I've got access to basic security routines. I'll loop their visuals so the cameras show a nice bland empty hallway. Can't vouch for how long it'll last."

"Good work." Green Arrow looked at the Flash. "Floor plan."

The Flash disappeared in a rush of wind.

Then he was back, breathing a little harder than normal.

"Okay." He took the tablet from Cisco and started to draw with his finger. Soon there was a rudimentary map. "I didn't see any servers. And everything came to dead ends."

Green Arrow glanced at the crude sketch, compared it to the layout of the castle and town in his head. He tapped a room. "Is this the lowest spot?"

"Yeah," the Flash said. "But only a drop of a couple feet."

Green Arrow tossed the tablet to Cisco. "Let's go."

Cisco nodded. Then his head shot up. "Oh my God!"

"What?" The Flash spun around.

The engineer's eyes gleamed. "This is like L.A.R.P. dungeons and dragons! Green Arrow is an elven ranger. The Flash is a human cleric. I'm a halfling thief. Spartan is a—"

"Let's go," Green Arrow repeated. "Straight. Corridor branches three ways. Take the right."

"That's just what an elven ranger would say," Cisco whispered.

Green Arrow took the lead down the short corridor, where he listened, then inched forward. Ignoring the branching halls on both sides, they went to the stairs straight ahead. Dim lights glowed on the walls. He crept to the top of the stairs. After another pause, he signaled the others after him.

Air flowed around them; there must have been ventilation operating. The stairs curved and the bottom wasn't visible. Green Arrow listened for the sound of footsteps. Nothing but silence.

Backs pressed against stones, Green Arrow slid along the curved walls. A faint glow shined up from the bottom. The blunt tip of a stun arrow swept over yet another empty room. Not just empty – a dead end. Green Arrow stepped cautiously into the room, checking corners and thick columns. No doors. No biometric pad.

There had to be a way through. The server would be at the lowest point for optimal protection.

A distant grinding sound started underfoot. Green Arrow motioned the Flash and Cisco behind one of the sturdy stone columns. He leapt onto a small ledge and bounded up into the shadowy vault overhead. With his legs pressed against the arches to anchor himself, Green Arrow aimed and waited.

Stones shifted and a section of the floor lifted slowly on a hinge. A simple trap door. Light filtered up and voices came out, speaking Markovian. Chatter and laughter. A man appeared through the trap door, looking down behind him and waving. Voices from below chuckled and faded away. The man climbed an unseen ladder into the room, smiling and humming. The thick hatch reached the top of its swing and started back down.

The man started across the room for the stairs. Green Arrow tracked the target, urging him to move faster. The Flash and Cisco slowly moved around the column to keep out of sight.

The man stopped at the foot of the stairs, patting his pockets as if he'd forgotten something. The hatch creaked toward the floor. Green Arrow drew the bowstring back another inch.

The man pulled his phone from his pocket and started up the stairs. Slowly his footsteps crunching on the stones drifted up and grew fainter.

The heavy hatch was inches from closing the gap.

An arrow flashed from the darkness, slipping into the barely visible space between the steel underside of the hatch and the edge of the hole. The hatch crunched into the thin arrow. Machinery whirred and the trapdoor began to rise again like a garage door.

Green Arrow dropped silently from the vault, holding up a hand to keep Barry and Cisco from moving. The hatch ground upward. Judging from the sound of the voices he'd heard below, the drop couldn't be more than fifteen feet. It wasn't. Arrow leapt into the open hatchway. He hit and crouched, bow at the ready.

This room was empty.

Green Arrow gave a soft whistle and soon the Flash and Cisco came clambering down the ladder. The hatch lowered into place and shut them in.

"Can you lock the hatch above?" Green Arrow whispered to Cisco, nodding toward a panel mounted next to the ladder.

Cisco tapped the screen for a few minutes and grinned. "Done. Until somebody notices I changed the code anyway."

Green Arrow paused at the open doorway leading out. "One way. Straight. Right. Straight. Server." He hoped anyway. "We'll hit cross corridors. Mind them. There are patrols down here."

"Guy's got an awesome memory for map directions," Cisco whispered to the Flash.

A quick glance from the front silenced the engineer. Green Arrow started down the corridor, hugging the wall. The Flash came next, looking out of place creeping at normal speed. Cisco tried to sneak behind him.

The main hallway turned right. Green Arrow's hand went up. *Halt. Listen. Check the corner.* Another long corridor stretched out, broken halfway with cross paths. The group moved on.

Green Arrow checked the time. The auction was going on. And they had less than ten minutes until the next patrol passed through the courtyard outside and would do a security check on the door reader leading to the sublevel. Arrow had watched them go through their routine many times. The patrol might detect the unusual entry and come to investigate.

That couldn't happen.

The branch to the left was dark. The one to the right dropped as it traveled out, but some light filtered up.

Green Arrow signaled down that corridor. "I'm on point. Then the Flash. Cisco, watch our backs."

"Me?" Cisco gaped and held up the tablet. "With *this*?"

Green Arrow led them down the shadowy hallway.

Felicity tried not to check the time on her phone again. But she did it anyway. Oliver would be leading the team in search of the server by now. She tapped her foot. Despite the noise all around her, the silence from the team frightened her. All her electronics were taken at the door except for her phone and it had a limited feed. She longed for mission chatter running through her head. She needed to hear Oliver and John and the others to be sure they were okay.

She tried to distract herself by scanning the room, marking various players who milled about. The crowd was smaller than the other night when Wallenstein demonstrated the generator. Only the team leaders were allowed in the auction. No advisors. No technicians. No muscle.

Felicity was facing off with top generals, spies, terrorists, and criminals from around the world. General Pyeng and Alistratov tried to look stoic. Simon

Fowler and Colonel Kolingba conferred in whispers. Felicity let out a nervous breath. Fortunately, Lyla would be here to help her.

Unfortunately, Lyla wasn't here yet. Felicity's foot tapped faster.

The wormhole generator rested in its usual spot at the front of the chamber. A single spotlight illuminated it dramatically from above. Ten body-armored guards stood around it with assault rifles strapped over their shoulders. A small desk was off to the side with a notebook computer on top.

Felicity checked her phone again, then dropped it to her lap with an annoyed huff. *Stop it*, she chided herself. *Act like a global mover-and-shaker. Not the girl from the IT department.*

"Felicity Smoak!" Malcolm Merlyn appeared next to her with a self-satisfied grin.

She jumped in surprise, although she should be used to him showing up out of nowhere by now. His suit was immaculate, as always. She rolled her eyes and looked away.

"How's the budget?" He leaned close. "Are you checking your bank account?" He nodded toward her phone.

"No, I was texting my people back home to clear a spot in my office for my new wormhole generator."

"Droll." Malcolm sat in the chair next to her. "It's heartening to see you can keep up the old Team Arrow spirit. Misguided though it may be."

"I was saving that seat."

"Really?" Malcolm made a show of glancing back toward the main door. "We're going into lockdown in a few minutes. How about I just wait here? You'll need a partner."

Felicity turned. Two of Wallenstein's guards flanked the double doors with their hands on the huge brass handles.

"What did you do to Lyla?" Felicity shot Malcolm an angry glare. She flashed on the memory of Cisco's vibe. The horror of Malcolm acquiring the generator.

"Do? Me? I resent the implication. Felicity, we're practically family. All these people are strangers. We should really be working together."

"Oh shut up." She turned back to the door, craning her neck, praying for Lyla to appear.

One of the guards glanced at the antique clock mounted high over the generator. He tilted his head as if listening to something in his ear, then he nodded to his partner. The two men began to pull the massive doors closed.

Felicity rose in alarm.

Just before the two oaken slabs touched, an arm jutted between them accompanied by a shout. One guard manhandled his door to a halt and pushed it open.

Lyla slipped inside the room.

Felicity sank back into her chair with a relieved sigh. Malcolm gave a little grunt of surprise. Lyla held out her auction card for the guards to scan. She caught sight of Felicity and weaved through the crowd. Some of the gathered grandees nodded to her. Others stared quietly. Lyla reached Felicity, but her eyes pinned Malcolm.

"You'll have to do better," Lyla said to him with a bland professional tone.

Malcolm shrugged. "I don't know what you mean."

"Let's just say you have an opening for a new assassin." She grinned savagely.

Malcolm nodded slow acceptance. With a wan purse of his lips, he stood and gallantly offered his seat to Lyla.

"I'm *impressed* you made it," he said.

"Malcolm." Felicity looked up with a smug smile. "You really need to work on your consistency. Either be a good guy or a bad guy. You're confusing."

"Thank you for that advice." Malcolm laughed, but his eyes were cold and unwavering. "Good luck with the auction." He gave a half bow and drifted into the crowd.

They watched him until he moved behind another man and didn't appear on the other side. Felicity shook her head at Malcolm's incredible ability to slip in and out of anyone's life he chose. Then she gripped Lyla's arm.

"Are you all right?" she asked. "Did one of Malcolm's goons attack you?"

"Just one." Lyla waved her hand dismissively. "He won't make that mistake again."

"No, he probably won't," Felicity agreed without humor. "Are you injured?"

"No." Lyla scoured the room, sizing up the

competition. "Merlyn's guy was good, but not great. I don't appreciate him trying to cut me out of the game though. How have you guys not taken him out by now?"

"It's complicated." Felicity took a deep breath as the lights in the chamber flickered like a theater signaling the end of intermission. She whispered, "Mainly because Oliver doesn't *take people out* anymore."

"Too bad." Lyla kept track of the suits and uniforms drifting toward their seats. "You'll regret not eliminating Merlyn."

"We already do. Every day. But it's not that easy. He's a master assassin with an army of ninja-type guys. He's also Thea's father."

"It *is* complicated, isn't it?"

"Yes. It's sort of *Dynasty* with hoods and arrows."

"You need to watch more recent TV." Lyla laughed. "Sounds more *Game of Thrones*."

The lights went out except for the theatrical spot centered on the generator. Cursing and the sounds of shins banging off furniture filled the room as the bidders finished bumbling to their seats. Frantic whispers drifted through the dark with last-minute negotiations.

Felicity checked her phone. Now there was no signal. Wallenstein had shut it down. Those surrounding her now found the same thing, followed by complaints and more cursing.

Bernhardt, Wallenstein's assistant, stepped out on stage and sat at the desk. He opened the laptop and tapped out a few phrases on the keyboard. Sitting back, he waited.

Count Wallenstein emerged from the dark and moved in front of the generator. Someone in the shadowy audience started to applaud before realizing it wasn't appropriate. Wallenstein smiled and nodded to people in the front.

"Welcome," Wallenstein announced. "Everyone check in, please."

Felicity held up her auction card. She pressed her thumb against the square in the center. Every participant did the same.

Bernhardt watched his computer screen. Finally, he nodded to the count.

"Good evening, everyone," he said. "I'm glad you all made it. After last night's festivities around the castle, I applaud your persistence… if not your aim."

Nervous laughter crept through the crowd.

Felicity scowled. There were people dead from the fighting, but it was just a clever joke to these people. None of them cared about any of their soldiers who may have been killed, except that they represented lost assets.

It reminded her again that while Oliver existed in this world, he was not a part of it.

"We all know the object of your desires." Wallenstein extended his arm toward the generator. "And there is no need for more delay. Shall we begin the bidding at twenty-five million American dollars?"

An overhead light clicked on and shined down onto

General Pyeng. Felicity noticed spotlights fixed on the ceiling above every chair.

"Thank you, General, for the opening bid," Wallenstein said. "Fifty million?"

Now General Pyeng went dark and Simon Fowler, the Englishman, lit up. The bidding continued quickly with the lights flicking on and off over members of the crowd with a strobe effect. The bidders sat with little movement and no discussion.

Seventy-five million.

One hundred.

Felicity pushed her thumb onto the biometric square on her card and found herself bathed in light. She nearly laughed with excitement. A diode readout on her card showed $125M in green as her bid and $150M in red as the next level. Felicity couldn't believe she could even offer to pay one hundred and twenty-five million dollars for a single object. Then she was in the dark again, already outbid. Felicity slumped, dejected by the end of her brief time in the lead.

Activity began to ripple through the room. Whispers. Consultations. People turned from one side to another. Some rose from their seats and sought out partners.

Fowler lit up again at the same time as Kolingba. The first alliance revealed.

Conversations grew even more animated as the bid reached two hundred million. Three hundred. Four.

Lyla bid five hundred million.

Her light was extinguished by the duo of General

Pyeng and Alistratov. At the same time, the Russian glanced off into the darkness. Malcolm's spectral figure lurked on the edge of the crowd. The assassin nodded with a faint smile. Alistratov consulted his card. One light switched off Pyeng, but stayed on Alistratov at the new price of one billion dollars.

Alistratov's light shifted to a blue tint.

Wallenstein regarded Bernhardt. He looked up from the computer and shook his head. The blue light went dark.

"What the hell!" Alistratov shouted from the dark and bolted to his feet. "What is this, Wallenstein?"

The count held up his hand. "You don't have the funds for your bid, sir. You are excused."

"Merlyn is with me!" Alistratov spun around. "Merlyn, where are you?"

There was no answer. Heads swiveled, searching for Malcolm. The Russian raised his arms in desperation. Then he pointed at General Pyeng.

"Come, I will join you again."

Pyeng glanced quickly at another man before raising innocent eyebrows. "I think not."

"But we were just allied!" Alistratov clenched a fist in the general's face.

"Get your money from Merlyn, you traitorous idiot! He played you out." General Pyeng batted Alistratov's hand away and followed it with a mistimed blow to his former partner's jaw.

Alistratov grabbed the general by the lapels. The

grappling men pushed into Felicity, who shoved against Lyla to get out of the way. Others cleared space around the two. The men jostled and grunted, exchanging angry accusations like spurned lovers.

In the dark, a patch of air glittered next to Felicity. Ghasi stood a few inches from her. He snatched Alistratov by the arm and yanked him free of the general. When Alistratov whirled angrily, Ghasi shifted his grip to the wrist and with a simple twist brought the Russian to his knees screaming.

Ghasi looked toward Count Wallenstein while holding the crying man.

"Show Mr. Alistratov out, please." Wallenstein hadn't moved an inch.

General Pyeng arranged his jumbled medals. He glared at the Russian and looked for his seat.

"General," Wallenstein said, "you are also excused."

"Me? I did nothing. I was attacked."

The count didn't reply; he merely stared. Ghasi crooked a finger at General Pyeng.

"No!" the general argued. "This isn't fair. I was attacked!"

"Sir." Ghasi's voice was steady and quiet. "Follow me."

The general spun to his fellow bidders, appealing to their good graces. "Gentlemen, are you comfortable with this?" No one made eye contact. He looked directly at Felicity. "Won't you speak up? You seem to be a fair-minded person."

"Sorry." Felicity smiled uncomfortably. "You did throw the first punch."

"I wish my man had killed you." General Pyeng glared at her.

"That was *you*?" Felicity surged to her feet, but Lyla grabbed her.

The general sniffed at her and retrieved his cap from the floor. He placed it carefully on his head. With a stiff back, he followed Ghasi, who was leading the moaning Alistratov by the wrist. Felicity tried to kick the old soldier as he passed, but Lyla shoved her back down.

"Stop it!" Lyla hissed.

"He tried to kill me!"

"You should be used to that by now. Relax or Wallenstein will boot you out."

When the doors boomed shut on General Pyeng and Alistratov, Wallenstein said, "I apologize for that interruption. Shall we continue? Our last legitimate bid was—"

"Seven fifty," Bernhardt replied, "to A.R.G.U.S."

The light bathed Lyla again, but quickly slipped off to another bidder. The auction proceeded with the light flicking from one person to another. As the price again topped one billion dollars, several bidders sat back in surrender, legs crossed, out of the running. Clearly Wallenstein had brought in many of them as fodder, merely to raise the price so the big money players would have to wield their financial power at full strength.

Billion one. Billion two.

More bidders tried to work their way into alliances. A few additional members were dismissed by Wallenstein for overextending their resources.

Billion three.

Lyla pressed her card and nudged Felicity. With a terrible sickness in her stomach, Felicity added her account to Lyla's bid. She stared at Bernhardt at the laptop, fearing the shake of his head and the air tingeing blue with rejection.

But the light stayed white.

Wallenstein observed the now mostly idle crowd of bidders. Heads swiveled as the seconds ticked off the antique clock looking for the next bid, if any.

Felicity sat on the edge of her seat. This was it. There were no counter-bids. They were going to win.

She found herself in sudden heart-wrenching darkness. She and Lyla spun around to see two men illuminated. A numbing cold seeped into Felicity.

Simon Fowler and Malcolm Merlyn.

Malcolm gave a pleasant tilt of his head.

All she could see was Oliver draped dead over the generator.

3 5

Green Arrow slid along the outer wall of the corridor while the Flash trailed on the inner. After a semicircle, the hallway opened into a room, large and poorly lit. The air hung thick and hot.

Blinking lights and bundles of cables nested amid the dark stone columns of the former dungeon. Old-fashioned torture racks had been replaced by metal shelves crowded with computer equipment stretching from wall to wall and reaching to the arched ceiling. The chamber vibrated from the machinery.

"Bingo!" Cisco edged past the Flash and Green Arrow, drawn by the siren call of the humming server array. He put a hand on his head and cooed, "Oh man, look at this setup! Somebody engineered the crap out of this thing! I don't know if S.T.A.R. Labs has this much power in such a small space."

Green Arrow reached into a pocket in his tunic and pulled out several objects. They were simple SD cards.

"Here. Find slots and load it up." He handed the devices out.

Everyone spread out across the bank of computers and searched for access. Quickly the proper slots were found and the cards went in. In just a few seconds all the drives lit green. They pulled the devices out. Green Arrow checked the time.

"That was pretty easy." Cisco tossed the SD card up and down in his hand.

"Help me," came a strained whisper from behind the server bank.

Green Arrow dropped to one knee with an arrow ready. The Flash reacted instinctively and rushed Cisco behind a stone column.

Beyond the humming wall of processors and routers, the floor dropped two steps before reaching the far wall. Three wide doors of steel with barred windows were set in that wall. Eyes peered out of the shadows behind the bars of the center door.

"Help me!" the figure inside the cell moaned. "Get me out of here. Hurry before they come."

"Who are you?" Green Arrow signaled the Flash to stay put. The archer rose slowly with bow drawn toward the voice.

"I'm a prisoner. Please help me."

"How long have you been here?"

"Years." The shadowy face dropped and sobbing started. Fingers clutched the bars. His hands were gnarled and misshapen, black as if burned and badly healed. "Please God help me."

"Can you walk?"

"Yes!" Terrified eyes rose and fingers tightened on the bars. "I can walk! Hurry or they will come. Surely they know you're here. *He* may come. He may be here now. He likes to stand here invisible and enjoy my tears."

Ghasi.

Green Arrow slipped around one of the time-darkened columns. With one foot on the bottom step, he asked, "What's your name?"

Teeth bared, the reply came back. "Why do you care about my name? Free me now if you have a soul!"

"What's your name?" Green Arrow repeated. He wanted to hear a simple answer to a simple question.

"Evgeni Valov. I'm Bulgarian. Do you want my home address in Sofia? Why do you care?"

"Why are you locked up here?" Green Arrow asked quietly. Something didn't feel right. Or it could have been the pressure of knowing Felicity was bidding for the key to saving Barry, while trying to keep a doomsday weapon out of murderous hands. Wallenstein's tangled crimes didn't compel Oliver to endanger his own plans in order to untangle them.

"You work for Wallenstein, don't you? He sent you to torment me." Valov bounced his forehead against the bars. He turned away from the door. "Go away. I won't tell you anything."

"We've got to let him out." The Flash moved toward the door.

"We'll come back for him."

"There may not be time," the Flash argued.

"We don't know—"

"What's there to know? Look at the guy. He's been tortured. If we don't help him, what's the purpose of any of this? I can run him out to safety." The Flash broke into Green Arrow's automatic contradiction, "I can't just stop running. He needs us."

Green Arrow didn't argue. He stood aside as the Flash pressed the tablet against the biometric scanner next to the cell door. The mechanism whirred.

The lock clicked. Green Arrow pulled the door open. The prisoner hunched, gnarled hands clutched in front of him. His face was scarred. Wispy hair sprouted in patches on his scabbed head.

Something strange caught the light. Wires protruded from his skin along his neck, his forearms, and the back of his head. The Flash stepped in to assist the man.

"Flash, wait!"

The wires sparked and a blackened arm slammed the Flash aside. Barry crunched against the cell wall. The dark figure rushed out, slamming the door behind him.

Green Arrow extended his bow, blocking an incoming fist. The impact shivered into his arm. As numbness tingled through his body, he ducked another blow, stepping back, and flipping aside. He caught the prisoner on the face with a boot. Valov spun around, his fist smashing a chunk off a stone column. Shrapnel slashed Oliver's face and knuckles that felt like iron battered his chin, blasting him against the steel door. His knees buckled and he dropped to the floor.

An alarmed shout came from the main entry. Beyond the blinking banks of computers, a technician stared in terror, yelling in Markovian.

Valov laughed and bounded across the floor. He caught the tech just as the man stumbled back. The prisoner backhanded the terrified man and slammed him against the stone wall. And then slammed him again with a triumphant grunt. The tech slumped lifelessly in Valov's grip.

Green Arrow dragged himself onto his knees, sighting through blood and blurred vision and blinking computers. He fired an arrow through the server rack. It struck the back of Valov's legs and a web of steel cables whipped out, constricting the man's thighs. Valov staggered, struggling against the cords.

Arrow rushed around the server array and launched himself. He kicked Valov in the chest. A powerful arm clamped around his ankle. Ignoring the lancing pain, he used the leverage to drive his other foot into the man's face. Bone crunched, but Valov hardly reacted.

Green Arrow ducked a blow that whistled past his ear. He drew a shock arrow from his quiver and jammed it against the man's neck. Sparks flew. Valov screamed. Green Arrow kicked away from him, rolling and firing a second grappling arrow that bound Valov's arms to his chest with steel cables.

"You can't stop me," Valov ground out. "He made

me and I have all the power I need." The wires in his arms and head sparked again. It reminded Green Arrow of Ghasi's shimmer effect. Valov grunted with effort. The cables sang from the strain and one snapped.

Across the room, the Flash rose into view behind the bars of the cell door. He squinted, fighting to regain his senses. The door started to quiver. He was vibrating it to pieces from the inside.

When Green Arrow drew a tranquilizer arrow and fired, Valov grinned.

He flexed his shoulders. Another line broke.

"I'm going to kill you and your friends." He shot a glance toward Cisco, who was frozen against the column. "And then I'll kill Ghasi. Then Count Wallenstein. He made me and then says I'm not good enough? I'll show him how good I am."

"We can help you." Green Arrow nocked another shock arrow. "We can get you out."

"I don't want to get out!" Valov shouted in a glorious rage, neck muscles bulging. Wires crackled with power. The web of cables around him snapped like string.

He didn't seem to notice that his skin was blistering. Yellowish smoke wafted off him. He staggered.

Valov's grin of triumph dropped off his slack face. Blisters rose and popped. Liquid dripped to the floor. He looked at the oozing sores on his arms. Moisture seeped through his shirt. His bare feet were wet from the fluid dribbling from his pant legs.

The cell door snapped open with the sound of metal

shards skittering over the stones. The Flash zipped out.

"Don't touch him!" Green Arrow called out.

The Flash maneuvered behind Valov. The man turned with obvious effort. He took a step and his knee gave out. Valov crashed to the floor in a wet heap.

"No no no," he muttered. "I was first. He cheated me. He could've finished me, but he wanted Ghasi." Valov put his head against the stones and looked up helplessly at Green Arrow. "I should've been him."

The man lay lifeless in a cloud of bruise-colored smoke.

"Good God," Cisco breathed. "What was he?"

"A Ghasi prototype." Green Arrow lowered his bow and gathered the arrows he had fired.

The Flash knelt next to the body of the technician, but sighed with pained resignation. The man was dead.

Next he looked at Valov slowly turning into a puddle.

"Oh my God," the Flash muttered. "His own biology destroyed him. Like me."

"Nothing like you." Green Arrow replaced arrows in his quiver. "Get away from him."

"What do we do with him?" the Flash asked.

"Nothing." Green Arrow marched for the door. "Let's clear this room. We've got two minutes before the next patrol outside."

Felicity stared at Malcolm's smug face and cursed.

"Let's go a billion five." There was desperation in her voice.

"We don't have it," Lyla said. "My budget is hard-capped. And I know what Palmer Tech has."

"You do?"

"Yes. And so does Count Wallenstein. Damn it, but I think Merlyn has us."

Wallenstein waited patiently while the clock ticked overhead.

"No, it can't happen," Felicity told Lyla. "Trust me. There's some rainy-day money you don't know about." She consulted her wristwatch. "I hope."

Lyla gave a suspicious squint. Felicity urged her on so she pressed her thumb against the card, bidding one billion five hundred million. Felicity joined in. The tech studied her screen as if confused, but then sat back satisfied. The lights fell on Felicity and Lyla.

Felicity glared back at Malcolm with satisfaction.

Malcolm conferred with Fowler, who shook his head doubtfully. Malcolm pressed. All eyes turned to the men, waiting for the end.

Felicity and Lyla went dark. Fowler and Malcolm again sat in the light. Felicity groaned. Her heart slammed inside her chest. She couldn't fail. Malcolm couldn't get the generator or Oliver would die. She had to do something.

Then the two men were bathed in blue. Malcolm leapt to his feet.

"No!" he shouted. "I have far more than enough to cover this!"

Bernhardt rechecked his screen and shook his head at Wallenstein.

"I'm sorry, Mr. Merlyn," the count said. "You do not."

"Your data is wrong." Malcolm crossed his arms, smug and self-assured. "I have retained enormous wealth from my old... businesses. I have more than enough to cover this."

"Perhaps." Wallenstein's eyes flicked at Ghasi, who edged closer to the blue light. "You should have deposited those rubies you stole from the League of Assassins in a reputable financial institution so I could tally them. You may count buried treasure on your ledger, but I cannot."

"Kolingba, I need you." Malcolm stepped around to face the Congolese warlord. "Join us. We'll make it worth your while."

Kolingba glared at Malcolm as if he was going to attack.

"I wouldn't help you for any reason, Merlyn. The League killed my brother in Mombasa last year."

"But I'm not with them any longer." Malcolm exhaled in annoyance. He looked beyond Kolingba, but everyone refused to look at him. Malcolm jabbed a finger at Wallenstein. "I won't be cheated. You are making a mistake you'll regret."

"You may go, Mr. Merlyn," Wallenstein said.

Ghasi reached out for Malcolm.

"Don't." Malcolm froze Ghasi with a stare. "I always

liked you in Star City, even though you wasted your time trying to be Oliver Queen. Don't make me kill you."

Ghasi's nose wrinkled; the only sign of anger.

"But you'll never be him." Malcolm looked the man up and down before glaring at Wallenstein and pushing past him. Malcolm didn't bother to glance at Felicity or Lyla as he left the room.

Felicity sat back in her chair with a deep sigh. She almost laughed. And tears of relief welled in her eyes.

Lyla whispered, "It is complicated with Merlyn, isn't it?"

"You have no idea."

With his partner gone, Fowler pushed forward to plead his case to Kolingba sitting in front of him.

"I'm not going against A.R.G.U.S.," Kolingba snorted. "The Americans are the top customer for my coltan."

Felicity and Lyla again shared the light. Felicity squeezed her hands together on her lap. Not only was Malcolm out, but the fact that she could cover this high a bid meant that Oliver had reached the server and one of her viruses was working, feeding Wallenstein false data about Palmer Tech's resources. She held her breath as the ornate second hand of the clock swept around its face. Most of the others sat stiff in the dark. A few leaned in to whisper to Fowler as he scurried from bidder to bidder, causing Felicity to twitch in terror.

The clock chimed.

"Congratulations." Wallenstein bowed toward Felicity and Lyla.

"Woo hoo!" Felicity leapt out of her chair and spun around with her hand up to Lyla for a high-five.

Lyla sat still. She cleared her throat with an expectant look.

Felicity stood, hand high and grin frozen on her face. Then she noticed the gathered generals, spymasters, warlords, terrorists, and crime bosses staring at her with genuine resentment.

"Sorry." Felicity chuckled sheepishly. "But I think deep down we all know it's better that none of you have it."

Vengeful eyes met hers.

"Okay." She smiled. "Let's agree to disagree."

The wormhole generator rested inside a wooden crate with no labels or identification. Lyla's A.R.G.U.S. team had carted it down to the cable car station where it waited on the platform. Her commandos formed a cordon around it.

Many of the other bidders had already departed Castle Wallenstein with their teams. General Pyeng. Alistratov. Colonel Kolingba, Simon Fowler. They all arrived at the station, glowered at the crate and its protectors, and as their cable car clanked away, they continued to stare longingly out the back window. Finally, they scowled or cursed and turned away, disappearing in the snowy air.

Two cars pulled to a stop in the narrow street outside the station. Felicity, Lyla, John, and Cisco got out of the first car. The second idled in the snow behind them. The driver stepped out and opened the back door for Count Wallenstein. Ghasi slid out of the passenger's seat.

Wallenstein, in his heavy topcoat and fur hat, joined Felicity's group on the platform. Both cable car berths were empty but the heavy wheels churned, drawing the thick steel cables along. Lyla went to confer with her men while John eyed the brown-suited members of Wallenstein's militia standing guard around the station.

"This is goodbye, Ms. Smoak." Wallenstein drew off his glove and extended his hand. "Congratulations again."

"Thank you for selling me *my own* property." Felicity shook and quickly returned her freezing hands to her coat pockets.

"Where is the rest of your team?" Ghasi strolled the platform. "Where's Oliver?"

"He went down early," Felicity answered, "to check on transportation."

"Very wise." Wallenstein nodded. "You realize that once you leave the castle, you are no longer under my protection."

"I do." She smiled sarcastically. "So if anyone kills me and takes the generator, you keep my money."

"I'd say you are amply protected." Wallenstein indicated the A.R.G.U.S. agents. "I'll say good day then, and bon voyage." He began to walk to his car. Then he stopped and turned back. He held up his hand to Felicity. "Oh, I believe this is yours."

A small SD card rested in his palm.

She froze.

"I'm sure you think you're very clever, Ms. Smoak." Wallenstein studied the data card. "But someone left this in one of my servers. I'm impressed that members of your team managed to get into the sublevels and override the security checks. And you might've gotten away with it longer if not for that nasty incident in the server room." His gaze flicked to Ghasi and then back. "At first we thought that Valov had escaped and killed a technician before burning himself out. But we decided to run checks, and found this."

He held out the chip and Felicity took it as if it were poison.

"We scoured the network," Wallenstein continued with calm precision, "and found your little virus."

"I don't know what you're talking about."

"Yes, yes. I could negate the sale, but I won't. I'm a fair man and I don't have definitive proof you did this. However, you are the only one here smart enough to have done it."

"Thank you." Felicity looked down, embarrassed. "But I still don't know what you're talking about."

Wallenstein chuckled and bowed before returning to his car. When the door shut and the driver settled inside, Ghasi started back too. He passed close to Felicity.

"I'm very sorry to have missed Oliver. He was lucky I was at the auction or he would never have made it to the servers. Tell him goodbye for me. I doubt we'll ever meet again, unless he comes to Tahiti."

Felicity didn't answer so Ghasi left the overhang of the station and joined Wallenstein in the car. The gleaming black Rolls Royce pulled away from the curb.

"After all the trouble we had getting in there," Cisco groaned. "I bet I'm the one who left that card. That's something I'd do."

Felicity winked at him. Then she shook her head with narrowed eyes to indicate they shouldn't discuss it with Wallenstein's men still lingering.

A cable car clanked to a stop in front of them. The A.R.G.U.S. crew assembled around the crate. Several men worked open the gondola, spreading the glass and metal doors wide. They wrestled the generator inside. It barely fit, nestling tight between the plastic bench seats on the sides of the car.

"That looks heavy." Cisco peered at the large wooden crate crowding the inside of the car. "Is this safe?"

"Sure." John eyed the gondola. "But we're not all going to fit, that's for sure."

"I want us all on that cable car," Lyla said. "I don't want to leave any valuable tidbits here that someone might try to snatch up."

"Tidbits?" Cisco muttered. "I think my feelings are hurt."

"Felicity has been a target already." Lyla herded people toward the gondola. "And others might try to hurt her out of revenge. And if Cisco gets taken or killed, your whole plan with the Flash goes up in smoke. Right?"

"Yeah, you're right." John selected one of the A.R.G.U.S. commandos to go with them.

"Taken or killed?" Cisco pressed a hand over his

heart. "I thought this whole caper was over. Are we still worried about that?"

"It's not over by a long shot," Lyla said, "until that generator is strapped in the A.R.G.U.S. Air Command and airborne back to the U.S."

"Um." Felicity held up her finger. "We're taking it back with us to Star City. On our plane. Remember?"

Lyla paused, looked at Felicity through mirrored lenses. John stiffened. Lyla removed her glasses.

"Of course." She gave a slight grin. "That is the plan."

"Let's go then." John stationed the A.R.G.U.S. agent at the curved front window of the gondola. He climbed in, skirting the crate by clambering over the bench, and placed himself at the rear. Lyla worked her way around to the far side while Felicity and Cisco had to sit on top of the crate, their heads nearly brushing the ceiling.

The commandos slid the doors shut. Couplings clicked into place overhead, locking the car to the cable, and the gondola lurched into motion.

When they pulled clear of the station, the car dropped and Cisco screamed, clutching the crate. The cable snapped taut after a few feet. The car swung but continued on. It topped the bastion wall, jostled through a tower junction, and then hummed smoothly down toward the distant town.

Felicity patted Cisco to calm him. He tried to smile, but failed. His eyes were locked on the swirling snow ahead. Visibility was poor and it did feel like the car was falling through a snowstorm. The loss of perspective unnerved Felicity too. There was no visual landmark to anchor yourself. The ground was lost in the snow, as were the surrounding mountains. The castle mount they had just left was now only a smudge in the white.

Felicity produced her tablet and activated a scanner app, checking the gondola for listening devices. It came up clean.

"Cisco," she said, "you didn't leave that SD card behind. Oliver did. Because I told him to."

"You did?" Cisco looked curiously at her. "Why?"

"Because Wallenstein was suspicious of me, so I wanted Wallenstein's people to find it so they would search their server and find the virus I planted there. One of the viruses. A sophisticated one, but not nearly as good as all the other ones I put on his system. I knew once they found the bait, they would clean their system and be all proud of themselves. But I don't think they can undo the other viruses I planted without a lot more work." She shrugged. "That's the plan anyway."

"So what do the other viruses do?"

"One of them virtually liquidated all Palmer Tech assets so Wallenstein's scans would show that I had a lot more money to spend than he thought I did."

"Is that legal?" Cisco asked, knowing the answer.

"Not strictly speaking. And if this doesn't work out, Palmer Tech will be ruined and I will be an international felon."

"So what are you going to do?"

"Well, the really good evilware I put on his server will let me sneak back into his system whenever I want. I will snatch up the plans for the generator, and then I will wipe them off his server. Forever. Oh, and I will get all our money back."

"The American taxpayer thanks you." Lyla nodded from the other side of the car.

"I'm glad you work for the good guys." Cisco tightened when the cable car shook in the wind.

"Thank you. I do look good in black though." Felicity put the tablet away and resumed rubbing Cisco's arm.

"Ma'am," the A.R.G.U.S. agent called to Lyla over his shoulder and tapped the front glass.

Ahead through the snow, a dark shape swirled into view. It was just off to the right, hanging in the air.

"It's the other cable car," John said. "It's coming back up."

"Something's weird." Lyla crept forward, moving her head as if trying to see between the snowflakes. "Johnny, there's something on top of it."

Felicity and Cisco slid to the front of the crate to stare out. John drew his sidearm and climbed along the bench to join Lyla. Through the storm, the big oblong bulk of the second gondola grew clearer. But it looked misshapen across the top, rough instead of smooth.

"There are men on it." Felicity reached for her phone.

Dark shapes that had been crouched low against the storm rose up on one knee and lifted bows. In front of the group loomed a familiar figure in a long black tunic and hood.

"Oh crap," John muttered. "It's Malcolm Merlyn."

A hail of arrows whistled through the air. Thin cables fluttered behind the arrows. Black-clad figures launched themselves into the sky between the cars, sailing like spiders on silk. Felicity heard the soft impacts of feet on the roof.

John and Lyla fired through the ceiling. A muffled *whump* shook the roof hatch. Smoke seeped between the seams. The hatch flew off and frigid air rushed into the cabin.

John and Lyla spun to train their pistols on the open section of the ceiling.

"Surrender the generator," Malcolm's voice wafted down with stray snowflakes. "No one needs to die."

John shot through the hatch.

"What is wrong with you people?" Malcolm called back. "There is no cavalry coming."

"Felicity?" John said as he continued to sight down his pistol barrel. "Cavalry?"

"Done." She thumbed a red button on the phone screen.

3 7

Green Arrow and Speedy crouched in the shadowy lee between the slate roofs. The cable car carrying Felicity and the generator had departed barely five minutes ago and the A.R.G.U.S. agents were gathered together on the platform to wait for the next car. He anticipated Felicity's signal that they had arrived safely, and he and Speedy would make sure no one sabotaged the cable system. The Flash was patrolling Fürchtenstadt below.

Green Arrow heard a buzz in his ear, as did Speedy. An emergency tone from Felicity. They leapt to their feet, sliding down the sloped roof. The archers vaulted the narrow lane, landing with a clatter on the flat metal roof of the cable car station. They legged it for the edge of the overhang where the cables ran out into empty space. As they ran, they tugged metal clamps from their belts.

The two reached the end of the station roof and leapt off into the air, caught hold of a moving cable, and clapped the metal brackets around it. Grasping the brackets, they slid along the cable out over the abyss.

The relay tower loomed up through the snow. Green Arrow slammed against it with his feet. Speedy rammed into his back. He steadied himself on the tower with one hand, unclamped the bracket, and swung around to the other side of the tower where he clamped onto the cable again. He spared a second to look back at Speedy.

"Don't wait for me!" she shouted through the wind, climbing up behind him. "Go!"

Green Arrow pushed off from the tower. The metal bracket skated along the steel cable with a ringing hiss. He sliced through the frigid air at the speed of freefall. The brutal cold didn't affect Oliver, only the thought that something threatened both Felicity and Barry's future, and that there was still space between him and them.

"I'm ready," Oliver heard Barry in his earpiece. "I'm down in town but I can run up to help."

"No, it's under control!" Green Arrow shouted with his feet dangling hundreds of feet above barren rocks.

"But I can—"

"No! Stay put."

Felicity's gondola appeared through the storm. Green Arrow released the bracket and went airborne. He crashed into a small group of black-coated assassins. Two men tumbled off the side. Arrow stopped his own wild slide by grasping a ladder that ran up the suspension arm to the cables.

Shrouded heads whipped around in surprise. Then Speedy rocketed in, flattening another fighter. Green Arrow caught her arm as she went by and pulled her next to him.

They launched into an immediate attack, taking down two more. The assassins toppled into empty space.

A blow struck Oliver from behind, driving him to his knees. Dodging to one side, a sword swept through the air where his head had been. He fell flat, threw back his legs, locking the assassin's ankles with a scissor catch. His move sent another man over the side and Green Arrow barely caught himself on a vent housing.

A dark shape dropped silently from the top of the ladder where he had disengaged the cable coupling to keep the car stationary. He focused on Green Arrow. Speedy used the ladder as an anchor to kick his cowled face, driving him a few steps back. She flipped upside down, bracing her feet through the upper rungs. With hands free, she battered the man, grasped his tunic, and flung him off the gondola.

Green Arrow started to bolt up for another man who zeroed in on Speedy when a boot slammed into Oliver's face.

"Amazing entrance," Malcolm said. "Here's your exit."

Oliver's hands clawed for purchase on the snow-covered roof. A nauseating blow in the stomach followed. Malcolm's foot caught Oliver's knees and shoved him over the side.

Green Arrow's fingers caught a narrow lip above the window that jerked him to a stop. His body slammed against the wide plexiglass.

Felicity saw him hanging. Her eyes went wide with terror. She shouted his name, silent to his ears.

John and Lyla fought two of Malcolm's dark assassins. A third lay dead or insensible over the crate. The A.R.G.U.S. agent was apparently dead too.

John glanced at Green Arrow before blocking a swipe from an assassin's long-bladed knife. John raised his pistol toward Oliver.

He fired.

The bullet punctured the plexiglass, passing a few inches from Green Arrow's torso. A network of cracks spread over the window. Oliver smashed his forehead into the plexiglass just as his fingers slipped. It shattered and he thudded against the bottom of the window frame and bounced back. Felicity stretched out and clutched his arms.

Green Arrow pressed his elbows to push himself up against the jagged teeth of plastic sticking out of the window frame. He lifted one knee inside. Felicity tugged him frantically. His arms burning from the strain, he dragged himself into the gondola and crumpled into the bench.

Oliver fumbled with frozen fingers to draw a dart from his bandolier. A flick of his wrist sent it flying into the assassin who pressed Lyla against the wall. The man staggered and Lyla cracked him in the face with the base of her palm. He grunted and fell. Lyla stooped out of sight and came up with a pistol.

She shot the assassin fighting John.

Green Arrow gave Felicity a reassuring smile before struggling onto the crate. Knees shaking from exertion, he stood and threw his arms up over the rim of the open hatchway in the ceiling.

On the roof of the cable car, only Speedy and Malcolm remained. Standing toe-to-toe with Malcolm, Speedy laced the air with her short sword. Malcolm used his bow as a staff, countering his daughter's skillful attacks. A subtle shift of Speedy's head gave Green Arrow the sense she had seen him, and he paused.

She feinted to the side and made a wild swing. Her foot slipped on a patch of ice. She fell hard onto her knees.

Malcolm struck at her, but she dodged awkwardly. Speedy banged against a guide wire and skidded toward the edge.

"Thea!" Malcolm dove for her.

Green Arrow vaulted from the hatch and slammed into Malcolm's back. Speedy yanked Malcolm's ankle and he toppled over her, spinning out into the air.

Oliver fell against the roof and grabbed Speedy's wrist. She smiled with exhausted relief.

"Thanks, Ollie."

"No problem."

Suddenly Green Arrow sensed something just in front of him. He looked up and saw the sharp tip of an arrow just an inch from his face. It hung in the air.

Beyond the glittering razor edge, he saw a red hand.

The Flash held the arrow. His hand shook and perspiration coated his face.

"You two get inside," Green Arrow ordered.

Across the chasm of empty space, Malcolm was falling with another arrow already nocked. Suddenly he jerked in the air and rocketed toward the other gondola. He was on a wire. He hit the bottom of his line and started spinning like a pendulum.

As he struggled to get control of his movements, all his assassins crawled up their own lines back to their own car.

Green Arrow pulled the bow off his back and snapped it open. Pulling an arrow, he steadied himself on one knee. He aimed for the coupling wheels above Malcolm's gondola and fired. The explosive tip detonated and the other car tilted, suspended but disabled.

He took hold of the ladder and dragged himself up to the coupling switches. Fighting his frozen muscles, he slammed the mechanism, feeling the shocks vibrate through his bones until the wheels clamped the moving cable. The car lurched and started down again. Malcolm and his assassins would soon be left behind, stranded.

Green Arrow slid down to the roof of the car. Speedy and the Flash climbed inside through the hatch. When Oliver jumped in, Felicity grabbed him. Cisco checked on Barry.

"I told you to stay put, Barry," Oliver said with all

the authority he could manage. "If you had blurred on that cable…"

The Flash managed only a brief lift of his hand to give reassurance. He tried to breathe properly, but he was gasping for air as if he had just surfaced after being too long under water.

Barry's arms and legs vibrated, and he wasn't shaking from the cold. Running up the cable had overexerted him. An act that would've been nothing to the speedster just a few weeks ago had left him spent.

Felicity put her arm around Oliver's shoulders. He actually trembled a little bit too.

"Wallenstein found the card." She fished the SD card out of her pocket.

"And?"

"As soon as we're airborne with the generator, I'm going to get into his network and put the Wallenstein family back to the Middle Ages." Felicity flipped the data card like a coin. "Steal my technology, will you. I'll show him what I think of that."

Oliver leaned against her, relishing the firmness. He needed something strong at the moment to hold him up.

3 8

Oliver Queen's childhood home rose from the horizon. The Queen mansion. Built during a bygone age, it embodied wealth and privilege and obligation, but to Oliver it was just home.

Now it was a skeleton, like the rest of his past. Blackened fingers reached up into the sky. The structure was a ruin, nearly destroyed by a fire.

"Oh man," the Flash exclaimed. "What happened?"

"Long story. The Queens fell a long way."

The Flash shook his head sadly.

Oliver couldn't help but glance again at the circular contraption crisscrossed over the lightning bolt insignia on the Flash's chest. "What is that thing again?"

"It's a magnetic inductor. It generates a magnetic field that will create a path for the plasma to exit my body. We believe that the plasma will seek to equalize regions of concentration by leaving me for its own dimension. It's called diffusion. You see, plasma—"

"That's okay. I don't need a physics lesson. It's going to help get the plasma out of you?"

"Yes. We hope." The Flash paused. "Without tearing me to pieces. Right, Cisco?"

"Right!" Cisco's voice chimed in their ears. "We've set cameras around the house so we'll see and hear everything that happens from here at the Arrowcave."

Felicity spoke up over the comm, "We'd rather be out there."

"I know," Oliver said. "You've got to operate from there because it's the only place with the computer power to manage the generator."

"But—" Felicity continued.

"Felicity, don't worry. Malcolm didn't get the generator. That means the rest of Cisco's vibe is moot. Right, Cisco?"

"Uh… yeah," Cisco said without conviction. "That future is changed. It's gone. It's a multiverse kind of thing."

"A multiverse kind of thing," Felicity muttered, clearly not assured.

"Thank you for volunteering your family estate, Oliver," Caitlin Snow offered in her usual apologetic tone, hesitant and a touch guilty. "And thanks for bringing me in from Central City to help."

Oliver heard the tension in Caitlin's voice. She had lost her husband the day the cataclysmic wormhole opened over Central City, the day Barry was infected by the plasma. But her commitment to Barry was extraordinary; and they needed her medical expertise.

He kicked through charred detritus on the overgrown lawn. The house was just an object now. Its loss meant little in the face of everything Oliver had accomplished for the city. The ruins of his childhood would serve one final practical function.

"Barry," Oliver said, "are you sure you don't want Detective West and Iris here? We can wait."

"No." The Flash shook his head with a sureness born of a painful decision finally made. "I talked to both of them last night. It's better for everyone that they stay in Central City."

Oliver didn't press. It wasn't his choice. Barry knew his family, and understood the limits of their stress. And of his own.

The air smelled acrid. Oliver slowed to let Thea come closer to him as they moved into the charred walls of the entry hall. She followed silently, arms folded over her chest, her eyes sadly sweeping the blackened artifacts of the house where she grew up.

John stayed quiet, giving the two siblings a moment.

Oliver kicked his way into the old sitting room. The acrid smell was worse here. He held out a hand to block the blank-faced Thea from continuing toward a large hole where the flooring had given way.

The hole had concrete walls and a block staircase down the sides that would've led to a door at one time. They started down the steps into the dark. Then they reached a large open space, nearly half the size of the mansion itself. It had been an underground garage where Robert Queen had stored vintage luxury cars and hotrods.

The wormhole generator sat in the center of the concrete space in the glare of temporary halogen lighting. Several computers were connected to the generator. Three large monitors were mounted on the walls.

The depth of the garage and the thick concrete walls and floor offered excellent protection should the generator malfunction and explode. Protection to anyone outside at any rate. Those inside the old garage would be vaporized.

Barry's future boiled down to this one event, and he stood quietly. Everyone knew what was at stake and all that could be done had been done.

"We really worked hard to get that place fixed up," Cisco squeaked in Oliver's ear again.

"Kid tested and mother approved," Thea responded, looking dubiously at the wormhole generator standing lonely in the center.

The monitors flickered on and Felicity, Cisco, and Caitlin appeared in HD via cams in the Arrowcave. Cameras mounted on the walls of the garage whirred to track Oliver and the team as they moved around the space. John sat on the bottom of the steps and waved at Felicity's monitor.

"Are we at least sure," he asked, "that we aren't going to suck Star City into a wormhole?"

"Absolutely," Felicity promised. But her eyes

went to the camera on her side, so she wasn't looking directly at anyone, which was a little disconcerting. "Right, Cisco?"

Oliver could hear the tapping at keys. More than likely everyone back at the Arrowcave was processing multiple data streams across their screens.

"In this case," Cisco said as he studied something off camera, "we're not worried about the wormhole growing out of control. Our problem will be keeping it open long enough. I made a few adjustments that should do that."

"We used the plasma samples I've taken from Barry," Caitlin said, "to calibrate the generator."

"Right." Cisco checked readouts on yet another screen. "The wormhole should have the same plasma signature as Barry. It will provide a nice, cozy home so the plasma inside Barry will be aching to leap out through the magnetic channel."

"That's good." The Flash tapped the magnetic regulator strapped to his chest. "So it won't rip me into little atomic pieces?"

"Dude, a little confidence, please." Cisco gave him a look of mock insult. "Who is the king of temporal tech?"

"You are," the Flash mumbled.

"Damn right I am." Cisco nodded emphatically. "Which reminds me—from the time you initiate the process, you've got fifteen minutes max. The generator uses a pretty nifty way of hyper-resonating magnetic energies off mu-metal containment to initiate the wormhole, but it can't sustain the stress of maintaining it. So the generator will start to shake apart, which means the wormhole will destabilize and collapse on its own."

"And then boom." Barry pulled back the cowl of his costume.

"Yes, boom." Then Cisco shook his head and wagged a finger in the air. "But there won't be a boom because you won't need that much time. You are the Fastest Man Alive. You got this, Barry."

The speedster gave his friend a weary smile.

Oliver set the timer on the smartwatch he wore over his glove. Cisco's pep talk was far more energetic and sincere than his could have been. He wasn't sure if he would have even managed a pep talk. Yao Fei didn't excel in motivational speeches.

"Don't worry." Felicity smiled down at him, which made the tightness in his gut recede a bit.

"What do we need to do?" Oliver asked.

"Most of this is on Barry," Cisco said. "We'll power up the generator and establish a small wormhole. Barry stands right at its horizon. The magnetic channel on his chest should automatically start to bleed the plasma out of him back to its natural environment."

"Sounds easy enough," Barry said without conviction.

"Well," Cisco responded, "*easy* in the sense that it's going to work. And we'll have the Flash back in top form in no time."

Cisco's constant optimism irritated Oliver but he said nothing.

Felicity finished her computations and looked up. "There's a black cable connected to the base of the generator. You'll need to attach it to Barry to ensure he doesn't get sucked into the wormhole."

Barry merely nodded, his face pensive. He made a circuit around the generator. Oliver doubted it was because he didn't trust his friends, but every eye on the situation meant his survival.

"Do I have a safety line?" Oliver asked. "What keeps me from being sucked into the wormhole?"

"Distance is your friend," Cisco replied. "There's a protective screen across the room. You stand behind that. Even once the wormhole is stabilized, it shouldn't have crazy matter-sucking powers. You should be fine."

"Okay." Oliver stared up at Felicity and she smiled uncomfortably. He asked, "What's the worst-case scenario?"

Oliver didn't like being the pessimist, especially in front of Barry, but he also had to be pragmatic.

"We have safety protocols built into our systems," Felicity was quick to answer. "In the unimaginable event that the wormhole expands beyond expected parameters, we'll shut it down remotely with a click of a button."

"And if that fails?"

"You pull the switch behind you." Felicity gestured through the monitor to a massive system of power cables feeding into a utility box that looked capable of powering Star City. "But you have to be careful. It will be dangerous in there."

"Yep," Cisco said. "The wormhole will generate immense energy. The plasma lightning could be intense. Stay behind the safety screen."

"I could control the lightning possibly," Barry said.

"You focus on getting the plasma out of you," Oliver retorted firmly. "Don't think about *saving* anyone."

"I know. I know."

Together, they both intoned, "Breathe. Be still."

John clapped Oliver on the arm. "Watch out for the lightning, man. Me and Speedy will be up top patrolling the grounds. Just in case."

"Good." Oliver nodded to him and put an arm around Speedy's red-garbed shoulders. "You two stay well away from the house. We don't know how much energy will come off this thing."

"Yes, we do," Cisco argued. "According to my calculations—"

"Enough," Oliver said, and turned back to Speedy. "Stay back anyway."

She smiled and patted her hand against Oliver's chest. "Have fun. Barry, good luck. See you in a few."

Barry returned her smile and caught John by the arm.

"If something happens to me, I want you to tell Joe."

"Look, man, nothing is going to happen."

"John." Barry stared at him. "Please tell Joe. He likes and respects you a great deal."

John started to object again, but instead he gave Barry a respectful nod.

"Sure," he said. "I'll take care of it."

"Thank you."

John and Thea climbed the concrete stairs out of the garage.

"Barry, we'll be monitoring your vital signs the entire time." Caitlin's head lifted from her computer. Her mouth was a thin line.

"Okay." The speedster came up beside Oliver with a wry grin. "Let's get this damn plasma out of me."

Oliver connected him to the safety strap and paused to look into Barry's eyes.

"Survive," he said.

Oliver retreated behind the thick steel and glass screen fifty feet away. Barry nodded at the camera. They were all set. Oliver pulled up his hood, feeling more comfortable viewing this event from inside its shadow.

"Good luck, you two," Felicity said. "Don't do anything… you know… just stay safe."

An eerie silence filled the sunken chamber until Cisco's voice came over the speaker.

"We're going to start it up slow."

Suddenly there was a definitive *snap*. A low hum built louder and higher. A pinpoint of light appeared in the air next to the generator. Rivulets of lightning crackled. Abruptly a fountainhead of swirling energy gushed forth.

To Green Arrow, the swirling mass looked like a death trap, a vortex of matter compacted into a morass no human could survive.

Barry looked calm. Determined, facing this monstrosity as if it were any normal day.

Barry actually turned, flashing a smile and a thumbs-up at Oliver before stepping up to the maelstrom. The energy surrounded him hungrily, pulling him forward. The Flash remained rooted at the spinning horizon. His red figure flickered and he thought he was seeing Barry front and back at the same time. The taut safety line held the speedster in place just as Cisco had said.

"All vitals are stable," Caitlin called out, though her voice sounded like she was speaking underwater. "Heartbeat is a little elevated."

"This thing is spitting out a hell of a lot of power," Green Arrow shouted. "Can Barry handle it?"

"Yes," Cisco reported.

The energy cascading around the accretion disk stretched Arrow's skin even from behind the screen. It actually hurt. Transfixed by the swirling energy, he was forced to shield his eyes from the deafening cracks of light snapping about the Flash like missiles.

He checked his watch. Barry had been in there only one minute. It felt like an hour.

A ripple of movement near the utility box brought the bow to his cheek. Green Arrow's eyes narrowed, searching the area, but the light show behind him made the whole room flicker with motion.

His body remained tense for another minute before he lowered his bow. He turned back to watch Barry standing suspended in the blackness of the maelstrom's opening. There was no change in the speedster's position or body language. He was frozen in place.

The crackling energy fractured into a thousand heaving shards of power that snapped out across the chamber. Oliver dove for cover, feeling the heat of the bolts cascading around him. A crash of lightning struck from the edge of the wormhole's bloom and the room shook. Equipment exploded in sparks and flames.

Fire licked the floor. Parts of the wall around Arrow smoldered. The monitors and cameras hung in shattered bits. Felicity and the others were blind.

"Can anyone hear me?" Green Arrow shouted through the comm.

Static crowded his ears.

He got to his feet and looked at Barry caught in the rapidly changing flux of the vortex. There was no change in him.

The power box smoldered, but appeared intact for the most part. There was no telling what damage had occurred from the surge. Oliver made his decision.

Pull the plug.

They could try again, safely, after the team repaired the damage.

Oliver ran for the utility box. He grasped a hefty double-handed lever.

An agonizing blossom of pain ripped across his back. He dropped to the ground as the air beside him undulated.

Ghasi appeared from the shadows, one of his short blades dripping with Oliver's blood.

"Leave it running."

3 9

The archer rolled to the side just as Ghasi's blade flashed again. Snapping his bow open, he raised it to block the downward strike.

The blow numbed his arm up to his shoulder. Oliver exploded to his feet, shoving Ghasi back with a furious shout, letting loose a flurry of attacks. The crack of the bow on the man's neck. The heel of a hand against his jaw. Spinning, his leg pounded across Ghasi's ribs. It felt like hitting an oak.

Ghasi thrust out his arms. His short blades crackled with electricity. He weaved them with terrible skill, striking quick, lunging out before darting back in before the echo of the last strike faded. His face twisted with hate, swinging his blades so they sang in the air.

Green Arrow parried desperately. The glowing blades were inches from his face. His cheek burnt from the neat edge of a swipe.

He dove to the side as a dagger sliced over his

head, scraping sparks along the wall. Flipping to his feet, he slammed the bow into Ghasi's midsection. Then he drew it up so that the horizontal haft snapped the assassin's head back violently. Blood spit from Ghasi's mouth. The man blinked several times, his arm grabbing out instinctively.

Oliver leapt out of reach. An arrow swept up to his bowstring and he let it fly. Ghasi deflected the shot to the side.

"Ghasi, I'm tired of you thinking you belong in my home. You don't."

Roaring, the man charged.

Oliver shot a cable up out of the pit. He rose thirty feet in seconds. He had to keep Ghasi away from the Flash. Looking back he saw a figure climbing after him. Ghasi leapt from the top landing, vaulting out of the open pit to face Green Arrow. Burnt furniture and fallen beams littered the floor of the old Queen sitting room.

"Your home is no longer what it was," Ghasi sneered. "Much like the man."

"The foundation is still solid."

"Then I'll shatter that too."

Ghasi threw two razor stars. Green Arrow knocked one out of the air with his bow and twisted to the right so the second just slipped past him to embed in the wall.

Oliver drew three arrows from his quiver in a single motion. He saw Ghasi pulling a small capsule so he didn't take aim, trusting all to instinct.

The first arrow caused Ghasi to step to the left. The

second flew high above his target. He quickly shot his last bolt to keep Ghasi in a narrow two-foot space.

Ghasi then saw a tangled mass of metal falling toward him. It was the massive chandelier Green Arrow had shot from its precarious place hanging from the damaged ceiling. He had a split second before the chandelier smashed on top of him.

Ghasi hurled the capsule up. Dark foam blossomed and seeped into the jagged edges of the falling wreckage. The goo-coated chandelier dropped against Ghasi and amazingly the entire bulk slid to the side as if it were a child's balloon. But the impact of the strange frictionless substance shrugged Ghasi aside too, sending him crashing into a pile of burnt beams and furniture that collapsed over him.

Oliver nocked another arrow, aiming into the rising dust and ash.

But nothing moved.

Oliver didn't breathe, focusing on the swirling motes in the air, looking for a disturbance. After several seconds, Oliver exhaled. He took a step forward.

Wreckage exploded outward and flew at Oliver. Throwing himself to the side, the debris crashed past him, but a long shrapnel spike caught his left leg. Lancing pain gripped his calf and he fell back against a charred wall.

Ghasi crawled from the wreckage, gasping, blood dripping from his neck. He pushed up onto one knee. Blackened detritus fell away.

"I told you to just play the game, but you couldn't stand it, could you? Not Oliver Queen. You had to be the best, the winner. You had to make sure I had nothing!"

"I don't know what you're talking about," Oliver snapped.

"Liar! Even now, when it doesn't matter, you can't stop lying. It wasn't enough that you got your generator. You had to kill Count Wallenstein!"

"Ghasi, I didn't kill Wallenstein. I didn't know he was dead until now!"

"Liar! I found him dead in his office. Merlyn told me you killed him."

Malcolm. Of course it was Malcolm.

"You don't seem like the type driven by sentimental revenge." Green Arrow gritted his teeth, trying to catch his breath and fight the pain.

"I couldn't care less that Wallenstein is dead. You looted his computers. You stole my money."

"We didn't take any money from the servers. It was Malcolm Merlyn. He must've killed Wallenstein. He diverted all the money. And he aimed you at me." Green Arrow struggled to clear his vision. "My God. So all of this really is just about money? That's the limits of your depth?"

"No! If you prefer, it's about you! You stole my future! You ruined everything for me again! And you have to pay for that once and for all." Ghasi shifted slightly, drawing his arms up from beneath him. "I pulled *this* out of Wallenstein's body and now I'll kill you with it!"

With a snap of Ghasi's wrist, something flew at Oliver. The archer was barely able to shift aside as an arrow pierced his shoulder instead of his heart where it had been aimed. His blood spurted across a blackened lump Oliver recognized as his mother's old armoire.

Oliver looked down. The arrow had his trademark green fletching.

As Ghasi started to rise to his feet, Green Arrow staggered away. He needed distance; he needed a moment to recover his strength. Climbing the ramshackle stairs, he stumbled to the nearly demolished second floor.

The green arrow was one of his. He tried to pull it out. The pain brought out a wet gasp. The head must've been caught on something. He couldn't break the metal shaft, but his arrows were designed to be interchangeable. With excruciating agony, he gripped the shaft and unscrewed it from the broadhead inside, which was held in place by his muscle or collarbone. Sucking air through gritted teeth, he dragged the metal shaft out of the bleeding hole and threw it aside.

He started off again, but his movement was slowed; he was fighting shock. The arrowhead inside him cutting against his flesh. He careened around the corner off a charred wall, causing another flush of agony.

This hallway once held nineteenth-century American landscapes; his father's prideful collection. Now they all lay as ash on the floor, bathed in the sun from the collapsed roof.

The pain started to numb his thoughts, making

them stray. He pulled a small dart of adrenaline from a loop on his tunic and jammed it into his thigh. Warmth spread to fight back the creeping chill.

"Spartan. Speedy!" The comm in his ear remained dead silent.

"They're not coming," Ghasi gloated from somewhere in the shadowy distance. "I made sure of it. You're alone now, Oliver. Just like me."

Green Arrow kept moving, kicking up clouds of soot in his wake. Bright red blood dripped down his arm to mix with the ashes, coating his fingers, making them tacky. The cloth under his Kevlar was soaked in sweat.

He twisted back to cover his retreat, his bow sweeping up and his wounded arm drawing back the bowstring with agonizing effort. A torturous moan slipped past his lips just as Ghasi rushed into view like a bellowing bull. Oliver released the new flight of arrows and they whipped away. The feathers hissed down the darkened hall.

Ghasi deflected the first arrow with steel bracers. The razors of the broadhead from the second split his cheek to the bone. The last arrow punched into the wall behind him and the stun grenade went off. Ghasi reeled, holding his head. He bounced off the wall and toppled back around the corner out of sight.

Green Arrow staggered forward, drawing an arrow. The muscles down his back and across his shoulders seared. A bead of sweat rolled down his face and landed on the feather of the arrow nestled against his chin.

He waited, listening for any sign of Ghasi.

The only sound was his own labored breathing. He needed for this battle to be done. With Arrowcave blind, Barry was alone below. And time was running out.

Moving to the far right side of the hallway, he angled for a clear view around the corner.

The space was empty. Ghasi was gone.

Green Arrow immediately spun around. The air rippled behind him and a fist slammed into his head, snapping his whole body into a twisting motion that ended when he collided with the wall. He choked on a mouthful of his blood.

Ghasi ran up on him, driving him deeper into the charred boards. Oliver grabbed Ghasi's arm in time to hold the glittering knife back. For the first time, he felt wires under Ghasi's skin.

Just like the man in the cell beneath Castle Wallenstein.

Green Arrow braced himself, struggling to keep the knife away. His muscles burned. The dagger pressed ever closer. Oliver dropped his bow and fumbled for his quiver, ignoring the agony of the embedded arrowhead ripping through more muscle in his shoulder joint. He slammed the tip of an arrow against Ghasi's face. Smoke curled up along with the man's scream. Acid ate Ghasi's flesh.

Ghasi lurched away and Green Arrow struggled to pull himself free of the crater in the wall. He stripped off his smoking glove and threw it aside.

He jerked his bow up and pulled an arrow. To his dismay, his arms quivered with fatigue.

In front of him, the figure of Ghasi vanished in a shimmering field.

The dust shifted microscopically in the air. He sent an arrow flying.

Cables snaked around an invisible shape. Green Arrow thumbed a remote on his bow and the cord cracked with current. Ghasi's form shook into visibility. His mouth gaped open in a frozen scream.

Hopefully five seconds locked in the grip of lightning would short-circuit the wiring inside Ghasi. But when the charge faded, he still stood.

With a flex of his shoulders, the cable snapped. The man's skin had blackened into raw patches, peeling away in others. Ghasi turned to Oliver, fury smeared across his face. He jerked as his body continued to be assailed by current. Now it was from inside.

Oliver loosed another arrow. The subsequent flash blinded Ghasi and nearly Oliver himself.

His reflexes were slowing.

Ghasi rushed him, arms swinging. Green Arrow ducked. Barely.

He stumbled, struggling to keep his feet. If he went down, it was over. Bending low, he fired a cable arrow through the open ceiling and hit the recoil on his bow.

The cable jerked him up into the air. Ghasi smashed a powerful blow into empty ground with a snarl of frustration.

The agony in Oliver's shoulder swelled. His vision caved in. He barely felt himself dragged onto the top of the house's outer wall. While most of the roof had caved in during the fire, charred crossbeams remained. The stone husk of the mansion had also crumbled in spots, but the tall rook tower still stood imposing over the front of the old place.

Shaking off the encroaching black from the edges of his vision, Green Arrow slowly drew himself up, rolling his legs over. Shoving himself back upright, he blinked hard, forcing his eyes to focus, brushing the cascading sweat and blood from them with his sleeve.

Barry. He needed to get back to Barry. How long had he been fighting?

Green Arrow stood on the narrow stone parapet that ran the length of the front façade. From this height, he could see the cemetery where his parents were buried. Where *he* was buried after they had declared him dead those years he was on the island.

The sound of crunching debris made him turn. Ghasi crawled up the inner wall toward him. Oliver fired down at him, but Ghasi leapt away, bounding off collapsed timbers until he came to rest in a hollow window on the far side of the house.

Ghasi sparked, the telltale sign that he had attempted to use his stealth but failed. Oliver grunted in satisfaction. He had short-circuited something at least.

Nocking his last explosive arrow, he let it loose.

It struck right in front of Ghasi, obliterating another chunk of his old home.

Ghasi leapt again, but missed a step as stones shifted under his foot. Thrusting out a hand, he shot a cable out of his bracer. The tip penetrated the top of the stone tower next to Oliver. Ghasi leapt into the chasm, drawing himself closer with the retracting cable.

Another arrow flew, slicing the cable. It snapped and Ghasi dropped with a roar of rage out of sight below a section of surviving roof. Running to the edge, Green Arrow looked down, and Ghasi erupted at Oliver.

Green Arrow swung his bow, chopping down on Ghasi's bladed arm, blocking a strike that would have disemboweled him. The archer made a desperate leap to a distant section of roof. When his feet touched, he barely found his balance before he spun and fired.

The arrow struck true, digging deep into Ghasi's leg. It should have brought him off his feet, but he stood solid. His fingers crunched into the mortar of the rook tower. With a thunderous roar of rage, he strained and sparked. His body smoldered. Then he wrenched off a chunk of the tower about the size of an SUV and lifted it over his head. Electricity arced from the wires that slid out of his flesh.

Green Arrow sprinted along a narrow beam, one foot slapping in front of the other. The stone wreckage landed behind him. The entire structure shimmied from the impact. Oliver went down to his knees as the beam abruptly snapped. The remaining sections of the roof collapsed in a domino of cracking timbers and tumbling stone.

Both men disappeared in the chaotic cascade of wreckage.

40

Even facing into the wormhole, Barry saw the space around him. Oliver. The generator. The abandoned garage.

Lightning cascaded across his vision. The energy of the wormhole pressed into him like a vice. At the same time, he expanded, pushing outward.

His hand brushed against the magnetic siphon on his chest. It wasn't vibrating or moving. Maybe it wasn't working. Maybe this was the one time the gimmick wouldn't work, the fix wouldn't take. If that was the case, he was doomed unless he thought of another way to get the plasma out. And he was running out of time.

His eyes flicked up. Suddenly the room was gone. No generator. No Oliver. All that remained was the wormhole that churned about him.

Wisps of plasma flowed around him like snakes.

Two bright orbs glowed in the haze. They were aimed at him, focused on him.

Eyes.

Reverse Flash appeared with the cruel grin of Harrison Wells under the cowl.

"This was easier than I'd hoped," Reverse Flash said. "I didn't even have to lure you or chase you. I've been trying to drag you into this dimension, but you opened a path and just walked in."

Barry turned, hoping to see the garage and Oliver, but there was only swirling plasma. He spun wildly, back and forth, searching for the light from his world.

Blackness surrounded him.

He looked down at his ankle and the cord was frayed and flapped uselessly. Barry was trapped.

"You're in my domain now." Reverse Flash leaned forward, barely an inch from Barry's face.

The Flash grabbed for the yellow specter, but he was gone like one of the wisps.

Suddenly Wells stood beside him again.

"I know what you're trying to do, but you're too smart for your own good, Mr. Allen." Reverse Flash offered a mocking snarl. "Here *I* am king."

The Flash swiped at him again, then again and again. Grasping. Snatching only empty space.

"Oh this is sad." Reverse Flash remained only a few inches away, but it could've been miles. "I'm glad your father isn't here to see this. Or Joe. Or Harrison Wells, for that matter."

A glint of emerald flickered in the Flash's peripheral. Green Arrow stood beside him, clad in his dark armor, staring at Barry through hooded eyes. For an instant

Barry panicked, his mind racing.

Oliver had been sucked into the anomaly as well. A normal human couldn't survive inside the wormhole. He was going to die just as Cisco had vibed. Barry gathered his dwindling speed force, ready to get Oliver to safety.

A yellow blur surged and Barry took a blow to the chin. He staggered. Another shot drove his head to the other side. His knees weakened. One after another, hammers crashed into him. Barry stumbled, trying to cover himself. Fists pistoned his stomach, bending him forward, pushing the air from his lungs. His vision darkened.

A crashing blow fell on his neck and Barry dropped to the ground where he hunched, gasping for breath.

Yellow-clad feet stepped in front of him. A boot pressed into the Flash's shoulder and shoved him onto his side.

"It's over," Reverse Flash said. "You're done."

Barry pressed a hand flat on the ground. Blood drizzled from his mouth onto the back of his glove. Red on red.

"No." The words crawled wet and strangled from the Flash's throat. He pushed himself up, dragging his knee under him. He had to save Oliver. Barry started to stand. Reverse Flash kicked him, knocking him flat with a painful groan.

"Yes." Wells's voice was calm and authoritative. He sounded almost supportive, trying to teach Barry yet again, to get through to the bull-headed kid. "Let it happen. Let the speed force go. It won't be so bad. I'll stay here with you." Reverse Flash crouched and held out his hand. "I won't let you be alone."

Barry gritted his teeth and gathered himself yet again. He struggled to push up onto his hands, bracing for another blow.

A hand touched his shoulder. Strong. Firm.

Green Arrow knelt next to him.

The Flash looked up at Reverse Flash, expecting him to attack. But the man in yellow merely stood observing.

"Barry, breathe. Be still." Then Oliver shook his head petulantly at the Flash. "But you can't lie here. You've got to run."

"What?" Barry groaned in disappointment. "No. I can't hear that anymore. Running faster isn't the answer. That's what he wants."

"I didn't say run *faster*. I said *run*."

"There's no difference!" Barry screamed and grasped his head, sick of the confusion. He gasped for breath and struggled to his feet. "What's the purpose of running? What good has it done? I can't win."

"There's no purpose." Oliver glanced dismissively at Reverse Flash. "There's no winning or losing."

"I don't understand you. I can't try harder."

"When you look through a microscope, do you see the truth clearer if you look hard?" Oliver regarded Barry with a curious squint. "The truth is there no matter what. You'll see it because you can't miss it."

The Flash saw a yellow streak from the corner of

his eye as Reverse Flash swung at him. Barry was still thinking about Oliver's words and his head tilted imperceptibly to the side.

The blow missed.

Reverse Flash stepped back and Barry saw something he hadn't seen before.

The man in yellow betrayed a surprising uncertainty.

The Flash looked for Oliver's reaction, but Green Arrow was gone. He had never been here. He was part of Barry's mind too. No one was in danger.

"You're in danger," Reverse Flash said in Harrison Wells's most pretentious tone, but there was a hint of apprehension. A rush of words to reassert his control. "Don't forget, I am you. I know your thoughts. I know your heart. I know your limits."

"You can't." He leveled a stare into the glowing eyes. "Because I don't know my limits."

Breathe. Be still.

Barry shook off the cobwebs from the beating. He stepped forward.

Reverse Flash backpedaled.

"Face it, Mr. Allen," his voice rose. "Stop being stubborn. You've lost. There's no way back."

"I don't believe you."

"How can you not believe me? I'm *you!*"

"I know." Barry grinned through bloody teeth. "But I've been wrong before."

He charged…

A light-speed punch came at Barry's face.

He skidded to an immediate halt, fire spewing from his feet. He bobbed his head and knuckles just scraped his temple. Another blow screamed toward him. The Flash easily slipped it. A barrage of fists came in microseconds that looked like a wall of yellow. Barry dodged so swiftly he seemed to be standing still.

Barry saw Reverse Flash standing with his arms hanging weakly by his side, a look of surprise on his face. The fatigue in Barry seemed to have traveled to Reverse Flash. Barry drew in a new breath. Free. Easy.

Reverse Flash instantly became a speck in the distance.

Barry laughed and ran after him.

The fear and the turmoil in his brain suddenly ebbed. He carried no burden over concern for the vast gap between him and his enemy, a gap he rationally knew he had no chance of covering. He didn't worry about the plasma flaring to life and savaging his cells that were charged with the speed force. He didn't think about speed.

He just ran.

A strange tingling sensation boiled up from deep inside. It touched every perception. The flexing of muscles. The vibrations singing through his bones. The roaring of blood powering the machine. The tingling was the plasma. He could hear it and feel it pushing inside him.

The Flash accepted the sensations. The plasma was part of him. He couldn't run away from it. He couldn't run toward it. He could only run.

One step after another.

Legs pumped and arms swung, metronomes powered by lightning. His feet whispered to the ground as he passed.

Barry had no thought for how fast he was running. There was no meter. No goal. No destination.

Only the road. Only the steps.

Suddenly he strode alongside the yellow haze of Reverse Flash. The glowing eyes glanced at Barry with shock just before the Flash veered to the right, perfectly matching the other speedster's move. Reverse Flash slipped left, but the Flash was already there at his shoulder.

Barry knew with exquisite clarity where his opponent was going even before Reverse Flash moved. He felt it. The vibrations from Reverse Flash poured over him and resonated inside him.

The Flash inched closer to Reverse Flash. Their arms touched.

The glowing eyes again looked at him, almost pleading for his life. The yellow man tried to run harder, but there was no escape.

As if peering through a powerful microscope, Barry could see the very particles that made up the physical reality of the two figures. Their molecules slipped between each other.

And more, he saw their essences like speeding souls racing through the ether.

The yellow figure grew fainter as the Flash's red consumed him. Their limbs were a pumping mass of pendulums and vibrations. Slowly, in seconds, their arms and legs blended together, moving together, merging into one.

One figure in red. Running.

Now the world flowed through Barry. Electricity sang in him.

The world darkened. Streamers of plasma grew into a solid mass roaring about him, a tunnel of deadly energy. The red of his arms started to fade.

He looked down. Instead of his scarlet costume he saw skin. Blackened now with dark veins bulging through like cords of hard muscle. The plasma consumed him.

Still he felt no fear, only stillness. His mind remained focused with attention on one thing, not a dozen, wrapped in a cocoon of serenity.

He no longer fed the beast within him. He stopped giving it power. It just was there, a part of him.

It wasn't a true part. It belonged elsewhere and now that the Flash wouldn't give refuge to the plasma, it was seized by the overpowering rules of nature and the strength of physical forces. It was attracted by the natural state surrounding it, and it found a ready path of escape, of release, into its own world.

A deep satisfying thud pounded into his chest. The magnetic coil tore at him.

An exquisite pain lanced Barry.

The plasma tore out of his body, burning through muscle and bone and blood. It poured out of the channel, flailing hot into the air around him. The plasma boiled into the swirling universe around Barry. Under the scorching touch of the escaping energy, his body continued to fight and drive. Despite the agony, his limbs churned on.

The Flash outran his own screams.

Noise crowded Green Arrow's world, a massive roar that stabbed into his skull like a pounding nail. Dragging his eyes open, he was assailed by bright flashing lights. Wind slapped his bare skin and rustled his torn clothes.

The wormhole shimmered into focus.

He wrenched himself to a sitting position and fresh agony washed over him. The arrowhead embedded in his shoulder had been shoved in even deeper. Blood drenched the front of his green Kevlar. He pushed his hood back.

The sky above him was gone. Debris sealed him in the garage now. It had become a covered tiger pit.

He struggled to shift his legs. To his relief they moved. Nothing was broken. Oliver crawled to his feet.

Barry was gone.

The safety cable flapped free. Lightning cracked all about the chamber. The vortex of the wormhole shuddered for a moment. The only light came from the flashes of energy swirling around the wormhole.

Ghasi stood by the generator. Exposed wires stuck out through his flesh. His skin blistered and sagged.

Ghasi smashed a heavy chunk of concrete against the generator. The crack barely registered over the roar of the wormhole.

Oliver habitually reached for his bow on his shoulder. There was nothing there. Despite the agony of merely bending, he grabbed a metal pipe off the floor. His gaze locked on Ghasi and he limped over, lifting his makeshift weapon. He slammed the pipe down on the assassin's head. The man's neck barely moved. But it got his attention.

A mask of burning skin turned to Oliver, the outline of Ghasi's skull clearly defined now. A growl emanated from flaccid lips.

Oliver struck again. The end of the pipe connected with his jaw and shifted it to the side with a loud crack. Ghasi didn't react save to swing his arm at the annoying fly. Oliver took a wide step to the side and slammed the pipe across Ghasi's lower back. The blow would have crippled a normal man.

"Your strength is failing," Ghasi slurred, his jaw jammed onto the right side of his face. If there was pain, the assassin didn't register it. He snatched the pipe, wrenching it from Oliver's hand.

"Look at yourself, Ghasi. Your biomechanics are frying you from the inside. If you stop now, you might live. We'll help you."

Ghasi responded by rushing him, but Oliver flung himself back. He dropped heavily to the ground. A scream of pain slipped out and Ghasi laughed. Oliver rolled frantically to avoid the pipe as it slammed down at him, missing his head by inches.

Oliver's throbbing shoulder brought a rush of nausea. The pipe lifted again. He continued his roll, leaving a smear of red on the floor. Scissoring his legs, Oliver swept Ghasi off his feet. The other man fell heavily onto his back. The smell of burning flesh crowded Oliver's nostrils, making his nausea flair again.

Oliver twisted and struck at Ghasi's exposed throat with a stiff arm. To his surprise he hit soft tissue. The assassin's body was finally vulnerable. Ghasi convulsed, wrenching away, coughing violently.

Oliver struggled to stand upright, using a large piece of stone and masonry to brace himself. It was the hunk of the tower that Ghasi had used to smash through the roof. His eye caught a glimpse of green metal lying in its shadow.

His bow.

It was bent and nearly broken in two. Snatching it up, Oliver fumbled his final arrow onto the bowstring. The tension on it was too great but he had no way of reducing it without breaking it completely.

"You're nothing without your rich-boy toys," Ghasi gloated through his melting face.

Something on the generator exploded, throwing up a spout of sparks and flames. The wormhole shuddered and rotated faster. Oliver looked sharply at the swirling disc. Barry was in there somewhere. The wind roared louder as the vortex started to drag objects toward it. Oliver hooked his leg around one of the support beams. Anything that wasn't secured started a slow slide toward the mouth of the wormhole.

Ghasi grinned at the swirling maw, reveling in its destructive power. His hand thrust downward, embedding his fingers in the floor, halting his slide. He sneered and started to drag himself toward Oliver, digging lumps of concrete out of the floor as he came.

Oliver had nowhere to go. If he released the column, he'd be sucked in with the rest of the helpless debris.

The wormhole began to shrink.

"Flash!" Green Arrow yelled into his comm. "Get out of there. It's starting to close!"

All he heard was Ghasi's laughter.

"I win, Oliver. You've lost the last friend who trusted you."

The massive stone beside Oliver began to shake. Rivers of dust cascaded down its craggy surface as it scraped toward the wormhole. His head snapped up toward Ghasi. Even with the bow haft bent, he knew his weapon as well as he knew the muscles and bones of his own arm. With the disruption tearing through the room, it wouldn't be a pretty shot. He let the strained tension of the bowstring speak to him. He felt the weaker points and compensated for them.

Trusting in his skill, the last arrow was released. He

already knew where it would strike home.

A bola burst from the arrow and whipped around the assassin's arms. The cables pinned his upper arms to his sides. But his fingers still dug into floor. He looked behind him. Torrential energy swirled around and into the event horizon. Dirt, stones, scrap metal all scraped or tumbled over the floor toward the wormhole.

Oliver jammed the end of his bow into a crevice in the stone chunk. He put his shoulder to the makeshift boulder and pushed. It rocked up and back. Oliver gritted his teeth and shoved again. The stone tumbled forward, and then rolled again, caught in the attractive power of the wormhole. It rumbled toward the swirling energy. The line pulled tight, yanking Ghasi with it.

He yelled, fighting against the cables wrapped around him, slapping bloody fingers impotently against the ground. The exposed wires sticking out of his body spit electricity, burning him, raising white-hot flashes and smoke.

The piece of the tower plunged through the wormhole and disappeared. The taut cable stretched back into the room, dragging the struggling Ghasi, his legs flailing like a doll.

"Oliver!" Ghasi screamed as he disappeared into the black abyss.

Oliver held onto the support column. The arrowhead in his shoulder cut through something and his arm went limp. He didn't have the strength. He could feel his trembling fingers slipping over the hard edge of the column. Soon he would be pulled loose and tumble into nothingness.

The wormhole suddenly collapsed into a pinpoint of light. The bright dot hung in the air and then went dark. The tempest vanished. Debris dropped lifeless to the floor. Dust and ash swirled in lazy circles in the growing darkness.

Lifting his head, Oliver's body shook. Wreckage surrounded him. Heavy beams and smashed timber. Stones and shattered concrete. There was no way out. He was trapped and alone.

Electricity flew off the generator with a high-pitched whine. The generator rocked back and forth and vibrated with increasing violence.

Oliver lay motionless.

Damn it, he thought. *Cisco was right after all.*

That wouldn't have bothered him except for the fact that he had failed.

Barry was lost.

He screamed, raging at his own incompetence, his own arrogance. And now another had paid the price for his pride.

"Hey, what's wrong?" Barry's cheerful voice sounded behind him.

Oliver sat up and spun around before he realized he was too injured to move.

There stood the speedster.

"You're all right!" Oliver cried.

"But you're not!" Barry took hold of his friend, his

eyes widening at the bloody mess that was Oliver Queen. "Where aren't you bleeding? What happened to you?"

"Ghasi." Oliver collapsed to the floor. Barry quickly knelt beside him.

"Oliver…"

The archer shook his head. He felt the vibrations coming out of the device. He pointed toward the generator.

"Oh crap!" Barry exclaimed. "I'll get us out of here."

He looked around and saw the bottom of the deadfall of heavy wreckage overhead. No exit.

"Oh crap," he repeated. "We're buried."

"Remember how I said to be still?" Oliver looked up at Barry. "Forget it. Go fast. Now."

Barry grabbed Oliver, picking him bodily off the ground in a desperate attempt to get them clear. Oliver stifled a moan as his body protested.

The generator exploded into a blinding fireball. He could see the wall of flame close enough to touch. He felt the rush of heat. And then the next moment, the world stopped.

The only noise he heard was a high-pitched scream of sound. Even his own heart seemed to have stopped beating. His brain felt like it was sloshing about inside his skull. He couldn't draw breath.

Then the world speeded up again, or more accurately, the Flash slowed down. A spinning red vortex that was Barry twirled to a stop. He clutched the battered Oliver in his arms. The archer gasped for breath as his lungs started working again.

"There," the Flash announced. "Nothing a spinning inertial shield can't fix."

He placed Oliver gently on the ground and darted to snuff out the flames around them. Oliver lay there trying to gather his wits, suppressing the wrenching nausea clutching his gut as he forced the world to stop spinning. Blinking, he tried to focus on what was happening inside the room. The Flash was a red blur and the fires winked out one by one.

Debris inside of the chamber had shifted due to the force of the Flash's spin. Small pinpricks of sunlight could be seen above them.

The Flash appeared beside him and dropped to the smoldering floor, exhausted.

"Are you okay?"

Oliver nodded. He closed his eyes as the figure of Barry kept threatening to shift about. He grabbed the man's arm, squeezing it. Partly to see if Barry was blurring, but as soon as he felt solid muscle under his hand, he knew the spinning was all him. Oliver swallowed hard and tried to regain control over his body.

"What happened?" Oliver asked. "What did you do?"

"Oh, I just spun around at superspeed to protect you from the blast. And managed to dissipate some of the energy from the explosion. No biggie."

"How about you? Did that... magnetic channel work?" Oliver tapped the twisted and burnt device on the Flash's chest. "Please tell me this… wasn't all for nothing."

"It worked like a charm. A very painful charm." The Flash unbuckled the siphon and gave Oliver a quirky grin. "But it was you that made this work."

"I didn't do anything except get my ass kicked."

"You really hate praise, don't you?" Barry rocked back on his heels and scowled as he looked at Oliver's bleeding, battered form. "I need to get you to a hospital now. Are there any other ways out of here? You know, secret passages."

"No." Oliver gasped out a laugh. "We're the Queens, not the Borgias."

The Flash lifted a hand to tap his comm. "Cisco? Felicity? Anyone out there?"

Oliver shook his head. "Communications went out… as soon as the wormhole appeared. Just find a way out. Ghasi boasted he took care of John and Thea. They're not answering."

"I don't see Ghasi. I assume he's out of the picture."

"He… fell into the wormhole."

"Oh. He *fell*?"

"Anyone alive down there?" a voice shouted from above.

Barry and Oliver looked up. Relief washed over the archer's face. John was visible as he shoved a chunk of wood aside. Speedy and Felicity joined him at the opening, staring down.

"We're both all right." The Flash waved. "But Oliver

needs medical attention pronto!"

Felicity half laughed and half sobbed with relief as Speedy hugged her.

"Oh my God," Felicity cried. "Oliver! Are you okay?"

Oliver struggled to roll onto his back, staring up at her face.

"See?" he croaked. "Both arms."

"We'll get a line down to you!" John shouted. "And then I'm going straight to church. It's a miracle you survived."

"We're going to make it." Barry pulled back his cowl and patted the archer's leg. "Just breathe."

Oliver closed his eyes and a weary smile creased his lips.

4 2

Barry weaved through the tables. His phone was clutched in his hand. He grinned as he hopped up onto the high bar chair.

"Just called Joe," he shouted over the pounding dance music. "Told him the good news that the plasma is gone. And I told him we'd be home tomorrow."

Caitlin and Cisco raised their drinks and toasted.

"That's wonderful." Caitlin nearly teared up. "He must've been so happy."

"Yeah." Barry stopped there, feeling the emotion from the phone call welling again. He grinned and lowered his head.

"Oh man." Cisco closed his eyes in ecstasy. "I cannot wait to get back to Big Belly Burger."

"We have Big Belly Burger here." Thea jerked her thumb over her shoulder. "There are two like a mile away from here."

"Yeah, I've tried both of those." Cisco shook his

head. "They're not the same. Maybe Central City cows are just better."

Felicity bopped in her seat to the music and joined the toast along with Thea, John, and Lyla. All the glasses touched in the center of the table.

"We're so happy for you, Barry," she called out.

"I can't thank you guys enough." Barry leaned into a hand on his neck from John and a kiss on the cheek from Thea.

"Any time, man," John said.

"*Any* time?" Cisco asked.

"Why do you say it like that?" John stared evenly at the engineer. "You vibing some new disaster off that bowl of peanuts?"

Cisco held up a peanut and squinted at it before popping it in his mouth. "All good."

Felicity took several peanuts and stared at them too.

"I'm just grateful," she said, "your vibe didn't come true."

"Yeah, we all are." Barry looked at Cisco. "You were way off this time, which is great, but what happened?"

"It's pretty obvious, isn't it?" Cisco replied defensively. "I was looking into events where a wormhole was involved. That thing threw everything off. How do you expect me to vibe a straight story with dimensional-temporal energies flying all over the place? But somewhere out on Earth X-24, that vibe really happened."

Felicity shook her head sadly. "Well, I feel sorry for the people on that Earth then."

"Man, one Earth is confusing enough for me, stop talking about all the others." John glanced at his phone, and then at Felicity. "Where is Oliver?"

"He's coming." She checked her phone for messages and exhaled with disappointment. "He said he had something to do."

"He's not out…" Barry shrugged. "You know." He mimed shooting a bow and arrow.

"No. No way." Felicity looked grim. "The man just got out of a hospital bed and he can barely walk. He promised he'd take it easy."

Thea and John exchanged quick glances. Felicity saw their doubt.

"No!" she shouted. "He promised. Like *really* promised. Not the usual Oliver Queen promise!"

Felicity looked at everyone. They all smiled awkwardly and checked their phones or suddenly noticed something interesting across the bar. Anything to avoid her eyes. She dropped her head into her hands.

"Oh. My. God. He's out fighting crime, isn't he?"

"He might not be," Barry offered. "I mean, you said he can barely walk."

"Oh that won't matter to him." Felicity snatched up her phone. "He'll use some kind of braces or exoskeleton or crutch arrows." She typed with furious thumbs as she muttered, "Where. Are. You? You. Better. Not. Be. Wearing. Green."

She set the phone on the table and stared hard at it.

No response came back. Long minutes passed and the phone sat black and empty.

"Where do you think he is?" Felicity asked John.

"He didn't say anything to me, but don't worry. Even Oliver isn't stupid enough to be *out* in his condition." John's easy confidence shaved the sharp edges off Felicity's anxiety. "He said he was coming, so he's coming. He's not going to miss these guys' last night in town."

"Okay." Felicity nodded. "I'm sure you're right."

"Yep." John put his hand over Lyla's. "But it's getting late for us. Maybe we should head home."

"Late?" Cisco checked the time. "It's barely ten."

"I'm an old married man, Ramon, and a father." John smiled with satisfaction as he stood and Lyla gathered her purse. "Got to get home to the baby."

"I've got to fly to Washington tomorrow," Lyla said with exhausted bemusement, "to explain to the National Security Council how their money bought a scorch mark in a garage."

"You've got the schematics." Felicity smiled with exaggerated hope. "That counts for something, doesn't it?"

"It does," Lyla said. "Plus Count Wallenstein is dead and his network is shattered, so that's a feather in the cap."

"You can thank dear old Dad," Thea muttered. "Malcolm didn't get his generator, but he eliminated a major competitor, so it's a win for him."

Lyla gave Barry a quick hug. "So good to see you well."

"Thanks, Lyla," he replied. "Thanks for everything."

"Seriously," Caitlin echoed. "You put yourself out there."

"Well," Lyla smiled, "got to keep the Fastest Man Alive alive."

John patted Barry's arm and gave a cheerful wave to Caitlin, Cisco, and Thea. He regarded Felicity.

"Talk to you tomorrow." He nodded toward her phone. "Call me if you need me."

Barry watched the couple leave and as soon as the door swung shut on them, he spun to Felicity.

"So you're really turning Straub's research over to A.R.G.U.S.? I mean, we trust Lyla, but she could be out tomorrow. And then what?"

"Yes, I am." Felicity raised her eyebrows as if put off by Barry's question. "And no, I'm not."

Barry rested his chin in his hand and waited for the inevitable Felicity follow-up. She signaled to bring everyone closer.

"Here's the deal," she said. "The government paid for co-ownership of the generator we saw in Markovia. That generator now consists of a few non-atomized bits and pieces, which A.R.G.U.S. has collected from the Queen estate. There were also technical specs provided by Count Wallenstein, and A.R.G.U.S. has copies of that."

"Oh man." Cisco bit his lower lip. "So they do have it."

Felicity raised a finger.

"They have some information," she said. "However, the material retrieved from Wallenstein's servers, including the original Straub operating system stolen from us, and the Straub device we recovered from the mine, are proprietary and exclusive IP of Queen Consolidated and, by extension, Palmer Tech. They are not entitled to any of that. And there won't be any more copies of it because I've sent out a little hunter-killer worm that will seek and destroy any bit of Straub's code wherever it might appear."

"What if the government sues you?" Barry asked. "Without that original code, they've got nothing."

"They can't sue for it if they don't know we have it." Felicity buffed her nails on her blouse with pride. "Lyla is the only government official who knows we recovered all the data."

"And she won't tell," Barry concluded.

"Lyla has a healthy distrust of secret power because she's seen what A.R.G.U.S. could be under questionable leadership. And luckily she trusts us because John trusts us." Felicity's glance flicked to her phone. She sighed at the blank screen.

"I was really hoping Oliver would be able to enjoy your last night in Star City," she said. "I'll text him again."

"No, hold up." Barry touched her arm. "I've got an idea where he is. Let me check. Be right back."

The crowd froze as Barry raced out into the night.

* * *

Oliver Queen sat alone in the booth near the bathroom door.

The Glossy Starling was quiet with only five customers drinking alone or sitting together but not talking. A small television over the bar showed a basketball game, but no one in the bar seemed to care. The game went on, droning through the air, playing to little recognition.

Oliver spun a glass of bourbon slowly with his fingertips. The oaky smell summoned memories, most of them bad.

He saw his phone on the table with Felicity's last message still showing: *You better not be wearing green.*

He straightened the phone on the chipped Formica tabletop and let it sit. The ache in his shoulder still made the tips of his fingers feel numb.

"Hon, you doing okay?" The waitress stood next to the table, a look of practiced sympathy on her face.

"I'm fine, thanks."

"I'll have a beer."

Barry sat across from Oliver.

The waitress froze, then stared hard at the young man. She looked all around her, wide-eyed.

"Oh, I'm sorry, hon. I didn't even see you sitting there. Have you been here? Did I ignore you before?"

"No." Barry waved a calming hand. "I just got here. What do you have on tap?"

"Um. Tap? Nothing."

"Bottle is fine."

"Can." She backed away, confused by Barry. "I'll be right back."

"No rush." Barry sat back and smiled at Oliver. "Hey."

"How'd you find me? Did you look everywhere in Star City?"

"Nope. Came here first. It's like your place. Must be the ambiance."

Oliver offered an amused smirk. "How do you feel, Barry?"

"Oh man, I feel great. Everything is back on track. I'm in top shape already. How about you?"

"I'm good." Oliver resumed rotating his glass in its pool of condensation.

"Really? Because, no offense, you look like you just went through a meat grinder."

Oliver caught his reflection in the grimy window. His eyes were blackened, nose covered in strips of gauze, his lower lip split, and small scars showed red on his forehead and jawline. His right arm was in a sling.

"Some of us heal fast," he said. "Some of us just forget we're hurt."

Barry took a can of cheap beer from the waitress, who was still unsure he was really there. He took a swig and grimaced.

"You know," he said, "in Central City there's a craft beer joint that's really great. Got cool things on the wall and everything. Next time you're in town, we're so going."

"Sure."

"I need to show you something other than S.T.A.R. Labs and our latest metahuman threat every time you visit."

Oliver sat back, content to let Barry talk. He liked listening to him.

"I've been patrolling the city the last few days while you were laid up," Barry said. "Everything seems pretty quiet."

"Thanks."

"No sweat. You guys really have a lot of warehouses in Star City."

"Yeah. It's our thing."

"Listen, Oliver," Barry said quietly, "I wanted to tell you I'm really sorry about Ghasi. I know he was your friend once. I wish it hadn't come down that way."

"I know. You told me."

"Oh yeah, but that was the other day. Wait, you were under sedation. You heard me?"

Oliver smiled. Barry quirked an eyebrow.

"So you heard all the stuff I said?" he asked. "About how grateful I am? And how you're an inspiration to me? And how there wouldn't be the Flash without the Green Arrow coming first?"

"Yes." Oliver picked up his perspiring glass and tapped it against Barry's beer can with an unsatisfying *tink*. "Thank you."

"You're welcome."

Oliver sat silently, not drinking.

"Can I ask you a question?" Barry said.

"Sure."

"This meditation thing you taught me, is it the key to being an effective Super Hero?"

"By itself?" Oliver leaned back in the seat. "No."

"But you meditate every day."

Oliver's lips tightened. He met Barry's gaze.

"No, I don't. In fact, I fell out of the habit completely until you needed it. But I should do it. And you should, whether I do or not."

"I did today."

"Good. Will you tomorrow?"

"Hope so. But, you know, the plasma is gone so—"

"It's not about the plasma. It was never about the plasma. It's about Barry Allen."

"Believe me, I know. I would've run myself to death. I would've blurred into nothingness without you."

After a soft sigh, Oliver started to say something.

"And I know," Barry continued, "that it's not that simple. But you gave me the start, and you kept on me. Step by step. Like you said. And who doesn't like to be more focused in a fight, right?"

"Your emotions set you apart, Barry. They drive you and they make the Flash important to everyone. Don't lose them. Just know they can work against you."

"Does that happen to you?"

"No," Oliver replied deadpan, "I don't have emotions."

Barry started to object vigorously until Oliver let slip the faintest of smiles. The young man laughed and nodded appreciation at the joke.

ACKNOWLEDGMENTS

Thanks to Nick Landau, Vivian Cheung, Laura Price, Natalie Laverick, Miranda Jewess, Julia Lloyd, and Rhys Thomas at Titan Books.

Thanks to Ben Sokolowski, Josh Anderson, Amy Weingartner, Carl Ogawa, Greg Berlanti, Andrew Kreisberg and Marc Guggenheim on the production teams of *The Flash* and *Arrow*, and at Warner Bros.

And thanks to our editors, Cat Camacho and Steve Saffel.

ABOUT THE AUTHORS

Clay and Susan Griffith are married co-authors of novels, short stories, comic books, and television. They were brought together by a single comic book, and they stayed together because of a shared love of heroes, villains, and adventure stories. They are the creators of the Vampire Empire series, the authors of the Crown & Key trilogy, and of *The Flash: The Haunting of Barry Allen*.

For more fantastic fiction, author events,
competitions, limited editions and more

VISIT OUR WEBSITE
titanbooks.com

LIKE US ON FACEBOOK
facebook.com/titanbooks

FOLLOW US ON TWITTER
@TitanBooks

EMAIL US
readerfeedback@titanemail.com